Rambling with Rebah

ADDISON J. CHAPPLE

WITH VICTORIA BAY

Copyright © 2022 by Level 4 Press, Inc.

Published by:
Level 4 Press, Inc.
14702 Haven Way
Jamul, CA 91935
www.level4press.com

Library of Congress Control Number: 2019943900
ISBN: 978-1-64630-018-1
eBook ISBN: 978-1-64630-019-8

Printed in the United States of America

Other books by
ADDISON J. CHAPPLE

THE MAN WHO WOULD BE KING
DESTINATION WEDDING
CON CRAZY
UNDER COVER
THE MOONBEAM SOCIETY
SANTA ANA
THE MOLLY MASTERSON MURDERS
MONTEZUMA'S REVENGE

Prologue

They say you're not supposed to make any major changes during the first year of grieving, but the day after his wife's funeral Aidan Cisneros stopped drinking.

In the sprawling kitchen of the Happy Valley Bed & Breakfast, once the most charming and accommodating luxury B&B in Napa Valley, he arranged fourteen bottles of wine, both red and white, in a shipping box and then clinked two bottles of whiskey into a shoebox that was left over from his last pair of size eleven Dockers. He even dug out from under the kitchen sink an enormous bottle of absinthe that his best friend, Kyle, had given him as a joke two Christmases ago. He'd told no one, but he'd actually tasted the stuff one dark night about a month before when the wine and whiskey had run dry. It had tasted as disgusting as it smelled, but it hadn't stopped him from drinking a generous quarter of it.

He dragged both boxes and the bottle out to the trash barrel that leaned against the spreading walnut tree that stood tall at the end of his driveway and stuffed the stash deep inside, covering what he now thought of as "evidence" with an empty industrial-sized plastic bag for bird food. To hell with recycling. Recycling required opening the bottles and pouring out the contents, watching the liquid mix with the red dirt of the yard and smelling the resulting paste, the tangy texture of loss and regret. It was too much.

It was all too much.

He ran his hands through shaggy blond hair that was always in need of a cut and turned to head back up his gravel driveway, gazing up at their home, his home, the Happy Valley. *I'll have to change the name*, he thought numbly. *Happy doesn't exist anymore.*

He couldn't believe it had only been a week since laughter had spilled from the open windows of their home. Only a week since the foundation of his life, his daughter's life, and the well-being of the B&B had been rocked and reduced to crumbly ash. Only a week since he'd leaned across the bed to deeply breathe in Jessica's hair, the skin of her neck. Now—gone.

The three-story Victorian farmhouse with cream siding and rusty-pink trim held sway over a quarter acre of yard and valley oak trees, now solely his responsibility. And he felt every ounce of that weight. He wondered idly if this particular responsibility would actually crush him, but he found that he didn't much care if it did. How blissful it would be to slip into his own long sleep, devoid of dreams or worries. He wouldn't have to feel so much. He wouldn't have to feel anything.

Still looking up at the house, Aidan spotted movement in a second-story window—a flash of pink that meant his daughter, Apple, was watching him. Apple, the reason he'd just dumped two weeks' worth of escape into the trash barrel. The sole member of the human race he now lived for. *You can't wish for death, asshole*, he thought. *You have a kid, and she has no one else.*

How was he possibly going to handle this? His daughter, the place, the business, being alone. He trudged up the drive toward the house, which had never before seemed threatening, but now it loomed over him, a look of judgment evident in its scowling windows and frowning doorway. Evident, at least, to Aidan.

"Apple?" he called as he came through the front door. It was just the two of them in the house, alone for the first time since the morning her mother had died. Death brings people, they'd discovered. People who are aching to help, people who come bearing fresh fruit, lasagna, and even a cozy pink blanket—a friend's comfort gift for Apple, who actually hated the color pink but had fallen into some kind of complicated dependent relationship with the blanket. It trailed her as she appeared on the second-floor balcony above him. Her face, framed by her long, brown, tangled hair, was flushed from recent tears.

"Hi, Dad," she said.

He answered by opening his arms wide, and she rushed down the staircase to fill the space in his chest. She was twelve and far too old to be carried by a parent, so he took her hand and led her to the mustard-colored, comfortable-but-elegant couch in the living room. Jessica's choice.

The house was filled with Jessica's choices. Across the room from the sofa stood a glass-fronted china cabinet filled with tiny wooden troll figures that Jessica had collected for most of her life. Aidan wondered, who was going to love those ugly creatures now?

"Dad?" Apple murmured, after they were settled beside each other.

"Anything," Aidan answered, knowing full well that he was currently capable of only nothing.

"I just want to let you know that if you need to send me somewhere else to live, I'd be okay."

He pivoted so he could see her face, which was serious and concentrated—she'd obviously rehearsed this conversation. "Why would I need to send you somewhere else to live?" he asked, genuinely curious.

"That's what's always happening to children in books. A mom dies and the father needs to work extra hours in the coal mines and of course is just completely destroyed by grief, so the poor children have to go live with an aging aunt in a huge house with a walled garden and no snacks." Apple blinked.

More than anything, Aidan wanted to ask his wife how he should respond to this. Jessica had always been the parent who knew exactly what to say, what to do, the right tone to take, when to intervene, and when to step back and let Apple figure things out for herself. He was shockingly unqualified for his new role as sole caretaker after twelve years of co-parenting.

He knew that whatever he said was bound to make everything worse. But not saying anything was probably the harshest thing he could do.

"Sweetie, we are very lucky to live in a time of labor laws and life insurance. No coal mines for me. No being shipped off to an aging aunt in a walled garden for you."

"I just didn't want you to feel badly if that was the way it had to go."

"Well, I truly appreciate that."

Aidan realized, his heart clenching anew, that there was no one with whom to share both the worries and the joys of parenthood anymore.

He had friends, of course. Kyle Dejesus, and his wife, Sharon, and their twins, who were a few years younger than Apple. They lived next door and worked at the B&B whenever they were needed. They had been foundational this past week as Aidan struggled to make even the simplest of choices about burial versus cremation, blue dress versus yellow dress. Sharon had brought over three meals every day, hearty soups and homemade bread that even Apple had managed to nibble. She'd even been the one to bring the pink blanket that Apple had developed a devotion to. They were Aidan's favorite people in the world after his wife and daughter.

But just then, with Apple snuggled beside him, the full force of his solitude struck him. He tried to keep his breathing steady. This was going to be hard.

This was going to be impossible.

Aidan thought of the bottles of wine now occupying the trash barrel at the end of the drive under the walnut tree. It wouldn't be difficult to retrieve them. Dive into one last escape. Welcome that numbness one last time. And truly, wasn't that why he hadn't dumped out the liquid before tossing the bottles? Just in case?

No. He'd had his last time.

He'd last obliterated himself the night after Jessica died, when he had wondered if he'd ever sleep again. Kyle, or Kye as everyone called him, had slept over, and Apple had gone to stay with Sharon and the twins. Kye knew that Aidan wasn't capable of purposefully hurting himself, and thus hurting Apple, especially not with such fresh pain running rampant through the family, but drinking and despair don't mix.

Aidan had vague, dream-like recollections of sitting on the back patio and sobbing uncontrollably into his hands, his face sodden and salty, his back and knees aching with the effort to remain upright, a war he finally conceded as he crumpled to the grass in defeat. He remembered the moon above, and Kye's doughy, kind face looking down from his six-foot-four height, worried. He remembered the coolness of the dewy lawn and how he kept thinking, *This grass is so damn lucky to never have to feel anything like this.*

And the next morning he'd woken up, half on and half off the couch he and Apple were now occupying, and he'd known that was his last time getting drunk. The promise to stop drinking that Jessica had tried to extract from him for years had finally been granted. And even though the week since had been many layers of awful, he hadn't broken that promise.

He gave Apple an extra-hard hug and she sighed, not quite happy but at least reassured, and the two of them sat on the couch as the house around them keenly felt its own loss and dusk descended over the oak trees, the sloping hills, and the vineyards in the distance where a hawk hung suspended against the purple gloaming sky. Just for a moment, Aidan thought they'd be okay, he thought everything might just be okay.

But the moment vanished, leaving only the taste of expected defeat and the scent of barely contained fear.

Chapter 1

Six Months Earlier

Jessica Cisneros brushed a stray blond hair away from her face with the back of one hand and smiled at Mr. Hawthorne as she offered a Meyer lemon-and-crab pastry bite from the silver platter she balanced in the other hand. "Richard, I know you can't resist these," she murmured and smiled across the table at her guest, whose girth indicated that Richard had never met a Michelin-rated appetizer he didn't like.

"Ah, you're an angel, Jessica. Aidan, you make the most delicious food on the West Coast. I know—I've tried it all." Mr. Hawthorne laughed generously at himself. His wife, Gwen, a thin woman with sleek black hair and a tiny butterfly painted at the corner of her left eye, joined in with a laugh that was surprisingly snorty.

Jessica shot a sly look at her husband, a warning that said, "No grimacing." Being married for fifteen years, they'd had a lot of practice using nonverbal dialogue, especially as their bed-and-breakfast business had grown, their daughter had aged into a near-teen, and Aidan's drinking had worsened. It could be tremendously complicated to maintain a family unit with a constant onslaught of guests, so a shared language of facial expressions helped.

Seated next to her, Aidan raised his eyebrows mockingly to express both his innocence and his dismay that she'd assume he was about to make fun of one of their most lucrative guests. "Richard, so glad you like the grub," he said. "I can give you the recipe, if you'd like."

This earned further snorting from Gwen. Her butterfly danced beside her delighted eye. "Oh, Aidan, we don't cook. Neither of us can stand the idea of being in a kitchen for longer than it takes to make a cup of tea."

The Hawthornes had chosen the enormously popular Happy Valley Bed & Breakfast for the past seven of their thirty wedding anniversaries. Looking at them, you might think they'd be content to spend a long, quiet weekend in Napa Valley visiting wineries and shopping for new dinnerware. But their style leaned more toward four-wheeling in the mountains. Gwen still had a smudge of crimson clay highlighting one sharp cheekbone.

Before getting sidetracked by Meyer lemon-and-crab pastry bites and Southern-style *gougères*, they'd been recounting their adventures avoiding a porcupine on the mountain trail. "He really did resemble my mother, didn't he, darling?" Gwen had giggled when describing the waddling, prickly creature.

Listening to them, Jessica could only hope her own marriage would be so fun when she and Aidan hit their thirtieth. She beamed at him and reached under the table to brush his fingers with her own. He smiled back at her. He looked tired, she'd noticed. What time had he come to bed last night?

She worried more and more about his drinking.

"The secret ingredient is a dash of benign neglect," he joked to the Hawthornes and was thankful when they chuckled. Aidan wasn't a natural at hospitality—which was strange since he and Jessica owned one of the most beloved bed-and-breakfasts in Napa Valley—and was inordinately proud whenever he managed to be authentic and natural.

Wine helped. He swallowed the last sip of the local vintage swirling in his hand-painted glass and glanced around the table to see if anyone else needed a refill, which would allow him to pour more for himself without directing unwanted attention toward the amount he'd managed to drink that night. So far.

At the other end of the table, amongst the murmurs of several contented guests, another couple was obviously embedded in an intense discussion. From what she could see as she peered at the other diners, Jessica figured it was a positive one, but you couldn't be too careful when it came to the dinner hour, so she delicately interrupted. "James, Micah, how are you finding the salmon? Have you tried the Dijon pickle butter sauce?"

James and Micah looked up from their intimate conversation, and James reached out to grasp his husband's hand. The two men were such opposites, Jessica reflected, not for the first time since she'd met them two years ago. James was sandy-haired and tall with a pronounced hunch to his back because he tried to convey a constant apology to the world for both his height and his very existence. Micah was brown-skinned and short, a powerful man who could throw a dare from afar to anyone tempted to apply their own biases and judgments onto him and anyone he loved. The two were no strangers to the Happy Valley and had come to consider it a haven in a world that sometimes felt too harsh.

"Jessica, it's my pleasure to announce—and it feels so right to announce this for the first time here—that we just decided to adopt a baby." James turned to Micah, both of them now teary and smiling, and then they looked back to Jessica as though her blessing would pave the path through the tangle of logistics they faced.

"What?! Oh, James, Micah, I can't even tell you how happy this makes me! A toast! To my beautiful friends, who are going to be incredible parents."

The table raised their glasses as one, and a chorus of cheers, well wishes, and good lucks was showered upon the men, who remained holding hands, a binary star formed of hope and determination.

Jessica turned back to Richard. "I love getting to be a part of life-changing moments. Don't you?"

Gwen raised her glass toward her in a more subtle toast. "Jessica, I can't even begin to understand how you and Aidan continue to surpass yourselves every year we come. You don't even know how much we look forward to our anniversaries here."

"We're incredibly lucky," Jessica said, looking at Aidan. "Both to have this place as our home and to have such wonderful guests as yourselves."

Aidan knew he was supposed to say something witty and meaningful. But what? "When we were looking for a place to buy, we almost settled on a burned-down horse farm, but the place still smelled like barbecued manure," he blurted, his face turning red as he heard himself. Jessica winced, almost unnoticeably. Who wants to hear about barbecued horse manure at the dinner table? "So, we decided to bet on this place." Could he just shut up already?

"It is an accomplishment to have built such a thriving hospitality business, even in this economy," Gwen remarked.

"Now, Richard, if you'll just nab this last spicy ginger-shrimp wonton, Aidan can refresh the tray." Jessica winked warmly, covering up her embarrassment.

Aidan took the tray and smiled at his wife, this woman with the sweetheart face and casually elegant knit skirt and draped shawl. He really did understand how deeply his luck ran beneath his skin. He knew that without Jessica, he'd be lost. Well, more lost.

As he rose from the table, he glanced over at Apple, who was chatting animatedly with the two people sitting across the table from her. Apple was twelve, though you'd guess twenty-seven if you overheard her conversations.

"What makes me so miffed is that the rule completely disregards the rights of Native people that were put in place by the same institution that is now trampling those rights and I just, I mean, where does it end, right?" Apple spooned a bite of fish into her mouth and just about vibrated with indignity, her brown eyes incredulous.

"But how might you solve the problem of the pipeline itself?" asked

Jemimah Jewels, a choreographer from Toronto. "We rely on that oil, don't we? We are more likely as a society to become better in terms of morality if there is a less painful way to do this."

Jemimah's brother, Jasper, chimed in, "And this is a practice that's been going on for hundreds of years. The U.S. government yanks the rug out from under First Peoples whenever it suits them economically. Even worse than Canada." He paused to take a sip of wine.

"Um, respectfully? Mr. Jewels? Morality has to come first. People are horrid. We are greedy and selfish and that's why we do terrible things like build a pipeline right across Native territory, and we'll keep doing terrible things until enough of us stand up and say, 'No more!'" Apple said these last words a bit louder than she meant to but look what was at stake! Only the soul of her country! And she did love her country, despite the deep disappointment she often felt for its actions. "All I know is I can't wait to go to Barnard, get a law degree, and start fixing some of these problems."

"Yeaaaaah . . . Apple, sweetie, you are probably doing more right now as a, how old are you? Fifteen? As a fifteen-year-old than most people three times your age," Jasper told her.

"Absolutely," agreed Jemimah. "You keep doing you, sweetheart. I can't wait to see how that turns out."

"I'm twelve, actually." Apple smiled at her friends and helped herself to another grilled pear with balsamic reduction sauce.

"Twelve going on forty," Aidan joked as he passed by her chair and winked over her head at Jasper and Jemimah.

"Dad, that is totally condescending." Apple scowled.

"I just meant I think you're smarter than me," her dad answered.

"Just because I listen to the news, read books, and keep up with more than one blog doesn't make me older than my years. It makes me informed! Something more people need to be!"

Jemimah interrupted. "Apple, you are so right. Listen, I need to know what blogs you read. Will you give me a list?"

Apple started counting them off on her fingers and Aidan kept moving so he didn't inadvertently embarrass her more. He didn't mean to be condescending—he just wasn't great with people. Any people. Even his daughter.

He felt deep gratitude that Apple was able to hold complex conversations with their guests. And that the Happy Valley attracted the kind of guests who were willing, even eager, to chat with this twelve-year-old girl who was quite possibly the smartest person in any room she occupied.

The kitchen was where all sense of awkwardness fell from Aidan's aura. It was his personal arena, which he navigated as a ship's captain guides his vessel through channels dominated by serpents and boulders. In the kitchen, Aidan felt at peace. He could breathe. He was alone.

He slipped a sheet of pine nut crackers into the broiler to toast and gave the olive tapenade a quick stir. He checked the blueberry crumble and washed a frying pan while he waited for the timer to ding. He was a fan of efficiency. His belief? True creativity could only erupt from a controlled set of variables. Brilliance was born of constraint.

To that end, the kitchen had developed into a well-oiled machine over which he presided. Mixing bowls and measuring devices occupied the row of drawers to the right of the stove while the specialized utensil drawer to the left of the sink was a marriage of utilization and artistry: whisks kept separate from basting brushes with bamboo dividers and ladles spooned together according to size. Taking his cue from the great Julia Child, Aidan had hung a pegboard and used a black marker to outline the various sizes of pots so no matter who was drying, they'd be able to hang the vessel in the correct position.

Which meant, of course, that as he was cooking, he'd be able to reach for the pot he needed without even having to look for it. The perfect blend of function and genius.

Not that he'd claim the label of genius, but he knew his food was good. Damn good.

He pulled the crackers out of the broiler and popped one into his mouth to test—perfect.

After layering them on a tray and swirling the tapenade into a blue ceramic serving dish, he reached to the shelf above his cookbook collection, chose a bottle of whiskey, and poured two fingers into his favorite glass, the one that had "#1 Dad" written on it, a gimmicky tourist-shop gift from Apple two birthdays ago.

The whiskey slid easily down his throat. Just one more shot. Then he could return to the dining room and be charming.

He turned and glared at the wooden troll that stared at him from the windowsill. Jessica liked to keep her trolls together in the china cabinet, but sometimes, Apple took one out and it would be found later in some crevice, a witness to their private moments. Like secret drinking.

After two more shots, he was ready.

"Dessert will be a few minutes, so in the meantime, everyone please try this new experiment of mine," he said to the crowd as he rejoined them. "I developed this new recipe for pine nut crackers and I'm just not sure—"

"Aidan, you are a sneak," said Kristabelle Johnson, an art dealer from New York who had spent her day scoping out new talent in local galleries. "We all know you're entirely sure of your work before presenting it to a room." She smiled at him and took a cracker from the tray along with a dab of tapenade, then pretended to swoon as she popped it into her mouth. "Oooooohhhh . . ." she moaned.

"'I'll have what she's having,'" quoted Miriam Radisson, a film producer.

The room laughed and Aidan smiled, though this level of attention and the showcasing of joy always made him uncomfortable.

Jessica cast a discerning glance around the room and let herself feel a moment of confident success. This didn't always happen. Sometimes a group of guests didn't quite gel into a gathering. It didn't matter if they were all polite, reasonably friendly, and interested in being there— sometimes something was just a bit off, and no matter how much charm she infused into the room, it was always slightly uncomfortable. But not this time. Tonight was perfect. The room, the company, the food—everything was a delight, and everyone felt lucky to be there.

Jessica would've called the evening an unmitigated success but for one thing: Aidan's face was flushed, his eyes were bright, and his left eye was just barely drooping. Not enough for anyone else to notice, but she did. These were the signs she kept watch for every night. Signs that he had poured too many glasses of wine for himself and snuck too many shots from the bottles he kept above the cookbooks. He was the chef, so of course he made frequent forays into the kitchen and she couldn't always follow him.

The guests were too distracted by the amazing food and their own banter to notice Jessica stand from her seat and float to Aidan's side to give him a warm kiss. "Honey, maybe slow down on the drinking?" she murmured.

Aidan nodded and tried to settle the quake he felt in the hollow of his stomach. This was not an unfamiliar moment. When he cooked, he poured himself a glass of wine, then two, then three. Another couple of glasses with dinner, and then partway through whatever delicate feast he'd prepared, he would down a shot or two, or three, or four, of whiskey. He didn't know why, exactly. It wasn't a matter of reason.

He only knew that bottles—of wine, of whiskey—wanted to be finished. They wanted to be empty. And he was the person to accomplish that.

Though he had developed effective methods of keeping his altered state a secret from his guests and friends, Jessica always knew. She could tell by the slope of his stance when he'd had more than he should, the way his smell changed, and the way he uttered her name—he was a different person. They'd had a few heated conversations about it, and he always promised to try harder, to do better. And he always meant it.

He might stay sober a couple of nights. Even a week. But the call of the bottle was insistent, and Aidan always returned to it.

Lately, their conversations had taken a firmer tone. She wanted him to go to A.A. She had even found a group in town, discovered the days and times they met, and jotted them on the back of an envelope that was now crammed partway through the pages of a book sitting on his bedside table, ignored.

Jessica was thinking about this as she turned back to her dining room full of guests, but as soon as she spotted her daughter, who had slipped away from her seat and was chatting amicably with Mr. and Mrs. Hawthorne, she was able to focus on the present.

"Apple, did you tell our friends about the mock debate you had in school last week?" she asked.

"Oh! I didn't! Mr. Hawthorne, how do you feel about the fact that a woman makes eighty-one cents for every dollar a man makes?"

Mr. Hawthorne, to his credit, didn't laugh or look bemused. He simply appeared interested.

"And how do you feel about the fact that women might lose nine-hundred-thousand dollars over their lifetime of working? Compared to men? How is that fair? Why are women penalized for taking time off to have babies? Babies that, by the way, men had a hand in creating, right?"

"So, you were debating that women should make money equal to men," Mr. Hawthorne said.

"No, I was on the other side. If women aren't logging as many hours or investing as much energy into their jobs, why should they get paid as much as the men who are logging hundreds of hours and investing a ton of thought and energy? And I truly believe that is soooo unfair, but it's healthy to debate the other side. And we won. But that could be because the people in my school are really closed-minded. We don't even compost lunch scraps!"

Mrs. Hawthorne couldn't help but smile at this, though she also pulled Apple aside and told her that if she needed a composting mentor, she had a connection that could be quite useful. "A compost czar," she whispered, and Apple looked suitably impressed.

* * *

Aidan excused himself from the dining room to plate the dessert in the kitchen, where he burned a finger arranging individual crocks of blueberry crumble on a silver tray. "Dammit," he muttered.

He'd first learned to cook in his grandmother's kitchen. She had raised him after his parents died in a house fire, and from her, he discovered the way foods move with each other, over each other, and around each other, each dance an intricate balance of surprise and comfort, texture and flavor.

Eventually, he trained as a chef at the New England Culinary Institute in Vermont, but he couldn't deal with the brutal winters there, so he came back west and worked in kitchens up and down the California coast, honing his skills and gaining layers of experience that coalesced into the stunning dinners he prepared nearly every night for their guests at the Happy Valley.

But still, despite the years since she had passed away peacefully in her sleep, Nana was always with him when he cooked, whether he was throwing together a macaroni casserole or lemony mushroom crostini. He could almost hear her now, telling him to run his finger under cold water to stop the burn from going deeper.

Instead, he reached for the whiskey bottle. Just one more shot.

As he was putting the shot glass into the dishwasher, Apple burst into the kitchen. "Come play, Dad!" she squealed.

"Baseball?"

"Dad . . ."

"Soccer?"

"Would you just—"

"Oh, of course. Parcheesi."

"Piano! Why do we have to go through this distinctly unfunny joke every time?"

He laughed, more at how much fun it was to spark exasperation in his daughter than at his actual joke, and nabbed the dessert tray as she towed him back to the dining room. Jessica rescued the tray before it became a victim of enthusiasm and Aidan and Apple sat on the bench in front of the Steinway upright that took up most of the eastern wall of the room. "What's tonight's song?" he asked his daughter.

"How about *Love's Old Sweet Song*? You've been practicing, right?" She smirked, knowing the answer was, "Yeah, not so much."

"Absolutely! 'Be prepared,' that's my motto."

"You and the Boy Scouts," she answered and dove both hands into the melody, letting Aidan catch up with the rhythm as well as he could. They found their groove—they always did. And Apple started to sing.

"Once in the dear dead days beyond recall,
When on the world the mists began to fall,
Out of the dreams that rose in happy throng
Low to our hearts love sang an old sweet song;
And in the dusk where fell the firelight gleam,
Softly it wove itself into our dream."

Aidan hummed where he could—singing was not his strong suit. But at least he could play.

"Just a song at twilight, when the lights are low,
And the flickering shadows softly come and go,
Tho' the heart be weary, sad the day and long,
Still to us at twilight comes love's old song,
Comes love's old sweet song."

Apple held the last note, both tremulous and strong, as Jessica swung by on her circuit of her guests and hit F-sharp at exactly the right moment, bringing the song to a delightful finish and their guests to their feet.

The three of them leaned toward each other instinctively, just for a moment. If a photographer had been in the room, this was the image he'd snap: a family of three, a triangle of love.

Jessica found early morning to be the best time to get a few things done that she didn't quite trust to anyone else. For example, putting away clean linens. Not a difficult task, of course, but Jessica liked to slip sprigs of lavender between each layer of folded sheets to keep the Egyptian cotton fresh and sweet. She could explain the process to Milly, their hired cleaner, but doing it herself felt like one of those personal touches the Happy Valley was known for, and she'd be devastated if it got forgotten. And to be honest, Milly, though a sweetheart, was not the most conscientious of cleaners. So, every morning Jessica picked several stems of lavender from the kitchen garden and relished the scent as she put away yesterday's linens.

As she straightened back up from the lower shelf of the linen closet that morning, she felt a nudge in the back of her head.

Stress? Aidan's drinking was getting worse and he didn't seem to want to listen to her or break the cycle he was stuck in. And she knew he was stuck. And Apple, while a terrific kid with a clearer head than most adults, was still just that—a kid. She needed so much. And Jessica sometimes wondered if she was up to this parenting gig. Especially with the teen years on the horizon.

She massaged the back of her neck with one hand, still holding the rest of the sheets in the other.

Or maybe it was the Happy Valley that was causing this slight blip in her morning. She loved the Happy Valley, but it was still a business, and sometimes a difficult one.

No. That was ridiculous. Jessica had never felt as at home as she did in this house. It was her place. Without it, she was a lesser entity, a puzzle piece alone in a box. And the house without her, well, she couldn't even imagine it. And she didn't have to, she reminded herself. She'd moved a lot as a kid because her dad had been stationed in different places all around the world, but once she'd met Aidan (it was a classic story of waitress and chef) and they'd found this place, she'd known she was home. She had banked on the fact that they'd never have to leave. And she worked hard to make that the reality.

Another nudge in her head, sharper this time. In the same place in her skull. Maybe she needed to drink more water. She leaned against the wall. Just for a moment, she thought. Then she'd get back downstairs and make sure Apple had set the table. But she was so tired, a pause would do wonders.

There was a stabbing in her head. Something wasn't right. But she had too much to do to be sick. She had too much to take care of. The people here, her guests, needed her. Her family. Her family.

From far, far away she heard Aidan. "Jessica?" he called, and she was desperate to answer. Every cell in her body tried to make a comprehensible word, tried to call out *Here!* but she wasn't sure she was making a sound. She heard him again, farther away. "Jess?" Why was he moving away?

Apple, where was Apple? Sweetest Apple with a crispy bite, that was what they'd called her as a baby. The three of them in a perfect bubble of constant sunlight and warmth.

The bubble burst.

Swaths of white linen floated down and landed on the dark hallway floor, arranged around Jessica's lifeless body as though an artist had decreed it.

Jessica didn't see Aidan and Apple come around the corner of the hall and discover her there. She did not witness the sudden flood of panic on Aidan's face or Apple's features tensed in confusion. She did not sense the house settling into grief around her, the house that was no longer whole, the house that had lost its heart.

Chapter 2

Five Years Later

Apple delicately removed a plastic container from the refrigerator with two fingers, holding her face away from the stench. "Really, Dad? You have got to be kidding me. Are you running science experiments in our fridge?"

She dumped it into the trash with only a hint of guilt for not dismantling the biohazardous materials for composting and recycling. The world would just have to deal. Because she couldn't. Not today. Not now.

She turned and glared at her father, her long, brown hair whipping with her angry motion. Aidan, in turn, was staring at a framed photograph mounted on the wall of the kitchen, directly over the wooden butcher block with the built-in knife holder. Which, like most other cooking tools in the room, was furry with a thick layer of dust.

"Dad! Food! Cook. You." She mimed breaking open an egg and then snapped her fingers in a diva move that paired pretty well with her black combat boots, fishnet stockings under purposefully torn cargo shorts, and a white tank top made socially acceptable via a pearly-gray cashmere cardigan that had belonged to her mother. Aidan looked up at her, still a thousand years away.

"Kai's been waiting outside for me for like fifteen minutes. I'm going to be late for school, and meanwhile you've slipped into *The Twilight Zone* for the nineteenth time this morning. Dad, guests need breakfast. It's in our name. Bed and, you know, breakfast."

Aidan ripped himself away from the picture of a roundly pregnant Jessica smiling at the younger him who held the camera. She leaned against the back of a bench at the Presidio, the Golden Gate Bridge in the distance. They'd talked that day about names for the baby. If it were a boy, if it were a girl. He'd wanted Sam for a boy and, well, Sam for a girl. Sam had been his father's name. But Jessica had been certain she was carrying a girl, and even more certain that the girl's name was not Sam. And Aidan had believed her—Jessica just knew things like that.

"Right. Sorry! Apple, I'm so sorry. Go. Go to school and be amazing. I've got this." He tore himself away from the photo and picked up a spatula from where it had been left last night on the table. Or maybe it was the night before? Anyway, there was eggy material crusted to it. He brandished it like a wand in front of his scowling daughter.

"You got this? For real?" Apple's gusty sigh was typical teenager but touched with something more, something deeper. A grief that had yet to abate. An acknowledgement that no matter how hard the two of them tried, without Jessica they still did not quite make a family. Not a functioning one, anyway. "Right, I'm going. I'll tell Milly on my way out that she's in charge of breakfast. Again."

Apple grabbed her messenger bag from the back of a kitchen chair and stomped out the door. Aidan heard her exchange with Milly in the hall and couldn't help but pick up on the obvious disdain with which she murmured something—probably about Aidan's lack of motivation, the usual story—to the housekeeper, who wasn't more than seven years her senior. And then he heard them laugh. Were they laughing at him? Probably.

Even so, it was incredibly sweet to hear his daughter laugh.

Very little laughter had echoed through the halls and rooms of the Happy Valley for the past five years, two months, one week, and two days. Since Jessica's death of a brain aneurism, overwhelming loss had eclipsed all other emotions in the house. Aidan had tried so hard to keep moving forward. Not only for himself and his daughter but also for Jessica and for the home she loved.

But he was failing. He knew he was failing. They couldn't go on like this. And he wasn't just being dramatic. Aidan wasn't a dramatic person.

For proof, he only had to look around the kitchen. Once a place that combined efficient industry with creative genius, the room was now infected with dinginess and dirt, layered with an air of neglect and abandonment. Bowls, measuring cups, baking sheets, plates, drinking glasses—cooking implements of all types crowded every inch of horizontal space. Even the floor was dotted with a few landmines of dirty mugs. As he stepped away from the butcher block to seek out ingredients for breakfast, he had to do a quick two-step to avoid a tower of saucers standing sentry near the counter. Ridiculous.

He opened the fridge and made a half-hearted scan of its contents, noting the lack of fresh produce, the carton of creamer with a sell-by date a week past, the pool of bloody juice under the steaks that had been defrosting for a few days now. There was nothing decent in there with which to create a breakfast for the measly four guests currently staying at the Happy Valley.

He turned to the cabinet. Powdered scrambled eggs it would have to be. Maybe he could dice some of the sardines he had spotted on the shelf above the boxed mashed potatoes to spice them up. Or maybe some capers—he spied a small bottle behind the cooking wine.

Wine. Aidan knew how terrible that wine would taste. It was meant for cooking, and to be honest, it wasn't even up to that. That particular bottle came from an emergency run to the local market three years ago when he was desperate for a marsala for a recipe. That wine would burn going down.

But he knew, too, the wave of relief he'd feel beginning on the roof of his mouth and spreading quickly through his head, his chest, all the way to his fingertips. He knew how good one sip would feel. Just. One. Sip.

Aidan reached into the pocket of his jeans and clutched the A.A. token he carried everywhere. He squeezed it. Five years, two months, one week, and one day. That's how long it had been since he'd had a drink.

Milly came bustling into the kitchen, interrupting his solitude and self-reflection with her usual mix of snapped gum, pink-tipped dreadlocks, and determined-but-distracted attitude.

Milly was not talented in the ways of food. Or cleanliness. Or decorating. Despite lacking these traits, she was the longest-serving staff member at the Happy Valley. Jessica had hired her years ago, when Milly was still in high school, and, despite being smart, Milly had never seen the point in going away to college, which was lucky for Aidan since he couldn't see how he'd ever find someone else willing to work for pennies. Without even the minimal efforts of caretaking Milly brought to the place every day, it would have fallen apart even further. And she was loyal. Aidan and Apple might not have seen it clearly enough to articulate, but Milly stayed on out of deep and abiding love for the two of them. She couldn't have stood to see them fail.

Well, fail worse, anyway.

"Mr. Cisneros!" she hooted at him. "How's tricks?"

"Ah, Milly, you breath of fresh air, you savior, you diva."

This was their standard greeting.

"So, what have we got to feed our lovely guests this morning?" she asked, proceeding to scramble through the same cabinet Aidan had just been taking stock of. "Plenty of powdered options still, I see."

"Yeah, I guess I haven't had a chance to get to the market yet this week." In fact, Aidan hadn't been to the market in six weeks. "I was thinking we could add some capers to some quick-and-dirty scrambled eggs? Give them a true Q-and-D start to the day?"

"Sure thing, Mr. C. Just like yesterday, right?"

"Yesterday we didn't garnish the plates, did we?"

"Ooooh, too fancy. Can't even, Mr. C. Hey, you start on the caper thing, and I'll nab some garnish from the garden, okey dokey?"

"Two steps ahead of you, Milly." Aidan was already reaching for the pickled buds. Then he poured powdered eggs into a silver metal bowl, the last clean one in the cupboard. It was painful to mix up a batch of powdered eggs. Every culinary instinct left in his brain shrieked along with the whisk. He'd have been happier breaking fresh eggs from the farm down the road, then adding cream that had still been in the cow as of yesterday. He'd have been thrilled to dice some onion and pepper and sauté the veggies on high heat to release the juices, then lower the temperature to layer the creamy egg mixture into the pan so the result was fluffy and delectable.

But he just couldn't get his act together to make that particular breakfast happen.

Aidan issued his standard silent apology to Jessica's memory as he beat the gelatinous pool of fake yellow with his whisk. *I'm sorry, sweetheart*, he whispered in his head as he poured the stuff into a not-quite-heated pan. *So, so sorry*, he murmured as he applied a spatula to the concoction and sprinkled a few wrinkly capers into the mixture. The smell was just about punishment enough for the sin of serving powdered eggs to guests.

Risking burning the food, Aidan leaned his head down on the counter for a moment, overcome by a not-unfamiliar sense of defeat. But he misjudged the distance to the countertop and ended up banging against it, making an audible knock against the oiled wood that sent a glancing pain through his forehead. *Great*, he thought. *Maybe I have a concussion now and an excuse to sleep for a week.*

"Okey dokey, here's what I found in that bramble bush you insist on calling a garden," Milly announced as she returned and spread a handful of lavender on a rare clear space on the counter.

Aidan stood upright and tried to pretend his head didn't hurt. "Milly, lavender isn't really a garnish," he began to explain, reaching to pluck a sprig from the purple chaos, but then thought, *What's the point? Why not?* Nothing about his world made sense anymore, so why insist on a certain species of garnish? He held a violet twig under his nose for a moment and breathed in the sweet, enduring scent and was treated with the briefest memory of his wife sliding the dusty green leaves between clean sheets she'd stacked in the linen closet. That was the kind of minute detail Jessica had always remembered. No one here was thinking like that now.

Together, they managed to get the eggs, the lavender, and a few slices of white toast onto each of the four plates. Paper plates, because every other piece of dishware was dirty, piled in the sink in a leaning tower of pitiful.

"Breakfast is served!" called Milly as the two of them entered the dining room, plates balanced in their arms.

"Finally," muttered a pinched-faced woman to her beefy husband, the two of them dressed in matching polo shirts and Teva sandals. "It's practically midmorning. We like to eat early, don't we, Tom, so we can get an early start on the day."

Aidan couldn't for the life of him remember the woman's name. "Well, there is a delightful bakery that serves breakfast sandwiches just down the road. You're welcome to eat there any morning you'd like."

"And get a discount, I assume?" the woman snorted. "After all, this is supposed to be a bed and *breakfast*. Or did I misread the sign?"

"Now, Carol, it's fine," said her husband. Tom was tucking into his eggs with gusto. It made Aidan's stomach hurt to watch this man consume such sub-quality food, even though the food, and its lack of quality, was his fault. Tom, however, seemed like he was enjoying his culinary adventure.

Carol sighed and flicked a clear-coated fingernail at her paper plate. "You know, we almost didn't book here because of that review on *Rambling with Rebah*. You know, the travel blogger? I just love her. But she, let me tell you, does not love you." She picked up a fork and proceeded to nibble at her food.

God, Aidan hated that name—Rebah. His fist tightened around

the butter dish. Rebah Reynolds had stayed there about a year ago, got drunk, threw up in a trash can, and spilled red wine on what had once been Jessica's favorite quilt. When Aidan had rightfully accused her of being a drunk the next morning, she'd been pissed. There's no one more righteous than an alcoholic accused of drinking, he knew from firsthand experience. She'd stormed out, after giving Aidan an earful of threats about how she was going to ruin him, and went on to publish a colossal takedown of the Happy Valley on her travel blog, *Rambling with Rebah*. Aidan had to admit that her threats had played out exactly as she'd said they would. Guest numbers—not super healthy to begin with—had plummeted, and the Happy Valley had limped along ever since.

The other guests were picking at the plates in front of them while Milly bustled around refreshing coffee cups. Aidan flashed back to what this dining room had looked like five years ago. Back then, there were no cobwebs in the corners. There was no grit underfoot. The table surfaces weren't sticky. The rugs weren't dusty. The piano wasn't out of tune. And the guests—even they had been different: vibrant and engaged, eager to discuss the day ahead or behind, happy to talk art, books, politics, geography. The current crop of visitors avoided eye contact except when issuing complaints about the food, the bedroom door that wouldn't close quite right, the stench coming from the space behind the toilet in their bathroom. All day long, complaints. Aidan was just about driven mad by it all.

So why do I stay? he asked himself as he retreated to the kitchen to attempt to clean a dish or two.

Because of Jessica. Leaving meant failing. Staying meant honoring her memory.

But how? Aidan's desk in the second-floor office was a museum of unpaid bills, all of them squawking at him whenever he tried to sit there and think of a plan. Creditors called daily, forcing him to get good at different accents. Just yesterday, he'd pulled off a pretty good cockney when Zenith Insurance called looking for their twelve thousand dollar annual payment.

Aidan gave up on the pile of encrusted plates that had taken up residence in the sink. He poured himself another cup of coffee and leaned against the windowsill, looking out on the front yard that was not looking its early spring best. There was so much shit to do. The grass needed raking. The walnut tree had a dead branch near the top that should really be lopped off. And he was just so goddamn exhausted. What he really wanted was a drink. Or ten.

The night before Jessica died, their very last conversation had been about his drinking. She wanted him to stop. She'd wanted him to stop for a long time, but that night she'd delivered a kind of ultimatum. She wanted him to promise to stop, or he was going to lose everything he loved. He still hadn't been able to see it. Because he was, well, drunk.

Not horribly drunk. But the Hawthornes had been staying that night, and Richard sometimes liked a nightcap after his wife, Gwen, had gone up to bed, so Aidan had been happy to accommodate. And when, finally, Richard had finished telling the story of how he'd made his first million, Aidan had been very, very comfortable. But that pleasant sensation had deteriorated into shame when Jessica met him at their bedroom door with a look of fury on her face.

"I have tried really hard to stay sweet about this, Aidan, but I'm sick of it. You almost served Kristabelle Johnson the peanut salad wonton cups, and you know she's allergic. You could have killed her. And you did it because you'd had too much to drink."

Aidan tried smiling. That was the only expression he thought he'd be able to manage. But it only enraged her further.

"No! Don't you make this into a ridiculous story! You have to stop drinking or we are going to lose this business!"

"Jess, it's okay, I'm fine. I didn't kill anyone." He tried to maneuver around her into the room—he was just getting to that point where lying down would be a welcome relief, but any longer on his feet and he'd need another brandy.

"Uh-uh. You find a different bed to sleep in tonight."

"But . . . we're a full house. There are no other beds."

"Hmmm. Not my problem. But, God help me, if a guest finds you on a couch or in a common area, you're going to be in even more trouble."

He'd found himself folded nearly in half in the back seat of his truck. It was the only place he could think of where he wouldn't be discovered by an early riser. And anyway, it wasn't so bad. He watched the moon rise over the walnut tree at the end of his driveway and heard an owl call out, again and again, over and over.

That had been their last conversation. If he'd known that night, as he lay with cramps in his calves and the door handle pressed into the top of his head, that his wife would die the next morning, he would have stayed in their bedroom, despite Jessica's fury.

But instead, the next morning he stumbled back to the house when he was awoken by the sun coming through the truck window. He'd snuck in through the front door, careful not to let it slam behind him. A glass of water helped, standing at the kitchen sink. He knew she'd be up already, getting a start on the avalanche of tasks that awaited anyone crazy enough to own a bed-and-breakfast.

All he wanted to do was find her. Tell her she was right. Tell her that he'd go to an A.A. meeting. Promise her he'd try.

He called her name softly as he climbed the stairs, not wanting to wake anyone else, but when he heard an unnatural thump and a guttural sound, he'd started to run. Apple had sleepily stumbled out of her bedroom as he passed, looking confused. "Where's Mommy?" he asked. Apple shook her head. She didn't know.

He climbed the stairs past the turn to the third floor. Maybe she was putting away linens? She liked to slip sprigs of lavender between the sheets.

"Jess?" he called, louder now.

And there she was.

On the floor. Eyes open. Eyes unseeing. Eyes that would never see again.

And he was beholden to a promise he could only make to her corpse.

But he'd kept that promise all these years, and he'd keep it today, too. He sighed and pushed himself up from his stance against the windowsill. Time to at least pretend to clean rooms and function as a decent host.

Chapter 3

Rebah Reynolds was an expert at driving with one eye on her phone. She navigated her cranberry Lexus through intersection after intersection around her suburban New York town, her finger swiping continuously through her phone alerts. At a stoplight, she managed to unscrew a tiny bottle and dribble the last of the vodka into her ceramic travel mug, the one she'd picked up at Heathrow last year, "Mind the gap!" scrawled on the side in messy print.

A horn blared behind her—the light had turned green. "I'm going!" Rebah shouted into the rearview mirror. "Jeez, if you can't have a modicum of patience with other people in society, don't leave home."

This was funny coming from Rebah. Patience wasn't something she could boast of having an excess of, except when it came to her work.

Or at least that's how it used to be.

Rebah swerved out of the lane she'd drifted into and, keeping one hand on the wheel and one eye on the road, slid a yellow legal pad out of her briefcase that sat in the passenger side footwell. Balancing a pen in her right hand, her phone in her left, and the steering wheel with her bare knee, she gave the order to dial her boss, or, rather, one of her bosses. "Call Frank." The ringing on the other end of the line filled her car with tension.

Rebah distracted herself with work while she waited for Frank to pick up. Scrolling, scrolling, swerving, braking, gassing. Her own site

popped up in her feed, and she clicked through it. It used to be she'd
feel a rush of delighted ownership whenever she looked at her site,
Rambling with Rebah, but now . . . now, she felt a pressure bloom in her
chest as she checked the status bar at the top: three million subscribers.

A year ago, that number was five million.

"This is Frank. Go."

"Frank! My man! You'd never guess what I ended up eating for dinner my last night in Cambodia . . . tarantulas!"

On the other end of the line, Frank sighed, and she could hear the
disgust in his voice. "Ugh. That's not going to make it into the article, is it? Because our readers are not going to think that's destination
material."

It occurred to her to wonder if that disgust was directed at the
crispy tarantulas or at her for eating them. "Frank, my readers love
culinary adventures. And they especially love adventuresome culinary
endeavors." Rebah was still looking at her site, half an eye on the con-
struction workers scrambling to get out of the road as she nearly ran
them over.

You wouldn't guess Rebah's stats had dipped so badly by looking
at her current post, "Rebah Rambles in the 10 Most Romantic Hot
Spots of Central Asia." There was a photo of her on a camel in the
Gobi Desert, a gauzy purple and gold head scarf flowing over her long,
auburn hair just so, her hauntingly dark blue eyes peering from her
healthily tanned face, a Mongolian guide with a chiseled jaw and icy-
green eyes that contrasted with his dark skin pressed against her back
in a pose that was both protective and seductive. Mostly what she
remembered about that trip was the enormous amount of sun block
she'd had to use to keep from burning.

Rebah scanned a year's worth of posts as she listened to Frank drone
on about corporate regulations and how eating tarantulas didn't really fit
with the Rebah brand, keeping a dab of attention on the traffic around
her. She was famous for her "Top 10" segments: "Rebah Rambles in
the 10 Most Beautiful Volcanos of Iceland," "Rebah Rambles in the

10 Most Haunted Castles of Scotland," "Rebah Rambles on the 10 Most Pristine Beaches of the Maldives." Photo after photo of herself, beaming under chic straw hats, smart visors, or a perfectly draped scarf, and always a different gorgeous man framing her body against the sweeping backdrop of an inspired destination.

But she wasn't always counting to ten as she traveled: "Eating Healthy in Helsinki," "Ecotourism Finds Its Stride," "Giving Back in Gabiro." And, for those with a healthy appetite for puns: "Yachts and Yachts of Fun with Rebah." Ah, yes—she'd been seasick for much of that week. The things she did for her readers.

"Frank, wait. What did you just say?"

The truck behind her leaned on its horn as she braked suddenly to avoid hitting the pedestrian she'd only just seen crossing in front of her. Her legal pad slid to the floor.

"Corporate wants you to do some kind of partnership with Stewart Starr. He's got this fantastic vlog, lots of laughs, and interaction with the audience. It's a hoot."

"Yeah, I don't do vlogs. Or partnerships."

"Well, Corporate thinks this could be a stellar collaboration."

"And I don't do anything with Stewy. That guy is a creep. Worse than a creep—he's a schmoozy, evil bastard."

"Hon, you don't understand—this isn't a request."

"What the hell, Frank?" Rebah yelled. "That idiot knows nothing about travel! He wouldn't recognize luxury if it was served to him in a crystal flute! I do not care about his interactive, ridiculous vlogcast thing, and I want no part of it. My readers want Rebah to be Rebah."

Damn. She knew she shouldn't talk to her boss like this, well, one of her bosses, but she couldn't stand the idea of being . . . bossed around like that.

She glared at her phone while the silence on the other end deepened. She winced at the tiny image of her beaming face staring back from her home page. When had this way of life become so exhausting?

When had traveling become such a chore? When had this job become a job? The traffic around her slowed.

"Frank? Frank. Let me be with frank with you."

No answer from Frank.

"You know me, right? You know what I do, what I am. Do you really think a vlogging collaborative will fly with my particular style? My essence?"

There was a deep sigh from Frank while the truck in the lane next to her honked as it swerved to avoid her drift.

"Hey, how about I come out there and explain directly to Corporate how bad this idea is?"

"You know, Rebah, there are plenty of bloggers, younger bloggers, who'd kill for a chance to work with Stewart."

That stung. At twenty-nine, Rebah knew her days of managing stunning photos of herself in the arms of desirable men were numbered, but Frank didn't have to point it out like that. Low blow. And why wasn't anyone killing for the chance to work with her? Not that she'd ever stoop to that. She was a loner, an individual. She liked to hunt in solitude.

Rebah spotted a liquor store and crossed two lanes of traffic, ignoring the stares, the horns, and the gestures sent her way from other drivers, to pull into the parking lot. This would help. She didn't let herself recognize that it was ten in the morning on a Tuesday. She refused to acknowledge the glimmer of worry in her belly that maybe something other than simple thirst was making her navigate the highway in a beeline to a liquor store.

"Frank, you're giving me a headache. Look, I'm in the middle of writing." She parked and opened her car door while trying to release the seat belt at the same time, but that was difficult with a phone and pen still in her hands. The car burst into a warning beep. "Dammit," she muttered, yanking on the belt, which seemed to tighten around her even farther. "What? No, of course I'm not driving. That would be dangerous. Listen, I'll fly out and talk to Corporate. I'll perform. I'll be the Rebah they want." Who even invented this crazy seat belt system anyway? "Frank, I said I'd do it!"

Rebah hung up with a sigh of relief and nabbed her coffee, still waiting patiently in its cup holder, and took a long gulp. Hot! Damn.

After stocking up at the liquor store—two cases of wine, a case of vodka, and, just for fun, a bottle of Unicorn Tears beer—Rebah settled back into her car and wondered what to do next. Another sip of coffee—perfect temperature. And the extra kick helped, too.

It was always like this coming home from a trip. Reentry could be a challenge. When you spent half your life traveling to exotic places and having experiences that your friends really couldn't relate to—Who else has had their hair washed in a glistening waterfall by local warriors using soap made from papaya?—it could be hard to have a normal conversation with normal people.

But at the moment, Rebah craved the company of friends. It had been way too long since she had had a chat with someone who had known her for years, pre-blog, and wanted to just hang out and gossip about shared acquaintances. She wanted to relax. She wanted to drink. She wanted to forget about all the responsibilities that kept creeping up in her mind. She wanted to moan to someone about how much she wanted a dog, even though her lifestyle really prohibited keeping any pets.

Rebah scrolled through her contact list, wondering who might want to hang out. There! Jocelyn! Jocelyn was always up for a good time. One of her best friends from college, Jocelyn had moved to a godforsaken suburb from the city after getting married to Mark, and Rebah had followed soon after, figuring that the party had moved elsewhere and therefore so would she. Besides, the city had been losing its charm for a couple of years. There was a hustle that was required of city dwellers that she had to admit did not come naturally. It was one thing to rush around for a week through a new city and another thing entirely to have to constantly be on just to keep up with the rest of the city dwellers. So she bought a house in the suburbs after just one weekend of house hunting alongside a real estate agent whose French bulldog accompanied them to the open houses.

Turned out, the suburbs were not a party unless you were into weekend barbecues with other families from your gated community. But still, for what Rebah had been paying for a walk-up in the West Village, she got a four-thousand, five-hundred-square-foot house with a pool, back deck, and full basement. Of course, who really needed all that space?

But Jocelyn had still proved to be a good friend. Whenever Rebah was in town, the two of them usually found an evening to go to the city for dinner and drinks, and more drinks, and more drinks, and usually they ended up dancing until dawn and paying an exorbitant amount of money for a cab back to the suburbs.

It had been a while, though, Rebah realized, since she'd seen her friend. Oh! Jocelyn had had a baby! That's right. Which was great since that meant Jocelyn would be home with the kid instead of at her job as a marketer for a big tech firm. Perfect. Rebah took another gulp of coffee and wondered how she could've forgotten that her friend had given birth to a baby. Had she even sent a gift?

Plan in place, Rebah revved her engine and pulled out of the parking lot with a squeal of tires. She sipped her now-cool coffee as she raced down the highway, windows open and her favorite playlist queued up—heavy on the Bowie with a smattering of Brandi Carlile to keep it real. It didn't take long for her to get to Jocelyn's complex, which was nautically named "Ocean's Destiny."

Rebah was beginning to suspect she had never dropped off a present for the baby. Damn. And Jocelyn liked presents, always had. Rebah vibrated with a flash of inspiration: the Unicorn Tears! A baby shower in a bottle, the perfect gift. Party saved.

She pulled up to the keypad and typed in the code Jocelyn had given her when she first moved to the 'burbs. The gates opened elegantly, and Rebah maneuvered her Lexus along smooth blacktop framed with flowering hedges, the occasional mansion rising from the sloping hills. Which one was Jocelyn's house? Man, how long had it been since they'd hung out?

Rebah pulled into the drive of the house she was pretty sure belonged to her friend and skipped up to the door holding two bottles of newly purchased wine and the Unicorn Tears, knowing a security camera was tracking her every move and an alarm had already sounded inside to alert the occupants of a visitor. Sure enough, as she approached the front steps the door opened and there was Jocelyn.

Holding a baby.

Wearing a dirty tank top and sweatpants.

With her obviously unwashed hair wrapped up in a scrunchie.

"Rebah?" Jocelyn asked, bewildered. "What are you doing here?"

Rebah swallowed her shock at seeing her usually adorable friend in such a disheveled state. "Joc! It's been too long! I'm back in town and was thinking I hadn't seen you in ages, so I picked up some wine and came by so we could throw on some tunes, lay around your living room, and you could tell me everything I've missed! And here! Happy baby!" She shoved the Unicorn Tears at Jocelyn, who tried to juggle the door, a stuffed animal, a pacifier, and the baby to take the bottle, but finally just shook her head, indicating that Rebah should hold on to it.

"But it's, like, eight in the morning? I don't even know what time it is. The baby was up all night."

"Pretty sure it's almost eleven. Party time!"

The baby was staring at Rebah and gumming some kind of orange chew toy that looked like it had some lint on it. Rebah tried waving with her free elbow. *Do babies like waving?* The kid scowled and opened its mouth wider and a sound came out like no sound Rebah had ever heard before—halfway between a howling coyote and a chainsaw.

"Oh, God, she's starting again. Okay, Rebah? Come in if you want, but I have to find her teddy bear and make it talk a certain way so she'll stop crying."

Rebah closed the door behind herself and called out to Jocelyn, who'd gone ahead with the howling creature, "I'll just get a couple glasses and pop this cork, shall I?" In fact, it was almost noon. Rebah mentally kicked herself for not picking up some cheese and olives, maybe even some of that delish artichoke tapenade from the local gourmet market. They were going to need provisions if they wanted to get through this wine without being sick.

The kitchen was a disaster: plates, cups, and water glasses everywhere, a pot of old spaghetti solidifying on the countertop. Rebah pulled open several drawers before she found the corkscrew. The wineglasses were easier to find since the cabinets were glass fronted. Rebah uncorked the bottle and then cleared a space on the table and set down the Unicorn Tears, the opaque white bottle looking bizarre against the backdrop of chaos. Was that—yes, a balled-up diaper, obviously used, took up half a plate at one of the table settings. This was really beyond the limit.

The wailing in the other room had stopped. Rebah carried the open bottle and two glasses to the living room. Jocelyn and the baby were snuggled together on the couch, a teddy bear between them, and, for a second, Rebah couldn't breathe. They were such a unit, a whole package of love, an entire continent of a family. Mother and baby were gazing at each other with similar expressions—a sort of "I love you, but you need to calm down" kind of face.

Rebah had never felt the urge to have children like she'd heard other women talk about. When she'd imagined her future in high school and college, it was always a solitary one, days spent doing work she loved and nights spent however she wanted, whether that was partying, reading, or going to a movie. She liked the idea of a man to do things with, but not everything. She thrived on independence, always had. So then why did she feel this sucking sensation in her belly, as if a tide had suddenly reversed direction? Why did she feel so . . . sad?

It wasn't the kid. The baby, actually, was kind of repulsive, all gummy and damp. But the complete whole they formed together—that's what was making her belly flip-flop.

"Wine will help," she announced, as much to herself as to her friend. She poured two overly generous glasses.

"Oh, Rebah, I really don't think I can do wine right now. She's not sleeping through the night, so I get woken up every hour, and I'm breastfeeding, so I really need to limit and—"

"Just a few sips, that's all I insist on." Rebah downed most of her own glass and watched as Jocelyn carefully took just that: a few sips. Huh. Looked like babies made people boring.

"So, tell me everything! Who have you seen lately? And how's that handsome husband of yours? What about Cassandra and Jack—how have they been? God, I never see anyone anymore. Must be all my traveling. Oh! Let me show you pics of Cambodia. I ate a tarantula! Swear to God!" Rebah reached over and dug in her purse for her phone but then realized Jocelyn wasn't actually listening. Instead, she was undoing the front of her shirt, hitching up her bra, and shoving the baby's head into her breast. "Oooooohhhh . . ." Rebah muttered.

"Oh, you don't mind, do you? If I don't feed her now, she'll be screaming again in a few minutes. So, Cambodia? That sounds amazing." Having successfully gotten the baby to latch on to her nipple, Jocelyn reached for her wineglass again and held it up toward Rebah. "Cheers!"

"Yes! Cheers!" Rebah held up her own glass in response and thought that maybe this visit was going okay after all.

But then the baby popped off Jocelyn's breast, and Jocelyn winced, jerking painfully away from the baby's brand-new teeth, and a glug of rosé wine splashed over the rim of her glass and landed on the beige couch.

"Oh! I'll get some paper towels." Rebah scrambled from her seat and dashed back to the kitchen, not just in an effort to be helpful but also because she did not want to look at her friend's boob. Not that she hadn't seen them before: a naked nighttime swim on a beach in Cabo came to mind, but that was a far different situation. Jocelyn had been sexy then.

No! Women were still sexy after having babies! Rebah had scanned enough magazines while waiting for the doctor to know this. God, this was all so complicated.

Mercifully, by the time she returned to the living room with paper towels and her newly filled glass, Jocelyn's chest was covered up again. Rebah patted at the stain ineffectively until Jocelyn put her hand out to stop.

"Look, Rebah, this was sweet of you, really, but to be honest, I'm not up for day drinking anymore."

"Um . . . okay?" Rebah took a large glug of wine and sat back in her spot.

"I mean, it's not like we're still in college. Life is different now. We're grown-ups. I have a baby!"

"Sure, of course. Totally understand." But she didn't. She didn't really understand how everything had changed so drastically since they were twenty. How had her friend veered onto this path of breastfeeding and beige couches?

Rebah remembered Jocelyn one particular night in college when they'd joined up with a Swedish women's volleyball team at a local party and held an impromptu volleyball tournament in the central campus quad. Jocelyn had been on fire, spiking balls and serving like a madwoman, scoring points on these near-professionals, and the next day she hadn't been able to remember a thing. "I was good at volleyball?" she'd asked confusedly in between eruptive visits to the toilet. "I've never been good at volleyball." But that was Jocelyn. Rise to the occasion. Meet the demand at hand. Surpass expectations as though those expectations were simply helpful suggestions.

But now her friend was trapped under a baby, who'd dozed off in that way babies do, all of a sudden and totally boneless. Jocelyn wouldn't even have been able to reach her wineglass, now balanced on the end table, since the baby made it impossible to move very far.

"Do you want me to get that for you?" Rebah asked, rising partially to deliver the wine.

"Oh, God, no. It's giving me heartburn."

Rebah drained her own glass and then casually reached for Jocelyn's and started drinking from it, trying not to be noticed. She needn't have worried. Jocelyn was looking only at her baby. Rebah tried to think of something to talk about. "Have you heard from any of the old gang?" she asked.

"Well, Tammi and Craig got married, finally, and they're buying a house in Maine, some kind of dilapidated farm they have big plans for. And Kristin is living at home again while she gets her business off the ground—that girl is super ambitious. And Jeremy, well, I haven't heard from Jeremy for a while, but according to social media he's got yet another gorgeous boyfriend and they're crazy in love." Jocelyn absentmindedly patted the baby as she talked, running her fingers over her eyebrows and leaning down to sniff her head. Rebah was almost embarrassed to watch. Like she was witnessing something intimate and personal.

"Wait, Kristin is starting her own business? I could give her some advice if she wants. So much could go wrong—I should know. Let her know she can call any time, I'm totally happy to help." Rebah poured herself another glass of wine and eyed the remaining inch or so in the bottle. She wondered if it would be okay to open the second one. Was that rude? Since she was the only one drinking?

"Yeah, I think she has a pretty good thing going." Jocelyn looked uncomfortable. "She's smart, and really driven. And you made it kind of clear a while back that you didn't think she'd succeed and I'm not sure she'd be into getting advice from you after that."

"Wait, what? I did? I don't remember!"

"Yeah, well, you were probably drunk. Remember our barbecue a couple years ago? Everyone was here? You were doing shots?"

"Oh, no, I remember. Totally."

"And Kristin had just started with the planning and researching, and you were really kind of down on it."

"Oh, shit, I'm sorry. I never meant to be discouraging." Truth was, Rebah had zero recollection of any conversation with Kristin about business. She remembered the first few shots, and she had a vague recollection of going swimming in her sundress, but beyond that, the barbecue was a blank space in her head. "But business really is hard. I mean, I'm a success, but I've been so lucky." Rebah grabbed both glasses and the empty bottle and said, "I'll just bring these to the kitchen."

Back in the kitchen, she went to work opening the second bottle.

As her fingers worked, she tried not to think of her dwindling subscriber numbers. Or about how many travel bloggers there were nowadays, all of them competing for that ever-shrinking slice of pie. Particularly Stewart Starr. God, that man made her so angry. Young, mean, successful, and creeping into her territory. If Oscar Wilde and Donald Trump had a love child who liked to travel, Stew's signature scoff would adorn its puffy face.

She tried not to think about how the thought of another trip made her feel deflated. It wasn't always like this—she used to travel because she loved it. She loved flying overnight and waking up to peek out the airplane window and see new land below, whether it was the turquoise blue of the Caribbean Sea or the steely gray of a mountainous village. She loved leaving an airport and finding herself immersed in a new language. She loved meeting people who had lives completely different from her own. She loved the air, the markets, the restaurants. She loved staying in little-known luxury hotels and resorts, tiny inns, and enchanting bed-and-breakfasts. She loved seeking out what made those places special and writing about those key details for her readers.

But lately . . . She poured herself a fresh glass and downed half of it in one go. Lately, she had been so tired. Traveling wasn't fun anymore. Traveling made her feel empty. Traveling, actually, kind of sucked.

Which might have been a good thing to realize before she'd agreed to be bought out by FEOR, the publishing conglomerate that focused on luxury travel magazines and websites. Because now she worked for them and had to do what Corporate wanted her to do. And really, it was not easy having a boss. Well, bosses. And it was not easy to explain her audience's drift away from her blog. She had no idea why people weren't flocking to her site like they used to. Maybe it was the overall economy that kept people from traveling to luxury spots? Maybe she needed to refine her keywords so more people could randomly discover her? Maybe she was simply losing her touch?

No. It couldn't be that. Rebah knew she could write the crap out of any topic, crap people wanted to read.

She took her glass and the bottle back to the living room, leaving the other glass on the kitchen counter surrounded by dirty dishes, where she discovered that Jocelyn had dozed off, her sleeping child nestled against her. Just like that. Rebah gazed at her friend for a minute. Part of her felt annoyed. She'd only just arrived! There was much Rebah wanted to tell her, about her latest trip, about the improvements to her house she'd been planning, about a guy she'd met on one of her connecting flights who'd told her that her eyes reminded him of stardust stored in a crystal box. And now, Jocelyn let out the faintest snore.

But also? Rebah recognized a pang of sadness. Could she even call Jocelyn a friend anymore? Could she call anyone a friend?

Rebah planted a kiss on her forehead. "Goodbye, Joc," she whispered. Only the child squirmed in response, eyes still closed. She left the Unicorn Tears where it stood on the kitchen counter, a tableau of life after baby, but took the nearly full wine bottle with her as she headed out the front door and back to her Lexus. She shook off the sneaking suspicion that something wasn't right, that she'd left something behind—her purse? Phone? Had she been wearing a scarf?

No, she had everything. Nothing was missing.

Dammit, enough. She was Rebah Reynolds. She had an amazing job and plenty of money. And she wasn't going to spend another minute feeling sorry for herself—because her life was fantastic, thanks very much.

Back in the house, the baby woke up and squalled when the sound of the front door slamming penetrated the sweet blanket of sleep. Jocelyn, startled and fuzzy after the too-quick nap, carried her daughter to the window to watch as Rebah sailed down the drive and out onto the quiet community street. "Oh, Rebah." She sighed, shifting the baby to the other hip. "I hope you find what you're looking for."

Chapter 4

Monday morning found sheets and towels gathered and thrown in the industrial washing machine in the basement and bleach in a spray bottle, multiple sponges, and rubber gloves employed in the battle against bathroom mildew and smudged surfaces. This was how Aidan started his days.

As usual, the aging vacuum cleaner objected to being called into service and showed its orneriness by belching gusts of dust behind itself as Aidan tried to believe that the carpets were now adequately dirt free. But even he could tell there was a lot left to be desired in terms of cleanliness as he looked behind him at the trail of black that marked his path down the upstairs hallway. "Tomorrow," he promised himself. "Tomorrow I'll fix the vacuum." Same promise he made every morning.

He could only afford to pay Milly for two hours' worth of cleaning, so most of the burden fell on him and he was not well-versed in the language of cleaning supplies, even after five years of trying. Complaints about room cleanliness were frequent—every time he assured the customer that he'd have a word with the housekeeping staff, knowing full well that he was the head of housekeeping. But still, pretenses were sometimes a necessity in life.

Only two more rooms to clean. Thank God. Then maybe he could take a nap.

Room 11 had a tricky wiring issue, which meant Aidan's neighbor, friend, and resident not-so-handyman, Kyle Dejesus, spent a lot of time in there with a meter and some tools, trying to fix the system enough so the lights worked when they needed to and would stay glowing even if someone flipped on the bathroom fan. Aidan wheeled the vacuum into the room, carting his bucket of supplies behind him, finding Kyle there brandishing a two-prong fork at an opened outlet.

"Just don't electrocute yourself, OK, Kye?" Aidan said. "Sharon will be so mad if you die on my watch."

"Now, Aidan, how many times have you known me to spark myself in service to the ever-disintegrating electrical grid you've got going here at Chez Cisneros?" Kye was a slow talker—that sentence took about twice as long as it took a snapping turtle to cross a freeway. Actually, he was slow at everything—talking, moving, making decisions, working. It was his wife, Sharon, who drove most aspects of their lives—from every decision about their twelve-year-old twins to what type of invest-ment they were going to make that year to where they were going on vacation. Without Sharon, Kye would have been stuck.

But he was the first to admit his preferred speed was first gear with lots of pauses, and he made no apologies. He and his family had moved to Napa to escape the pressure cooker that was San Francisco, and he had sworn never to subject himself or anyone he loved to those levels of stress again. So far, he was making good on that promise. Which meant that half the time the repairs Aidan needed him to make didn't actually get done, or Aidan tried to make them himself. Which often ended in worse damage than there had been at the outset.

"Well, I promise you, as soon as business picks up and I start mak-ing more money than this place costs to run, the electricity is going to be the first thing we fix, okay?" Aidan started stripping the bed down to the mattress.

"Yeah, well. That's a good dream to have. Profitability is definitely a positive goal." Kye added a few more twists to the wire he was holding in his fingers and then tucked it back into the wall.

"Yeah, it's just been a tough year."

"Tough five years."

"Oh, absolutely, but we might have done okay if we hadn't been panned."

Kye had been around long enough to know that while the downturn in profitability had plenty to do with Jessica's death, what really kicked the Happy Valley off the financial cliff was a bad review one year ago. And not just any bad review. A bad review by Rebah Reynolds, travel blogger and social media influencer.

"Yep, bet you'd do things a tad differently with Ms. Rebah if you had the chance to go back in time." Kye chuckled. It was his favorite story, how Aidan had managed to mortify and anger Rebah Reynolds so deeply that she retaliated with a scathing entry on her blog: "From Happy Valley to Death Valley: Top 10 Reasons to Stay Away."

"Yeah, well, it wasn't my fault she got blind drunk and ruined a perfectly good trash can."

"You didn't really care about that trash can." Kye screwed the faceplate back over the outlet and tapped it with the butt end of his screwdriver, a kind of wish-you-would-work gesture he often made at the end of a job. Frequently, the magic didn't happen.

But what he said about the trash can was absolutely correct. Aidan didn't give a crap about it. But he did care about the paisley quilt Rebah had stained when she spilled her Cabernet. The quilt had been Jessica's favorite. That had been the quilt he'd wrapped himself in those dark weeks after her sudden death, the quilt that had smelled like her long after she was buried, the quilt he'd cried into. That quilt meant more to him than anyone's opinion, including Rebah Reynolds's, and when he'd discovered that she'd spilled red wine on it while drinking in bed, he'd lost all respect for her.

And for himself. Why had he put the quilt in a guest room in the first place? Why? Stupid move. He'd thought it was a way of keeping her spirit alive in the house, but, really, he was just endangering something she'd loved.

So, then he'd opened his mouth at the breakfast table in front of twelve other guests and made Rebah feel lower than dirt, and he'd been paying for it ever since.

But honestly? Yeah, he'd do it again. "The problem with Rebah Reynolds is that she's an entitled snob who thinks the world is her playground and that she's allowed to do whatever she wants, whenever she wants." Aidan furiously squirted the mirror with his spray bottle as though he could wipe out Rebah's review. "I mean, come on, you know she probably hasn't worked a real job even one day in her life. Instead, she's paid to travel the world and eat amazing food and swim with dolphins and be carried atop a litter up mountains by economically depressed populations so she can have a champagne breakfast at sunrise and catch the view of Tibet at twenty-thousand feet."

"Well, to be fair . . ."

"But that's just it. It isn't fair. She has everything, an amazing life, and then she comes here, to my home, and ruins a quilt and doesn't even bother to say sorry. Not a word! So, yeah, that makes me mad. And then, and then! She slams us in a review! Not my fault she can't see further than her makeup. Not my fault she doesn't know what it means to own something, to work for something. I tell you, she better not show her face here ever again or I'll have to serve bleach in her mai tai. And you know she'd drink it down. Anything with alcohol, right?"

Kye let him rant, and for that Aidan was grateful. He was grateful to Kye for a lot of reasons. Kye and Sharon were the only people he'd trusted to take care of Apple after Jessica's death. And he loved their kids, too. Twin twelve-year-olds, Miranda and Mason, who both idolized Apple and tried their best to copy the way she dressed in white tank tops, ripped jean shorts, fishnet stockings, combat boots— even Mason.

"Jesus, why am I still thinking about Rebah Reynolds?" Aidan moaned. "That's it. Shaking it off. Who cares what she does with her life? We'll be just fine. We'll recover from that stupid review. Right?"

"'Course," Kye answered.

"Thanks, man." Aidan stopped wiping the counter to look directly at his friend.

"Dude. Any time."

The bro moment was interrupted by Apple's emphatic shout up the stairs. "Dad! We're going to be late! Come on!"

Aidan sighed and started putting away his supplies. "Duty calls."

"You're pretty lucky to have that duty," Kye pointed out.

"No, I know." What Aidan didn't say was that he'd been even luckier when there was someone to share that duty with. Jessica had not only excelled at making the Happy Valley the go-to destination for the world's most elite travelers, she'd also been amazing at getting Apple wherever she needed to be, and on time, too. And Aidan, despite trying his utmost the past five years, still hadn't figured out the parenting trick to being in seven places at the same time.

"Dad!" Apple called again.

"Coming!" Aidan yelled back and gave Kye a two-finger salute as he backed out of Room 11.

The rolling hills of Napa Valley were a blur as Aidan raced along Highway 29 in his forest-green 2002 Jeep Wrangler. San Francisco was more than an hour away, and he still had to finish changing sheets and he should really get supplies from the market and he was exhausted to his very bones.

He'd almost suggested Apple skip her lesson, just this once. He was so tired and had so much to do. But she'd been taking advanced piano lessons from a master composer in the city for six years and hadn't missed even one appointment, except once when she had the flu and, of course, the week her mother died. Who was he to suggest she waffle on a commitment? But, God, he needed a nap. For the rest of his life.

"Dad, you want me to drive?" Apple asked from the passenger seat. She was scrolling through her phone, trying to find the piece she wanted to listen to for the ride. It was important to her that she listen to exactly the right music, something that was inspiring but not too expert so that she went into the practice room with her nerves turned up. This was her weekly lesson, and she relished it.

Ah, perfect—Apple vibrated slightly with chills as "The Promise" by Michael Nyman finally began streaming out of the ancient speakers. Despite the squawks and static, the music was deeply beautiful.

Even Aidan felt his shoulders relax, just a little.

"No, sweetie, I'm fine. Just, you know, a little tired. The Morrisons kept me up late last night complaining about the smell of damp in their room. What does damp even smell like? And really, we're in a drought—damp would be a stroke of luck." Aidan snorted. "Damn tourists."

"Dad, those damn tourists pay your damn salary," Apple reminded him. "They're going to be paying my college tuition pretty soon, too. Speaking of which . . . I still haven't heard from any of them."

By "any of them," Apple meant Barnard. That was the only place she'd ever really wanted to go, and she was crazy scared the university wouldn't accept her and she'd be stuck at Solano Community College next year or, worse, still tending guests at the Happy Valley. "What if nobody wants me? What if I don't get in anywhere? What if I'm already a failure and we've just been fooling ourselves that I had any kind of future beyond the Happy Valley?" She threw her arms over her head as though she were hiding from all the daggers of defeat that were swirling around the Jeep. The piano music crashed on in the background.

"Hey. No. I totally and completely reject that path of thought," Aidan said. "Honey, you are one of the smartest, most passionate people I know. And I'm not even being your dad when I say that. Hey, did we bring the popcorn?"

"*Mais oui.*" Apple dug in her backpack for the family-sized bag of cheddar cheese popcorn that had become their go-to road snack on piano lesson days. She spread her old, now-ragged pink blanket on her lap as a napkin. "And, yes, thank you for reminding me that I'm amazing, but then why haven't any of the colleges I've applied to accepted me yet? Or even answered in any way?" She shoved a fistful of popcorn into her mouth and chewed around her words. "No offense, but it is time for me to get the hell out of Napa."

"Oh, sure, no offense. Why, only because I live here and you were raised here and here is the only place you've ever known? Why should that be offensive?" Aidan teased, matching Apple in popcorn, mouthful by mouthful. Every bite shot a tiny reminder to his brain that he used to care deeply about the taste of everything he put in his mouth. Now, he didn't even notice when popcorn was stale. If he let himself think too much, he'd really feel the loss of his cooking life.

"Look," he continued, "the system is slow. College acceptance takes time. Try to enjoy these last few . . . months? Oh, man, you're leaving in months?"

"Well, that's assuming I get in."

"I can't think of a bet that's surer." Aidan was quiet for a moment, watching rolling vineyards fly by alongside the highway. He cracked the Jeep's window to let in the smell of early spring in wine country— that mixture of dirt and sweet air and budding fruit, everything alive and not yet dusty with an aging summer. Just a few months until Apple was gone. How was he going to deal with that? How could he possibly deal with that?

On top of that, how could he possibly pay for the privilege of Apple's education?

"Dad!" Apple snapped at him. "Dad, quit zoning out like that. Dude, you have got to be more on point."

"Yeah, sorry, I know, I just get lost sometimes. Look, I want to tell you something." Aidan took a long slug from his water bottle, washing out the popcorn particles so he'd be able to breathe around his next words. "I just want to tell you how sorry I am. For not, you know— being the parent you needed all these years. I know your mom would have done better, and I really have tried, but there's no way to match your mom."

"Oh, my God, Dad, really? We're doing this again?"

"What do you mean again?"

"It's like every month or so you get it in your head that you're a terrible parent and that if Mom were alive we'd all be better off psychologically and financially and the Happy Valley would be, you know, happier. You don't really get it, do you?"

Aidan was confused. He thought he was sharing something tender and important with his daughter, an apology for everything he'd failed at. But she just seemed annoyed. Was this a teenager thing? There were so many teenager things.

"Look, you've been a great dad. I know things are hard. I'm not an idiot. I totally get that you have worked your butt off and struggled to keep things going and to, you know, raise me, whatever that even means. And we're good!" Apple held up a finger for a moment—she loved this part in the music. She closed her eyes to enjoy it more deeply and Aidan was moved at how she could escape into herself like that, in the Jeep on the highway with cars on either side of them and him in the driver's seat in the middle of a conversation. Just escape. As though the world would wait. And for Apple, it did.

"God, that's amazing," she said once the moment had passed. "I hope I can do something that powerful someday. Not piano necessarily, but something ginormous that touches people. Pass a law or something." She dumped more popcorn in her mouth. "Anyway, yeah, the B&B could use some TLC, and don't even get me started on your lack of a love life, but I'm doing great, or I would be if only Barnard would send me an acceptance letter. It's you. You're the one you should be apologizing to."

"I don't . . . Why would I . . . How do you figure I'm the one who needs an apology?"

"It's like you're not even letting yourself live." Apple picked an unpopped kernel from her teeth.

"What do you mean? I live plenty. I have the Valley, I have you, I have friends. I'm doing great."

"Uh-huh."

"Uh, yeah." Aidan ignored the uncomfortable worm of suspicion that wiggled against his back.

"When was the last time you had a date, other than a dude date with Kye?"

"I've been on a few. At least two. And, okay, yeah, it's been a while, but you know, you don't really need a romantic relationship to be fulfilled in life."

"Yeah, like, what self-help podcast are you listening to these days?"

"Look, when your mom died, I just decided I needed to focus on you, me, and our home. That's it." Aidan glanced in the rearview mirror to make sure he wasn't blocking anyone with his less-than-speedy driving. He wasn't a slow driver, exactly, but the world always seemed to want to go faster than he did. And, mostly, he was willing to get out of its way.

"I'm fully cooked, you're still sober, and the inn is falling apart anyway," Apple said. "Two out of three ain't bad."

They didn't usually talk about Aidan's alcoholism directly. Apple knew her dad went to meetings, she knew he carried his token everywhere, at all times, and she suspected his commitment had a lot to do with her mom dying. But it wasn't something they ever discussed head-on. So to hear Apple say the words out loud hit Aidan in the gut in a way that felt awkward but necessary. He shifted in his seat, uncomfortable but also relieved. He didn't want her to think he was trying to keep this huge part of his life a secret from her, or from anyone. He wasn't. It was just another thing he was trying to handle.

"But seriously, Apple, I just want you to know how much it matters to me that you're happy," he said, unconsciously evading that part of the conversation.

Apple groaned and starting swiping through her phone again. The final movement was coming up and she wanted to get another piece in the queue. "I get it. And I miss Mom, too. Still. I never won't. You never won't. But you know what? It's time to stop using me as an excuse not to move on."

Aidan braked hard as an older Ford Escape cut him off. He resisted the urge to lean on the horn, scream out the open window, or make all manner of obscene hand gestures at the driver, who, he could see now, was an older guy in a ball cap who probably had no clue he'd nearly caused an accident.

Was Apple right? Had he been hiding behind her all these years, using her as an excuse to avoid any semblance of a normal life? He was just trying to take care of her, making her his priority—isn't that what good parents were supposed to do?

Parking in downtown San Francisco was not for the weak of heart, but Aidan was well-practiced after so many years of taking Apple to her piano lessons. He found a spot on a busy street not far from the music school and stretched his arm along the back of the passenger seat to guide the hind end of the Jeep into the space, then—bam! A yellow blur filled his vision out the back window and the Jeep jerked with the impact.

"Dammit!" he swore. He threw the car into park then popped out the door, furious.

Apple craned her neck to try and see what had caused the bump. "Dad?"

Aidan looked back to reassure his daughter. "It's okay, just some idiot who thinks sneaking into a parking space headfirst gives them the right to dent my bumper." He straightened and his eyes narrowed at the bright yellow beamer wedged behind him. "Hey!" he said gruffly to the figure emerging from the driver's door. "You go so far as to hit me so that you can steal my parking space? What the hell do you think this is?"

"What the actual hell?" The woman driving the beamer matched Aidan's tone. "What is up with this shitty city? Did you not see my car? Does yellow not register in your catalog of things to avoid?"

Aidan stared at the woman, his mind clicking over in a series of recognitive moments that ended in one insane result: "Rebah Reynolds."

Rebah whipped her head around to face him instead of examining the teensy scratch on her front fender. "Well, isn't that just perfect. You know my name. You a fan?"

"A fan? Why in the world would you think I was a fan?"

"Well, how else would you recognize me but from my blog?"

"Oh, Rebah, I'd recognize you from anywhere." Aidan felt like spitting out the bitter taste that rose in his mouth at the sight of her. That auburn hair, those blue eyes, the flawless skin—he hated every inch of her perfectly toned body. A domino effect of memories distracted him from the busy street and crowded sidewalk as people paused to survey the drama and then moved on, caught up in their own worlds.

"Jesus, this day. Look, I don't know who you are, but this is a rental, and, no, I did not accept the full coverage they try to scam you into buying so you're just going to have to give me whatever pathetic insurance you carry on that dune buggy and do it fast because I am late."

"Uh-huh. So no recognition whatsoever?" Aidan let out a sharp bark that was the opposite of laughter. "Heh. I suppose I shouldn't be surprised. You were blotto most of your time at the Happy Valley. Blackouts are a bitch, am I right?"

"Who the hell are you to talk to me like that?" Rebah planted a well-manicured hand on her hip. Aidan noticed she was careful not to scrunch the brown suede of her skirt. Snob. "What exactly are you accusing me of?"

"Oh, Rebah Reynolds, you are funny. If only you could get past that selfish wall of defense and access all those memories you try to drown in booze, you'd be mortified. Mort-if-fied." Aidan dug his wallet out of his back pocket and slid out a business card.

"I can't even begin to understand who you are or what your problem is, but you know what? I do not have time in my day, or in my life, for losers. You, sir, can go to hell." Rebah snatched a satchel out of the passenger seat and slammed the driver-side door.

Aidan tried to control his breathing, but anyone with eyes could tell it wasn't going well. Time to be done with this toxicity. Time to scribble the name and number of his lawyer on the back of the card and find a different parking space and get his daughter to her piano lesson. Focus. Don't be distracted by this mess of a woman. Don't think about what she did to you a year ago. Don't think. Don't engage. Don't . . .

"Oooohhhh. You know what? I totally remember you. Huh. Maybe it was the bitter, snarky tone that clued me in." Rebah was looking at him now, her eyes narrowed to slits and teeth slightly bared. "You're the nasty guy who owned that miserable B&B in Napa, right? The asshole who thought it was okay to insult one of his most important customers. Huh. How'd that work out for you?" Rebah smiled, not without a small amount of disdain, and held out her fingers to pluck Aidan's card from his hand. She showed no intention of giving away her own.

She glanced down at the card. "Still in business? Still the Happy Valley? I'm shocked, I don't mind admitting. I guess the next time I decide to use my powers for good and take down a sorry excuse for luxury accommodations, I'll have to deploy different tactics."

"Forget it. You can't bait me. I know exactly what you think of me and my place. You just don't get it. The Happy Valley isn't for people like you."

"People like me? You're the one who doesn't get it. I'm saving people like me from having to experience the malignancy of your inn. People like me are the only people there are. And we're not going to that hellhole anytime soon."

"Yeah? Well, you know what?" Aidan was red in the face, his eyes frantic with excess energy.

Apple watched, not so much concerned as interested. Her dad hadn't been this animated in a very long time. What was going on?

Why did this woman, obviously a past guest, have such a crazy effect on her dad?

"I'll have you know that you do not have nearly as much power as you think you have!" Aidan practically spat. "The Happy Valley is thriving! We're doing great—fully booked every week! We have to turn people away, and I'm not talking about Mr. and Mrs. Ohio. You know Kate, right? Kate Winslet? Yeah, she cried when I told her we couldn't fit her in for three years. In fact, we have a whole celebration weekend coming up because of how good business has been!"

Rebah rolled her eyes, unconvinced, and looked at her phone. "You know what? This? Has been a delight. No, for reals. It's nice to get a chance to follow up and make sure the warning I issued—what, a year ago?—stands firm. You should not be in the business, Aidan Cisneros. Look at yourself. Disgraceful."

Aidan's eyes turned dark gray as he drew himself up to his full height of six-foot-two. "Disgraceful? Absolutely. What you did—ruining my wife's quilt and then giving me a bad review? Absolutely disgraceful."

"Look, I have to go. I was supposed to be in this meeting fifteen minutes ago." She dug in her leather handbag and came up with a pink business card. "Take my card and do the thing. I don't want to deal—the rental company will work it out. And next time you decide to parallel park, take a clue and don't back in—that's not the way to do it." Aidan watched with furious, stabbing eyes as she maneuvered around her yellow BMW, pausing to kick the back tire with her over-the-knee brown leather heeled boot. "Oh, and Mr. Happy Valley? If your business is booming, why are you driving such a beat-up wreck? More to the point: Why are you still so pissed at me?"

As Rebah strode onto the busy sidewalk, a custom hubcap fell away from the BMW and rolled into the street, narrowly missed by a stream of drivers hurrying to their next destination.

"So, that was interesting," Apple drawled from the passenger door of the Jeep. "Friend of yours?"

* * *

The sidewalk in front of the offices of FEOR was pristine. Not a splat of gum, not a stray leaf, not an offensive tab of litter—not even dust. Rebah noticed how clean it was as she hustled over the pavement, and she might have stopped to wonder who got paid to ensure this level of cleanliness if she hadn't been so late and so flustered by the fender bender and, of all people, Aidan Cisneros.

God! Of all the people in the world to run into! Literally. The man who'd made her feel worse about herself than anyone else had in a very long time. Who the hell did he think he was? Accusing her of getting drunk and ruining some stupid blanket. And he was still bitter, obviously. But really, that review had been her only line of defense. No one insulted her and got away with it.

Rebah took a gulp of coffee (special coffee, with additives), hoping it would calm her nerves. She had to be on. She had to be charming. These were her bosses, and they hadn't been super happy with her performance lately. She had to be impressive. As much as her current feelings of ambivalence clouded her desire to work, she needed her job. This was what she did!

Through the revolving door, smile, smile, smile. The elevator was full, of course, with women too skinny for pancakes and men polished to a wincing gleam. Rebah smiled more as she squeezed herself in, her five-foot-five, one hundred, thirty-pound frame feeling like a mistake in the gene pool. She tried to match her confidence with that which she sensed on all sides.

Floor twenty-two, her stop. Carpets hushed her hurried steps and camouflaged the way she almost tripped a few feet before the front desk. A long drink from her coffee cup only made her stomach roil. That was not the magic she needed.

"Ah, yes, Ms. Reynolds," the coiffed receptionist murmured. "They're expecting you."

"Yep!" chirped Rebah. "They're expecting me!" Why did her voice sound so loud?

"Down the hall, can't miss it," the receptionist nearly whispered.

"Great!" Rebah tossed her empty cup in a discreet trash can, gritted her teeth, and started the trek down the hallway. And, no, missing the boardroom with its bank of windows was not an option. And there wasn't a chance that the roomful of men missed her echoing hiccup as she approached the door.

"Ah, Rebah. Good to see you. Flight okay?" Charles Lanican was the vice president of FEOR, and it showed. Flanking him on either side were his powerful minions, her usual contact, Frank Melinisi, among them. The only empty seat—the only other seat, period—was on the side of the table opposite the array of suits.

"Flight great!" Rebah chirped, wishing she could stop speaking in exclamation points. And what was the deal with skipping verbs? Was the human species slipping into short-form language before her very eyes, her own voice part of the pack? She slipped into her seat and tried to seem capable of greatness. Or at least competence.

"We've put together a presentation to show you just how far you've slipped in terms of standards, metrics, and audience," said Frank.

What?

"As you can see from slide one, *Rambling with Rebah* peaked in terms of hits back in April of last year and never quite reached its apex again. In fact, it's slipped in rankings every month since then. That downward trajectory is unacceptable."

Whoa.

"Here, we delineate the kernel of the problem, Ms. Reynolds. Your content is simply too . . . positive."

What the . . . "You realize this is a luxury travel website?" Rebah's voice wasn't quite a squeak, but it wasn't too far off. "Luxury travel does tend to be fairly positive." She looked around for a pitcher of water, a selection of bottles, but there were no accommodations for her visit. Perhaps water was reserved for those bloggers whose analytics weren't on a downward trajectory.

"Viewers have different needs now than they did ten years ago. Viewers want to be incensed." Frank made a tent with his fingers and nodded sagely.

"Incensed? I'm not sure I . . ."

"You see, Ms. Reynolds, it's a matter of getting the click. Hooking the scroller. Feeding the fumes of consumer upset. It's a fine line, and you're nowhere near it."

"So, you want me to be . . . meaner?"

"Ah, she's not unteachable." The row of men nodded in agreement. Rebah's nervousness was taking a turn. She felt something akin to incensed herself. "What we really want is for you to apply your own unique Rebah brand in a way more similar to something like, I don't know, *In the Stew with Stewa*—"

"What?! Are you actually kidding me with this right now? You want me to be more like Stew? Have any of you even watched his vlog? It's hideous. It's disgusting. Stew takes *moron* to new heights. He's—"

"Raking in the views, Ms. Reynolds." Charles Lanican's voice boomed over her own.

"Ah, of course, the almighty view count. How could I not see? That's what readers want. To be counted. And all of you, hiding in your fish tank, are the ones to decide what my audience wants. Of course you know, because spreadsheets! PowerPoints! Designer glasses frames! How well you all connect with the average upper-middle-class white woman with two point six kids and a husband on Viagra who is desperate for twenty minutes of living vicariously, living my life, through my blog." Rebah took a deep breath and wondered how hard she should try and stop herself.

"Now just one minute, Ms. Reynolds, there's no need to attack—"

"You know, there's a reason you bought me. I mean, my site. I was raking it in doing exactly what I do best, showing people that they, too, can have a good time, that there are places in the world, amazing, gorgeous places, where someone can feel like they are on top, they are first, they matter more. People need to feel that. People crave that. Everyone!"

"We aren't saying that you don't connect with your—"

"And they found it on my blog. They didn't have to travel halfway around the world. They can just swipe, hover, and click, and boom, they are with me, along for the ride of their lives."

Frank made a gesture at someone through the glass walls of the conference room and within a moment a selection of artisan spring water bottles was in front of her, delivered by a skinny woman wearing impossible heels.

"You bought me, I mean my site, because you knew this was the way to go, this was what people wanted. And you can't tell me that people have changed all that much in the last ten years. I mean, that's just not how any of this works."

"Ms. Reynolds, we bought you, well, your site, because you attracted sponsors due to your stats," Frank said. Rebah noticed that he called her "Ms. Reynolds" in front of his cronies and "Rebah" when they spoke on the phone. "That is no longer the case. We have a perfectly valid suggestion as a way for you to improve those stats, but I'm sensing resistance."

Rebah leaned her head back and took a deep breath, blowing it out at the ceiling. What was she doing there? How did she get there? And why did she keep finding herself asking questions like this?

She straightened her neck and took a moment to look each man in the eye, up and down the room in front of her. At least two of them had the consideration to squirm uncomfortably while pinned by her gaze.

But not Frank. And not Charles Lanican.

"Look. You buy my site. You see the numbers go down as I cheerfully accept your suggestions and try to change a few things to better fall under your definitions of a lifestyle travel blog. I make accommodations, I quit listening to every one of my instincts, I include certain things and leave others out to satisfy some voice you are all intent on listening to. Why? Because you pay me good money. But if you think I'm going to sit here and be degraded for having taste, style, experience, expertise, and damn good eyes and ears, you are sorely mistaken."

She paused and took a sip of water, noticing that she felt steadier and more confident than she had in weeks. Certainly since entering the building.

"You can complain all you want about my numbers, but I reach people, okay? I reach out, and people listen because they want to hear which venues have sheets that feel like chicken gristle against a naked body, which beaches are overrun with jellyfish and the stench of decaying whale blubber, which in-house restaurants consider guacamole to be a vegetable and wine to be superfluous to a meal. My readers want to hear about B&B owners who neglect their own bodily hygiene to the detriment of anyone in the room with them." Here she turned a steely eye toward a blond man at the end of the table who was definitely sweating through his shirt under his sport coat. She could see moisture beading on his forehead. "They want me to tell them the events to avoid. Where they're most likely to get food poisoning. Which tour company is most likely to leave them on top of a mountain in the middle of a sudden snow squall. And, of course, where they can feel as though the world is simply working for them. Where they can go to experience true and absolute luxury, to feel as though the sunset was painted exclusively for their enjoyment." Rebah took another sip of water. "And you? All of you, sitting at this table? You have no idea what it's like outside this office, outside your comfortable homes where your wives greet you with bourbon and lie about their own happiness. And you dare tell me to be meaner. Well. If that's what you want."

"Huh," said Charles Lanican.

"Well," said Frank.

Had she made enough of a point? She didn't even know what point she was trying to make. But it had felt good to speak her mind for three minutes. She looked up and down the row of suited men and was about to smile at the way they were all at least slightly dumbstruck when a wave of excitement visibly stirred each of their faces.

"Oh, there's Stew! Hey, Stew!" called Frank, as he leapt from his chair and waved to someone outside the glass walls that stretched behind Rebah. "Excuse me, one sec, I've got to talk to this guy. Charles, Angus, have you all met Stew?"

As Frank and Charles and, apparently, Angus, plus one or two of the other men circled from behind the board table and left the room to gush at their new star vlogger, Rebah fumed. She'd felt like she'd made a connection. Like she'd taken charge of something. For the first time in a long time, she'd recognized that spark of passion for her work that had been missing for at least a year. She was defending a job she remembered loving. But these people, they didn't care. They were only interested in money. And Stewart the Skunk made more money than she. Okay then.

She stood and firmly planted herself on her heels. "Gentlemen," she murmured to the remaining men in the conference room, all of whom looked miserable at being left behind by what was obviously the inner circle. Then she turned and sashayed out the glass door and confronted the clot of men in the hallway. At the heart of the clot was her nemesis, Stew. A compact, fit man with an impeccable bow tie and constantly raised eyebrows, he smirked as Rebah approached. "As for you two," Rebah practically spat at Frank and Charles. "You just see how mean I can be. And, Stew, honey, you've got a little bit of mayonnaise in the corner of your mouth." Rebah pursed her lips and blew the group a kiss as she turned and walked down the hall, making damn sure her hips were moving exactly right. It wouldn't do any good for Stew, but maybe the others would be distracted on a certain level.

Frank and Charles looked at each other and nodded. This was the Rebah they wanted. "Frank," Charles said, turning from Stew, "let that girl know we look forward to seeing her next blog. And keep her in

California through the weekend. Give her some of those leads we just got, and let's see what she can do. Could be she's back."

Stew looked like he was eating dirt, but he smiled as well as he was able while trying to find the errant mayo with the tip of his tongue.

But Rebah had been lying. He was clean.

Chapter 5

I t was evening by the time Aidan and Apple got home to the Happy Valley after Apple's music lesson, and they made the walk toward the house in silence. Well, not quite silence. Apple hummed the music she'd made her dad listen to again on the way home, scuffing her combat boots into the clumps of dirt that were sifting up among the driveway pebbles. Aidan added "redo driveway surfacing" to his mental list of tasks.

But at that moment, he felt peaceful. Seeing Rebah again hadn't been easy. He'd had to work to push down the feelings of rage that threatened to engulf him after they'd parked the Jeep on a different street and Apple had gone in for her lesson. He'd sat in the car for a while, clenching and unclenching his fists around the steering wheel, breathing—in two, three, four, out two, three, four—until he'd felt reasonably calm again. Then he'd gone for a walk and stumbled upon an antiques store, the kind that carried farm implements instead of Victorian couches, and spent a distracted half hour rummaging through bins of small pieces whose function had long been forgotten. He'd bought an oval metal disc that was smooth to the touch for fifty cents and now carried it in his pocket, nestled against his A.A. chip. He couldn't have explained why he'd wanted to own it. It just felt good in his hand.

The peace he was feeling as he and his daughter walked up their driveway was shattered by a piercing shriek coming from inside the B&B. He broke into a sprint. What now? See, disaster found the weak spots. He'd had a moment of feeling as though most things were almost okay in the world, and now look.

"Apple, Apple, Apple, Apple!" It was Milly. She met them on the porch, every inch of her vibrating, down to her purple-tipped, dreadlocked ponytail.

"Milly! What's going on?" Aidan reached out to try and settle the poor woman, who resembled a flustered, punk chicken.

Instead of answering, she thrust an envelope toward him—an open envelope addressed to Apple.

"Milly, you opened it?"

She nodded, her eyes wide.

Apple snatched the envelope from her dad and ripped out the letter. "Oh, my God," she said, looking up at Aidan with eyes that knew no bottom. "I got in. Barnard. They want me."

For a moment, the world went still for Aidan, even as Milly and Apple whooped together and hugged. Even as a guest exclaimed loudly through the living room window that all the noise meant he couldn't concentrate on the evening ball game he was watching on his phone. Even as the oven timer blared from the kitchen and the smell of charred food—What was that, fish?—gushed onto the porch. Aidan was a pillar of stone in a hurricane. He was so proud of his daughter, and so sad that Jessica wasn't there to share the success. So proud.

"Dad?" Apple turned toward him with questions in her eyes, but he pulled her close and kissed her hair.

"I'm so, so proud of you, sweetie." *She did it, Jessica,* he thought. *Our little girl is going to Barnard.*

Apple pulled away and tried to smile at him, but suddenly the reality of the acceptance letter hit, and she couldn't find the breath to speak. "Oh," she gasped. "I don't think . . . I didn't really think . . ."

"Apps, you got into college!"

"No, I know, but it's in New York City. It's all the way across the country. Barnard is on a different coast, Dad!"

"Well, yeah. It hasn't moved since you first started talking about going twelve years ago."

"I just never thought about how far away it was."

"It'll be fine, Apps. We'll figure it out."

"And, oh, God, it's so expensive!" Apple shook the letter in front of her as though maybe some cash had been included but gotten lost in the folds.

"Again, we'll figure it out."

"I mean for just one year, tuition plus room and board is like seventy-thousand!"

Aidan gulped. The click in his throat was audible.

"That's a lot of money!" called out the baseball-watching guest through the living room window.

He wasn't wrong. That was a lot of money.

"Apple, this is your dream," Aidan said. "And college, it's an invest-ment. You pay money so you can make money, right? And, you know, there are ways to pay for college. There are brochures and stuff. I know I have a stack that your guidance counselor gave us once."

"I just . . ."

"You know what? Sweetie? I got this. You're going to Barnard. You're going to be amazing. Let me work out the logistics. You? You focus on studying your butt off. The world needs your brain."

Apple caught her dad in a big hug, and everything faded around the two of them as they shared this moment, this achievement.

And Aidan almost managed to turn off the high-frequency voice inside his brain that was wondering just how the hell he was going to manage this.

Tuesday morning the smell of lemon furniture polish permeated every square inch of the Happy Valley. The far-flung corners of the living room's vaulted ceiling were no longer cluttered with cobwebs, and every window gleamed, smudge- and smear-free. The floors were swept, the carpets vacuumed, and someone had even put some effort into erasing a few of the worst stains, like the one that had resulted from an overeager twenty-something from Oregon proposing to his girlfriend of three months by putting a ring in a crock of chili and expecting her to find it before swallowing. She swallowed—and said "No" when informed what exactly the foreign object that had just slid down her throat was. And then she threw the rest of her bowl to the floor. Who proposes via chili?

But now the carpets looked better, the rooms looked better, and someone arriving for the first time might mistake this B&B as a place someone cared deeply about. If they didn't look too closely and notice the crack in the dining room window, the patterns of scuffs on the baseboards, the way the kitchen floor creaked and groaned as though warning of the apocalypse.

Aidan rearranged a burst of sunflowers stuffed in a vase and positioned it in the entryway one more time. Then he adjusted the drape of the curtains in the living room. He was about to give the piano one last polish with the microfiber dusting cloth, but then he noticed his watch. "Milly!" he called to the kitchen. "Cookies!"

"Okey dokey, Mr. C," came the answer. A crash sounded as Milly opened the oven door and slid the tray of frozen cookie dough lumps inside.

Aidan checked the Crock-Pot that was positioned behind the Japanese privacy screen in the dining room and added a few more slices of apple to the warm water inside. This was a trick he had learned from Jessica, a way to keep the air fresh and smelling like hope. And that day, he needed all the tricks he had at his disposal.

Yesterday had been exhausting but, in a way, also exhilarating. After Apple had disappeared into her room to text a series of friends about Barnard, Aidan had walked the property outside and thought hard. *What are you doing?* he'd asked himself, leaning against the walnut tree at the foot of the drive. *Why are you holding on so hard to something that doesn't really do it for you?*

When Jessica was alive, this had been a great place to live and work, the cooking was fun, he could be on, and he could be around people. Sure, he drank, but not so bad that the guests ever noticed—it wasn't like his drinking was a cry for help because he was trapped in a life he hated, it was just the way he was. It was a disease.

But now? It was time to face facts. Aidan had paused in the near dark and looked around at the series of silhouettes that acted as a decorative fence for his view of the world. The house, darkly outlined against the deep blue sky. The row of cedars along the back edge of the sloping yard. The trees on the other side of the vineyard that lay adjacent to his unkempt lawn. He gazed upward and noticed he'd never arranged for anyone to come and remove the obviously dead branch from the walnut tree.

"Time to go," he muttered to himself.

Once he made the decision to sell the Happy Valley, it was easy to kick himself into a higher gear and accomplish some of the ever-present have-to's. It was too bad he hadn't been able to feel this kind of motivation before. It might have helped save the inn. With help from Milly and Kye, he transformed the B&B into a somewhat comfortable, somewhat clean space. It helped that there were no guests scheduled for a few weeks.

Milly bustled out of the kitchen, her dreads tipped with blue and tied into a kind of bun today. It was her way of showing respect to the authority wielded by the realtor, who was expected to arrive at any moment.

"This place, Mr. C? Looks real good. Like, I'd stay here."

"Agreed," said Kye, who'd just landed on the bottom step of the staircase. He'd been replacing a blown-out light bulb in a guest room. He'd been working on that task all morning.

"And you know who would have loved to see it this way again?" Milly went on.

Aidan wanted to stop her from uttering her next words. Not because they weren't true, not because they'd bring bad luck, but because they were going to hurt.

"Mrs. C would be, like, super proud of you."

"Agreed," nodded Kye.

Aidan winced as his belly flip-flopped with anxiety. He knew Milly was right. And he felt ashamed that he'd let the place get so run-down.

"Milly, Kye, thanks for all your help this morning. I really would have been stuck if you guys hadn't been willing to put in the extra time."

"No worries, Mr. C. To be honest, the only thing on my agenda this week outside of work is to pick up a new rescue. Some big jerky-jerk in Pasadena couldn't handle feeding a lizard once a day and the poor thing just about starved." Milly, in her spare time, ran a one-woman lizard rescue organization. Aidan had never been to her apartment, but according to Kyle, who sometimes lizard-sat when Milly had to travel to pick up new ones, it was wall-to-wall lizard. "Why are people so cruel to lizards?" she asked with a note of true wonder in her voice.

"Maybe because lizards don't wag their tails," offered Kye.

"Or maybe because they aren't furry and feel pretty weird to touch," said Aidan.

"Weird? They feel amazing!" Milly gushed.

Aidan knew from experience that Milly could be kind of obsessive if you got her talking about the positive traits of lizards, so he was relieved when he heard the sound of wheels on gravel.

The realtor had arrived.

Jax Pitts maneuvered his silver Porsche into a spot far from Aidan's Jeep and Milly's dusty blue, ten-year-old Honda Civic. As he guided his tall frame out of his car, he seemed to push the rising dust away from his pristine suit with only his mind. A wry smirk appeared on his bespectacled face, which had an odd way of looking younger than his fifty years. "Mr. Cisneros!" he called up to Aidan, who had opened the front door. "Let's find a way to make a deal."

Briefcase in hand, Pitts strode up the front steps and into the dining room as though the place was his to sell and chose the chair at the head of the table. Aidan followed, feeling like a puppy who had no idea how the world worked. Milly and Kye grimaced at the obvious display of power and retreated to the kitchen, where Aidan knew they'd be listening at the door. He knew they had just as much emotional investment in the place as he did.

"So, Mr. Cisneros," Pitts began.

"Oh, you can call me Aidan."

Pitts continued as though Aidan hadn't spoken. "You want to sell, you need money to send your daughter to college, plus you're looking at moving east. Do daughters generally like it when their fathers follow them to college?" He looked at Aidan through narrow eyes, and Aidan felt a shiver run the width of his shoulders.

"Well, Apple and I are quite close," he said awkwardly. "She's going to need some kind of support when she's out there. I mean, she's never been away from home before, and, you know, with her mother having passed away, we're . . . quite close." God, he sounded like an overprotective, suffocating parent who was going to make his kid's life miserable. And it wasn't like he hadn't been thinking about this since last night when the idea had first occurred to him as he stood in the dark and looked around at the place he suspected he wasn't really worthy to own anymore. Where else would he go? He'd go help Apple be the success he knew she was going to be. "So, about the inn . . ." he prompted.

"Ah, yes. The Happy Valley." Pitts planted his briefcase on the newly waxed table and clicked open the clasps. "The last few years haven't been good to you, have they?"

Aidan pulled out a chair and sat, thinking maybe he could think more clearly if he didn't have to focus so much on standing upright. This wasn't going as well as he'd thought it would. Pitts hadn't even seemed to notice how clean and shiny everything was.

"Let's face reality, Mr. Cisneros. You have deep debt on this place and you won't be able to sell for enough to pay even half of that."

"Wait, what? How can . . ."

"Before you bother pointing out the size of the parcel, the demand for land in this county, and the historical value of a one-hundred-year-old building, let me remind you that you are selling a business, not a lifeless stretch of highway." Pitts adjusted his wire-framed glasses, surely designer, then reached into his briefcase and removed several oversized spreadsheets with a lot of red numbers. "Your occupancy rate has been on the decline for four years, taking a massive dive just one year ago. You charge less now than you did five years ago, not even accounting for inflation, and do you know why you charge less now than you did five years ago?" He tapped the pages together on the shiny wooden table. "Because that's all that people will pay. Your service is subpar, the grounds and building are in desperate need of a full overhaul, you do not seem to have a clue about marketing and advertising, and your staff really do fall short of charming."

A yelp came from the kitchen. Aidan knew Milly had heard that one.

"Truth be told, Mr. Cisneros, if you had managed to maintain revenue at the level you'd reached five years ago, you could get what you want to ask for. Maybe even more. But as it is . . ."

"No, I know, I haven't been as on top of things as I should have been. I mean, after my wife died, I kind of lost . . . I mean, it was hard. Raising a kid, keeping up with this place—it's been hard."

"And a year ago when revenue truly took a walk into the ocean with stones in its pocket—that had more to do with a devastating review, didn't it? One by travel blogger Rebah Reynolds?"

Aidan's hand tightened into a fist. Why did Rebah Reynolds ever have to set foot here? That woman was the bane of his existence.

"It's truly difficult for a luxury B&B in Napa Valley to be considered a decent business opportunity if it's hostile to online tastemakers like Rebah Reynolds. And, Mr. Cisneros, word is you ridiculed her for drinking wine—in wine country."

"Oh, for crying out loud!" Aidan couldn't take another moment of being berated for calling out a selfish guest by making a simple joke a year ago. "I am not a hostile person! Rebah Reynolds is a total joke and

I don't care how many followers she has, that's no excuse for behaving badly, and why the hell should I pay for her mistake?" He slammed his fist onto the gleaming table, creating a gust of air that upset Pitts's spreadsheets, sending them floating to the Oriental rug below.

"Really, Mr. Cisneros," Pitts muttered as he bent to retrieve his papers.

Aidan sighed deeply. "Look, Mr. Pitts, I know something about drinking too much and I know something about stopping. I'm an alcoholic. My wife asked me to stop drinking right before she died, and to be honest, that's the only thing I've really managed to do well since then." Even as he spoke, Aidan didn't know why he was baring his soul to this sorry excuse for a human, but he was upset. He was done with the past inserting itself at the most inconvenient times. Yes, he'd called Rebah Reynolds a drunk, and he had done it in front of a room full of breakfasting guests. But she was a drunk! Didn't that make his comment to her, so long ago, at least mostly justified? "I haven't had a drink in five years, and I'm better for it, even if my business is failing. And I'm fine with other people enjoying a bottle of wine, a decent whiskey—hell, I'll even pour it for them. I like seeing other people appreciate good things. But when someone loses control of their drinking and causes damage, and especially when they do it in my home—yes, the Happy Valley is more than just a business, it's my home—well, then, I say something. Enjoying a drink is fine, until you make an ass of yourself . . . like she did." He mumbled that last part.

Pitts collected his spreadsheets and arranged everything back in his briefcase and snapped it shut. "Nevertheless, Mr. Cisneros. The revenue simply isn't there to support the numbers you want." Pitts stood and glanced around the room. Now that Aidan was looking at the space through Pitts's eyes, it didn't look quite as polished and welcoming as he'd thought. "If, and this is a formidable if, you can get revenue back to previous heights, I could, potentially, find a buyer at your asking price. That is simply the best I can do, given your current situation."

Aidan held out his hand to shake, but before Pitts could deign to reciprocate, the smoke alarm blared and the smell of burning cookies wafted from the kitchen door, which had burst open to reveal Milly and Kye, who were trying their best to look like they hadn't been listening.

"Goodbye, Mr. Cisneros!" Pitts shouted above the sound of the alarm. "And good luck. You are certainly going to need it."

Chapter 6

The Sprawling Oak Bed & Breakfast lived up to its name. For a mere two thousand, five hundred a night, you could stay in the When the Bough Breaks Prenatal Suite or the Rusted Rhododendron Rave Room or the Lumbering Jack Chestnut Lounge. Tree house–themed luxury wasn't exactly Rebah's idea of a good time, but her boss, well, bosses, insisted that this was the newest thing making chatter in certain circles. Plus, Sprawling Oak had just bought a high-tier advertising package. It was time for Rebah to earn her paycheck.

And to be honest, after a couple of nights in San Francisco's Hyatt, Rebah was ready for something different. Not that there was anything wrong with the hotel, but it was just so . . . ordinary. The desk clerks wore polyester uniforms and checked people in and out without quite making eye contact while the lobby fountain gasped every other wave, something in its motor dying a slow and agonizing death. Rebah had tried to make the hours she'd spent there waiting for the powers that be to decide where she'd be staying next productive ones, but gah. She was done with run-of-the-mill.

And Sprawling Oaks was certainly not run-of-the-mill.

The lobby was all swooping beams and vaulted tents, concierges with iPads immediately available as new guests entered via the Magical

Forest Path. "Oh, this place is divine," gushed Rebah to the nearest attendant. "The smell of it! As though we were deep in the redwoods."

"Yes!" the blond forest imp exclaimed excitedly. "That's exactly how we're modeled. We want you to have the full-immersion experience of a forest wonderland. You can call me Pine."

"I've got to say, this beats the Desert Oasis place I stayed at in Kabul a couple of years ago. I mean, they did a decent job but there just isn't any way to keep the sand out of the sheets, or the drinks, or your underwear."

Pine tittered. "No sand here! Nothing but pure loam. Now, you're all checked in, and I can send a lumberjack to get your bags if you'd like." She twirled on tiptoes and snapped her fingers in the air to alert one of the men standing at attention alongside the stream—complete with floating, fall-colored leaves—that a guest needed servicing. Rebah was delighted to see one of them break ranks and head toward her. He was classically handsome, dressed in leather chaps and a plaid chamois shirt that looked like it was perfect for burying a face into against a brisk breeze.

"Perfect, although I do travel light—just the one I'm holding. Our lumberjack won't quite get the chance to show off his biceps, I'm afraid." The lumberjack was perfect lumber chic as he swung her satchel from her arm and bowed his head, his dark locks topped with a leafy kind of crown that wouldn't have looked out of place on the head of Puck. "Well," Rebah whispered, forcefully directing her attention back to Pine. "Can I ask a few questions? Where do we gather for sunset cocktails?"

"We offer complimentary wine and delectables on the East Branch and then you're welcome to join us on the North Branch for one of our five-star culinary picnics! All of our food is, of course, tree-themed. You'll just die for the Black Forest ham and honey sauté, or maybe you'd prefer the vegan option, made entirely from plant-based ingredients. Chef calls it the Rose of Sharon."

"Oh, I'm an omnivore."

"Well, don't eat me!" squealed Pine.

Rebah grinned at her new best friend while surreptitiously scanning the room, looking for things to be mean about. But, man—this place was based on trees. How could she be mean about trees? She had as much concern for the environment as anyone. Trees were heroes! Though she didn't really want to live in one. Maybe that was the hook. The mean hook. Let the trees be trees. Keep your feet on the ground. Don't ask so much of a hammock. Okay, maybe she could do this.

"Oh, excuse me for two secs, I just have to go say goodbye to a very special guest," Pine said in a super-excited voice. She dashed toward a slim figure skulking across the lobby floor. Even the lumberjack could be heard sighing a sweet goodbye in the figure's general direction. Rebah squinted her eyes to see who could possibly be more special than an award-winning blogger only to see . . . Stewart Starr.

"Rebah!" gushed Stew as his entourage surrounded him. "Goodness, honey, are you just checking in? Well, looks like we're double-dipping! I'm actually just checking out. One and done, sealed with a Stew." Stewart smiled the kind of smile crocodiles were known for, just before they tasted your closest limb.

"Wait, did the corporation send you here? Why would they send both of us?"

"Oh, no, I caught whiff of this gorgeous place on my own. It's called having my finger on the pulse of the luxury accommodation industry. Some of us are just more in tune with what our viewers crave!" Stew chuckled a false note of laughter and the crowd of forest imps around him burst into a flurry of giggles. "Anyhoo, I've got to jet. These vlogs won't make themselves, you know." Stew tossed a wink toward Rebah and continued on his way down the Magical Forest Path.

"So, shall we continue with check-in?" Pine was back in formation.

"Actually, you know what I just realized?" Rebah retrieved her bag from the arm of the disconcerted lumberjack and slung the strap over her shoulder. "I just remembered . . . a tree house is a terrible theme." She hit Pine with her hardest glare and twirled around to leave.

"But . . ."

"What?" Rebah snapped, ready to storm off.

"You forgot your license." Pine handed over Rebah's ID with a pout, and Rebah had the feeling she'd managed to burn a branch.

"That's R-E-B-A-H Reynolds, like Reynolds Wrap. Yep. That's right. She ran right into me. I called you on Monday, right after it happened. It's now Wednesday—I'd have thought you'd have processed the claim by now." Aidan held the phone up like he was strangling it as the insurance drone on the other end of the call hemmed and hawed. He was in the driveway, walking in circles around his Jeep to make sure he didn't miss any potential scratch or dent that could help squeeze money from Rebah Reynolds' insurance company. "Yeah, and I'd just had it painted, too."

Kye rubbed a microfiber cloth around the bumper, smoothing out the last of the damage. He shook his head at Aidan.

"Aaaannnndddd now he's going to call me back," Aidan moaned, tapping the off button on his phone. "What is it with insurance adjusters? This is a tactic. He's hoping I don't notice he never calls back and I forget to file a claim. This is what they do. But he doesn't know how much I have it in for Rebah Reynolds."

"Rebah Reynolds. Still gorgeous after all these years. Well, one year."

Aidan whipped his head from where he was examining Kye's work on his car. "Dude."

"Well, dude."

"Dude, you know I didn't find her attractive. I mean, she was pretty, but also the devil incarnate."

"Yeah, but maybe that was, you know, a rough weekend for her. We've all had those. You especially should understand what it can be like when something else takes over and makes all your decisions for you." Kye mopped his brow with a red-checkered handkerchief and stuffed it in his back pocket. "I'm just saying."

"Yeah, but she was out of control. Like, for real. And she ruined Jessica's quilt and then had the gall to slam us in that review. Jesus." Aidan scowled at his friend. "I can't stand her."

"No, no, I get it." Kye stretched his arms up and bent his head from side to side to get the kinks out. "Hey, Shar!"

Sharon and the twins were en route from the cabin next door. Kye and Sharon had bought the place with the bundle they'd made when they'd sold their place in San Francisco, and the two couples had quickly made friends. Sharon and Jessica had been pretty diametrically opposed in terms of personality, style, taste, parenting views, and just about everything else, but something about the foursome's friendship had worked. These are the people, Aidan sometimes reminded himself, who are going to write your eulogy.

"Hey, sweets. We figured we'd come by and learn some auto repair. That's a good lesson, right?" Sharon homeschooled the twelve-year-old twins, Miranda and Mason, and treated the entire world as their classroom. It was really the most convenient way to do it.

"Dad, can we take apart the catalytic converter?" Miranda asked.

"Yeah, no," interrupted Aidan. "But you can totally take apart the lawn mower if you want."

"But that's so boring. I need a bigger engine. A challenge." Miranda was fascinated by engines, which could be useful when something went wrong with the toaster or the string trimmer. It could also be disastrous when she got bored and decided to take equipment apart for fun, but then got tired of the process and left it in pieces.

"Is Apple around?" asked Mason. He stood with his hip cocked, twisting one of his long red locks around his forefinger.

"She's inside." Aidan motioned with his head toward the house. "I think she's getting ready to go out with Kai."

"I don't have plans with Apple," Kye said, looking confused.

"No, Kai. *Kai!*" Kai was Apple's boyfriend, and it had been super amusing when they'd first started dating to have homophone names in their friend circle. But now? It was a little annoying.

"I wanted to, like, try on that new beaded vest she scored from the thrift store. Oh. My. God. I can't believe she found one before me." Mason huffed his breath toward the heavens and closed his eyes dramatically at the injustice of it all.

"She's in there somewhere. Go catch her before she's ready to go."

Mason and Miranda raced each other to the porch steps—but, really, there was no contest. Miranda was deeply involved in sports and held a starting position on every team she managed to convince her mother to let her join, whether that was soccer, baseball, or basketball. With her short-capped brown hair and wheeling arms and legs, she sped toward the porch like a bullet. Mason, on the other hand, had zero interest in any sort of physical exertion, but he did love to rummage through Apple's closet, and so he tried to keep pace with his sister, his long hair flying behind him.

But she won easily.

Sharon watched her kids with a bemused smile on her face, her blond hair, shaped in a practical page boy, fluttering in the light breeze. Never known for her fashion sense, a fact mourned by her son, she was wearing a colorful combination of pink overalls, a man's orange waffle-weave undershirt, and green rubber gardening shoes.

"Aidan, I've been meaning to ask—is Rebah Reynolds in any position to sue you? Does she have a case?" Once upon a time, Sharon had been a lawyer. Never had anyone been so glad to remove herself from an oppressive system as she was.

"No! She hit me! I was backing into a parking space and wham—freaking Rebah Reynolds reenters my life."

"Okay, good."

"Good?"

"Good in the sense that you don't want to be on the wrong end of her litigious stick," Sharon clarified. She brushed her hair away from her brow with a hand filthy from planting carrot seeds in her organic garden. "In all other senses, ugh."

Aidan had to snort at the ridiculousness of the entire episode.

"Yeah. 'Of all the gin joints in all the towns in all the world,' right?" He smacked the heel of his hand to his forehead. "And kind of the worst thing? I can't even believe this. I told her the Happy Valley was doing better than ever. I lied that—get this—we were having a grand celebration weekend. You know, because business is so good."

"Huh." Kye nodded. "Well, that's confirmed then. You are a pure and unadulterated idiot."

"Hey, let's not resort to name-calling," Sharon said. "But, Aidan, why? Why lie about something that, first of all, is the furthest thing from the truth and, second of all, is very easy to prove a lie if she had any interest in pursuing it? And Rebah Reynolds being Rebah Reynolds, I wouldn't put it past her to feature the Happy Valley in her next article, something about 'The Valley Digs Itself Even Deeper with a Series of Mistruths.'"

Aidan moaned into his hands and shook his head, wishing he could rewind time so he could undo that entire encounter. Find a different parking spot on a different street. Better yet, admit to Apple he just wasn't up to a trip to the city that day and skip the whole thing altogether. Why had he lied? What did he have to prove to that woman? Maybe he would give up on the insurance adjuster. Just so he didn't ever again have to utter the name Rebah Reynolds.

Kye reached out to pat him on the shoulder. "You sure know how to impress the people you swear you aren't trying to impress."

Apple's boyfriend, Kai, swooped up the driveway, his slim torso balanced over his longboard. He floated to a stop in front of the group, his tall lanky form surpassing all the adults in height. "Hey," he murmured and took a drag from a vape he magicked out of his low-slung cargo shorts. "You three look happy." Kai tossed a hank of blond hair off his forehead and beamed, his bright blue eyes, the exact shade of his hoodie, hiding no sense of irony.

"Hey, Kai," Aidan answered. "How's life? You know, vaping is bad for you."

"Same, same. Life, I mean. Same. And, hey, vaping is way better for me than, you know, cigarettes, or even, like, marijuana. Soooo . . . pick your poison, am I right?"

Kye held out his hand to bump fists with Kai. "You are so right, Kai. My poison? Organic broccoli. It's so freaking addictive."

"Yeah, man, Kye knows."

"And free-range chicken breasts, locally sourced."

"Aw, man, making me hungry." Kai grinned and tucked his vape away in his sweatshirt pocket.

"Seriously, Kai," Aidan said. "I better never see Apple doing that. Be a good influence on my daughter, right?"

"Oh, totally. You know Apple, right? She's got bigger things on her mind than vaping. Anything that might keep her from pursuing dreams A, B, and C, she's going to avoid like diseased lizards."

"Good plan." Sharon nodded.

All of them looked up as a murder of crows alighted from the walnut tree at the end of the drive and swooped out toward the neighboring vineyard.

"So, Kai, where are you guys heading this morning?" Aidan asked.

"I'm supposed to be going somewhere?" Kye answered.

"No, I meant Kai."

"What?" asked Kai.

"You guys doing something fun today?"

"You know, I have this friend who set up this movie theater in his basement with like a projector and, like, snacks. He's showing some vampire movie? I think it's called *Dracula*? Apple thought it would be cool. You know, to go watch."

"That does sound kind of cool," said Kye. "Sharon, how about you and I leave the kids home and check it out? I can steam some broccoli to take along."

Sharon grimaced at her husband, who knew very well that she actually loved vampire movies and the societal metaphors they offered but hated basements filled with strangers. "Yeah, that's a hard pass."

"Chicks dig vampires," said Kai.

"Chicks dig vampires." Kye nodded wisely.

Aidan and Sharon shot each other long-suffering looks.

Just then, Apple bounded out of the doors and leaped down the front steps to land in front of Aidan, her own longboard tucked under her arm, the twins trailing behind, Mason earthily resplendent in the beaded vest. "Dad, don't forget, Room 2B still needs a fresh set of sheets since the last guests checked out. You got that? And I know you haven't fixed that air conditioner yet."

"Yeah, but it's spring. Who needs an air conditioner?"

"Sheets, Dad. Just accomplish the sheets."

She turned to Kai and grinned in a way Aidan hadn't seen in a long time. "Ready for a morning of theater magic?"

Kai reached out and tugged one of her long dark braids. "Your wish? My command." And the two planted their longboards on the pavement and thrust off down the driveway.

Aidan turned to Kye. "She looks so happy."

"And you look so worried," Sharon added.

"I just want to be able to give her what she wants. I need to afford Barnard."

"There are other options." One look at Sharon's face and you could tell she was creating spreadsheets in her mind. The woman was a logistical genius and, to be honest, the Happy Valley probably would've gone under by then if she hadn't helped out occasionally with the books. "Scholarships, for one. And other universities—she could do community college for a year, get all of her general education requirements out of the way, and then go on to Barnard."

"But Barnard has been her dream since she was tiny. How do I say no to her dream?"

"That's a tough one." Kye rocked back and forth on his heels. "A question for the parenting gurus that live next door to you, am I right?"

"You're referring to yourself as a parenting guru?"

"Well, maybe not me. But definitely my wife."

Sharon raised her eyebrows. "And this guru says first you need to go change the sheets."

Aidan grimaced. "Yeah, well, Kye? How about you come with me and fix that air conditioner?"

"Didn't I just hear you point out the benefits of spring in all its temperate weather patterns?"

"Both of you. Upstairs," Sharon directed. "The twins and I are going to go do some research into college scholarships. Kids, what's your first search term going to be?"

Mason spoke up. "'Where to shop for a beaded vest.'"

Chapter 7

"A cannabis-themed B&B?" Rebah muttered. "Of all the things . . ."

But it was true. Take a Toke Bed & Breakfast described itself as the "Relaxation Destination," and by the looks of the two staff members manning the entryway, that was an apt description. Apparently, high-end no longer meant awake and aware—the girl, dressed in genie pants and a halter top, was dozing with her eyes closed and the older man next to her was giggling at an ant winding its way around his wrist. Neither noticed Rebah's arrival. This high-end B&B just seemed . . . high.

But despite the inattentive staff, it was a sweet entryway. A shallow waterfall, stone-tiled floor and half-walls, exactly the right shade of lighting—Rebah felt her shoulders relax with every step. Maybe this was exactly what she needed. A chance to escape, to press the reset button, to mingle with wealthy people out of their minds on weed. Marijuana didn't assert any kind of pull on her, but surely she could get a bottle of wine, settle into her room, and just . . . decompress. Forget about seeing Stewart at the ridiculous tree house. Forget about that ridiculous meeting with her bosses. Forget about running into that ridiculous guy, Aidan Cisneros. Of all the luck. And he was still just as much of a jerk, that entitled, smug, self-centered . . .

Rebah's shoulders reversed their downward creep and ended suddenly in her ears. Time to quit thinking so much.

"I think you're expecting me?" she asked the one greeter who was at least awake.

After a few false starts and miscommunications, she eventually got her key (on a key chain shaped like a miniature bong, of course) and opened the door to the "420 Room" where she was confronted by decor that seemed a cross between the 1970s and the future. A sunken bed did look comfortable, but a vending machine? In the room? Filled with snack bags of potato chips and Cheez Doodles? Not to mention several posters on the walls that, when she tried a few light switches and discovered one controlled a black light, revealed themselves as fluorescent artwork.

"Don't be judgmental," she muttered to herself and slipped her yellow legal pad out of the front pocket of her satchel. "This is perfectly lovely. Just a different kind of lovely than you're used to."

She kicked off her low heels and rubbed a foot, suddenly exhausted. Just a few minutes lying on the bed, jotting down some thoughts, and then she'd find a place to eat. And a place to get a bottle. She looked around and spotted a pair of wineglasses hanging by their bases from a surprisingly elegant rack. She appreciated the glasses, but complimentary wine would have been nice. She sighed and flopped on the bed and started writing some notes. "Not so subtle in its motivation for existence, the Take a Toke B&B offers a plethora of . . ."

What was that? A drop of water landed on her notepad, messing up the Bs. Another drop. And then another. "What the?"

Rebah craned her neck up just in time to see several cracks run across the surface of the ceiling just before a wall of water escaped and cascaded around her, soaking the bed, her legal pad, and, of course, her body.

* * *

"Dammit, Frank, this is ridiculous! Not only do I not have a subject for a blog post, but I don't have a place to sleep tonight." Rebah signaled to move into the fast lane so she could beat a path around the slowpoke Audi in front of her, but a truck barreled past just as she was about to ease over. "Ugh."

"Rebah, of course you're upset. Burst pipes do not make for an enjoyable stay."

"I don't think you understand the gravity of the situation, Frank."

"No, I do, I do. You need a new place to stay and you need it now."

"I need it ten minutes ago." Rebah finally pulled out and around the Audi and floored it as she passed. "I'm soaking wet, I'm hungry, and I could really use a glass of wine." *In fact, there must be a liquor store around here somewhere.*

"Well, Rebah, I am working as hard as I can to find you a place. Let's just hold on now. How about this: a B&B that's more motel than B&B?"

"Why would anyone run a B&B as a motel?"

"Apparently it was a Holiday Inn that was rebranded as a Home Comfort Stay Inn and then rebranded once again as . . . the world's largest B&B."

"Yeah, sounds super intimate."

"Well, Rebah, the Jazz Festival is this week and we're a little late trying to find a place, so . . ."

"Frank, it is not my fault that a pipe burst and it's not my fault that Sticky Stewart got to the tree house before me and it is not my fault that the Jazz Festival is going on. Just find me a decent place."

"Ah, here we go. The SFCA DIY B&B."

"Frank. English, please."

"No, that's its name. It's an acronym. The San Francisco, California, Do-It-Yourself B&B. Totally high-end. Apparently, you get to make your bed with thousand-count silk sheets, you cook your breakfast from locally sourced organic ingredients, and you clean your bathroom with non-toxic solutions based on milk from humanely bred goats."

"I am not paying to clean my own bathroom!"

"Well, you're not paying anyway. Right?"

God, that twist of power came so easily to her boss. Well, bosses. "Is there nothing else available?"

"Oh, this looks delightful. The world's first B&B&B."

"I can't even imagine."

"No, really, listen. 'Into apiaries? Buzzed about beeswax? Then you'll feel right at home on Napa's Bee You, Bee Free, Honeybee Farm. Relax among nature's hardest workers as you spend time at our day spa, complete with a honey facial and beeswax waxings, and then settle on our veranda with a glass of our best mead as you listen to the sounds of the delicate industry all around you.' Doesn't that sound spectacular? Oh, and you get a pair of beekeeper-style pajamas. This sounds right up your alley!"

"Hate to break it to you, Frank," Rebah said, swerving to avoid hitting the car slowing in front of her. "But I'm deathly allergic to beestings."

Rebah pulled onto a long, winding driveway that led through fields of strawberries to a series of man-made caves. Caves? Frank hadn't mentioned caves when he offered up this place as a last resort. But apparently a B&B with the theme of Homer the blind poet was structured with caves. Did people in ancient Greece really live in caves? Her class on ancient civilizations was years ago, but she remembered some really fantastic architecture, none of which was evident in this particular interpretation.

Rebah parked in the sparsely populated lot in front of the largest cave and looked around. The caves were a warm, reddish-brown color, some in the shape of large mounds and others resembling small mushroom caps. A system of well-tended pathways connected them, and prayer flags danced along wires strung between occasional stone columns that rose out of the ground. She groaned, put her hands up to her face, and took a couple of deep breaths. *This will work*, she told herself. *This will be fine.* Already the headlines were starting to percolate in the back of her brain: "There's No Place Like Homer." "Homer is Where the Art Is." "Two Ancients, One Stone: Homer or Plato, You Decide."

She grabbed her bag and purse and locked the rental as she looked around for any kind of signage but—it was all Greek. Literally. She saw some prayer flags lining a doorway and figured she'd start there.

"Hello?" she called out as she approached. It was eerily quiet. Not a soul marked the view of rolling hills rising behind the strange caves in front of her, with the exception of a lone tractor making its way across a field in the distance. "Anyone around?" This was bizarre. It was Rebah's extensive experience that B&B owners and workers were generally more welcoming than absent, but maybe this was all part of the . . . charm?

A door she hadn't noticed before opened on the front of one of the larger caves, and a bell tinkled. A bald man in a brown rucksack-like robe smiled and gestured at her to come. Oh, this was rich. He motioned to a sign, the only one in English she'd seen so far: "Dear Guests, please honor our code of silence. Namaste."

"Kind of a clash of cultures, don't you think?" Rebah asked. She was trying, she really was, but a code of silence from a bald man dressed like Friar Tuck standing in a cave amongst an army of Greek signs was just a little much.

Friar Tuck gestured again at the sign asking for silence, and Rebah once again put her head down in her hands and inhaled a deep, controlled breath, counting rapidly to twenty and wishing hard for a glass of wine to magically appear in her hand. Right. What were her choices? She could try the bee place, but that was sure to end in a trip to the emergency room. She could call Frank and demand another alternative, but she didn't really want to talk to him again and, anyway, she had to admit he was right. It was Jazz Festival week—there would be no other options.

She lifted her head, straightened her shoulders, and smiled that blog-famous smile: her delighted face. "Charming!" she shrieked with only her eyes. "So unique," she clarified with her uplifted hands. Not a sound passed her lips.

The man—not unhandsome, but entirely too wrapped up in his own brand of Zen—handed her a clipboard and a pen and bowed his head in a gesture that obviously meant, "Fill this out."

Rebah hadn't encountered a paper and pen check-in system since the early aughts. It felt so . . . germy.

But she flashed a "When in Rome" smile at her host and went to work with her name, DOB, license number, car plate number, car color, credit card number, and two phone numbers (she wondered if the code of silence could be broken to use the phone) and by the time the form was complete, her hand ached and her temper was barely in check. What the actual hellish planet had she landed on?

Friar Tuck clapped sharply and a woman appeared, dressed in the same style as the friar though with flowing locks of red. In fact, the woman was quite pretty and smiled wryly at Rebah as she held out a hand to take the bag, which Rebah refused by tightening her grip. Red Hair shrugged, took a key from a pegboard leaning against one wall of the cave, and with her head indicated that Rebah should follow.

All of this not-talking was exhausting. Rebah could feel a headache coming on.

It was a short walk down a wooden boardwalk lined with olive trees to Rebah's cave. Red Hair unlocked the door and entered first, smiling in a slightly creepy way that made Rebah wonder if she was about to be murdered. But instead Red Hair held her arms out wide and twirled around in a show of "See? It's not so bad."

And it wasn't. Caves have a reputation for being dank and dark, but this one was well lit with LED lights tastefully placed at appropriate intervals, and it smelled like an old bookshop on the verge of being discovered by hipsters, not dank at all. A hammock hung from hooks that were screwed into the cave's plaster wall, a stark wooden table offered the only surface on which she could place her things, and a curtain held the promise of modern plumbing just a few feet away.

"Lovely." Rebah shrugged.

Red Hair leaned in and whispered conspiratorially, "We're not supposed to talk, as you might have guessed, but signing all of this takes forever and you seem reasonable, so: Boozy Breakfast at eight, a communal reading of *The Odyssey* at ten, Liquid Lunch at one, Bathing with Sea Monsters at three, and the option to join our Drinking Dinner at seven. Oh, and the Siren Sing-Along directly afterward. It's a hoot."

"Thanks," Rebah whispered. "Hey, is there Wi-Fi?"

"But of course. Password is αγάπη." Red Hair winked and slipped out the door before Rebah could ask how the hell to spell that.

Alone in her cave, Rebah groaned again and tried to find some kind of solace in her phone, but—of course—no signal. She dug through her bag and pulled out her yellow legal pad and a pen and started making some notes standing right there on the hard stone floor, but seriously, her hand ached after filling in all those tiny boxes on the registration form. How did people used to do that every time they stayed somewhere? What if they were traveling cross-country and had to stay at a different place every night? Every night, repeating all that information with tiny, tiny letters in tiny, tiny boxes.

Rebah knew work wasn't going to get done in her current state. Maybe there was an office center somewhere? A large cave with laptops and scanners? Maybe even a coffee maker? It was time to explore.

She braced herself, then opened the door to her cave and stepped into the Napa sun, the sound of crows cawing overhead, cicadas in the olive branches, and . . . rhythmic chanting? What fresh hell?

She followed the sound farther back into the maze of caves until she came upon a raised platform on which a dozen or so figures clad in those same brown robes were kneeling, rising, kneeling again, leaning their foreheads on the platform, rising, and chanting unintelligible words the entire time. "This place has an identity problem," Rebah muttered to herself, only to be shushed by a robed woman on the platform spot closest to her. "Sorry," Rebah hissed.

"Shhhhhhhhhh . . ." buzzed several of the chanting members. So Rebah mouthed her apology, completely silent, only to be scolded one more time. "SSSSSSHHHHHHHHHH . . ."

"Oh, for Christ's sake!" she said out loud. She turned without waiting to see what kind of effect she'd had on the congregation, winding back the way she'd come. It was too bad this place so obviously had a personality disorder—it was quite lovely with the sculpted rock and the wooden pathway and the olive trees bending their branches over the cedar bark mulch that surrounded the native plantings—Rebah spotted yerba maté, eucalyptus, and cattails waving in the breeze.

Back at the office, she found Friar Tuck having a silent conversation with another member of staff who had clearly made some kind of foul mistake. Scowls, aggressive hand gestures, and lots of pointing dominated the exchange. Rebah backed away, not wanting to interrupt, but Friar spotted her and his face immediately, strangely transitioned into one of warm welcome. So weird. The shamed staff member slipped out the door.

How does one politely, silently ask where one might acquire a bottle of wine to better handle the bizarre customs of this strange place? Rebah chose hands over heart, then one hand mimed holding a wineglass, bringing it to her lips, sipping, and then she rolled her eyes in obvious relief. She looked at her host questioningly.

Friar Tuck looked confused. He raised his hands in a gesture of perplexity.

Rebah tried again: hand aloft, sipping the wine, pouring more from an invisible bottle, and then more sipping, more pouring, more sipping, until she had drunk an entire imaginary bottle of wine and Friar Tuck looked more befuddled and perhaps a little—was that irritation on his previously placid face?

Rebah was about to break all kinds of codes by laying into this man who stood in the way of relief when off to the side of the office, a curtain was yanked across its wooden bar, emitting an audible rip. A gorgeous woman with bright green fingernails, flaming red lipstick, and a skintight blue halter dress stood framed by the fake rock. She looked like a slutty Audrey Hepburn.

"You!" she shrieked.

Well, this just got interesting, Rebah thought.

Friar Tuck looked very, very afraid. He even nabbed a clipboard and held it in front of him like a shield.

"You have stood me up for the last time. What exactly do you think I am? Someone you pay by the hour? Someone you keep on retainer? Someone who comes when you call and retreats when you shoo me off?" Slutty Audrey Hepburn took a step closer to the two of them and Rebah caught a whiff of—Could it be?—alcohol on her breath. Aha. This was a woman she wanted to talk to. "Well, you have missed your last chance, jerk. That's it! I'm done!"

Friar Tuck came alive, finally. "It's not my fault!" he squeaked. His voice was way higher than Rebah would have expected. "I got stuck here with a last-minute check-in and you know what happens if I let the other staff try to handle things like that. You can't break up with me because of this! I'm just being responsible."

"It's not just because of this. It's because of everything. It's because of you." Slutty Audrey Hepburn slumped where she stood and swayed slightly, her face crumpled into a painted oval of pain. "I can't keep being second to all the other things in your life."

"But you aren't really. I don't even have that much in my life. There's my job, my bike. My dog. My sister and her problems, God help me, and my mom's cancer and Dad's dementia, and I know my ex still comes around sometimes but you're not second to anything, baby. You're first all the way."

"But when we're supposed to meet and you stand me up and I have to drive out to this godforsaken place to find you, it doesn't feel like I'm first."

"Excuse me," Rebah softly interrupted. "Can I just ask, is there a liquor store nearby?"

"Baby, of course you're first. There's no contest. Seriously, not even my dog."

"Not even your ex?"

Rebah tried again. "I know you guys are in the throes of making up and that is super awesome because, honestly, you seem like a great couple, but before you slip away to seal the deal, seriously, just point me in the right direction? Phone service is lousy out here and I could really use—"

"My ex? Dead to me. There's only you. I totally mean that."

"So, can we go on that date?" Slutty Audrey looked like a glow stick had been cracked behind her face, all beaming with a happy glow.

"Wait, you mean now?"

"I mean really, just point toward the liquor store. That's all I need. Just a direction." Rebah could feel her headache deepening. Jeez, these people. Was it too much to ask? For the answer to one simple question? Should she remind this desk clerk how much his business counted on her for a good review of this measly place? This was a disgrace. She was Rebah Reynolds.

"Of course now! This was supposed to be the night we tried that new restaurant, the one where they cook the food on your car bumper and serve it through your window. Why are you even hesitating?"

"Baby, I'm so sorry. I know we meant to do that but tonight got kind of hairy with that group doing the meditating and this last-minute chick."

Rebah cleared her throat. "You know that last-minute chick is right here, right? You know I can hear every word?"

"I swear, I'd love to skip out, but the boss will kill me and I—"

"So I don't come first. I never came first. That was a line to get me to calm down." Slutty Audrey Hepburn's voice slipped into high gear. "And I can tell you I am not calm!"

"Liquor store!" Rebah's voice matched Audrey's. "Tell me now! And then I'll get my things and you"—She jabbed her finger toward Friar Tuck, who looked shocked that she was even there—"won't have to worry about this last-minute chick."

"Don't you yell at my boyfriend like that!" Audrey turned on Rebah and advanced as though she meant business, the kind of business that usually ended in a lawsuit. Rebah shot a look at Friar Tuck, but he was watching the scene unfold with a half-smile on his face.

"Right. First off, Slutty Audrey, you must know that you are far superior to this specimen of humanity, simply by the fact that you did not take a vow of silence to appease the employment gods. Second? Those earrings are killer. Love them. And finally—all I want, all I need is directions to a liquor store to get a bottle of wine in an attempt to at least half-save this delightful lodging experience." Rebah took a deep, square breath—in two, three, four, and out two, three, four—and continued. "But as I reflect on the past hour of my life, I realize there's no need. This place is lost. A hellhole. And I have a very special spot on my blog for exactly this kind of encounter."

On the path back to her cave to get her stuff she glanced behind her, but Slutty Audrey had, apparently, stayed behind to defend her man from anyone else who tried to interrupt, and her man, Friar Tuck, was busy gazing after Rebah with a look that blended "Oh, man, this will not look good to the boss" and "Hey, can I get your number?"

"Insanity," Rebah muttered. And the worst part, she realized, was that she was still without a place to stay the night.

In his heart, Kye knew that it was time for Aidan to move past the granite block that had stood in his path for the past five years. He'd watched his friend struggle through the deepest of valleys, the darkest of fogs—life had been pretty bleak at times since Jessica's death, and there were weeks Kye had watched Aidan consciously choose to live.

And his sole reason? Apple.

Aidan was damaged, desperate, lonely, broken, but he was also a dad, and a good one. He knew Apple needed her one remaining parent to stay sober, stay alive, and stay at least moderately functional. And he had managed to rise to the occasion, including the days when the urge to drink mixed with memories of his dead wife to make a stew of desperation that he choked down, even though it was trying to kill him.

Kye had seen this, had watched his friend go through this hell, and knew that it was time to nudge. Aidan needed something. Something big. Something monumental.

When Aidan was outside trying half-heartedly to do some weed whacking around the overgrown lawn, Kye palmed Rebah's business card from the front table where Aidan had left it.

"Yes, hi, this Kye Dejesus, head of marketing at the Happy Valley B&B." He spoke smoothly into the phone as he stood in a hallway in the Happy Valley. Milly, who was standing next to him on her tiptoes with her hands clasped under her chin, cocked her head and grinned at how businessy he sounded. "I was wondering if I might speak to Ms. Rebah Reynolds. No? Ah, she's on the road? Well, that's why I'm calling, actually. I'm trying to, well, build a bridge, so to speak. We feel terrible about the unfortunate car accident that occurred this past week with our owner, Aidan Cisneros?" Kye moved the phone away from his face to shush Milly, who had inadvertently let out a squeal. "Mr. Cisneros is just miserable at the thought that he caused Ms. Reynolds any hardship and would like to extend an invitation. Yes, to stay. Yes, here. Well, yes, we do remember that review, and, yes, we do understand that this seems a bit out of the blue, but, with the Happy Valley doing so well, we truly feel that there is space in this relationship for growth. Business relationship, I mean, of course. And, as a gesture of good faith, we'll waive the nightly room fee. That's right. Of course. Lovely. Terrific. Absolutely. Lovely. Yes. Well, we'll see her then then. Have a lovely day!"

"You're pretty good at being snooty," said Milly as he hung up the phone. She plucked Rebah's business card from his fingers and studied it.

"Did I ever tell you about the summer I spent waiting tables at a private island up in the Pacific Northwest? You haven't seen snooty until you've seen private islanders." Kye ran his large hands through his sandy hair. "That was the booking agent at the company she works for. She used to work for herself, didn't she? Strange that she works for a company now. But anyway, she's coming."

Milly squealed and bounced on her toes, green dreadlocks dancing around her face in excitement. "Kye, Kye, Kye, this is going to be amazing. It will totally work, I know it!"

"Well, easy there. We still have to break the news to you-know-who. He's not going to take this lightly."

"Take what lightly?" Aidan asked, coming around the corner from the kitchen.

Milly yipped and whipped Rebah's business card around her back. "Nothing!" she answered in a pitch that could attract dogs.

"Ah, listen, Aidan? We've got some news," Kye began. "See—"

"Wait, what did you do?" Aidan reached around and easily nabbed the card from Milly's nervous fingers. "Rebah Reynolds? Why were you calling Rebah Reynolds?"

"Because you need a miracle and I think Rebah Reynolds is your miracle worker," Kye told him confidently.

"No way. Uh-uh. Miracles don't actually exist and Rebah Reynolds is in no way the person to provide me with one if they did exist. Call her back. Whatever you told her, call her back and untell her."

"Wait, wait, wait, wait. Just listen to the plan. Because we do have a plan, right, Milly?"

Milly's head bounced up and down so hard her glasses slipped down her nose and nearly off. Which was fine because they had no glass inside the frames. "We invited her here for your grand celebration this weekend."

"You did what! And how is that supposed to make me feel better? Knowing the plan is not making me feel better."

"I just know that if we can clean up the place a bit more and get her here and show her a good time, but not like a dirty good time, just a normal good time, she'll write a glowing review and all the business you lost a year ago will come flooding back and who will want to see that? You know who. Jack Shit, or whatever his name is."

"Look, hey, there are so many things wrong with this idea. Let's start with how much she hates me."

"She doesn't hate you—she hates her memory of you, of being mortified in front of other guests at a B&B that's supposed to be classy."

"Second, this place—have you looked around lately?"

Kye and Milly glanced about the entranceway. They peered down the hall toward the dining room. They craned their necks to see into the front parlor. They settled their gaze in the living room. While they'd spick-and-spanned the place in preparation for Jax Pitts, there was still a lot left to be desired. Especially for someone with eyesight as keen as Rebah Reynolds's.

"Nothing a little paint and Windex can't cure," Milly offered.

"Third—I don't like Rebah Reynolds. She's a drunk, she's mean, she's a diva in a business that I have no respect for. She's the opposite of everything I enjoy about life."

"You know, casting her as a drunk is a little shortsighted, my friend," Kye said, putting a hand on Aidan's shoulder. "You of all people know the depths of that word."

Aidan looked down at the worn carpet under his feet. "I know, I know. That's how much I dislike this person, that I would say something like that. I can't do this, Kye. I know you two mean well, but it's just not going to work out."

A clatter erupted from the front door as Apple and Kai burst into the hallway, glowing with the confidence and energy of being young, in love, and on the cusp of the rest of their lives. "Dad!" Apple laughed. "The basement movie theater was so cool! This guy totally takes it seriously. He prints tickets and everything. And he has a popcorn maker!"

"How was *Dracula*?" Aidan asked, still glaring at Kye and Milly.

"No joy in *Dracula* town," Apple told him. "That movie didn't work—we couldn't get past the first bite. So he played *Footloose*. Have you seen it? It's about this place where no one is allowed to dance until this guy moves there and is like, what? No dancing? There's no life without dancing!"

She broke into a shimmying dance, and Kai joined her, at a much slower, Kai-like pace, and the two of them dancing in the bedraggled hallway to no music but what they could hear in their heads nearly brought Aidan to tears. This girl, his daughter—she deserved the entire world laid at her feet.

He looked over at Kye, who was watching him, and at Milly, whose dreads were flying because she hadn't been able to resist joining Apple and Kai in their boogying. Apple dashed over to the piano and started pounding out a lively zydeco tune so Milly and Kai would move even faster.

Kye nodded at Aidan, and Aidan nodded at Kye, and with that, the decision was made. Rebah would come. And just maybe they could knock her socks off and she'd write up a fantastic review and bam, the Happy Valley would once again be the warm, welcoming place it once was.

Just in time to sell it.

Rebah got off the phone with the booking agent at FEOR, perplexed. Why did Aidan Cisneros want her to come back to his sad little bed-and-breakfast? Didn't she do enough damage the last time she'd written about him and his ridiculous business? She knew that a review on *Rambling with Rebah* was a great way to boost bookings, but hadn't he said the place was going great? Strange.

But then again, who was she to scoff at a place to stay for the weekend? She'd had such bad luck this week. And she was sick of staying at the Hyatt—they did not vacuum their carpets often enough and getting an extra towel was a lesson in negotiating the impossible. Now, at least she had somewhere decent to stay for the weekend. Or at least there wouldn't be angry pseudo-monks or flooded beds, right?

But check-in wasn't until Friday, so it was back to the Hyatt for two more nights. At least she knew of a liquor store that was on the way.

Chapter 8

Early Thursday morning, Aidan armed himself with a clipboard and pen and announced to his troops—Kye, Milly, and Apple (Sharon and the kids would help after they'd returned from the dentist)—that the first thing they needed to do to create a dazzling celebration weekend was make a list of what they needed to do. "Your mom always said nothing could be accomplished without a list, and it was one of her many wise habits," he told Apple. They were all standing mostly at attention at the kitchen table, Kye munching on a Bosc pear.

Aidan drew a series of tiny boxes down the left-hand side of his paper and tried to imagine them all checked off. Even though no tasks had been set yet.

Apple knew that this weekend was important, that they were trying to impress Rebah Reynolds. What she did not know, however, was why. Selling the Happy Valley had never crossed her mind. She just thought her dad's interest in their B&B had been rekindled and that scoring a good review from the infamous Rebah was critical for Operation Reboot.

"First on the list?" she said. "Food!"

Aidan rubbed his hand across his forehead, leaving a smudge of dirt. "Okay, I'm putting it on the list. Food. There. Now we know it's a problem we have to solve. Okay, next problem?"

"Cleaning."

"Entertainment."

"That smell coming from under the front porch." Milly snapped her gum and twirled her hair—crimson today—with two fingers.

"Wait, when do we actually solve these problems?" Apple asked. "Or do we just keep listing them until we're so depressed at the amount of work we need to do that we just give up?" She reached over to the fruit bowl on the table and helped herself to a pear. "Mmm, juicy."

"Your smart daughter has a point," Kye drawled. "Maybe we solve the food problem before moving on to the next problem. Then we'll build up, what do you call it?" He snapped his fingers. "Momentum."

"Well, sure, we need to solve the problems we put on the list, but how do we solve such a huge problem like food?" Aidan pointed out. "I don't have time to plan a menu, get to the market, and prepare food all weekend. It's impossible. It would've been impossible even before . . ." Everyone in the room knew he was going to say "before Jessica died." He didn't have to utter her name for them all to be reminded of what was missing from their lives. How much joy she would have taken in whipping the place into shape. How much fun all of them would have had. They stood still for a moment, even Milly, who always fidgeted, as they silently acknowledged for perhaps the billionth time what had been lost when she died.

"Okay, the food thing—I have an idea," Milly said, breaking the spell. She tossed her dreads behind her back. "Maybe we don't shop and plan and cook this weekend. Maybe we, you know. Hire out."

"What, pay someone else to cook everything?"

"Well, sure. I mean, people hire caterers all the time. This wouldn't, like, be any different."

"Huh. Not a bad idea," Kye said.

"Okay, Milly, that's all you," said Aidan. "Call around and see if anyone can do it on such short notice. Something elegant but unassuming, flavorful but foundational. And no microgreens. I just . . . can't."

Milly dashed to the living room to get her phone to find the perfect caterer, and Aidan, Apple, and Kye reverted their attention to the house. Aidan turned to his troops. "Walk with me," he said.

Leaky faucets. Mold crawling up the wall in the dining room. Carpets that smelled of mildew. Threadbare sofa cushions, scuffed oak floorboards that had lost their sheen many moons ago, a flickering bulb in the upstairs hallway lamp, and a great swath of wallpaper hanging loose in Room 2. Plus, scratchy towels that didn't wrap all the way around anybody larger than a child, sheets thin as tissue, and pillows flat as tortillas.

"I think I've been avoiding actually seeing this place for, like, five years," Apple remarked. "It's awful."

Back down in the living room, Aidan tried to light the gas fireplace, thinking maybe some dry heat would make the mold evaporate on its own and add some cozy ambience to the place. He got a meager flame going, only to be interrupted by the shrieking sound of the carbon monoxide detector.

"Dammit," he muttered, turning the fireplace off.

"Hey, at least we know it works," Apple laughed from the living room doorway. She had donned rubber gloves and was holding a broom aloft, stabbing at the cobwebs that feathered every corner of the room. Kye was kneeling on the floor, lifting up the edge of the carpet, for all the world looking like he was trying to calculate how much dirt and disaster they could literally hide under the rug.

Aidan gazed at Apple for a moment, trying to figure out what was different about her. Sure, the news about Barnard had put a light in her eyes, but there was something else. She looked happy to be digging into the impossible project of fixing up the Happy Valley. Like she was enjoying herself. Maybe she'd inherited more of Jessica's passion for place and design than Aidan had expected.

"Okay, so we need cleaning supplies, paint, wallpaper glue, some new sheets and towels, maybe some new throw pillows?" he threw out to the team. "What else?"

"Cut flowers, clean vases, area rugs, some artwork that doesn't bring funeral parlors to mind," Apple added.

"Wait, what?" Aidan objected. "We have amazing, original artwork here."

"But it's all black-and-white and a lot of it is kind of depressing."

"It's street photography! It's only depressing if the people on the street are depressed!"

"Yeah, good try, Dad. I'm just saying, a print or two wouldn't hurt. Something with color. Abstract would be good."

"I think I'm gonna need a cup of coffee," Kye admitted.

Just then, Milly returned from the kitchen, phone in hand. "Okay, Mr. C, don't freak out but I got you the best caterer Napa Valley has to offer and they said they could do dinner Friday night and a sandwich lunch on Saturday, all for the super fair price of only five grand!"

"Shuuuuu . . ." Aidan tried to express his discontent, but shock got in the way.

Kye jumped in before Aidan's words could find their way out of his mouth. "Dude, you gotta spend some dough to make this weekend work, right? It's an investment. You're investing in your place. And," he continued in a quiet voice that only Aidan could hear, "you're investing in your daughter."

He was right. Of course he was right. And it would only be the first big price tag Aidan would have to swallow to make the weekend a success. But in the end, it would be worth it, right? Right?!

"Okay. Good. It's all good. Right. Let's do this." Aidan gave himself a shake and started delegating. "Apple and Milly, take my credit card and head to the hardware store and the home goods store. Hardware store: paint, wallpaper glue, caulk, and some industrial-strength cleaning supplies. Home goods: whatever the hell you want."

Apple's eyes lit up with the thought of having free rein to alter the interior of the Happy Valley. She backpedaled out the door, towing Milly as she went, before her dad could change his mind. "We'll be back!"

Aidan pretended to dust the mantel above the non-working

fireplace. He ran a rag along the beveled edge and tried to see the place through Apple's eyes. Did she really think the street photography was depressing? His grandmother was the photographer. The same grandmother who had raised him after his parents had died. She hadn't lived long enough to meet Apple, and that was something he had always regretted. She would've loved Apple.

The sound of Milly's junker roaring to life in the driveway woke Aidan from his downward spiral. "Kye, how long until Sharon gets here?"

"Already on her way. The twins are with her and they're bringing some tools."

Sharon was actually a better handyman than her husband. She was good at pretty much everything she attempted. And Kye was the kind of husband who appreciated that.

The next two hours were filled with the sounds of home repairs: hammering, drilling, and swearing. Aidan, Kye, Sharon, and even the twins fell into the spirit of sprucing up the place. When Apple and Milly returned, the enthusiasm in the group went up to eleven. Kye wandered around with a bucket of paint and a paintbrush, swiping at anything that looked like it needed covering up, while Aidan followed with his own paint tray and roller to fix any mistakes Kye made. Finally, he sent Kye to get his toolbox so he could do something about the gas fireplaces, ideally making it so they wouldn't leak over the weekend. The last thing they needed was to gas Rebah Reynolds by accident. If she objected so strongly to being called a drunk, imagine how she might react to carbon monoxide poisoning.

As the smells of paint and cleaning products gave way to the scents of lavender room spray and pine candles and fresh flowers, Aidan had to admit that he was thrilled to see the old place achieve this level of hominess again. It had been so long since the Happy Valley had felt comfortable, like a place he wanted to be. Like a place anyone would be happy to stay for a night or two. He stood a minute in the front doorway and gazed down the hall toward the dining room, noticing how the soft, newly replaced hallway lamp cast a shadow that looked like an opera singer onto the freshly painted wall. His eyes found the delicate drape of the brocade wall hanging Apple had produced from the attic and beaten with a spatula in the yard. It was the perfect way to hide the slight dent in the wall made by Aidan during one of his more frustrated drunken moments, a memento of time past. And the living room—he loved the new bonsai garden that occupied the deep-set windowsill, and the fabricated cherry-tree branches were a nice way to distract anyone who might look too closely at the crumbling molding.

Yes, the place looked good. And he was beyond grateful to have Apple working beside him the whole morning.

But one thing lodged in his brain, like a stone in his shoe. Yes, the Happy Valley looked good—but the prettiness and freshness were all meant to hide what the place was really like. Anything could look good with a fresh coat of paint and a spray of decorative flowers. But he knew what was going on underneath that. He knew that his neglect of the past five years had caused some major structural issues that were going to need a lot more than a few hours' worth of labor from him and his friends.

"Hey, Mr. C?" interrupted Milly as she bustled by wielding a toilet brush. "This is supposed to be a big grand party thing, right? Like, a celebration?"

"Well, yeah." Aidan reached out with his roller to paint around the entranceway mirror. "That's the plan."

"But grand celebrations usually have lots of people at them, right?"

"Sure, you want it to look like people are fighting over who gets a room at your B&B."

"Cause I gotta say, Mr. C—it doesn't look like anyone's fighting over who gets a room at the Happy Valley."

Aidan finally directed all of his attention at his employee, and his face went pale. "Oh, God, you're right," he said, and the two rushed to the desk in the hallway to check the register on the laptop.

"Yep, look at that," Milly said, clicking through several pages of calendars. "Ms. Reynolds is our only guest for, well . . . For the next two months. Until that bachelor party from Oxbow that rented three rooms. And honestly, Mr. C, I know we need the income, but I do not trust any bachelor party who registers under the name The Magic Mikes."

"Milly, we've got bigger problems than that bachelor party. That's it. We can't do this." Aidan threw up his hands in frustration and the paint roller he was carrying sent off a few flecks of white, speckling the dark wooden floor.

"Wait, why?" asked Apple, who'd overheard from the other side of the living room where she'd been dusting the piano. She came over and wiped at the paint spots with her dust rag. "What the heck, Dad?"

"Rebah Reynolds is going to smell the phony from the driveway if we don't have anyone else staying at the B&B this weekend. And we can't just conjure guests from thin air."

Kye had been listening from the dining room, where he was fiddling with the ceiling fan. Mason had been ordered by his mother to stand by and knock his father over if any kind of electrocution commenced. "Well, that may not be entirely true," Kye said. He nodded at Apple. "You have friends, right?"

"Sure."

"Friends who'd like to earn a few bucks while staying in the most luxurious venue this side of the Rockies?"

Apple grinned. "I could shoot some texts."

Kye turned to Aidan. "Problem solved."

Aidan sighed. "Yeah, I don't think a bunch of teenagers is going to convince Rebah that she's landed in the newest, hottest place."

"I have some friends," offered Mason.

"Thanks, Mase, but again, we need people who are a little older. Adults." Aidan rubbed his face with his hands. He was getting stressed. More than ever, he was convinced this was the most terrible idea anyone could have possibly come up with.

"Some of my friends are adults," Mason said with arched eyebrows.

"What? Who? Does your mother know?" Kye scowled at his son.

"Of course. They're her friends, too. From Tuesdays." Tuesdays were group day. Sharon and, by extension, Kye believed that every human should be issued a therapist upon birth, so they'd been going to group sessions on Tuesdays for years, since shortly after the twins were born. Actually, it had become more of a weekly date for Mason and Sharon since Miranda had decided a couple of years ago that her chosen form of therapy was going to be team sports and Kye hadn't so much decided to stop going as simply gotten lazy about it.

"Yeah, I'm not so sure your Tuesday friends are the right crowd, either."

"What's wrong with my Tuesday friends?"

Aidan held up his hands. "There's nothing wrong with them! It's just, we need a certain kind of guest to impress Rebah freakin' Reynolds."

"I'm not sure I'm going to like Rebah freakin' Reynolds," Mason announced.

"Well, get in line." Aidan sighed. "Look, I need a break. I'll be back, I just need to regroup my head." He snatched the keys to his Jeep from the hook behind the desk and shrugged into his brown leather jacket.

"Hey, you okay?" asked Kye.

Aidan knew that what he was really asking was, Are you needing a drink? Do you need to call someone? Do you need to be with someone?

"Yeah, totally okay. I'm going to town to do a drop-in."

"Excellent idea. We'll keep going here and I'll think of more people to invite for an overnight. I have a cousin in a biker gang. That's a lot of people we can net with one call—"

Aidan shook his head and walked away, checking that he had his phone and wallet as he headed toward the driveway. He just needed an hour.

The Napa Congregational Church was pink. Very pink. When it first got a new coat of paint back in 1986, the townspeople had objected to quite that level of character, but now it was a community beacon and every time it needed to be repainted and someone suggested an alternative color, they got shouted down by those who felt the pink church was truly representative of the entire community. The church was pink, and it was where Aidan went when he needed a meeting.

"Hi, my name is Aidan and I'm an alcoholic. It's been five years, two months, three weeks, and five days since my last drink," he announced to the people gathered around him in a circle.

"Welcome, Aidan," said the group leader as others in the circle murmured greetings.

"I know I haven't been here in a while." Aidan paused to count his breaths in and out for a beat. "I can't really explain why. It's not like life has been going all that great, but at the same time, it's not like I've wanted to take a drink any worse than before. I've been managing without really having to manage, you know?"

A few people nodded. There was a pretty good turnout—something about the upcoming weekend, maybe. Weekends weren't always the kind of release people needed.

"My daughter, she just got accepted to the college she's wanted to go to since she was this high." He gestured with a hand toward one of his knees. "And, of course, it's expensive. And, of course, it's all the way on the other side of the country. But kids, you do anything for them, right? So, I decided. It's time to sell my business. My home." Aidan swallowed hard. He forgot, sometimes, that the Happy Valley was his home. It had been so long since it felt that way. "Turns out, it's not that easy to convince a real estate agent to get someone to pay you twice what your asset is currently worth."

A heavyset guy dressed in an orange corduroy leisure suit sitting in the front row snorted and muttered, "Amen," just loud enough to get some chuckles.

"Especially since a while back we had a pretty bad hiccup, a hiccup in the form of an overly critical blogger who hit us with the ultimate shitty review." Aidan knew the people in the circle would understand. This was Napa. Hospitality ran through the veins of ninety percent of its residents. These people knew the devastating power of a bad review. "So I need to fix the past before I can fix the present, and that's what this weekend is all about, fixing the past to fix the present, and the whole idea, well, led me here."

Aidan took a long sip from his water bottle and tried to make out the time on the clock posted on the far wall. It was getting late. "I mean, it's just stress, right? We all live with a certain level of stress in our lives. And at the moment, I've got more stress than I've had in a while. I feel like I'm trying to rewrite history. Not all of my history, I mean, I've got a kid and people I love and, of course, you don't write that kind of thing out of your past. But some moves I've made, sure. My wife dying, absolutely. I'd need buckets of Wite-Out to take care of all the missteps I've made as a B&B owner. And I know, I know, we're not supposed to want to change the past because that's what makes us who we are, right? But for real, I feel like that's what I'm doing. And doubting myself for it."

Aidan could feel a headache coming on. This happened just about every time he came to a meeting. He'd share too much, get a headache, and then be host to a mix of feelings: relief that he'd talked, gratitude for the support, and a dull sense of shame for having to reexperience his defeats yet again. No, not defeats. He had to stop thinking like that. Also, he had to wrap this up.

"But I've just got to keep moving forward, right? Isn't that all any of us have to do? Thanks."

Everyone clapped and murmured their good wishes while Aidan took a seat. A few more people got up to share. Chelsea, who introduced herself as a recovering victim of domestic abuse, was marking her two-week sobriety but was broken up that she couldn't share this milestone with her ex-husband, who'd beaten her badly enough last year that he was now serving a dime in the state penitentiary. Nicholas, who couldn't have been more than early twenties, had nearly a full year sober but was frightened that he'd let it all slip to the bottom of a whiskey bottle this weekend as he said his final goodbye to his dad, who was in hospice with liver cancer.

And Mariah.

Mariah and Aidan had known each other for a few years, not just through A.A., but also because he'd hired her a few times to help out with serving at the B&B on the rare occasion when Milly took a vacation. Mariah was in her fifties and passionate about two things: her dogs and community theater. She ran a local troupe that put on an original (she wrote all the plays) show every eight weeks, complete with dazzling costumes, a soundtrack you could jive to, and decent acting.

"Most of you know my story. I come from a long line of hardened drinkers who thought smacking their kids was the sign of a healthy upbringing, who substituted meanness for love and potato chips for vegetables." Mariah raised her tiny form—all ninety pounds of herself—to stand in front of her seat as she talked. A few people in the crowd laughed. Mariah was a favorite here. "And most of you know how I willingly accepted my role as carrier of my family's drunken legacy. And how weirded out I was when my own daughter refused to pick up that mantle and flow it around her own shoulders. And how, since she was age thirteen, she has refused to see me, or even acknowledge me." Mariah bent her head and stared at her hands that were clasped tightly in front of her. "And now she's twenty-eight years old. Fifteen years of being denied my child, by my child. And now . . . I heard this week that she has her own child."

The room was so silent you could hear a clang in the pipes in the walls, as though a creature were trapped and trying to alert them to its periled existence.

"I know I won't be allowed to have a relationship with my grandchild. I don't even know if it's a girl or a boy. I know I won't be invited to any birthday parties or the first Christmas or to barbecues. I haven't had a sip for fourteen years, but none of that matters to my daughter. What matters to her is the way I was during her childhood, the way I treated her and the people she loved. I was awful. I mean, I don't remember much of it, but I'm sure I was awful because it was awful when I was a kid, too. I know what it's like. But my grandchild won't know what it's like and I admire the hell out of my daughter for making that possible. For breaking that particular chain, that pattern. My grandchild will grow up feeling safe. And loved. Thank you."

Mariah sat down to a chorus of applause, but her face was sealed inward. Aidan watched, knowing how much it took for her to make that speech.

But Mariah was strong.

And well-connected in the community.

And provenly capable of performing miracles on short notice.

Huh.

During the coffee connection after the meeting, Aidan managed to maneuver himself to her side. "Mariah, how are you?" he asked.

"Aidan! It is so good to see you here tonight. I can say that, right? I still have trouble remembering the rules. But anyway. It's always a joy to see you and hear about your life, and, oh, my heartiest congratulations on your daughter's acceptance. I am truly, deeply glad for you." Mariah actually clapped her hands, her tight black curls bouncing.

"Listen, I'm sorry. About your daughter and your grandchild."

"Ah. You're kind. I know, it's a sad story. But it's also a good story. My kid chose better than I could offer, and that's all we want for our children, right? But listen, enough with the sob fest. It's exhausting. You got one of your headaches?"

"Not too bad. It's funny, guzzling water helps a lot. Maybe I'm just dehydrated whenever I stop in here. Maybe that's why I get headaches." To prove he was being proactive, he took another long glug from his water bottle.

"Or maybe this is a place of emotional weight and a headache is a natural reaction to digging deep into one's psyche for reasons and solutions that might not even exist. Crikes, I sound deathly. I can say that, right? That I sound deathly? To someone who lost their wife?" Mariah shrugged adorably.

"Mariah, you can say whatever you want to me, you know that. Especially since I'm about to ask you a huge favor."

"Huge?"

"Super huge."

"You know I'm a lesbian, right?" Mariah took a sip of coffee and made a face. "Gah, how hard is it to make a decent cup of joe?"

"It hadn't actually occurred to me, but my favor has nothing to do with sex. Or penises in general."

"You do know, my dear Aidan, that a preference for pussy doesn't exactly translate into an abhorrence of penises. But I appreciate your sensitivity. Now, what's the favor you're going to beg me for?" She led him over to a couch and gestured for him to sit next to her.

"It's . . . complicated?" Aidan sat and ignored the crackling sounds his knees made. Jeez, was he really that old? When had forty become the new seventy? "Basically, I need to convince this weekend's guest of honor that the Happy Valley is doing remarkably well and she's lucky to have gotten a damn seat at the table so she'll write a stellar review and mostly cancel out her previous horrific review so I can sell the place for almost what it's worth and send Apple to college and maybe find a decent apartment in a new city on the East Coast where no one knows me except my daughter, who, thank God, is very forgiving."

"Ah! The classic runaway methodology! I love it! But, darling, how can I possibly help you?"

"Well. I need people. I need interesting people in interesting costumes saying interesting things."

"Oh!"

"To be honest, this is not my fault."

"Oh?"

"For real. It was my handyman's idea. You remember Kye?"

"Ah. Adorable, not speedy, but loyal, and perhaps not the best judge of any given situation? I believe I pegged him as a basset hound."

"Ha! That totally fits. Anyway, it was his idea to invite Rebah Reynolds and impress her with our amazing comeback. But it won't work if she's the only guest there, right? That's more than a little suspicious."

"Indeed. Wait. Let me think." Mariah took a long sip of coffee and swirled it in her mouth, moving her red-painted lips in curls, first up this cheek and then up this one, pouting, grimacing, pursing. She swallowed. "I accept your offer of this challenge."

"Yes! Thank you!" Aidan reached out to hug her, but she put up a decent home-manicured hand.

"However."

"However?"

"I need to state my case. You came to this meeting for a reason. I'm not sure you know the reason, but I am sure it has to do with change. The Happy Valley is changing. Your daughter's life is changing. Your own life, that, too, is changing. And while you are making this substantial effort to rise to the occasion of the multitudes of changes, I'm not sure you're going about it the right way."

"Well, no, respectfully—I think I'm just trying to manage as best I can."

"No doubt, but you are, simultaneously, setting up a series of misinformational moments for this person, Rebah, to trick her into a falsified record of her stay, a record that could hurt her irreparably in terms of her profession."

"Well, she hurt me irreparably in terms of my profession first!"

"Do you know why?"

"Well, she . . . I mean . . . She didn't have a good stay, but it was because she was drunk, not because of anything I did."

"My dear man. You do know where you are, don't you?"

Aidan's shoulders fell halfway down his back and he looked around at his fellow travelers on the ravaged road to recovery. "Ach," he moaned and buried his face in his hands.

"Listen. I'll help you because you are a good man, and you and your daughter deserve a chance. But think about it, hmm? Think about what this woman may very well go through every day of her life. Think about grace versus revenge. Think about the life you want to lead versus the life you are tempted to simply follow."

Aidan put his fingertips to the bridge of his nose and closed his eyes. He could feel a wave of despair rising like a tide inside his chest. Why was everything so hard? Why did he have to work so hard to simply keep things moving in somewhat the right direction? This was why people turned to alcohol, drugs, sex, food—you name it. Because this work, this work of living, was so bloody exhausting.

"Mariah, you are fabulous, and I do appreciate . . . everything. I know I have work to do, but that work can wait until I know I can pay for Apple's college. Right now, that's taking precedence over everything. Do you understand?"

She reached over and patted his hand, where he still wore his wedding ring. "Of course, dear one. I completely understand. Now, let's start the party."

Chapter 9

They'd never staged a play at the Happy Valley before. Jessica had had the idea once, back when she'd been pregnant with Apple. "What do you think," she'd asked Aidan one morning as they drank their coffee together on the front porch, "about having a theater evening? A sort of immersive theater experience? I think it could be so much fun."

"You do realize we're going to have a baby hanging around all the time in another month or so," Aidan replied, smoothing his hand over her prominent belly.

"Well, sure, but so? I mean, it'll be a baby, not a disruptive mother-in-law or anything." Jessica smiled at her worrisome husband, and then shifted on the porch loveseat. "I don't plan on giving anything up, you know."

"Except maybe sleep? A regular routine? Late-night movie snacks in bed?"

"What are you even talking about? We're still doing all that stuff every night."

"But seriously, Jessica. Life is going to change."

"Life is going to get ever more amazing, my love. So, a theater night. A theater weekend! We can hire actors and have a whole plot worked out." Her eyes shined.

"Well . . . I'm just not sure, Jess." Actually, he was sure. He didn't want to do a theater weekend. He didn't want to host a bunch of actors and actor wannabes. He didn't want to duck grand flourishes and offer polite claps every time someone decided to partake in a soliloquy.

"You don't have to be sure. You just have to be willing. You know, willing to make me happy."

"Ah, in that case." Aidan laughed and leaned over to kiss his wife's hair. "You know I can't even remotely deny that kind of argument."

"That's why I use it so often, my love."

But the theater weekend hadn't happened, because that was the Friday night Jessica went into labor. Milly had called the list of expectant guests to offer apologies while Jessica and Aidan spent the night in the birthing wing of the local hospital, circling the hallways at a slow and steady pace, leaning into each other while Jessica moaned, and kneeling in a large bathtub full of warm lavender-scented water, where Jessica found the tiniest bit of relief. The real relief was the arrival of Apple.

Aidan thought of that as he pulled back into his driveway and watched his home for a moment in the late afternoon light. Kye was outside on a ladder, touching up the paint on the worst spots of trim. Milly was planting marigolds in the long-empty railing boxes that lined the front porch. And Apple and Kai were laughing together as they tried to prop up the rotting grape arbor in a way that made it look less rotten. All around he saw people he loved trying their hardest to patch up a place he had once loved, and he wondered, not for the first time, if it would be enough. If any of this would be enough to launch his daughter into the next year.

"Dad!" Apple spotted him and came running over. "Okay, so you remember how I told you that Kai's in this new band and they are actually really talented, and they said they'd come for the weekend and hang out here as guests? But also? I thought it would be super amazing and impressive to have live music here. Reviewers love live music. And they agreed—the band will totally play this weekend. I might even set up that electric keyboard we've had forever and join them on a few songs. And then you remember my friend Boutique? Turns out she needs a place to escape to this weekend because her stepmother is having a total freak-out over Boutique's new job."

"What's her new job?" Aidan got out of the car and started up the drive. He'd stopped at the Asian grocery store on his way home and the two bags he carried contained loads of ingredients he hadn't been tempted to think about in years. But for some reason, that day seemed like a good day to browse the shelves for red lentils, kimchi, lotus root, and roasted coconut juice.

"Well, it's not like there's anything wrong with it. Her stepmother is totally over-reacting and saying that Boutique is selling her soul, but she's really just doing a teensy bit of work for the Republicans. Just, I don't know, handing out flyers or whatever? But she could really use some away time and she looks like she's thirty and über successful."

"Yeah, I don't know if we want to open the door to Republicans at this point. Are we that desperate?" Aidan grinned.

"Dad, you know how much I hate when you purposefully act closed-minded, and anyway the Republicans Boutique is working for aren't the weird kind and anyway there are weird people on both sides of the political divide and, honestly, if it weren't for me you'd have no idea who was even president much less governor, never mind their views on leading issues and—"

"Apple."

"I just think it's a little bit ridiculous of you to discount an entire group of—"

"Honey."

"Oh."

"I look forward to meeting Boutique."

Apple made a face that meant she knew he'd been riling her up on purpose.

"And," Aidan went on, "I've got a plan for producing other guests out of thin air. With a little help from an amateur professional."

"You say amateur like it's a bad thing!" called a woman riding an electric bike up the drive.

"Never!" exclaimed Aidan. "Amateur is everything!"

Mariah unstrapped her leather backpack from the back of her bike after coming to a stop and turning it off. "Damn right," she said. "Hi, Apple. I haven't seen you in a hot minute. Your father is lucky to have you."

"I completely agree, and it's nice to meet someone who recognizes my value." Apple raised her eyebrows at her dad, who was looking adequately chagrined. "I'm sorry, it sounds like we've met before, but I don't remember who you are."

"I used to help out here when things got busy, but I guess it's been a while since things were busy. I'm an old friend of your dad's. And your mom's. My name is Mariah. I run Pickerel Players Community Theater downtown, and I have a distinct eye for value."

"You knew Mom?"

"Excellent woman. Exquisite taste. That rare ability to like everyone and be liked by everyone. I know it was years ago, but I'm truly sorry for your loss. You look like her. Lucky you."

Aidan noticed Apple looked pleased at the thought that she looked like her mother. For the briefest moment, it was as though Jessica were there, with them. Helping them.

Mariah broke the spell by shifting her gaze from Apple to the house. Kye had borrowed a pressure washer from a neighbor and dinged all the moss and dirt from the shingles so the place practically gleamed, and Sharon had managed to do a super-speedy paint job on all the trim. The twins had hacked away at the front bushes to make them look reasonably well-tended, Kai had mowed most of the front lawn, and Apple had strung white fairy lights between the porch posts. "Aidan, your place is looking lovely. I can't believe you've been keeping me away for the last five years. Really? Poor Milly hasn't been on vacation in that long? No need for an extra set of hands?"

"More like no money to pay those hands," Aidan admitted. "Let's just hope this place does its job this weekend. We need some good welcoming juju if I'm going to get through it."

"Good juju is my constant goal. Now, take me inside. Let me see what else we're working with." Despite being the most recent addition to the plan, Mariah was the one who led the way up the front steps and into the house, where the smell of fresh paint and cleaning fluids was still strong. "Okay, let's set the scene. Rebah arrives. Where do you want her to first see you?"

"Me?"

"Well, yes, you. You're the one on the pedestal, baby. You're the one we have to sell."

"Oh, no, really it's this place we want her to love enough to write a good review about." Aidan scoffed at the idea that he was the one who was supposed to be in the spotlight. He hated spotlights. He hated most forms of attention.

"Yeah, no, that's not how it works. People respond to people. You could have a bed-and-breakfast that lived up to the name El Dumpo and put the right people in charge and you'll have a reservation list a mile long."

"Yeah, but—" Aidan had to remind himself to unclench his shoulders.

"Sweetie, there's nothing to fear. I see the panic on your face. You're going to have a stellar supporting cast, and, honey, you're a doll. Rebah is human, right? Give her a chance to adore you. And that girl of yours—actually, that might be an easier sell."

"Apple is definitely better at people than I am."

"Of course she is. Now . . ." Mariah's gaze swept over the dining room and landed on the always elegant—now smudged—double-glass doors that led onto the back deck. "Let's see what the outside has to offer out back."

Aidan tended to avoid the backyard. It always seemed as though there was so much to accomplish on the inside, he'd never even get to the outside, so why bother worrying about it?

The two of them stepped onto a wide, partially covered back porch where several mismatched types of outdoor furniture awaited guests, including a white wicker rocking chair that lived in Apple's room when she was a baby. The rocker had landed in different places in the house at different times, once even serving as a dining room chair on a particularly busy night, but after Jessica died, Aidan couldn't stand the sight of it and had excommunicated it to the back porch. Too many memories of her rocking Apple to sleep in that chair.

But Mariah was drawn to it immediately. She walked over and ran her hand along the wooden arch of the back and raised her eyebrows as she said, "This piece would have been perfect on the set of my latest show. I'm going to have to remember you when I need help at the theater, Aidan. Though I've noticed you haven't been around there much. Perhaps you've lost interest in the arts?"

"You know me, Mariah. I kind of lost interest in everything." Aidan sighed. "You're welcome to it. To anything. Oh, man, if I end up moving, I'm going to have to sell all of this stuff, aren't I?" Aidan realized what he'd said and quickly looked around to see if Apple was within earshot. But she was busy fluffing flower arrangements with Sharon in the living room. The thought of a pending yard sale deflated a certain pocket in his chest. "Why is change so much work?"

"Well, if it weren't, we'd be doing it more often and things would be in a constant state of chaos. More chaotic than now. Oh, a brick patio! Damn, son, here's your stage."

Aidan looked around and tried to see what Mariah saw. He saw overgrown grass, a garden that was ninety percent weeds, tipsy bricks set at odd angles to form a slanted, asynchronous patio, a small barn whose structural integrity was just beginning to collapse, several apple trees that tried and failed to gel into an actual orchard, a raspberry patch that was half brambles, and a shaky seam of wooden columns stretching around the perimeter that seemed to have no purpose but had used to be whimsical when Jessica was alive to string white lights between them.

"Yep. This is where the party's at," Mariah reiterated.

"I'm not really seeing it?"

"Because you're not using the right kind of eyes. First thing, we need to get the mower back here. Where's that man of yours? Never mind, he's too slow. What about his wife? My bet is she's the one who can move at a reasonable pace. Pure Jack Russell that one."

"I can mow, but what about everything else? It's all so . . . depressing."

"Depressing! Hardly! It's ancient English garden chic. It's Edwardian downfall chic. It's colonial hardship chic. Trust me. But, no, you can't mow. We have to hold auditions."

"Auditions?"

"Auditions. Our first actor arrives in . . ." Mariah glanced at her watch. "Ten minutes. Now, what's the play? Are we leaning more toward Neil Simon or Simon Gray? Caryl Churchill or Sarah Kane?"

"Who?"

"Right, leave it to me. For the plot, I'm seeing a down-on-his-luck widower making a last-ditch effort to improve his station in life all for the benefit of his lovely and intelligent daughter, aided in his efforts by a cast of rambunctious, but loyal, friends."

Aidan felt a case of whiplash coming on. That's exactly what he was—a down-on-his-luck widower. "Kind of a stretch, don't you think?"

Mariah grinned wryly. "So we're going to need B&B guests that are quirky and delightful, not too over the top but certainly not dull. How about a trapeze artist paired with a lion tamer, but they're pansexual so there's some intrigue with other lovers?"

"Pan-what?"

"Oh, and my favorite archetype, a young musical prodigy, but not too young, and his aging groupie. There's that jazz festival going on. We can cannibalize from that pool."

"Cannibals?"

"Oh, Aidan, keep up, my dear. Not actual cannibals. That would be strange. Oh, look, our first victim!"

Two victims, actually. A man and woman who appeared not to be any age at all rounded the corner of the house and picked their way through the overgrown grass, swatting at nonexistent mosquitoes and gazing around with slightly pained looks. The woman wore a skintight leopard-pattern sweater and a flowy purple skirt, her hair tied up into some kind of porcupine hairdo complete with trailing ribbons. The man was a bit more conservative in a pink polo shirt and cargo pants, his only apparent nod to fashion a spiked dog collar around his neck and rainbow Adidases on his feet.

"Mariah, where exactly have you brought us to?" The woman spoke first, her voice deep and raspy. Aidan wondered if she were a lifelong smoker. "I mean, you said diamond in the rough, but I was at least expecting a path through the damn weeds."

"Claire, Michael, meet Aidan, Aidan meet Claire and Michael—two of my finest actors, but don't tell them I said that because it will go straight to their heads and they'll be unbearable. Dear ones, I know it's a little unkempt at the moment, but a man with a mower is scheduled to begin the transformation within mere moments and trust me, a few strands of fairy lights will make all the difference in the world. Audition time!"

Mariah led Aidan, Claire, and Michael back into the Happy Valley and settled herself and Aidan on the couch, gesturing that the two actors should remain standing.

"Now. Improv," she ordered.

Aidan felt bad for the poor actors and tried to intervene. "Wait, Mariah, should we decide on some characters? Weren't you saying something—"

Claire interrupted him with a shriek. "Cats! The cats! Cats everywhere! Oh, the cats! Jameson, don't let the cats take their revenge!"

Michael came awake as though someone had thrown a switch. "Oh, sweetheart, my darling Verity, it's a nightmare, just a nightmare," he soothed his distraught partner, who had slipped to the floor in an impressive display of acrobatics and was lying prone at Michael's feet.

Or Jameson's feet, as the case may have been. The actor crouched next to Claire, or Verity, and brushed her spiky hair away from her face.

"The cats, Jameson. Even after all these months, they still haunt me," she murmured.

"You tell the cats all the things we've done to fix their world. Tell them about the sanctuaries! The Punishment for Poachers program! Soothe them with tales of your own suffering!"

Just above the impressive scene unfolding in front of him, Aidan could hear the mower start up out back. He felt better knowing something obviously productive was going on while he was trapped, held hostage by Mariah's vision.

"Oh, you poor kitties, I did murder your brethren, but look! I'm making it as right as I possibly can. We are pouring money into the cause like cream into a bowl! We are betraying our origins as hunters to effect change in your world!"

"Well, don't mislead them, dear." Michael continued to stroke Claire's hair, but he had a grimace on his face. "Don't forget, I never held a gun in my life."

"You aimed and shot a different kind of gun, Jameson! The gun of blind faith and zealotry!"

"Oh, you're speaking of my missionary years."

"Of course! You and your family did far more to contribute to the economic fallout of the mid-African region with your insistence on spreading the word!"

"I'm not sure that's entirely fair, dearest Verity."

"If it's not true, why are you working just as hard as I am to outpace your guilt? Why are we setting up those job training programs for young mothers? Why do you begin each meal not with a prayer but an apology?"

"You have shed enough blood for both of us!"

"Your damage goes deeper!"

"Well, you are visited by imaginary cats!"

"And you by imaginary bibles! That have teeth!"

"Verity, I feel a feeling coming on."

"Oh! Which kind of feeling?"

"The feeling I get when I'm about to make a sizable donation."

"That's my favorite! How sizable?"

"The size of Vermont's state budget!"

Verity/Claire squealed and bounced back to her feet, embracing Jameson/Michael with passion. Obviously, substantial donations were the perfect foreplay for this couple.

"And cut!"

Mariah's order startled Aidan. He'd slipped into a kind of dream, completely captivated by the two actors, momentarily forgetting what all of this was for. The mower buzzed in the backyard.

"That was actually pretty amazing," Aidan said. "I mean, the whole plot was ridiculous—come on, a reformed big-game hunter and an ex-missionary trying to resolve their damage through charitable donations—but I totally fell for it because you guys were so convincing."

"Wait, I don't understand. What's off about the scenario?" Claire asked as she brushed floor dust from her skirt.

"Well, it's just so unlikely."

"Actually, this is based on my parents. Yep, the great love story of my life is how my folks merged through their shared suffering and erupted into a force that was greater than the sum of their parts."

"Huh," answered Aidan.

Apple came bounding into the room from the front porch. "Dad, there's, like, some people here to audition?"

"Great, you two are hired!" Mariah barked at Claire and Michael. "Next!"

"Wait, Mariah—hired? Are we . . . am I . . . paying these people?"

"God, Aidan, you didn't think they'd work for nothing, did you?"

"Well, isn't that how amateur actors do it? For exposure?"

"Listen, sweetie, I'm going to pretend you didn't just insult the creative class with a worn-out cliché fit only for a cheap gag on late night television. Actors are workers. We pay people for their work. I mean, when you have a customer—a real customer, I mean"—She glared at him—"do you offer your services simply for the exposure? No. You demand your fee. A quite hefty fee, if I'm not mistaken."

"Yeah, it is pretty steep, actually—" Apple started, but Aidan cut her off.

"Okay, of course, my apologies. I get it. I really am sorry. You're absolutely right. People deserve to be paid for their creative work. That's fine! Everything's fine! We'll manage!" Aidan's grin was more of a grimace, and Claire and Michael beat a hasty retreat from the odd inn owner. And just as quickly, they were replaced by a tall, handsome man carrying a saxophone case, followed by a large, older woman with long hair in swinging braids.

"Tyrone, Frankie, so glad you could make it! I know you two will be perfect in this setup," Mariah gushed.

Tyrone held up a well-manicured hand then bent over to undo the straps on his saxophone case, but then the woman, Frankie, rushed over to do it for him. She lifted the gleaming instrument from its cozy cavern and used a microfiber cloth to shine it up a little before handing it over. Tyrone nodded and smiled his thanks, then turned back to his audience of two. "My hosts," he breathed.

Aidan felt his shoulders relax at the sound of the man's low-timbred voice. He thought, *This man has more coolness in one finger than I can ever hope to develop in my lifetime.*

And then Tyrone started to play. For a moment, Aidan wanted to cry, and then he wanted to exhale with the knowledge that everything would be okay, that this insane scheme of his would work, and then he wanted to find Apple, who'd slipped back out to work more on the house, and wrap her in a huge bear hug. All of this he felt as he watched Tyrone's elegant fingers call music forth from the horn.

Tyrone played for a good five minutes, and by the end, both Frankie and Mariah were in tears and Aidan was discreetly wiping his eyes with the back of his hand.

"Oh, Tyrone, you never fail to move me with that music of yours,"

Mariah whispered. She turned to Aidan. "Meet Tyrone and Frankie. Tyrone, as you've just seen, plays the saxophone. By all accounts, he should be a part of the jazz festival going on this weekend, but what was their excuse, Frankie?"

"We missed the deadline," Frankie scowled, her voice scratchy and worn like a failing foghorn.

"They missed the deadline. Well, their loss is our gain. Meet Mellow Michel and his faithful follower, Buttercup. They've been on the road for decades, never mind how young he looks, and he doesn't talk much. Anything he needs to say, he says it with music. That part's true, anyway."

Frankie nodded vigorously. "It's kind of all true, isn't it?"

"Well, we changed the names to protect the innocent, right?" Mariah winked.

"Innocent!" Frankie snorted. "You've met us, right?"

"I'll stay hush if you will," Mariah smirked. The two of them leaned over in giggles.

Aidan interrupted. "Wait, so Tyrone and Frankie are going to play Michel and Buttercup? But also, they really are a jazz musician and a groupie?"

"Oh, I prefer the term 'companion.'" Frankie snorted again and Mariah lost it once more.

"Okay. Good to know." Aidan wasn't sure about these particular personas, but Tyrone nodded reassuringly at him. He was obviously used to his companion's brand of humor. And Mariah's, too, apparently. Aidan heard the sound of the saxophone in his head and figured Tyrone could always just play more music if anyone started asking questions or if the stories started to slide sideways.

Frankie spoke up. "One more thing. We get fed, right? We always get fed at these kinds of things."

These kinds of things? How many times had they helped pull off a massive scam to trick a travel blogger into writing a stellar review of a failing bed-and-breakfast so that said bed-and-breakfast could be sold to the highest bidder? Was this a common occurrence?

"Of course there will be food!" Mariah promised. "Acres of food. Aidan here is a renowned chef. I'm sure he's got a bountiful table planned."

Aidan winced and didn't bother to correct Mariah about his most recent cooking experiences—of which there were none. The caterers would come and set up in the kitchen and he could slip in to check things out and then reappear with a waft of delicious smells swirling around him and people would be convinced. Rebah would be convinced. Right?

"Okay, sweetie, see you back here in full regalia." Mariah and Frankie stood, and Mariah kissed the other woman's cheek. "I know you'll be simply divine."

Tyrone had strapped his instrument back in its case and swung it around to balance on his shoulder. "Pleasure," he said, reaching out to shake Aidan's hand. It was the third word he'd spoken the entire visit.

"Okay!" Mariah exclaimed once the odd pair had left the room. "Shall we meet our next victims?"

"Can I just ask? I mean, this is probably totally rude, and I don't mean it to be rude at all, but is Frankie your girlfriend?"

"Frankie?! Ha!" Mariah's face was pure delight. "Hell, no. I mean, I love the girl dearly. We've been friends for eons, but she's all about younger men. Younger men who play music. Younger men who play jazz music. She's pretty specific, really."

"Damn, he was good, wasn't he? Tyrone?"

"Oh, honey, you don't even know the heartache his songs have gotten me through." Mariah sighed and briefly deflated as though the strain of keeping those heartaches below the surface was too great at the moment. But she shook herself and revived. "Okay, one more couple. I think you'll like these two. They are just the funniest people in the room, no matter what room you find yourself in. Let's see what they've got for us." She shouted toward the closed door, "Mackenzie!"

Aidan wasn't sure what he was expecting, but it wasn't the bland man in the beige suit and beige tie, brown briefcase in hand, followed by another man about the same age—mid-twenties—also dressed in a beige suit and tie. But with no briefcase.

"Mackenzie! Jasper!" Mariah greeted them warmly. "I'm so glad you decided to join us! I have no doubt you two will be the showcase."

Aidan couldn't really see it. These two were as unremarkable as they came. Blondish hair, pale complexion, average height. You'd pass them on the street and not even realize you'd passed anyone on the street. Vanilla.

"Aidan, Mariah, you are blessed for allowing us to join what promises to be a tremendous experience of divine company, refreshments, and that certain frisson that holds together a wonderful party," said Jasper. His voice was ethereal. It seemed to come as an echo from someplace outside the room.

"Jasper, is it?" Aidan said. "Thank you so much for joining us this weekend. There will be plenty of great food and, of course, we'll pay you at the end. We also have some excursions planned that you are welcome to be part of and—"

"Oh, Mr. Cisneros, you mistake our intentions!" This was from Mackenzie, whose voice was heartier than Jasper's but still overly refined. "We are not here to perform for payment of any kind. And we have brought a cooler of our own food, as we are on a fairly strict diet of cuisine sourced only from a certain region of the world: Naples, Florida. No, no, we are not here to burden you. We actually consider this a favor from you to us."

"I'm doing you a favor?"

"Indeed." Jasper again. The men were making Aidan nervous. They still stood, side by side, hands clasped in front of their waists, elbows touching, faces impassive but polite, their shoes too shiny to have walked far. "We are, you see, hiding."

"Hiding?"

"From the law."

"From the law?!"

"But not because we've done anything illegal. Or even wrong, in the eyes of most."

Mackenzie took over trying to explain. Mariah, meanwhile, could barely hide her amusement at Aidan's discomfort. "We are deeply in love, Mr. Cisneros. With each other. But our place of work frowns upon such passion between inmates and guards."

"Whoa." Aidan stood and tried to be impressively large. "Hey, look, I'm all for loving who you love, but I would really prefer to stick to a no-criminals rule this weekend. Honestly, it's already entirely likely that things will go badly wrong and adding an element of illegality just strikes me as a really bad idea. You can take your need to hide from the law and walk yourself back out that door and find someplace else to hide this weekend."

"Perfect!" shrieked Mariah delightedly, leaping from her spot on the couch.

"Perfect?" Aidan was confused.

"Didn't I tell you these two would be the ultimate? Can you even? I thought up their whole scenario on my bike on the way over and I texted them their roles. I was so hoping they'd show up just like this, in character, and they did not disappoint. They never do." Mariah reached over and took ahold of Mackenzie's cheeks and gave him an audible kiss on the nose. "You two are just wasted in community the-ater, aren't you, my little penguins?"

The two men had eased their stance and were grinning at Aidan. "Hey, mate, just to be clear, you can completely trust us around your guests—we aren't actually criminals, either of us," Jasper said in an Australian accent. "But your face, your face was the goal of every show I've ever done. That complete buy-in!"

"I was very nearly worried you were going to toss us out on our ears." Mackenzie's accent was still American but nowhere near as posh. "Oh, just to be crystal clear, we will absolutely be accepting payment at the end of the weekend."

"And the cooler full of food from Naples, Florida?" Aidan still felt . . . confused. Was that the point of theater?

"Nice touch, isn't it?" said Jasper. "Nah, we'll fill it with stuff from your kitchen, but we'll mash it up right so it looks like it traveled a ways."

Aidan sighed. Not for the first time he wondered if this was all going to be worth it.

Chapter 10

Rebah spent Thursday in her room at the Hyatt, trying to work on some evergreen content for the blog. By Friday morning, she admitted to herself that she was producing crap, so she set out after breakfast and drove a couple of hours through the gorgeous Napa countryside, then tooled around a little downtown area where she spotted a bar/restaurant that didn't look too much like a place where a biker brawl would break out or a gaggle of girls would be setting up a baby shower. The sign outside announced the place as Twain's and through the windows she could glimpse low lighting, several couches, squat, sturdy tables, and, best of all, a minimum number of people enjoying an early afternoon escape.

She settled herself at a bar table near a window and pulled out her legal pad to make some notes while she tried to figure out what the weekend might have in store. To be honest, she didn't remember her last visit to Happy Valley all that well. She'd gone there only a week after a particularly rough breakup with her boyfriend at the time and, yes, she had definitely drunk a little too much that weekend, though certainly not enough to warrant that man calling her a drunk. That moment she did remember. He'd let loose at her during breakfast, going off about some blanket she'd spilled a little wine on. And the trash can? Had she barfed in the trash can? Better there than on the carpet, right?

Rebah knew she was a lot of things, but mostly she knew she wasn't a drunk. She took pride in maintaining a semblance of order and grace, even when she was tipsy. Really, it wasn't that hard, and she never did think much of people who got sloppy and disgusting after just a few glasses of wine. But that wasn't her. And so, when Aidan Cisneros had shown the side of himself that was capable of fury and called her a pathetic drunk, and in front of all those other guests, too, she got her revenge with a scathing review.

Set, match.

"What can I get you?" An adorable bartender in a black vest and purple bowtie interrupted her thoughts. His name tag read "Christopher."

"A Cabernet, please. Your choice. Bring me something excellent."

"Something excellent? What level of excellence are we talking here?"

Rebah spotted a calculation in the tilt of Christopher's head. This was a man looking for a generous percentage off a decent bill.

"I like to explore floors three through five when I'm enjoying a Cabernet," she answered. She took some delight in Christopher's momentarily confused face but turned back to her notebook before she'd be required to clarify. He seemed like a smart guy. He'd figure out some way to earn his tip. And indeed, the waiter quickly recovered his facade and turned away with a knowing nod.

The man who had caused the broken heart she'd been suffering from that weekend was named Richard, and if she stopped to think about it, which she didn't like to do, he was the last authentic romance in her life. Of course, she'd had fun and flirted with plenty and hooked up with a few, but in terms of love—real, intense, brilliant love—he was it. He was the last. She still couldn't think of him without a tiny clutch in her belly. Would that get in the way this weekend? Would being back there dredge up memories of heartbreak? She doubted it. She'd always been pretty good at compartmentalization and inoculation against bad memories.

"This is the Larkmead 2016 Cab. I think you'll appreciate the blended aromas of pencil and sage, backed by a core of mineral and crushed rock, while equally available are the currant and plum, all dusted with dark chocolate." Christopher uncorked the wine and offered her a minute swirl in her glass, which she sniffed and downed and smiled at. "I'll leave the bottle?"

"Perfect. I do like that crushed rock undertone. Listen, Christopher, you fine with me being stationed here for a bit? I'm avoiding my demoralizing hotel room and I'd really appreciate the chance to just sit and not make friends. Is that okay?"

"I completely understand. Making friends is torture for some people." He grinned at her, and she smiled back. "Stay as long as you want, and I'll keep an eye on you."

"Ah, you're a peach. Thanks, dear."

"Dear? You're pretty young for a granny."

"I like to call men *dear*. I find it reinforces my power."

"Oh, I see. Intimidate the patriarchy through terms of endearment."

"Something like that. Aren't you feeling just the tiniest bit threatened?"

"Threatened? No. You're in my bar, dear."

"Damn the rule of territory."

"But I can assure you I'm not on the side of the patriarchy."

"Yes, but you are a man, right?"

"Well, sure, but . . ."

"You don't want to sit and have a glass of wine and remind me why I chose a career over a life of passion, do you?"

"I can't think of anything I'd enjoy more. Unfortunately, we can't all be privileged enough to drink a one hundred and fifty dollar bottle of wine in the middle of the afternoon."

"Huh. A hundred and fifty? That's very impressive of me."

They grinned at each other and Christopher retreated to another table to ask after the couple's bottle of rosé. *Sweet boy*, she thought. *I bet he does well with any guy he picks.*

Rebah took another sip of the delicious wine and sketched a line down her pad of paper to make two columns. This was a habit of hers.

It was how she wrangled her thoughts into some kind of working order to make them more accessible and less mysterious. And that's what she needed right now: to know herself better. Because she had a sinking feeling she was losing the thread to her own tapestry of life.

When she was a kid, she hadn't been one of those little girls who played with dolls and threw pretend weddings and imagined a life of marriage and constraints. Instead, she'd loved horses. And dolphins. And hot-air balloons. And trains. And the thought of going to another country. She used to beg her parents to take her to Europe or Asia, or how about Australia, somewhere, please, where things didn't look so familiar. So for her high school graduation gift, her parents had sent her to Ireland on a package tour with twenty people in their late sixties to mid-seventies.

You might think an eighteen-year-old girl would be bored out of her gourd on an excursion with a population that was essentially as old as her grandparents, but Rebah was perfectly content to ooh and aah over the Blarney Stone alongside members of the hippie generation whose hair was now capped and neat and gray. She was delighted to be served Guinness in pubs and to allow a kindly uncle figure to pick up her tab. She felt protected and also obliged to provide these good people the chance to relive their youth through her. Thus, she spent several nights dancing to the wee hours in discotheques, swore more than she ever had in her life, went hiking in heels, and was the first in line at every attraction, determined to suck the juice out of this mango of a trip, her first overseas.

And the old people had loved that about her.

She wrote a list in the left-hand column: freedom, luxury, fame, creativity, and a question mark. In the right column, she listed routine, ownership, freedom, and, in smaller letters, friends.

She sipped from her glass again and watched a family get seated a few tables over from her. There was a mom, a dad, an infant in the dad's arms, and a toddler who was arching his? her? its back against the indignity of a booster seat. Rebah didn't blame it. Those blocky plastic chairs were humiliating. *Just play it cool with the booster*, she thought toward the mom. *Is this really the hill you want to die on?* And finally, the mom relented and the kid was allowed to sit in a regular seat.

Christopher appeared beside her and raised his eyebrows and Rebah nodded, the effortless, unspoken conversation a joy, an understanding between bartender and drinker: You good? Fine, for now.

Christopher twirled away to greet his new table, shuddering almost invisibly at the child who talked to him in a fast dialect with words that pelted anyone within twenty feet, a language designed to create chaos and anarchy, but which its parents seemed well-practiced at ignoring. Rebah watched as the adults ordered a bottle of white and the child ordered what sounded like "orange marshmallows on a lake of noodles." Christopher looked to the parents for help in translating, and the mother said, "Whatever juice you have, as long as it's in a cup with a top and a straw."

"Paper straw okay?" Christopher checked.

"Shit," the dad said.

"You don't have plastic?"

"Ah, we've phased out all single-use plastics. I can offer you a sip top?"

"This is going to be bad," the mom said to the dad.

"He really needs to learn," he answered.

Aha. The child was a boy.

"Yeah, but in the middle of a restaurant?"

The word *restaurant* reminded Rebah that she was hungry. When had she last eaten? Breakfast? She broke off from watching the family to look at the menu and then added another word to her left-sided column: culinary variety.

"You need food, gorgeous?" Christopher paused by her table on his way to get drinks, no straws, for the new family.

"I do, but come get me after. I can't decide between the six-cheese macaroni or the crab salad."

"I'm not going to embarrass myself by admitting which one I had for lunch."

"There is no embarrassment in decadence, dear."

"Tell that to my poor arteries." And he was off.

Rebah gazed out at the street scene in front of her. A woman in a business suit and Converse sneakers was striding along the sidewalk, talking on her phone. A young man with terrible skin was trying to get his dog to quit leaping on people as they walked by, without much success. Rebah leaned forward as the Converse woman approached the dog-boy duo, completely absorbed in her own conversation. Would the dog leap on the beautiful, obviously expensive suit? Would the young man manage to control the canine? Would it all come to blows?

Rebah should've known to give Converse woman more credit. She sailed by the boy and his dog, effortlessly shooting out a canvas-covered foot when the dog sprang from its crouch, catching the furry creature in the shoulder and easily deflecting the attack. The woman didn't miss a beat. Simply walked on with the knowledge that the animal world would bow to her authority. The boy looked flabbergasted. The dog quickly righted itself and looked around, confused as to what exactly had happened. The woman was already a dozen steps away.

Rebah wrote in the right-hand column: dogs.

"Okay, I await your decision with bated breath." Christopher was back.

"Crab cake salad," Rebah said. "And the key lime crème brûlée."

"Excellent choices." He winked as he retreated.

Huh. Aidan Cisneros was supposed to be a renowned chef. Why didn't she remember any of the food from that long-ago weekend? Maybe he wasn't as good as he was talked up to be? That would put him in the same category as an Egyptian restaurant she'd gone to last year where the chef was supposed to have perfected the art of steaming sea urchin custards in the shell.

He hadn't. It was a disgusting, gelatinous mess.

But she couldn't remember any food from her previous weekend at the Happy Valley. Not even a gelatinous mess. She would have paid attention to the food—of course she would have. Wouldn't she? Food was a significant part of her reviews.

Rebah whipped her phone out and started scrolling through the notes app to see if she'd jotted anything down and saved it. Then she swiped through her photos—she was a star at meal porn and always made a point of snapping a few pics of every dish. But there wasn't anything that matched to that weekend.

Had she really been that blotto?

She looked at her list again, ran her finger down the right-hand column, and added, in teeny-tiny script: sober.

And then she scrubbed through the word as though it was a devil's curse and she'd endangered herself just by writing the thought. Ridiculous. She was Rebah Reynolds. Rebah Reynolds was not an alcoholic. Not part of the brand.

At the table with the family, the child had wrought an unusual amount of noise and energy—at least, Rebah thought it was unusual. Maybe this was normal in toddlerland. But the boy was shrieking, and then the baby was responding with shrieks of its own.

"Hon, we need to just go!" the husband yelled above the children. "We're making everyone else miserable."

The wife made a show of looking around and then gestured at the restaurant, empty now but for Rebah and Christopher. "I just want to have one meal that takes place outside our house!" She looked as though she were about to start shrieking, too. "One meal that we don't have to cook. That we don't have to stare at the dirty dishes from. One!"

"But that's not responsible parenting," the dad managed to make heard through gritted teeth.

"I need a damn break, Marcel. A damn break."

Rebah tilted her head as she watched this family unit brought to its knees by one small, loud person. Who even knew what the kid was crying about?

"Do you like keys?" she asked the child. But there was no use using her own voice. Digging in her bag she came out with the cave key on the smooth wooden-stick key ring. She hadn't returned it to Friar Tuck. She rose and approached the table, holding up her offering. "Hey! Do you like keys?" she yelled.

Silence. Lovely silence. Even the baby had stopped its sympathy bawling.

Rebah held out the key ring. "You can have this. It can be your very own. But only if you're quiet."

"Oh, we don't actually bribe our kids into the behavior we want . . ."

"Shhhhh!" the wife reprimanded her husband.

"I got it from a bed-and-breakfast I have no intention of ever returning to. It's infinitely replaceable. So this one can be yours."

"Bfskridka zemoiny fluuuuuup."

"That's right. Yours."

The child held the key in one hand and lifted it toward the ceiling, toward the back of the restaurant, toward his mother and father in turn, and toward himself. He was unlocking secrets only he could see. But it kept him quiet.

"Thank you," said the mother. She took a long sip of her wine, eyes closed, and Rebah felt a sting of recognition. "Really, thank you."

"Absolutely no problem." Rebah smiled at the two of them. "I've heard the crab cake salad is divine."

And it was.

Chapter 11

Rebah first noticed the flowers. Then the music—expert classical piano seeped out the open windows and onto the front porch of the Happy Valley B&B.

The window boxes along the railing of the porch were stuffed with marigolds, and her first instinct was to scoff. Marigolds? Not a springtime flower. But as she pulled her satchel out of the trunk of her car and climbed the five foot-worn steps, she was hit with their delicate scent.

They say the nose is the conduit to your past, and for Rebah, the smell of marigolds took her back to her grandfather's rock garden. She was suddenly thrust into a memory of being, how old? Five? Six? Seven? and helping Poppa weed the carefully executed network of paths and plank bridges and knee-high walls of rock, which were a meticulous reflection of her Poppa's soul, hard-packed earth, granite, lacy ferns, and marigolds.

"Can we plant daisies?" young Rebah sometimes asked. Or sunflowers, or roses, or lilies? And the answer was always the same.

"Marigolds keep away the monsters," he'd say in his rumbly voice.

As a girl, Rebah had never questioned this logic. Of course, if you knew a flower to be effective in keeping away monsters, you'd plant as many as you could possibly squeeze into the back garden of an Upper East Side apartment. It was only as she grew older and encountered all the living lushness the world had to offer—the dripping gardens of the rainforest inn she'd stayed at last year, or the green oasis in the Sahara, where the garden water had to be helicoptered in—that she wondered what kind of monsters would be afraid of a marigold.

Marigolds were small, bunched-up flowers that did not assume any kind of top-tier entitlement.

But the marigolds there at the Happy Valley were different. Rebah paused to run her hands across the tops of the blooms, encouraging them to release more of their scent. Freshly planted, she could tell—perhaps as part of the planning for the grand celebration weekend? She held her hand to her nose and breathed deeply. She was glad the marigolds were there. "They'll keep away the monsters," she heard Poppa say once again.

The piano music stopped and the front door opened. "You must be Rebah!" said a girl's voice, and Rebah turned, slightly embarrassed to have been caught in a whimsical moment. "I'm Apple."

"Apple! What a delightful name!" Rebah gushed. She brushed her hand on the side of her silk pants as if to rub off the smell of the flowers. "Though I bet you have a lot of nicknames."

"It's my cross to bear," Apple said and reached out to take Rebah's bag. "My dad is inside somewhere, but I can check you in. Can I offer you a lime-avocado spritzer? We offer the drink virgin or with alcohol."

Rebah felt a stab of fury. Was this a reference to the last time she was there? Was this going to be the theme of the weekend—veiled references to Rebah's affection for a good drink?

Her smile tightened, but she felt the anger fade as quickly as it had arrived. This girl couldn't possibly remember her out of all the guests they must see every month. And Rebah didn't even remember a teenager being around her last visit. No, Apple was just being polite. She was well-trained to offer options for guests to choose from. She was actually delightful, with her corduroy overall shorts, combat boots, delicate cotton cardigan, and string of pearls around her neck. Rebah wasn't great with teenagers—or younger kids, or in-between kids—but here was someone who seemed at least awake to the possibilities of existence. Most teens she met never looked up from their phones.

"That sounds delicious. I'll have one with rum." Rebah ignored the warning dip in her belly. She'd started the day with a Bloody Mary at breakfast and then finished off that bottle of wine at lunch. But now it was seven in the evening! And the week had been horrendous! She deserved a real drink to take away the sharp corners of memory that were starting to poke her in the ribs.

She kept wanting to duck, but what could she possibly be avoiding? She'd been in the right. She'd been the one insulted and humiliated. She was the one who should be walking around with her head held high, no regrets. She gave her shoulders a slight shimmy as if to shake off the lingering sense that she should not be accepting an alcoholic beverage in this place. She was a grown woman with a dazzling career who needed to get to work, and a drink was exactly the right starting point.

Rebah followed Apple into the house and was struck by music coming from somewhere in the back. This place was full of music. Also striking? The smell of fresh paint. But of course they'd been painting. No matter how much care and upkeep were applied to any B&B, there was always an intense amount of prep work for a big weekend. And, well, she was there, wasn't she? The weekend was huge indeed.

Rebah looked around while Apple slipped through a swinging door to fetch the drink. The couch felt familiar, and the glass cabinet full of ugly wooden trolls was still there. God, why? Those things were just weird. All those eyes watching you.

Apple came back through the door and handed her a frosty glass filled with a cloudy iced beverage. With just one sip, it became Rebah's new favorite. It was the perfect spring drink.

"Let me show you where you're staying, and then we'd love to have you join us on the back veranda," Apple said. "Can you hear the music? We're thrilled that the newest thing in soulful Dutch boy bands is staying with us tonight and needed some rehearsal time. Oh. My. God.

They really are divine. Even more divine, they're going to let me play a few songs with them this weekend. I'm a pianist."

She twirled away to get an old-fashioned skeleton key from the desk. "Okay, right this way," she said, turning back to her guest.

Rebah followed Apple up the grand wooden stairs, noticing that the banister was well-shined and the black-and-white photos of different people and places were all dusted and straight. And really, really wonderful. Rebah didn't remember those from last time. She didn't really remember much of this place, actually. But minds are funny. *They are protective*, Rebah mused. They blank out the episodes that are best forgotten, like when someone mortifies you in front of strangers.

Her room, though, she remembered as the same she'd had last time, right down to the quilt on the bed. A flush of shame crossed her cheeks when she spied the yellow and orange colors of that blanket, obviously handmade, a piece that really belonged in a museum or at least hanging on a wall where no one could spill red wine on it.

"We have you in the Autumn Room. This was one of my mother's favorite rooms," said Apple.

"Thank you, Apple. It's sweet." It was sweet, but Rebah felt a chill. This wasn't a site of happy memories.

"So we've got music and appetizers in the garden, and then dinner will be served in another hour." Apple subconsciously smoothed down the quilt on the bed, though there were no folds or bunches. "Join us as soon as you'd like!" Apple shot one last parting look at Rebah, and Rebah could sense that there was a wealth of questions behind that calm, hostessy face. Maybe Apple wanted to ask, What's it like flying around the world for your job? What does it feel like to stay in a new place every month, to eat food you'd never heard of, and ride different forms of transportation? Did she worry over the number of hours she spent in flight, what impact that had on her carbon footprint? What about the different kinds of government she encountered on her travels? Could Rebah tell just by the view from the streets which countries were socialist, which were democracies, which were on the brink of change? Maybe Apple's dad had warned her against grilling the famous travel blogger too hard on first meeting. But Apple seemed delightful, and Rebah wouldn't have minded at all giving her a sneak peek into her glamorous-on-the-outside life. Maybe after another couple drinks.

Rebah waited until Apple had left the room before taking a peek at the underside of the quilt—no stain. Someone must be a laundry champion. The stain she remembered. She hadn't meant to spill wine on the quilt, of course she hadn't. She wasn't a monster. And she'd apologized. Well, she was pretty sure she'd apologized. Hadn't she? And even if she hadn't exactly apologized, Aidan shouldn't have embarrassed her the next morning, calling her a drunk in front of the other guests. But still, whenever she thought of the stain, she felt bad. He'd made it a point to let her know it was one of his favorites when she'd first checked in that time. One of his wife's favorites. His dead wife's favorite quilt, and she'd spilled red wine on it. She was a truly terrible person.

No! She hated feeling this way. She refused to wander down this path of self-doubt and pity. There was too much at stake. She was there for one reason: to write a shaming review of the place, which, no matter how much paint they slapped on the walls, would never rise to the heights of her readers' standards. Aidan Cisneros could plant all the marigolds he wanted, but it still wouldn't cover up the fact that this was an aging structure in need of some upgrades. No matter how sweet his daughter seemed or how delicious the welcome cocktail had tasted, she was there to peer behind the niceties and dig into the cracks to find the dirt.

And it was time to get to work.

Rebah sifted through her satchel, tossing her yellow legal pad on the quilt and shaking out her go-to little black dress that had served her in countless social situations. Not the same dress, of course. She had a standing order to have a new one delivered to her home every month. Slipping it over her head, she wondered when this had become her uniform and when she had started feeling trapped by it.

No! She was not going to do that thing where she looked back on all of her decisions thus far and picked them apart for errors. Not here, not now.

A few brushes of blush, new mascara, hair tied back in a casual-yet-elegant French twist, a pair of simple ballet flats, a silver bracelet on her arm, and a golden sunflower pendant around her neck—she was ready. She was Rebah.

She gulped the rest of the delicious drink as she wandered down the hall back toward the stairs, wondering if there'd be another waiting for her wherever she happened to sit. There'd better be.

Aidan used the back of his hand to wipe invisible sweat from his brow. How many million things could go wrong tonight? He couldn't even think about tomorrow. Why did he agree to this? How was he going to pull it off? And foremost: What would it be like to stand here in his backyard and make nice with Rebah Reynolds?

"You have to admit, Aids, this place looks damn good," Kye said, handing him an ice water.

Aidan downed the drink like a man in the desert and looked around. Kye was right. Tea lights glowed along the edges of the back porch, paper balloons dangled from the crisscross of fairy lights that Apple and Milly had strung between those odd wooden pillars, a hastily erected grape arbor—without grapes—covered part of the stone terrace, and tiki torches burned in every corner. Dusk was just beginning to descend, providing the perfect background for the cast of characters who'd gathered at the Happy Valley.

And characters they were. A high-pitched squeal came from the cozy couple—Verity and Jameson—snuggled up on an iron bench under the apple tree. A vibrato laugh emitted from Jasper and Mackenzie, seated on stools at a tall table, deep into a game of Go Fish, with shots. Apple's friend Boutique really did look thirty years old, especially dressed in a slinky, silvery dress and heels, holding forth to Michel and Buttercup on the identity politics of jazz festivals. And the band—Aidan had to admit the band was a stroke of genius on Apple's part.

For one thing, Kai and his friends were actually good. Really good. Aidan felt bad for refusing to let them rehearse there when they'd begged him a few months ago, but he'd assumed the worst and just couldn't stand the thought of constant feedback from death metal-grunge near his home. But the band—they called themselves Shade of Night—was amazing. He reminded himself to check with Apple later to see if they had any songs available to download. And he was excited to see her play keyboard with them later on.

He turned and was about to comment as such to Kye when Rebah made her grand entrance, framed momentarily in the wisteria that outlined the back doors. She looked around and a smile crept onto her face, a smile that was so genuinely delighted that Aidan thought maybe he had been mistaken about everything he knew to be Rebah Reynolds. But then she realized Aidan was watching. Aidan could see her stiffen, sharpen, and shrink into a column of hatred. The change in her was slight, perhaps only discernible to him, but it reaffirmed his deeply held knowledge that Rebah cared only for herself. But: game face.

"Rebah Reynolds!" he called out in what he hoped was a joyful, but not too jubilant, manner. "What a pleasure to see you again, here. In my home."

Rebah's plastic grin stretched to acknowledge Aidan's obviously faked delight in her presence and her eyes swept the scene, absorbing every detail of the impromptu party that had sprung up in the rather well-tended yard. "Ah, Mr. Cisneros!" she called as she crossed the patio toward him. "I can't even tell you how charming your bed-and-breakfast is! How delightful! How sweet! How really, truly remarkable! Why, I wouldn't have recognized it from a year ago. Well done, you. I can only imagine the effort you had to make this past year to surpass my wildest dreams!"

Aidan tried to keep his smile from morphing into a grimace. Kye reached out and pinched his elbow to keep him on task.

"Ms. Reynolds," Aidan said. "If anyone can judge a place, it's you. Has anyone offered you a drink?"

"Ah, yes. Your daughter is a remarkable creature, Mr. Cisneros. I'm not sure I've met her before. She was the perfect greeter. Showed me to a positively delightful room, put a refreshing drink in my hands, and let me know where I could find you once I was ready."

"You must be ready for another, then."

Rebah's eyes sparked at him and her jawline went tight. "Aren't we familiar," she said through lips that no one but Aidan noticed were thin with anger. She swallowed her rage back down and lifted her voice. "If you're offering, I wouldn't say no!"

Aidan made his way to a slab of oak that was laid across two sawhorses and covered with a white tablecloth and that was serving as the bar, Apple manning the bottles. "Is this even legal?" he asked her. "Never mind appropriate?"

"Don't worry, Dad, alcohol is not my thing. And this way I can make sure none of the band members fool someone into serving them." She iced a glass while they chatted, eyes roving around the yard, keeping watch to make sure that everyone was behaving. For about the millionth time, Aidan marveled at how smart his daughter was.

He followed her glance and had to admit: The place looked spectacular. "I can't believe we actually pulled it off," he murmured. "And Kai's band? I'm really impressed."

"Yeah, they've pulled it together the last couple of months. I know you kind of think Kai is a loser, but there's a reason I like hanging out with him. And with his friends. They all have some hard-core passion in their lives, Dad." Apple swirled the glass with rum, added cucumber mixer, and stabbed a pineapple chunk with a toothpick for a garnish. "Like how I want to go to Barnard and go into politics and come back here and clean up this county? They all want something, too. Kai is going places, and it might be someplace with that band."

"You younger generation." Aidan beamed as he took the frosty glass from his daughter. "I swear to God, you're going to save the world and the rest of us sad slobs in the process."

"Go make nice with Rebah," she told him, waving him off. "Remember, she's your guest. And I don't even see what there is to hate about her. I like her."

"Oh, dear Apple, you are a kind and forgiving soul who sees the best in everyone. Believe me, she is not worth your time."

"Whatever, go talk to her and be charming."

Aidan did as he was told, dodging Verity and Jameson as he turned to make his way back to the guest of honor. They now seemed to be dancing some version of the tango.

"Whoops!" Verity cried as they swerved far more dramatically than Aidan had dodged.

"Weaving already?" laughed Jameson. He had to puff out his mouth to displace a few strands from a feathery pink boa Verity was wearing around her neck.

"Glad to see you're having fun," Aidan muttered. Was he really paying all these people to drink and act happy in his backyard? *Theater people are nuts.*

A spark of anxious panic zipped across his gut. *What if this all fails spectacularly?* It was more than possible. What would Rebah think if it all came crashing down on him?

Focus, Aidan. Focus on getting that glowing review. Make her love this place. Sell yourself. That's why they are all here, all the misfit toys in one backyard.

"Mr. C," whispered Milly, who had appeared at his elbow. She was smiling in a wide-stretched clench, her eyes darting around to make sure no one heard what she had to say to her boss. "The dinner is here. Caterers arrived early."

"Oh, okay," Aidan said. "No worries. We'll sit early."

"But cocktail hour is supposed to last past eight, isn't it? What is everyone going to think?!"

"First of all, there is no everyone, okay? All of these people are getting paid. There is only one person we have to think about, and I can make something up about this is how we do it in Napa. Or something. Don't people in Zimbabwe eat dinner on the early side? We can use that excuse."

"But you've never been to Zimbabwe! Why on Earth would we model dinner schedules after Zimbabwe?!" Milly was displaying a surprising amount of stress. Aidan always thought of her as the *c'est la vie* one around there.

"Okay, calm down. You go organize the caterers and I'll handle Rebah. Just make sure they stay out of sight. I'm supposed to be cooking for this thing, remember? What did I cook anyway?"

"Lobster risotto and caprese salads with buffalo mozzarella. Oh, and deep-fried squash blossoms. And cheesecake, but not real cheesecake? I think it has duck eggs in it?"

"Jesus. Aren't I sophisticated."

"Okay, I'm going to grab Kye to help me."

"Wait, Kai's in the middle of a set," said Aidan, his eyes on the stage.

"No, I meant Kye."

"Right."

"So you're on your own for a few minutes," Milly prodded.

"Right?"

"So don't say anything weird to Rebah."

"What makes you think I'd say anything weird to her?"

"Well, you just seem like you're going to be weird around her, that's all. Just be chill."

"Milly, look at me. I am the definition of chill."

"Yeah, except for that vibrating muscle in your cheek and the way you keep fixing your hair."

"I am not fixing my hair! I'm just . . . there's mosquitoes."

"Nope, we had it sprayed with that organic deterrent—no mosquitoes!"

"How much did it cost to spray organic juice at the mosquitoes in my backyard?"

"Okay, I'm gonna deal with dinner!"

Milly trotted off and Aidan tried to calculate the expenses rolling through his mental spreadsheet for the weekend.

Across the yard, he spotted Rebah chatting with Mariah, who had decided her persona would be that of a reclusive Pulitzer Prize–winning novelist who usually spent her days alone on an island off the coast of Maine. Apparently, she bred goats and sold award-winning goat's milk in her spare time. Aidan had to admit, at least from across the yard, she looked the part of an introverted-goat-herder-slash-brilliant-novelist from Maine. In fact, she could have stepped from the creases of time, a relic from ancient history when people dressed in what they were able to kill and had flat teeth to better grind raw food into a manageable pulp.

"I don't like to leave my space," he overheard her saying to Rebah as he crept closer with the drink, which was really starting to sweat under his careful fingers. "Or my babies. I truly think that routine and consistency are the best ways to raise a kid, don't you?"

"Oh, I don't have children," Rebah answered. She noticed Aidan and straightened her back and Aidan felt a momentary zing. But she was reaching for the glass he was automatically holding out to her. That's where her interest was focused. Of course. Aidan knew that she needed whatever was in that glass to feel normal, to feel in control of herself and her surroundings. He remembered, even after nearly six years, that tug toward a drink. That promise. He felt a stab of empathy for her, before he mentally shook himself.

"Mariah, my favorite writer, how are you?" he asked the short-but-commanding figure draped in sheepskin cinched at the waist with a rawhide belt, a knife holster dangling casually by her hip. "Are we expecting a battle?"

"Aidan, you know I love you, but you are an innocent. I'd go so far as to say weak. I'd never use my knife in battle—I'm a pacifist. I carry it out of precaution. You never know when an animal will be injured beyond repair and need immediate extraction."

"Extraction?" Rebah asked, her lips settling on the rim of her drink.

"Termination," Mariah clarified. She took a swig from a giraffe bladder that hung on her other hip. "Ah, that's the stuff. I only drink goat's milk. Good for the heart."

"So, you're a novelist?" Rebah asked. "That's fascinating. Would I know any of your books?"

"Oh, of course you would, but I don't reveal my titles in casual conversation." Mariah's eyes fixed on Rebah's with an uncomfortable intensity. "I don't know who I can trust, you see. Who might be disguised as a distractedly interested B&B guest."

"Ah," said Rebah. She looked over at Aidan, amused. He shrugged, and they shared a slight smile before they each realized they were consorting with the enemy and stiffened back up. "I completely understand," Rebah told Mariah. "To tell you the truth, I don't trust anyone at a party either." She took what Aidan felt was an overly aggressive sip of her drink.

"So, you know!" Mariah exclaimed, and Aidan felt a stab of warning. She seemed caught up in her own fantasy world, a little too Methody in her acting for his comfort level. Surely Mariah could be trusted not to spill the whole secret.

"Rebah, have you tried the mushroom quiches?" he interrupted and nodded to Mariah as he steered Rebah in the direction of Michel and Buttercup, who were nibbling hors d'oeuvres (Milly had found some premade apps at the local grocery) off a silver serving tray held aloft by Apple's friend Boutique.

"You know what, I'm just going to pop off to the ladies' room for a moment, Aidan," Rebah said and handed him her empty glass. Unspoken: She would appreciate a refill. He watched as she made her way back toward the house and his stomach unclenched only slightly. She didn't seem to suspect a thing.

But she was Rebah Reynolds. He knew not to underestimate her powers of destruction.

In the bathroom, Rebah made sure the door was locked and then settled onto a well-placed stool and pulled out her phone. Time to show her boss, well, bosses, that she was earning her keep. God, she hated this. Why was she even there? Why did she care what her bosses thought of her work? "Huh," she muttered to herself. "That's got to be some kind of sign—not caring what your bosses think of your work . . ."

She chose a few photos she had surreptitiously taken of the different people at the gathering—she'd caught a great one of the goat-milk woman with her hand resting on her carving knife, an expression borrowed directly from ancient warrior princesses. "Going to battle in Napa's B&B scene," she muttered as she tapped out a caption. "This should keep the wolves at bay for a little while."

She paused her typing and looked at the black-and-white photograph on the wall. The house was full of black-and-white photography, mostly street scenes from a bygone era—Rebah guessed it was the dead wife who'd had that artistic interest—but this photo was different. It was small enough that you had to be close to see that it was of a woman. Closer to see that the woman was crying. Sobbing, maybe, her face a patchwork of despair and defeat. She cupped one hand around her brow as if to protect herself from a further onslaught of horror, but anyone looking at her could see that it was useless, evil had already been committed, the woman was already doomed.

"What a terrible photo," Rebah muttered. She snapped her own picture of it with her phone and was about to upload it to her bosses' account but hesitated. She looked again at the woman. Was there something familiar about her? Had she met this woman before? Seen her in a photo somewhere else? This wasn't Aidan's deceased wife, was it? No, there were plenty of photos of her around the house, and this woman had very different features—handsome, where Jessica had been pretty, chiseled, where Jessica had been ethereal. And this woman was showing a level of pain she suspected Jessica Cisneros hadn't been capable of knowing. Some people were just born to be happy.

Rebah couldn't put her finger on why the desperate woman in the photo seemed so familiar, but she put her phone away without sending any more snaps to her bosses. It wasn't such a terrible photo. It was just an uncomfortable photo. Maybe she could get its story from someone. Maybe Apple would know.

Chapter 12

The kitchen was a scene of carnage and devastation. Cardboard boxes in varying stages of flatness lined the floor while the countertops all held trays of . . . something?

"What the hell is that?" Aidan asked.

"Okay, don't panic," said Milly. She, Kye, and Sharon circled him.

"Panic? I see no reason to panic." Aidan's voice was barely above a whisper. "We ordered the four-star gourmet option, right?" He was getting louder. "Where's my lobster risotto and caprese salads with buffalo mozzarella and deep-fried squash blossoms and not-real cheesecake? Why, exactly, should I panic when all I see is onion rings and corn dogs? I mean, really, what exactly is there for me to panic about when a cotton-candy machine is taking up half my kitchen?" This last question was issued in a shout.

"Okay, I know this looks bad," Kye began. "Here's the deal. The caterer accidentally switched the main meal with another one they delivered tonight that was supposed to go to a kid's birthday party—I think they were doing a carnival theme. That's pretty cool, right? For a kid's party? Sharon, we should think about that for the twins . . ."

"Kye, focus!" Aidan yelped. "What are we going to do? I mean, people are coming in for dinner *now*! Rebah, she's out there, in the dining room just waiting to judge! I can only imagine the headline on that stupid blog of hers. 'From Fancy to Fairgrounds: How Low Can You Go with the Happy Valley?' I mean, this is a bloody nightmare!"

"Well, listen. We can do this," Milly said. "We just need to spin it."

Aidan took a deep breath. Square breathing, he reminded himself. In, two, three, four, out, two, three, four. The entire room could feel his pulse lower—but only slightly. "Milly, award-winning B&Bs do not need to spin their meal presentations. This?" He gestured toward the mounded platters of fried chicken, fried zucchini sticks, fried dough, and fried sandwich cookies. "This is not acceptable at this tier."

"No, she's right," Sharon said. "You've got to announce the dinner theme."

"I'm a Michelin-trained chef. I don't do themes."

"Yeah, well, this Michelin-trained chef didn't exactly cook this meal, did he?" Sharon shot him a look.

Not for the first time, Aidan acknowledged that she was far less forgiving than her sweet husband. Also, maybe, a tiny bit smarter. Okay, a lot smarter.

"Maybe Milly could do it," he suggested. "She's good at making crazy look digestible."

"Nope." Sharon wouldn't let him off that easily. "It's got to be you. You're owner, manager, and head chef. You need to be the voice of the Happy Valley."

Aidan pressed both hands onto the countertop and leaned over the steaming platters of breaded food, all of it brown, all of which would surely lead its consumers to an early heart attack.

"Aidan! Focus!" Sharon had elevated her attack. "You have got to pull it together. This isn't a disaster. This is a freakin' opportunity and you need to step up or you lose. You lose everything." Sharon looked deep into his face. "You know that daughter you love so much? She loses if you don't present this disgusting meal as the epitome of class and fun. Because that's the Happy Valley. We are the epitome of class and fun and sometimes we show it through fried food."

But how could he face Rebah with this? She was going to laugh at him. She was going to see right through the ruse and expose him for what he really was—a fraud.

The kitchen door swung open and Apple came in, saw the problem, immediately understood what must have happened, and said, "Oh, man, the band is going to flip over this meal."

Aidan gazed at his daughter. She had no idea what this meal might actually cost them. Her.

"Okay," he said, straightening up and dusting his hands together as though he'd been actually cooking. "Let's do this. But we'll need some props. And music. Apple, what's that circus song you used to play on repeat?"

"You mean *Entry of the Gladiators*?"

"Yep, that's the one. Still in your repertoire?"

"I never forget an amazing song, Dad."

"Excellent. You're on keys. And can you get Kai to accompany you on his guitar?"

"Boss, I don't play guitar," said Kye, holding his hands up in defense.

"No one thinks you do, dude. Sharon, nab that clown wig from the top shelf of the hall closet. The one Apple wore to that Halloween dance that year, what, three years ago? Kye, can you still do handsprings?"

"Does the government have an accuracy problem?" Kye demonstrated his limberness by diving into a backbend and then zipping back up with a grin on his face.

Wandering down the hallway on her way back to the party, Rebah heard a crash coming from the kitchen. She hesitated, then veered toward the door. Just as she was about to reach it, it burst open and a tall man with a shaggy beard and plaid shirt came barreling through, screeching to a stop just before smashing into her.

"Ah!" said Kye. "Ms. Reynolds. Can I help you with anything?"

"Is everything okay? I heard a crash."

"A crash?"

"Yes, a crash. Loud. Crashingly loud."

"No, I don't think you did."

Behind the door, several loud bangs happened in succession, as though an army of giant babies was navigating a drum kit. "You don't think I heard a sound just like that?"

"Just like what?" Kye asked nonchalantly. He cast his eyes around the room, settling his gaze out the window. "Goodness, I wonder if it will be warm again tomorrow?" A thump bumped the door behind him partly open, hitting him in the backside as a yelp came from the other side. Rebah raised her eyebrows.

"Hon?" squeaked a short woman with a sensible haircut and green eyelids that somehow worked for her. She squeezed around the immovable Kye. "We might need your— Oh! Hello!"

"Ms. Reynolds, I'd like to introduce my wife, the lovely Sharon." Kye carefully maneuvered Sharon in front of his body without letting Rebah get a glimpse into the kitchen, where they could hear high-intensity scuffling going on. Something was afoot.

"Call me Rebah, please." She reached out to shake Sharon's hand, her attention still darting around Kye, trying to figure out what was going so wrong.

"Rebah, so lovely to meet you. I hope you're having a good time *chez* Happy Valley. But it looks like your hands are empty!" Sharon reached out and casually touched the smooth silk of Rebah's arm. "Let's get you a drink! Follow me out to the garden?"

Rebah knew something was up. A year ago, she would have barged through that swinging wooden door like she owned the place, demanding an explanation for whatever sights might have met her eyes on the other side. She'd have barked and berated, snapped photos, formed clever headlines in her head all while serving as witness to (and player in) the business's downfall. But now?

Now, she wanted to go back out to the garden party and sip another drink. She couldn't really describe the change in herself, other than it was partly a revolt against her boss, well, bosses, and partly a manifestation of the list of pros and cons she'd created in the bar. What might happen if . . .

The people here were strange and something was definitely going on behind the scenes, but the music was good, the décor was lovely, and she was having a good time. Also? She was hungry. So she allowed herself to be steered away from the mysterious kitchen door.

She and Sharon headed back to the garden, where the band had slipped into a slow ballad and three couples danced under the twinkly lights. The tangoing duo had relaxed into a gentler form of dance and made space for others.

The two women made their way through the dusky backyard air toward the bar, where Boutique, who had taken over for Apple, saw them coming and began to put together the ingredients for another cocktail. But Rebah shook her head. "Just a glass of wine, please, sweetie," she said. "It's funny, the older I get the more I appreciate the classic taste of a good red. And the more my head appreciates not having to deal with the morning-after spirits fog."

Boutique tipped her head and nodded. "I can't really commiserate, but I can pour you a glass of red. This one is a blend. It's supposed to be quite firm with a hint of zesty orange but nothing overwhelming. And if you hold it for just a hair longer than usual, you'll let the blackberry come through, and it's really delightful." Sharon narrowed her eyes at Boutique's sommelier talk. This was Apple's friend, right? An eighteen-year-old?

Rebah took a sip. "Oh, perfect. Will you excuse me? I want to wander a bit before dinner. I find that you can really get a sense of place as guests begin to get hungry." She took her glass and ambled toward the edge of the yard.

Sharon turned to Boutique. "How do you know so much about wine?" she asked, scowling slightly.

"Have you noticed where I grew up?" Boutique reasoned.

Sharon's scowl changed into a wink. "Well, that makes sense. You children are all so much more sophisticated than me. Hey, have you seen my kids? The twins? They were supposed to be helping with the—" Sharon caught herself just in time, right before she uttered the word "caterers." "They were supposed to be helping serve appetizers, but they've managed to disappear."

"Those two are adorable," Boutique said. "Your daughter is like a powerhouse, and your son gave me some excellent makeup tips. Yeah, my guess? You'll find them in Apple's closet."

"Oh, those two. I've told them, no fishnet until they're fourteen. Kids these days, am I right?"

"So right."

As Boutique and Sharon bantered, Rebah sipped her wine on the other side of the yard and watched, catching some of their conversation. The people here—not the guests, but the man in the kitchen, Sharon, Aidan, Apple—they were all so obviously a family, even if they weren't necessarily related by blood. There was a foundation of love there. This place was a home.

Across the yard, Aidan skidded to a stop after bursting through the patio doors. Buttercup threw up her drink in surprise and the delicate glass disintegrated as it struck the flat stone floor. The scent of gin blended with that of the roses blooming along the white border fence, and, for a moment, everyone froze as though in a snapshot. One of those old-time snapshots where people had to stand still until their muscles ached and their smiles melted.

"Dinner is served!" Aidan announced with a bow, and the photograph shattered into living pieces again, the people whole and present and hungry.

Rebah included. She followed the stream of a dozen bodies into the house, though not before topping off her glass with more wine.

"Clown wig!" shouted Apple, chucking it at Aidan, who sealed it onto his head.

"Okay," he said. "We've got this. Apple, get the door and then slip over to the piano. Everyone, grab a tray. This food isn't serving itself."

The parade danced into the dining room accompanied by the rousing rhythm of *Entry of the Gladiators*, Kye leading the way with a series of backflips and roundoffs that would make any tween with aspirations of joining the circus envious.

"Hear ye, hear ye!" Aidan called over the laughter and applause. "I hereby announce, dinner is served! And not just any dinner. There are some evenings that call for a very special brand of joy." He placed his platter on the table in front of Rebah, who looked confused to see a pile of Italian sausage, onions, and green peppers in front of her, hoagie rolls at the side. "How much of your childhood do you remember? Even my daughter, as close to her early years as anyone in this room, can't recall the days and months and years of simple joy that are the hallmark of every healthy childhood. And with this dinner, we are reclaiming that simple joy. We are pausing the onslaught of money problems, relationship issues, and work disasters that are a part of adulthood and living, for at least one meal, in the endless summer of being a kid. Dig in!"

The room erupted in applause. As Aidan took his seat at the head of the table, he noticed Rebah's look of initial confusion morphing into something akin to appreciation. Was she actually moved by his speech? Was this insane scheme working?

Fairground fare, while delightfully greasy and crispy and delicious when first introduced to your mouth, does tend to morph into a plug of material deep in the gullet a few hours after initial contact. That's the first thing that drove Rebah from her bed in the slim hours of the morning—heartburn.

The second thing? Thirst. She was so damn thirsty, and the bathroom water just wasn't cutting it. There had to be a filtered container in the fridge.

And the third thing: She was nosy. This wasn't an unusual tactic for her. There was a lot to learn about a B&B by wandering around on your own after hours when the owners weren't there to distract from peeling wallpaper or faded chintz curtains or mice scurrying in the walls. After hours was Rebah's favorite time at a new place, the moments when she made a space her own and dove deep into what it had to offer.

One night in Sri Lanka, she had discovered a brothel in the basement of a four-star place that advertised itself as an oasis of female freedom. Another time in Nova Scotia, she had stumbled upon the definitively creepy habit of the owner of an intimate chalet—he preferred to sleep sitting upright on a barstool in the den with a shotgun laid across his lap in case the ghost of his dead great-great-grandfather tried once again to burn the place down out of spite because the woman he loved had run away with a guest one hundred and twenty years ago.

What might she find at Aidan's place?

She threw a light robe over her tank top and pajama bottoms and crept down the hallway, careful to tread lightly on the wide wooden boards. Trying not to think about the dozens of eyes that were watching her from the photographs on the walls, she slipped down the stairs one by one, hesitating when she heard a sigh coming from a room behind her—but it was only one of the guests easing into a deeper sleep. And why shouldn't they? This place, though slightly odd, was peaceful.

Downstairs, she made the rounds in the dining room, the smell of fairground grease still hovering in the air. Nothing of note in this room, except, of course, the bar, where Rebah paused for a moment before deciding what she really needed was a glass of water. She continued to the kitchen. Kitchens were great places to find dirt—often literally. Kitchens were where B&B owners and managers spent a lot of time, and that's where proof of their incompetence was likely to have been left exposed, forgotten, waiting to be discovered.

But Aidan's kitchen was in fairly good order. Dishes were washed and stacked on different surfaces, a dishcloth hung by a hook above the sink, the stove was wiped down, and the air smelled of soap with a hint of olive oil. Rebah didn't reach for the light as she didn't want to give her wanderings away to the world at large, but she spotted a clean glass that was tipped upside down in the dish drainer and opened the refrigerator to see if she could find a jug of filtered water inside.

"Thanks, dude," said a gravelly voice behind her.

Rebah shrieked as she turned to find one of the band members, the bassist, standing behind her—completely naked.

"You couldn't sleep either?" the guy asked.

Rebah shrank away from him, but the only direction for her to go was deeper into the fridge. He reached around her—thankfully without touching her—and nabbed a milk jug. He popped off the cap and shamelessly chugged half the bottle, his throat clicking away in the kitchen that was otherwise silent but for Rebah's shocked breathing.

The kitchen door swung open, and there was Aidan, pulling a sweater over his T-shirt, one sock on while the other foot remained bare.

"What the . . ." he started, but the naked dude simply let out a ripping burp, handed Rebah the milk jug, said, "Peace," to no one in particular, and went back through the door.

Rebah and Aidan stared at each other for a moment in shock. "Rock and roll," Aidan muttered, shaking his head. He was going to have to have a talk with Apple about her friends.

Rebah, however, burst out laughing. "Did you see his tattoo?" she sputtered.

"He had a tattoo?" Aidan asked, confused.

"Right next to his belly button! It was a barcode with the word 'Priceless' under it!" She erupted into new waves of giggles, and Aidan couldn't help but join in. Of all the scenarios he'd thought to worry about this weekend, encountering a naked bassist in the kitchen hadn't made the cut.

"Um . . . was there anything I could help you with?" he asked suddenly. After all, the naked guy wasn't the only thing out of place in his after-hours kitchen.

"Oh—water. I was hoping to find some filtered water. That food was amazing, brought me right back to the county fairs we used to go to when I was a kid, but it really makes you thirsty, doesn't it?"

"Sure. Right here." He retrieved the glass from the dish drainer, reached around Rebah—far more politely than the naked bassist had—to fetch a water jug from the fridge, and poured her a glass. "Just let me know if there's anything else I can do for you, okay? It's been nice having people around again."

"Again?" Rebah asked innocently enough, but her mind had snagged on the phrase. It sounded like Aidan wasn't used to this many guests.

"Well, I mean . . . since we really turned things around and came back stronger than ever. I mean, it was quiet for a while, but now, yeah, we're booked solid constantly. All the time. No breaks, really. So, back to bed?" Almost blew it. Had he managed to save it?

"Yep, definitely ready for bed. I have water, I have a great story about a naked guy drinking milk in the kitchen, and now I can sleep." Rebah smiled at him. She considered telling him not to worry, that she wouldn't use the story in her blog, but then held off, just in case it was a promise she couldn't keep. Though he didn't need to worry. Naked dudes drinking milk were funny, not frightening, to her kind of up-for-adventure readers.

"Okay, then. I'll see you in exactly three hours."

"Three hours? Why so early?" The pair walked back up the stairs and whispered so they wouldn't wake anyone else.

"Ah, you're forgetting about our sunrise balloon ride. Four o'clock on the front porch to meet the van to take us to the launch field. It's going to be amazing."

"Oh, okay. Yep. Four o'clock. That's three hours from now. Plenty of time to get some refreshing sleep."

"You can snooze in the van on the way to the field. See you then!"

Aidan gave a little wave, an actual jaunty wave, and slipped back into his own room, leaving Rebah in the hallway to realize that for one, she hadn't dug up any useful dirt on the Happy Valley, and second, she was actually looking forward to a sunrise balloon ride. And in Rebah's world, this was a moment to remember for its rarity.

Chapter 13

"Four in the morning is just not my time," Apple grumbled as she fastened her seat belt in the van her dad kept on hand to chauffeur guests.

In the seat next to her, Rebah nodded in sympathy, though, to be honest, she felt pretty good about life at that particular four in the morning. She hadn't had more than five drinks the night before, and the incident in the kitchen had given her brain the kind of shake-up that meant she'd slept soundly afterward, more soundly than she'd slept in a long time. When her alarm went off, it had been easy to slip out of bed and into warm jeans and a sweatshirt. Now, she felt a thrill to be heading down the Napa highway on the way to the balloon field. But she still knew how Apple felt.

"Yeah, but think of it—breakfast in a hot-air balloon!" she whispered.

"If I spill my coffee, that's a long way back to a dry pair of pants." Apple and Rebah snorted together in laughter.

Up front, in the driver's seat, Aidan glanced at the two in the rear-view mirror. Part of him wanted to call Apple to sit closer to him. Despite their shared laugh last night—and he really needed to talk to Apple's friends about wandering around naked—he was still convinced that Rebah couldn't be trusted. Rebah was just as likely to write something foul about you as she was something glowing. Rebah also drank too much and had no respect for other people's belongings.

But it's hard for a parent to interrupt their kid's good mood, and Rebah was making Apple happy, he could tell. Her phone was no-where to be seen and she was telling Rebah a story that involved a lot of hand gestures and exaggerated facial expressions. Let them be. How much damage could Rebah do?

Aidan let out an involuntary shudder.

The other passengers leaned against each other or the walls of the van in varying levels of awakeness. Michel and Buttercup seemed to be fully asleep, leaning against each other. Verity and Jameson were taking photos of each other with their phones. Mariah was gazing ferociously out the window. Mackenzie and Jasper, with their cooler of food from "Florida" between them, muttered quietly to each other. Even at the front of the van, Aidan caught snatches of conversation about best practice escapes and the crabbing season in Naples. Mackenzie sneezed suddenly and Jasper handed him a rainbow handkerchief and patted his shoulder. *Sweet*, Aidan thought. Though the cooler still felt like a weird gimmick.

The balloon field emerged through the early morning fog, a dozen deflated giants spread out on the ground—rainbow, pale blue, deep red, and one that mimicked a sunset. Above their snoozing cousins, two floating orbs patiently awaited the travelers, their navy-colored surfaces dark against the sky. "Oh," breathed Rebah. Again Aidan glanced back and this time saw a look of wonderment on her face. Apple looked just as delighted, and that's not nothing from a teenager.

"Dad, this was a really great idea!" she called up to him.

It had better be, he thought, *at four-hundred dollars per person.*

The cast stumbled out of the van, all of them wide awake now that they were there and could see the contraptions that would take them high in the sky. "Goodness, they make me think of the dirigibles we boarded in Kenya, don't you think, dear Jameson?" Verity exclaimed. "These are much smaller, of course, but still impressive. I just love mag-nificent things."

"I, too, love magnificent things, and I love the idea of gazing down

at Earth from a vantage point that allows the fissures in the social construct to reveal themselves to those fortunate enough to glimpse them,"
Jameson pontificated.

"Yes!" agreed Verity, nearly tripping as one ankle buckled on a clump
of grass. "Perhaps we'll spot a new population in need. How high do
these things go? Will we be able to see any failing elephant herds?"

"You do know we're in California?" asked Rebah with a quizzical
look on her face.

Aidan felt a pang in his gut. Was she catching on? These people
really were ridiculous. How could she not suspect something was off?

"Maybe you're thinking of mountain lions?" she suggested.

"Oh, are you interested in philanthropic husbandry?"

"Well, I do like mountain lions," Rebah answered.

As they made their way across the damp grass, a tall man with
a long blond ponytail came striding toward them from the balloons.
"Aloha!" he called out.

Dude, we are so not in Hawaii, thought Aidan. But he smiled at
the guy who would navigate the vehicles that would carry him and his
daughter into the atmosphere and back. It's always best not to mock
the person who holds the keys to survival. "Yeah, hi, we booked a balloon breakfast for this morning?"

"That's right, that's right. Are you beautiful people ready for a
life-changing experience?"

"Always," snorted Apple, her face coated in teenaged rebellion
against the forced cheer of their host.

That's my girl, Aidan thought.

"I, for one, am always eager to change my life," said Buttercup.
Though she was technically supposed to simply play the role of Michel
the jazz musician's groupie—er, companion—she was really coming
into her own character, which seemed to be the persona of a nonbinary
soul who raised gladiolas whenever they weren't tutoring middle-school
kids in the fine art of *bataireacht,* a kind of Irish stick fighting.

"Fantastic," said the ponytailed man. "I'm Christian, and I'll be one of your pilots. My colleague, Jason, will be piloting the other balloon. And we will both be doing our utmost to ensure you have an amazing, transcendent time. Aloha."

Christian gave a slight bow before turning and leading them to the closest basket, which was anchored to the earth with a series of guy ropes, with a set of removable wooden steps leading to a docking station.

"Oh, this is awesome," said Rebah. "I went on a balloon ride once in the Amazon, but it was nothing as sophisticated as this. Back then, I had to climb into the basket like I was mounting a horse, and let me tell you, that is not easy when you're wearing your best beach skirt."

Christian flashed a grin at Rebah and Rebah grinned back, lowering her lashes to her cheeks and glancing upward quickly in an obvious display of availability that wasn't lost on Aidan. *Keep it in your pants*, he thought silently at Rebah. *And, really, Mr. Aloha has got to be ten years younger than you.*

That was weird, the flash of jealousy he'd felt watching Rebah be Rebah. Of course she was a flirt. A flirt and a tease and a drunk and an all-around annoying waste of skin. Why should he care if she looks a certain way at a certain surfer wannabe? This was Rebah Reynolds. His nemesis. Let her flirt with whomever she wanted. He couldn't care less.

"Up you go," murmured Christian as he helped Rebah into the basket. Half their group had been steered toward the other basket, where Christian's counterpart, similar in every respect except with a red ponytail instead of blond, was helping Verity get settled. Aidan was heading for the basket where Rebah and his daughter had both ended up, but Christian held out an arm. "Okay, and you'll be in the other basket. We need to distribute the weight appropriately. Otherwise, crash and burn, baby."

"Well, that doesn't make sense. There's just as many people in that basket as there are in this one. What difference does it make which I'm in?"

"Yeah, you aren't the one who's piloted dozens of hot-air balloon rides, are you?" Christian smirked.

"I can certainly count."

"Can you, though?" Christian gestured again toward the other basket, where Jason was now motioning to Aidan to join them. But Aidan really wanted to go in this basket, with Apple and Rebah and Jasper and Mackenzie, not the other one with Verity and Jameson and Michel and Buttercup and Mariah.

"Okay, all set? Setting sail!" Christian ignored Aidan's fuming face and began to go down his checklist of safety items, launching into a spiel about hands in, faces outward, no pulling on any dangling cords. Apple looked at her dad, confused. Why was he making such a big deal about this?

Aidan saw her watching him and realized there was no way to win, so he stomped down the wooden ladder and crossed over to the other basket, where he wedged himself into a definitely more crowded space than the other one had offered. He suspected his placement had nothing to do with weight distribution and everything to do with the fact that Christian thought Rebah was adorable and wanted as few unattached males in his ride as possible.

"Okay, everyone, ready, set, go," droned Jason, obviously not as fanatical as his partner about safety. From the other basket, Aidan could hear Rebah's laughter even above the sudden roar of the flame.

And with a quiet, rising sensation that he might have missed had he not been looking at the ground, they were afloat.

It was hard to fathom, the view. After a lifetime of seeing the world from the earth, with the occasional ascent in an airplane, to be suspended from above with no plates of glass or plastic between his face and the face of the planet was astounding. Aidan leaned on the edge of the basket and tried to open his eyes even wider to take it all in—the patterns of vineyards etched between neighborhoods, the sculptured hills rising and falling, everything in greens and browns except for the sky. The sky was its own breathtaking landscape, pure and thin until the hint of sun on the horizon became the main event with a rush of deep orange and red.

Everyone was quiet as they watched the sunrise, and just as they were starting to feel the warmth of the orb on their faces, they broke into spontaneous applause at this most perfect show. Aidan glanced around, wanting to share this moment with Apple, before remembering that she was in the other basket.

"Doesn't it simply escape words?" asked Buttercup.

Beside her, Michel let out a kind of cool, appreciative moan.

Aidan nodded and smiled, though he wondered about the validity of commenting with words on an event that "escaped words."

Breakfast was served in small brown paper bags, handed out by Christian and Jason in their respective balloons. It was a disappointing meal of cold, slightly slimy egg-and-cheese wraps and tepid coffee, but no one cared. Jameson and Verity scarfed theirs down like they were starving. The whole group seemed to be basking in the newborn sun.

Well, Aidan cared a bit. After all, when you pay a lot of money for a breakfast-sunrise balloon ride, you expect to be able to eat the breakfast without fear of food poisoning.

After they'd been floating for a while, the air was chilled enough that the view wasn't quite the distraction that was needed, and no one complained as they made the descent back to the waiting field. The groups remerged into one and people blinked at each other in a sort of embarrassed acknowledgment that they'd been moved by the experience.

And it was moving.

But it was also time to go horseback riding.

Milly had really come through as activities director, Aidan reflected. First, the balloon ride, now horseback riding. He admitted to himself that he was actually having fun. It had been ages since he'd done anything besides work.

And, more importantly, Rebah seemed to be having fun. She and Apple had paired up again in the van, and at the horse barn they gravitated toward the same section where the animals stood loosely connected to the walls via crossties attached to loops on their halters.

A young girl dressed in riding tights and a filthy T-shirt, who couldn't have been more than ten, took expert charge of their group and directed them to their individual horses. Apple had a small chestnut pony, Rebah had a gray beauty, and Aidan was granted a mottled patchwork steed with a scar over one eye.

"Okay, pony, you know I'm new here, right?" He spoke softly at the horse. He hadn't done any real riding in his life, and while he wasn't exactly scared, he also wasn't sure what plans this four-legged creature who outweighed him by hundreds of pounds might have for him.

"You'll be fine," the ten-year-old barn helper barked at him. "This is Clyde, but we call him Scarface. Because, you know, the scar." The girl patted Scarface hard on the neck and the horse responded by bending his face toward her and blowing out his nostrils. "He likes a firm hand. So when you're brushing him, don't be all soft and delicate. Brush him like you mean it."

Aidan had no idea what this actually meant, but he got a brush from a milk crate hanging on the stall wall and tried his best to be firm with it against the horse's coat. As he smoothed it over Scarface's rump, he could hear Apple and Rebah laughing softly together. That was good, right? The whole point of the weekend was to impress this woman, and Aidan should have felt lucky that she'd found his daughter so charming. But honestly? He felt a little bit left out. It should have been him and Apple laughing together at the horses. Or him and Rebah.

Okay, that was just ridiculous.

"Right!" barked the head instructor, a forbidding woman named Abigail in skintight leggings, a green polo shirt, and a white plastic helmet. "Lead your mounts to the ring and we'll cover the mounting basics." She didn't crack a smile, even though a few giggles erupted down the aisle.

"I have a question!" called Mackenzie. "Can the word *mount* really be both a verb and a noun?"

"You want to mount, you need to listen." Abigail scowled.

"It's like the word '*wave*,'" explained Jasper. "You can wave at a wave on the beach. Or conduct your conduct. Or object to an object. Or insult an insult."

"Ah. Mount. I'm going to have to work this into conversation more often," said Mackenzie.

"While you make your plans, bring your mount out so we can learn how to mount," Jasper teased then shot Mackenzie a look that was pure flirtation, and Aidan laughed along with the rest of their crew.

As he checked to make sure the girth around his horse's barrel was tight, he noticed Rebah watching Jasper and Mackenzie with a certain look. Not one of her usual criticism, and not the mask of ridiculous horror from the night before when they'd encountered the Naked Kitchen Man (he still had to talk with Apple about keeping her band friends in line), but a different expression, one that was perhaps more vulnerable than anything he'd ever seen on her.

Aidan got in line behind Michel and Buttercup, both of them apparently completely unimpressed with the idea of riding, standing and holding their horses' reins as though holding a cocktail glass. Luckily, their rides looked half asleep on the other end of the leather.

"Excuse me? I think my horse is defective," said Buttercup. "It keeps wagging its tail like there's something wrong. Could it possibly be in pain? I do have plenty of experience with animals in pain and tail wagging is indicative of a deeper issue. Excuse me? Barn staff? I think my horse needs X-rays."

Abigail came over and ran her massive hands along the horse's neck and chest, then down the front legs, and watched as it did indeed swish its tail up and around its rump. "There's your problem," she crooned, and slap! killed an annoying bug dead with one blow. "Just flies," she muttered, looking at Buttercup from under bushy eyebrows.

"Oh. Well. That's good. Better safe than sorry."

Aidan snorted under his breath.

Apple was up ahead of them, but Rebah had come out of the barn afterward and slid in behind Aidan. He was surprised to see her reach up her left leg, stick her foot in the stirrup, and, with a couple of well-timed hops, suddenly vault onto the horse's back and settle in her saddle.

"So, you've done this before?" he asked. Then it hit him—half the photos of Rebah in exotic locales included pictures of horses. Of course, she'd done this before. But she surprised him with her answer.

"Actually, I grew up on a horse farm. Kind of. My aunt had a farm and I spent summers there. It was all I could think about for the rest of the year. The horses, the barn, the riding. The other girls who rode there. It was amazing." Her eyes gleamed under her helmet's overhang. "You just know the school months couldn't compete."

"To be honest, I've never even been on a horse," Aidan admitted. "And to be even more honest, I'm scared to death."

"No! Don't be scared! Your horse looks mellow, and it's perfectly safe anyway. This kind of place knows how to take care of people. You can tell—the workers all look pretty happy. It's really bad for employee morale if someone falls off and dies."

"That actually makes me feel better." Aidan waved some flies away from his face.

"And it's even worse for business if you fall off and get merely maimed. Way more insurance bills to cover. Better to take a knock to the head and that's all she wrote."

Aidan brushed the horse's forelock from its forehead and looked the animal in the eyes. He could see his whole upper body reflected there.

"Oh, God, I'm so sorry. I'm an idiot." Rebah looked horrified at her words. Her horse sidestepped underneath her and she easily followed the motion with her body. "I really didn't mean . . . I know that your wife . . . Sometimes I just say the most awkward things."

"Oh, no, it's okay, honestly. I didn't even make the connection."

"Okay, good, but I'm still so, so sorry."

"Rebah, there's really no reason to apologize. She died of a brain aneurysm, and it was a long time ago, and of course I'll always miss her, but I can't not talk about death for the rest of my days, can I?"

"You know, I think that's the first time I've ever heard you call me Rebah."

Aidan's hands paused their patting of his horse's mane. "Huh."

"It's nice, actually. I never really feel the part of Ms. Reynolds."

Aidan was silent a moment and then he smiled at her, pulled his hands out of the horse's hair, and dusted them off, the reins looped through his elbow. "This is great, isn't it?" he asked, talking to himself more than Rebah.

"Riding horses?"

"Well, the whole thing. The whole weekend. I forget how much fun this can be, having guests and doing cool things. I forget that Napa is a pretty cool place to live."

"So you don't usually have guests?" Rebah looked confused. "I thought your business had been going really well lately."

"Oh, I meant . . . guests that I enjoy spending time with. Like we're doing. You know, usually it's more business and less pleasure." Aidan could've kicked himself for coming so close to blowing it. Again.

Rebah's face looked as though she suspected something was off, but a slight breeze twirled through the yard and the look was gone. *Close*, Aidan thought. *Stop being stupid around Rebah Reynolds.*

"I get what you mean. I travel so much and stay in so many gorgeous places and meet so many gorgeous people that I forget how much I actually love traveling—it becomes so tiresome. At least, I used to love traveling. I don't know, lately . . ." She trailed off, not sure how much she wanted to reveal to this man who just one day ago was an enemy.

But he was still the enemy, wasn't he? Sure, he was actually kind of a sweet guy. And he'd been nothing but a gracious host since she'd arrived last night. But really, did all of these positives truly erase the way he'd called her a drunk the last time?

Right then, watching him whisper to his horse and pretend that it was whispering back, she didn't feel angry anymore.

"Dad, check it out!" Apple called out from where she was perched on her chestnut pony. "I am officially going through my horse stage right now. Can we get a pony?"

"Absolutely. Just let Barnard know you won't be attending, and I'll buy you all the ponies you want."

"You are a riot, Dad. But don't I look good up here? And isn't this horse the coolest horse you've ever seen?"

She did look good up there. Her signature combat boots were perfectly placed against the horse's sides and her elbows were bent at a gentle angle, her hat tipped in a jaunty slope that made Aidan wonder if it was actually tight enough. Rebah turned to him and smiled and for a moment it felt like they were two people on the same team, proud of their kid.

And then the moment went awkward. Why were they looking at each other like that? Aidan coughed into his fist and then craned his neck to see how the others were doing. Rebah looked up, around, down at her horse's neck, then over to where a few of the mounted guests had gathered near the trailhead. Clicking her tongue, she maneuvered her mare toward them. Safety in numbers. Aidan watched as she pulled up beside Apple.

"You look good on a horse," Rebah said to Apple, smiling. "Here's what you want to do." She explained how Apple should sit, how she should hold her hands, how much pressure she should put on the horse's bit. "Now stretch your calf muscles down so your heel drops below your toe—good. And turn your heel out, knee in. Feel how you sit more deeply? That's what will keep you from falling. Remember, it's never your hands that hold you to your horse, it's always your seat."

"Why did I not try horseback riding before? This is amazing." Apple couldn't stop beaming. "I'm going to get bugs in my teeth if I keep grinning like this," she laughed.

"I know exactly how you feel right this minute," Rebah said.

"Horses are the best things in the world. I was so lucky to get so much riding time when I was younger. Man, have I missed it."

"But why don't you still ride?"

"Well, I travel a lot. Owning a horse is a real commitment, and that wouldn't be fair, to have a horse and never spend enough time with him."

"No, but if it makes you happy, I bet there's a way."

Rebah considered Apple's argument. If something makes you happy, you find a way. She knew the premise was strong and that the younger woman was right. But it just felt like that simple step wasn't easy at all. The transition from the kind of life she had to the kind of life she needed if she wanted to own a horse, have a boyfriend longer than a few months, read a book in bed on a weekend afternoon, have a restaurant she went to every Tuesday evening for drinks—that transition seemed insurmountable. She would have to change everything. Not the least of which? Her job. And what would she have left if she didn't have her job?

Chapter 14

"Yes, the security code is eight seven nine. That's right. And can you repeat the balance one more time?" Aidan winced visibly, though there was no one in the kitchen just then to see it, and the person on the other end of the phone was blind to any expressions of pain he made.

But still. Aidan knew Barnard was expensive. Hell, every college is expensive. But he hadn't really stopped to think about what that expense was actually going to look like on his credit card bill. Now? That was all he could think about. And this was just the deposit.

Aidan hung up with the treasurer's office. People had scattered after their return from horseback riding, mostly toward the backyard where the caterers had left a picnic sandwich buffet set up under the grape arbor. Aidan could hear music picking up again and the sound of people murmuring in hungry delight. He wasn't quite ready to join them yet. He straightened some of the clean dishes that had been stacked on the kitchen table. He took a damp rag and wiped down the stovetop, the sink, the faucet, the counter. He folded Apple's old pink blanket that had somehow made its way from her room to the kitchen. He absentmindedly poked through the refrigerator to see what was there. There was some of that food he'd picked up at the Asian grocery yesterday, and Milly had gone to the market last night so they'd have something other than powdered and catered options to serve guests, but he hadn't taken a look since the groceries had been put away. And was she expecting him to cook? Did anyone expect him to just slip back into that role?

Fresh basil. Heavy cream. Peaches—where had Milly gotten peaches? A baguette he knew had been baked just down the road. A jar of pickles that had been put up last summer by an elderly farmer out on Route 120. Onions, zucchini, marinated artichokes, tomatoes. Milly had shopped wildly and without a plan, apparently.

Aidan took out the cream and some eggs and washed the zucchini in the sink. He diced an onion, the feel of the knife between his fingers foreign after so many years of avoiding what had once been his passion. Why? Why did cooking fall apart after Jessica died? Maybe because everything had fallen apart. It was him—he'd fallen apart. Abandoning cooking was a symptom; grief was the disease.

But this felt good. He sautéed the onion and added some thinly sliced zucchini, took the veggies off the heat, and tossed in a chopped tomato. He added tarragon, chives, and freshly ground black pepper. Then he let that sit while he whisked a dozen eggs with heavy cream and added a pinch of salt, making the mixture frothy and light enough to defy all expectations. He put the veggie pan back on low heat, carefully coated everything with the egg mixture, and then put a lid over the whole shebang.

Cheese? They must have cheese. Aidan found a lump of fresh mozzarella made from buffalo milk in the fridge door and went to work slicing it into a heap of tiny wedges. Then he had to try a taste. It was required of chefs to ensure their ingredients were as fresh as possible.

As soon as the cheese hit his lips, he regretted his impulse. Because suddenly he was cast back in time to a sunny, breezy day when he and Jessica had driven upstate, Apple strapped into her car seat in the back of Jessica's Volvo. A rare day when no guests had been registered—they figured it was time for a break. Just a day trip. Just a reminder that there was life outside the Happy Valley. They'd ended up at a buffalo farm.

"I didn't even know these were a thing," Jessica had said. "A buffalo farm? Who farms buffalos?"

"Are buffalos native to this region?" Aidan wondered.

Apple, from the back seat, added an emphatic "Mooooooo!" to the conversation.

"That makes perfect sense, Apple Crisp," answered Aidan. "Moo."

They parked the car behind a strand of red plastic tape and wandered toward what seemed to be the buffalo barn, a rocky green field stretching far behind it. "Moo!" squealed Apple. And she was right—there was a buffalo!

"A buffalo!" shouted Jessica and turned to him with her mouth wide open and her eyes delighted. Aidan had been startled anew by how young his wife looked, how easily charmed she was with the world and all it had to offer.

Even more startling? The creature that was observing their approach. It was enormous, with horns that stretched away from its head and eyes that looked extremely intelligent and slightly bored. Shaggy clumps of hair hung off its body and its cloven feet stomped in the grass. It turned and ambled away, a great hulking body, and Aidan wondered if the few strands of electric wire that hung between it and them were enough.

"Let's check out the barn," Jessica said. The smell as they approached was bovine with a slight hint of other—Aidan couldn't place it. Each buffalo had its own open stall, and many of them were sacked out on what looked like—"Are those waterbeds?" he asked out loud, incredulous.

"Sure are," answered a voice, and the family turned to find a young man in work clothes and brown boots watching them with a bemused expression. "You wouldn't want to snooze on hard concrete, would you?"

"Well, no, but why not hay or, what, shavings? Wouldn't you use shavings in an animal's stall?" Aidan asked.

"Moo," Apple reminded everyone.

"Waterbeds are better for their joints, and they're actually easier to clean. Plastic. Just washes right off." The farmer gestured toward the rest of the barn. "Give you a tour?" He turned to lead the small family deeper into the depths of his barn, his pride in the place both obvious and steadfast.

Aidan slammed back into the kitchen at the Happy Valley where his frittata was just about on the verge of burning. "No, you don't," he scolded the pan of eggs, rescuing the meal at the last second and layering the slices of mozzarella over the top.

That day at the farm had been a good day. Sunshine, the smell of green fields and cared-for animals, and, by the end, the conviction Aidan had gained that mozzarella should only ever be made with buffalo milk. And on the way home, Jessica had found a small buffalo troll in a gift shop in the local downtown. Another one to add to her collection.

Rebah closed the door to her room and sighed with relief at being alone for a little while. She had announced her intention to nap so that she could recover from getting up in the tiny hours of the morning for the admittedly spectacular hot-air balloon sunrise, but, really, she needed to get some work done. Her bosses at FEOR Media Company had been texting her repeatedly with orders to call them at her earliest convenience, and while she would have loved to dispatch a two-word answer ("Always inconvenienced . . ."), she did have that pesky professional obligation to take care of.

"Rebah!" Frank crowed into the phone. She held it away from her ear in annoyance. "How's tricks? Digging up plenty of dirt?"

"Dirt? Yeah, sure, Frank. Lots of dirt. Practically a pig farm around here. Dirt like you wouldn't believe. Have you been getting my photos?" She absentmindedly played with the beaded fringe hanging from the edge of the bedside lamp. It was a lovely lamp, and Rebah could tell it came from someplace authentic. None of that fake chic in this place.

"Listen, Trevor here—you know Trevor, right? Trevor had this great idea for a regular takedown for your blogs. It's a list, right, but not like your Top 10 lists, because this list would be all about the vastly overrated—and let us not forget expensive—tourist traps that mar our great global economy. In fact . . . it's brilliant. Because it's about everything that's overrated, we'll call the column *Over It!* Get it? Overrated, *Over It!* This will destroy businesses. I can't even tell you how excited this makes me."

Rebah pulled the phone away from her ear again and looked at it incredulously. This was her life?

"Listen, Frank, I don't know, this sounds pretty—"

"Rebah, you're not getting it. *Over It!* is the key. It's what's going to put you back on the map. I mean, sure, keep your *Rambling with Rebah* for your, you know, current readers, but *Over It!* is the kind of thing to go viral, to be made into memes, to bring in those advertising dollars. It's going to be huge. Huge!"

Rebah considered. When did the Internet get so mean? When did outrage become the highest form of entertainment? When she published her first blog post ten years ago—all about this campground she'd found by accident, tucked away in the Colorado foothills, where you had your choice of woven hammocks strung between poplar trees—people were still nice to each other. Readers wanted to be charmed. They didn't want to be yelled at or disparaged. They weren't out for hospitality blood, or any other kind of blood.

And now? Was this really what people wanted? This was a few steps beyond Rebah's signature sarcasm. Even her bad reviews had a thread of humanity—most of them anyway. But an actual list of all the things terribly wrong with a place? That was too much. But it was hard to argue with Frank's data. Numbers didn't lie, right?

Frank was still droning on about *Over It!*, so Rebah had to interrupt. "Frank, listen. Give me a week to think about it. I mean, this is really a big step toward the dark side for me. I don't want to alienate any of my readers. And I've got to say, my instincts are really shooting up warning flags."

"Rebah, I'm not sure you understand. Instinct really isn't what we pay you for."

There it was again—control. She was being controlled by money. "Right, well, you are paying me for my content, and if I don't feel good about producing that content, we have a problem."

"Yes. We do have a distinct problem." Frank fell quiet on the other end of the line and Rebah wondered what his facial expression was. She imagined he looked . . . stern? Disappointed? Frustrated? No. He had probably put her on mute and was talking to someone else in his office. Maybe he was talking to that numbskull Stewart.

"Okay, Frank, I know, I know. I should trust your business sense, which is far more honed than mine." She didn't really believe that. "Give me a week to think it through. There's a lot of logistics."

"Logistics is just another word for an excuse. You have until tomorrow." And the phone cut off.

Rebah didn't really hate anyone. She was excellent at acting tough and calling people out on their bull, and she had no patience with incompetence, but seeking out problems with the places she stayed for the sole purpose of making her articles go viral was a whole new level of gross that she really, really didn't feel comfortable with.

Even through the closed door of her room, she could smell something delicious cooking downstairs. Funny—even though Aidan was the chef, he didn't seem to spend much time in the kitchen. And being there, she'd discovered that even though that long-ago weekend had largely disappeared from her recollection, sensory memories of his food had seeped into her consciousness—smoked pork loin and garlic-parsley fries, crabmeat pastries, the elegantly spun dessert that tasted like a lemon cloud. Why wasn't she seeing food like that this weekend?

Rebah settled into a wingback chair by the window and gazed at the backyard. The garden was overgrown, but it looked like someone had made an attempt to get it into shape recently. She liked the idea of a yard-to-table theme—Aidan could pull it off if he put some effort into it. Munching spinach greens that had been growing twenty feet away just thirty minutes before was a meal she could spin into something magical in a blog post.

And that falling-down barn. What was it about potentially fatal structures in weathered gray that was so compelling? She wanted to explore that building, even though all exterior appearances warned her off. She'd have to ask Aidan about it tonight at dinner.

The band was playing on the patio, unplugged. It looked like they were just friends hanging out and playing music. The guitarist strummed a few chords, and the singer broke into a rap while the drummer tapped out a beat on a tiny xylophone he held in his lap. The bassist grinned and shimmied as he provided a driving foundational rhythm. The effect was funky and magical, a mixed call and answer that blended like perfect flavors. Where had Aidan found this band? They were so much fun.

Rebah's stomach growled. How long had it been since the half-baked breakfast sandwich she'd eaten in the hot-air balloon? She was starving. Time to find some lunch.

Chapter 15

*A*idan heard a car pull into the driveway and he glanced out the kitchen window to see Jax Pitts's silver Porsche come to a halt with a spray of gravel, much of which landed in the front border gardens. "What the . . ." he muttered. He left the frittata on the table and headed out to meet the rascal before he could infiltrate the house.

"Ah, Mr. Cisneros. Just the person I was hoping to find here." Pitts was already out of his car and peering at the marigolds.

"I do live here, you know. Where else would I be?"

"Yes, super funny. Charming wit. A very delicate sense of sarcasm you've got there. I was in the area and thought I'd check in." He didn't seem inclined to offer any more of an explanation as to why he was standing at the foot of Aidan's front steps.

"Is that usual behavior for a realtor?" Aidan asked. "Especially when this is the sale you swore wouldn't happen unless there was a sudden change in circumstances?"

"Extra-special care for extra-special people." Pitts smiled without a hint of kindness in his face. He looked up and around Aidan's body and tilted his head. "Huh. Looks like someone's made an effort."

"You have no idea the effort I make on a daily basis."

"Yes, of course, but I mean the place. It looks . . . different. And is that music I hear? And voices? I've got to admit your Happy Valley seems quite a bit jollier than it did the last time I was here."

"Yeah, well, we've got some guests staying, got a band in, and we're showing everyone a good time. It's what we do here." Aidan knew he should be finding some selling points to lay on the guy, but he couldn't stand the man. Since when did people become so inauthentic? Was it always this way? And it wasn't just Pitts, though he was a special breed of entitled human. Aidan saw that behavior in many of his guests. People who traveled with the weight of need. Who demanded the world bend to their inclinations. Who wanted an experience, but not a vastly different experience from the one they'd get in the comfort of their own home.

But some people weren't like that. Rebah, for example. She had a thirst for experience, for adventure. For joy.

"Huh. Mind if I pop around and take a look?" And with that, Pitts was off, practically sprinting down the stone path toward the backyard as though he didn't want to wait for fear Aidan would say no. Which Aidan wouldn't have done anyway. But he certainly followed the realtor close behind. What the hell was he up to?

"Aids!" called Kye, who was tightening the bolts on the metal frame holding up Apple's electronic keyboard.

"Your friends call you *AIDS*?" Pitts couldn't contain the scorn in his voice.

"No, they don't. No one calls me *AIDS*."

"Where did all these people come from?" Pitts gestured at the yard where the band was playing, where Mariah was weaving brightly colored wool with a handloom, where Boutique lounged on a chaise wearing not much, her smooth skin goose-pimpled in the spring sun. The ex-big-game hunter and her ex-missionary partner were practicing a waltz on the porch and the con artist was trying to juggle while his boyfriend was trying just as hard to foil the trick.

"Ahhh . . . all over. You know, from everywhere. It's what happens at a B&B."

"Huh."

"Listen, I'd love to stand around and chat about nothing, but as you can see, we're pretty busy. In fact, I've got a frittata I need to serve before it gets cold. So, if you don't mind?" Without waiting to see if Pitts would follow, Aidan turned and headed back to the front of the house. He wanted him gone. What if Apple saw him and asked why he was sniffing around?

Pitts did follow and finally made his big reveal at his car. "So, I didn't stop by today because I was in the neighborhood."

"Really."

"I might have a buyer for you."

"Really?" *I should be happy*, Aidan thought. *This is the whole goal, right?* "A buyer as in . . ."

"Someone interested in buying your place. For money. And I tell you, I like what I see. Guests, activity, a general sense of aliveness. This is good, this is what you needed to do. Good job."

Jeez, was this guy going to pat him on the top of the head? Good luck with that. Aidan stood at least a foot taller than Pitts.

"Let me report back—all positive, of course—and we'll be in touch." Pitts slid behind the wheel of his Porsche, revved the engine, and bolted down the driveway at a dangerous speed.

Dude.

"Who was that dude?" asked Apple, coming up behind him.

"Who?"

"The guy who just left."

"Sorry, what?"

"Dad, why are you being weird?"

"Oh! I almost forgot. Are you hungry?"

"I mean, yeah, I was just on my way to get a sandwich. These caters can be pretty good when they're not mixing up the order."

"How about something a little fancier than sandwiches?"

"Interested . . ."

"Okay, come with me."

In the kitchen, they both automatically inhaled the delicious scent. "Wait, what smells so good?" Apple asked.

"Voilà," announced Aidan as he lifted the cover off the frittata pan.

"Dad. You cooked? This smells amazing. Wait, did you use powdered eggs? You know I hate that stuff."

"No! No powder! This, my dear, is the real thing. Farm-fresh eggs and cream plus a bunch of other stuff I threw in. Food of the gods, right here."

"I'm gobsmacked. Why? What, like, moved you to cook? Because it's kind of been a while."

"It's another thing coming unburied this weekend, I guess." Truth was, Aidan had no idea why he'd suddenly picked up the knife and the whisk and made a meal. But it felt amazing. It felt like home. "Okay, let's fill our mouths with something other than words." He slid the frittata onto a platter and used a butter knife to cut two slices, which he moved onto two plates while Apple retrieved forks. They made their way out to the back porch where the music was still going and people were laughing and munching oven-roasted ham, marinated artichokes, pesto turkey, and almond-encrusted salmon sandwiches made on thick slabs of ciabatta, focaccia, and multigrain roll. But the sandwiches, however fabulous, were no match for Aidan's frittata.

"Dad, I know why we're doing all of these things this weekend," Apple said, surprising him.

"Wait, you do?"

"Yeah. I'm not stupid. I know you've got it in your head that our time here is just about up."

How could Apple know that he was trying to sell the Happy Valley?

"I mean, I'm going to college. That's a huge change. This place isn't going to be the same without me."

Ah. Perhaps Apple knew less than she thought.

"But you've still got Kye and Sharon and the twins. And you need to keep this place going. You know, for Mom."

Those were not the words he wanted to hear. Apple found a spot on the table next to Mariah and dug into her frittata. "Dad made it," Apple told her. Mariah looked toward Aidan, raising her eyebrows in a way that let him know she was impressed. Aidan stayed by the door, feeling like he'd accidentally stepped off the edge of a deep, malignant crater and was now dealing with the sensation of falling forever.

"Oh, wow, frittata?" asked Rebah, appearing beside him.

"Ah, yes. Um, sorry. Sorry, I was a million miles away in my head just now."

"That's a pretty big head," she smiled.

"No, yeah, I see what you mean." Aidan couldn't shake the feeling that every mistake he'd ever made was coming to light. But he had to stick to the plan, right? He had to sell the place. Even if Apple thought he should keep it, she didn't actually have any awareness of their financial straits or what it cost him to even pretend to keep the Happy Valley open. She had no idea how he stayed awake at night worrying about her future, his future, the future of Kye's family—even Milly's future, for crying out loud.

"Ooookay, you are obviously still a million miles away. I'm just going to make myself a sandwich for lunch."

"Hey, you want to try a bite of this?" Wait, what did he just do? He'd had no intention of offering the lunch he'd made to Rebah. He'd figured the frittata was special, only for family. Everyone else could attack the picnic buffet. But it felt instinctual to offer Rebah the food he'd made.

"Really? Is that what smelled so amazing in the house?" She reached out, nabbed his fork, and before he really understood what was happening, she'd picked a bite off his plate and popped it in her mouth. "Oh, my God. That is amazing. Now, let me ask, do you go by a recipe or do you just make this sort of thing up in your head?"

"Recipe. No, scratch that. My head. Yup, everything just comes out of my head. I don't know why I said recipe. Listen, there's a whole frittata in the kitchen, just help yourself. Even better, take mine. Take this plate. Take it!" Aidan thrust the plate at Rebah, who barely managed to clutch it before he let go and took off back into the house.

She watched him go, surprised. Then she shrugged and did indeed tuck into the frittata on the plate. Delicious.

Back in the kitchen, Aidan packed the rest of the frittata in a plastic container and scrubbed the frittata pan to within an inch of its polish. *What was that all about?* he scolded himself under his breath. *Too much,* he decided. Too damn much going on. Between stupid Pitts showing up and Apple's revelation and the gulp in his chest when Rebah leaned close to grasp his fork—it was just too damn much.

Apple, unbeknownst to both Aidan and Rebah, had seen the whole exchange. *Interesting,* she thought.

Aidan hadn't had an actual date in the five years since her mom died. There was one woman who had been invited to dinner one night—what was her name? Jaelynn? Geri-Lynn? Something kind of country music-ish? Aidan had met her at this adult education class he'd taken on investment strategies (an ill-conceived attempt at expanding his portfolio, but it turned out you need money in the first place to be able to invest). Jaelynn/Geri-Lynn had sat next to him and proved to be a distraction from his obvious financial dilemmas, and at the end of the course, as all the students were saying goodbye, he'd asked her, without even looking up from his phone: "Dinner?"

And she'd said yes, and the evening had been a resounding disaster. Jaelynn/Geri-Lynn knew Aidan was supposed to be an accomplished chef, and her disappointment at the food he'd served her was evident on her face. Because frozen ravioli, boiled and smothered in red sauce from a jar, really wasn't the way to impress anyone. And things had only gone downhill when she'd begun asking about the carved wooden trolls in the glass case. "Where's this one from? And this one? And this one?" It was like she had been hired by an estate manager to make an inventory.

Aidan had answered every question with as few syllables as possible, and the dispassionate tension was palpable. Apple, serving as audience to the train wreck, cringed the entire evening and breathed a gusty sigh of relief when Jaelynn/Geri-Lynn finally offered up a tight smile and claimed she had to be up early the next morning for hot yoga and should therefore be getting home. It was seven o'clock.

Later, watching her dad stack the dishes at the dining room table and carry them to the kitchen where he left them piled in a monument to defeat, Apple thought maybe she understood why the evening had been such a failure. She saw him bend his head, chin to chest, and recognized his posture as that of someone who missed the person he was still in love with. Deeply.

So to see the way he reacted to Rebah was very interesting. Even as the friction between them reared up regularly, there was something tender there, too. She could see that her dad's face changed in a certain way when he was near Rebah. His eyebrows lifted and the tense lines usually found around his mouth smoothed into an expression of interest. Or maybe even hope.

And Rebah, for all the bluster and polish that she obviously wore very comfortably around crowds, was really stripped back to a singular essence when she was talking alone with Aidan. She looked capable of pain in those moments, as though anything thrown at her would stick, as opposed to the Teflon aura she usually sported.

Apple wondered. She thought. She scraped the last of her lunch onto her fork and looked around at her friends, old and new, as they occupied both their personas. People can be comfortable shifting from character to character, she thought, but not too comfortable. People are happiest when they're playing only themselves. When they're authentic. But you can't be authentic around certain people. She thought of her boyfriend, Kai, and watched as he strummed a new rhythm on his guitar, then took several moments to help the bassist get the same rhythm. She could be authentic with Kai. Could her dad be authentic with Rebah?

She stood suddenly and turned to Rebah, who was delicately scooping the end of the frittata into her mouth. "This is fantastic, Apple. I can't believe your dad let me have his lunch. Wow, he is a really amazing chef, isn't he?"

"Yep, totally amazing. So, Rebah, for this afternoon's excursion, we've got something special planned."

"Another excursion? Boy, you guys really go all out, don't you? Where are we headed?"

"It's less where are we headed and more where are you headed. This is a slightly more exclusive outing. Just you and my dad."

"I'm not sure—"

"No, it's fine. He wants to share a very special place with you. He doesn't want a lot of people knowing about it."

"He doesn't want a lot of people to know about it, but he's willing to share it with a travel blogger?"

"Oh, yeah, I see how that's confusing." Apple tried to think around that wrench.

"If he really wants to show me something, I can promise not to write about it. I mean, I get it. There are places that just aren't meant for general consumption. I've been known to leave out a morsel or two from my blog."

"Okay, excellent. Let me go see if he's ready."

Apple went in search of her dad, sure that once she sprang her plan for him to take Rebah hiking, he'd think it was brilliant. She knew he was ready for a break from the hordes of people who'd been at their place for the past twenty-four hours. He was a total introvert. He'd welcome the opportunity to escape! And to escape with Rebah—that would be even better. She found him in the kitchen, washing dishes.

"You know, I think Milly would be happy to do that for you if you want," she said.

He looked up and shrugged. "Actually, I always liked doing dishes. I know you might not guess that from my behavior of the past few years, but I find it . . . calming. Like meditation. I like it when things are in order."

"Dad, you've never meditated in your life."

"But I've done plenty of dishes. I'm pretty sure it's the same feeling. Kye meditates, and afterward he's totally mellow, like I'm totally mellow right now. It's all about the brain."

"Uh-huh. Whatever. Look, I had an idea."

"Oh, God, is this to do with more people doing more things, all of us together? I'm getting a little burnt out. I'm thinking we just wait until dinner and then have more music afterward and that could be it. I mean, that's all super impressive, right?"

"Or you could get out of here for a few hours. Escape the masses. Go for a hike up Atlas Peak!"

"Actually, that sounds amazing."

"And take Rebah with you!"

"Wait, what?"

"No, it's perfect. You get some quiet time, she gets to be impressed. It's all good."

"I don't know, honey. That sounds way too much like . . . a date."

"Noooo, that's ridiculous."

"What's ridiculous?" asked Kye as he came through the swinging kitchen door carrying a couple gallons of milk from the local market.

"Nothing!" yelped Aidan.

"My dad taking Rebah on a hiking trip."

"Oh, man, a hike sounds amazing. I could use a break," Kye said, setting down the vegetables.

"No, not you. Not me. Not anybody else. Just Dad and Rebah."

"See?" said Aidan. "Ridiculous."

"Actually . . ." mused Kye. "I can see it."

"See?" Apple crowed with triumph.

"No, no seeing. No hiking."

"Here, let me pack you some snacks. Sparkling water, the mozzarella, some sun-dried tomatoes, crackers. Perfect." Kye was throwing together the quintessential lovers' picnic without giving Aidan time to object. Apple was thrilled. This was perfect.

"Whoa. Okay, let me think." Aidan poured himself a glass of water and glared at the two of them over the rim as he drank. "Okay, I agree to go on a hike with Rebah, but only if you two stop assuming this is a romantic thing." He banged the empty glass on top of the wooden table. "I mean it. I'm not ready for any kind of involvement."

Apple and Kye both looked at him with wide eyes, as though the thought hadn't occurred to them. "Dad, you're the only one in the room thinking about dates. Me and Kye? We just want Rebah to be impressed so she'll write a great review and you'll get your business back. Right, Kye?"

Kye looked uncomfortable, but he nodded emphatically. "Right."

Aidan sighed. "Okay, Kye. Make that picnic a little less romance and a little more functional. I'll go see if Rebah's up for it."

He found her coming inside from the backyard, carrying her empty plate, which he took from her. "So, Rebah. How would you like to see a view of Napa Valley you've probably never seen before?"

"I'm always up for new perspectives," she said. "Just let me change my shoes, since I'm guessing ballet flats won't do the trick?"

"Excellent guess. And Kye is packing a picnic."

"Oh, wow, more food? Because that frittata was amazing. You really are talented."

"Well, that's kind, but really, it's hard to screw up eggs and cheese." Aidan swallowed hard, thinking of all the powdered eggs he'd served over the past few years. Turned out it was pretty easy to screw up eggs and cheese.

Rebah went up to change her shoes and Aidan was left alone for the first time in what felt like a week. Damn, he was tired. A hike would actually feel really good. He let his gaze roam around the room, settling on the cabinet full of carved wooden trolls. Those had been Jessica's hobby. Wherever they traveled, she found them—in gift shops, museums, organic grocery co-ops, one even sitting on its own at the bottom of a slide at a playground where they'd taken Apple when she wasn't even a year old.

He'd never understood his wife's fascination with them. For someone who was sweet, kind, and empathic, ugly little ogres didn't seem like her decoration of choice.

"They're misunderstood," she'd told him once. They were at a rented cottage on Lake Berryessa for a long weekend away. This was before Apple, before Kye, before the Happy Valley, before they really even knew each other—they'd been married six months and were still getting the feel for each other's particular space.

Marriage wasn't exactly what Aidan had expected. After his parents died when he was young, he had lived with his grandmother, who had never married, so his impressions of being a husband came mostly from TV sitcoms and the occasional dinner at a friend's house. He was happy with just his grandmother as his family and didn't really see the benefit in having two adults around to tell him what to do. But Jessica had taught him from the beginning of their relationship that mutual respect, listening, compassion, and honesty were the goals, marriage was generally a good thing, and living with someone meant compromise. He loved her from deep within himself, so he was on board with whatever she wanted. But the first six months had been difficult for him. Being married was way more intense than being a boyfriend had ever been.

"They remind me how easy it is to accept what others think of you as the ultimate truth," Jessica went on about the trolls. She was braiding her hair while they sat on the porch and listened to loons calling through the evening dimness.

"But you've never been ugly," Aidan answered. He was sipping a beer.

"You haven't known me forever, and besides, ugliness—and beauty—is a construct. Who decides what's ugly? In some countries, I might be hideous."

"We'll avoid those places."

"No, it's good to have different perspectives. What I'm trying to say is that it's all relative. Lots of people think trolls are ugly, and maybe they're right if they're thinking of those awful plastic ones in rainbow colors. But I think trolls are beautiful."

"And the trolls? How do they rate themselves?" Aidan reached behind his chair and felt for the next beer he'd stashed there. He popped the top and pretended not to see Jessica's quizzical look. They were on vacation, after all. This was what people did. They drank beer and had conversations.

"The trolls refuse to acknowledge any rating system. They simply exist." Jessica laughed and tossed her braid over a shoulder. "So, let's talk about that house in Napa. I really think we could make it into something special."

A sudden burst of people into the living room tossed Aidan back into the present. "A game is afoot!" Mackenzie called out. Aidan shook off the memory of sitting on a porch with his wife, a steely-gray lake stretched before them in the dimming dusk.

"Actually, guys, sorry, you're going to have to entertain yourselves for a while," he said, wondering how he might be able to extract himself and Rebah from the crowd without anyone else demanding to join them. Mariah's actor friends were doing an amazing job in their roles as weekend guests, but, jeez, he could really use a break.

"But it's all arranged!" whined Jasper.

"Mariah called in a favor," added Buttercup, hanging onto Michel's arm. Michel nodded and smiled a chill smile.

"What kind of a favor?" Aidan asked suspiciously. This could only mean yet another transfer of a large amount of money from his bank account to someone else's.

"Have you heard of the Independent Acres Winery?" Mariah explained, gesturing with her knife. "Over past Route 14?"

"Is that the make-your-own-wine place?"

"Yes! Isn't that delightful? You get to be a part of the process from the very beginning. That's their motto: 'From first pick to last sip.'"

Aidan couldn't really think of anything he'd rather skip than a trip to a DIY winery. Why be forced to have a hand in the process if you weren't partaking of the end result? A cooking demonstration was way more up his alley.

"Oh!" said Rebah when she reentered the living room, complete with a chic pair of soft hiking shoes. "Are we all going on the hike?"

"Ah, yeah, Rebah, about that. Apparently, some of my guests have decided to arrange a visit to a local do-it-yourself winery. 'From first pick to last sip,' that's their slogan. Cute, right? But we don't have to tag along . . ." Aidan trailed off, feeling awkward all of a sudden.

Rebah seemed to hesitate before answering. Aidan wondered what she was thinking. Had she really been looking forward to hiking alone with him? She couldn't be interested in him, could she? Something had shifted when they stood near each other in the lineup at the horse farm. They were totally wrong for each other. But there was something in the way she looked at him, a shy upward turn of her face when they were having a real conversation, as though she cared what he thought of her.

Ridiculous. He'd spent the last year hating her because of that review she'd posted of his place. You didn't just suddenly fall for someone you'd invested energy in hating.

Still, he found himself wishing Rebah would choose hiking alone with him over another group excursion.

"A winery sounds fun," she said and Aidan carefully kept his face completely neutral.

"Onward, then!" called out Jameson, and the crowd poured out of the B&B and piled into the dusty van.

Chapter 16

As with everywhere in Napa, the smell of grapes was the first thing the passengers noticed as they pulled into a parking space at Independent Acres Winery and threw the van doors open wide.

Everyone had decided to come on this excursion.

And the place was a treat. The vineyard sprawled in all directions and the winery itself was both sleek and architecturally interesting—stone columns framed the front entrance and a wall of windows peeked in at a tasting room, which was well-designed with tall tables and stools, couches, and a napping cat curled up in a basket by the farthest window.

The B&B guests made a motley line of amateur winemakers as they shimmied over to the outdoor tasting table, which was well-populated with bottles and glasses under a blue tent in the front yard. "We start with a goal!" exclaimed a man who was apparently their designated host, a tall man with white hair and a habit of clapping his hands. "My name is Michaels and I will be your guide. I truly believe it's easier to visualize the process if you know the end result. Now, gather round, claim your glass, sniff, and sip."

"Or gulp," snarked Jameson.

"As if anyone wouldn't already know the end result," snorted Verity. The two leaned against each other in an effort to hold back their giggles.

Aidan watched from his post at the other end of the table next to Rebah. Were they already tipsy? Had someone opened a bottle back at the house?

"That's right, everyone, taste," Michaels instructed. "Everyone, taste. Anyone here prefer a red? We've got a lovely pinot you might want to try. Anyone?"

Rebah reached out to claim a glass and nabbed one for Aidan, who took the offering but didn't raise the wine to his lips after she clinked her glass against his and murmured, "Cheers." She didn't seem to notice. She took a long sip of her wine, and her eyes closed in a look that Aidan recognized from his own days of drinking: relief. "This is a nice one," she remarked, holding the pinot up to the light to check for residue and viscosity. "I generally prefer the heavier reds, but I could drink this."

Michaels clapped his hands. "Now, the first step in our winemaking process is, of course, the harvest. The grapes you will be harvesting today are not the grapes you will be drinking—it takes longer than the hours we have in one afternoon to make wine correctly—but you will get an experiential sense of each of the five stages of winemaking as we venture onto the grounds. Tallyho!" He gestured toward a fleet of golf carts. Jasper and Mackenzie led the way and the rest of the crowd followed, Aidan and Rebah bringing up the tail.

Aidan had always loved vineyards—the smell, the orderly rows, the dirt, the pure growingness of the place—but even he had to admit this vineyard was exceptionally well cared for. The grapes were golden and lush, practically dripping off sturdy vines that held themselves fast to the fencing. For early spring, this was an incredible harvest.

As the golf carts made their way deeper into a field, Michaels called back so everyone behind him could hear. "You are all probably wondering why we are harvesting grapes in April, traditionally known as the cruelest month. These grapes have been encouraged in ways not quite found in nature, purely for the sake of our guests' enjoyment.

Usually, we harvest grapes in late summer, early fall. But today, we offer you magic."

It was really an impressive vineyard.

"When do we get to stomp on them?" asked Jasper to everyone's giggly delight.

"Tut-tut," scolded Michaels in a way that made it understood he had heard any and every joke that might be made about winemaking. "Let's not get ahead of ourselves."

The three golf carts carrying the Happy Valley guests came to a stop alongside a particularly vibrant row of translucent white grapes and the gang rolled off their magnificent electric steeds and claimed one of the dozens of woven baskets made available along the edge of the vineyard. Rebah looked delighted at the rustic design of the receptacles, charmed by the winemaking adventure. Aidan noticed she still held her glass in one hand, perhaps hoping for a refill.

But why not? Aidan shook off the feeling of disapproval. Rebah was a grown woman. Let her make her own decisions.

Michaels explained how to properly pick the grapes. "Cradle the babies as you would a new lover, holding them secure but not stifled, supportive but not stymied, and gently pull, pull, pull, until pop! You are now holding a sphere of pure and unadulterated joy."

Jasper and Mackenzie discreetly fed each other a grape or two, their fingers lingering on each other's lips. Aidan glanced up at them just as they stole a kiss and beamed at each other with delighted eyes. Aidan felt a pang of longing to be close like that with someone again. That wasn't an unfamiliar ache, though. And this time? He was surprised to find that images of Jessica didn't automatically follow.

Rebah had noticed the love between the two men as well, but she seemed distracted by the juggling act she was performing with her wineglass and basket. "Do you think they'll offer more wine before the end of the tour?" she whispered to Aidan.

"You can always lick off your feet after the grape stomping," he answered.

Rebah's face looked shocked, but then it broke into a smile. "I may be thirsty, but I'm not desperate." She pushed him gently on the arm with an elbow.

Michaels directed them again. "Once you have a little bundle of babies gathered in your basket, gently deposit them into the communal tractor bed and they will be transported with minimal jostling to the crushing center, where we will next perform our winemaking duties."

"Isn't all of this supposed to be mechanized?" asked Buttercup. "You know, for . . . sanitary reasons?" You could tell she wanted to whip out a disinfectant wipe. Michel produced a handkerchief from his vest pocket for her to scrub her hands on.

"Well, yes, but that wouldn't make for a very interesting make-your-own-wine excursion, now would it?" Michaels clasped his hands. "We do try to imagine ourselves hurtled back a hundred years or so when sanitation was not a priority and being one with the earth, with the grapes, with the process was. Now, shall we move on? We do require anyone entering the vats to wear a pair of specially provided booties."

"Wait," demanded Mariah. "We are actually encouraged to stomp on the grapes? With our feet?"

"With your bootied feet, yes."

Mariah's eyes lit up and her hand wandered over to where her hunting knife usually lay against her thigh. But Aidan had made a special request that she leave it home when venturing with the group into public places. You could tell, though, that she wanted to add a slicing and dicing step to the process of grape manipulation. This was a very primal outing.

The group wended their way past several more rows of grapes until they came to an old red barn with a long, low roof.

Aidan walked beside Rebah and kept stealing glances at her profile. She seemed so relaxed, such a different person from the stressed-out witch who'd run into him just a few days ago in San Francisco. He was happy to spend time with her. The image he'd held of her for the past year of an angry, spiteful, mean drunk was so completely wrong, it made him wonder what else in his life he'd gotten wrong.

She stumbled on a clump of dirt and Aidan instinctively reached out to steady her. The skin of her upper arm felt soft and electric, and for a moment he couldn't breathe. She looked up at him, her face open and joyful. "Hey, thanks for catching me," she murmured.

"Any time. Really." He eased his thumb along her arm for a moment, enjoying the reaction on her face, the look of confusion mixed with wonder.

And then he let his hand drop. Neither of them noticed Mariah some steps behind, aiming her phone and snapping a picture of the two of them smiling at each other.

In the barn, the first stop was the sorting table, where they picked through a wide tray of grapes, though not the ones they'd just harvested. "We only want the fruit. We only want the fruit," Michaels murmured as he strolled behind his flock, who were putting their fingers to the test in attempts to separate the sharp stems from the soft grapes. His words were a strange sort of incantation that had a lulling effect on the group—even Mariah's eyes seemed to relax into a kind of stasis.

"We only want the fruit," Rebah whispered to Aidan, and he giggled. Not that it was a funny line, but when she said it she made it sound so . . . sexual. She looked at him with raised eyebrows and an impossibly innocent face.

"Focus," reminded Michaels. He rubbed two fingers of his left hand along his hairline, an obviously impatient gesture. "Have we made an acceptable amount of progress? Shall we continue on?"

"Ready for stomping," Verity announced.

The stomping quarters were a large, cavernous room with metal vats lining the walls, each with a trough underneath and hoses leading to a collecting container at the end of the row. A box of disposable booties sat near a bench, and the members of the party tossed off their shoes and covered their feet in preparation. Low-slung bars served as handles to access the vats, but Jasper and Mackenzie were already helping each other up and over the side of the first tub, grimacing as they lowered themselves into the grapes. "Is it supposed to feel quite so disgusting?" asked Jasper.

"I feel like I'm crushing tiny embryo skulls," moaned Mackenzie.

"Indeed, it's not the most pleasant of sensations," admitted Michaels. "That's a common misconception, that treading on grapes is a kind of aphrodisiac or, at the very least, a way to ease bunions. But, no, in reality it's really quite obnoxious." He visibly shivered. "So, everyone, don your booties and pop into your vats! Two per container, please. Otherwise things go awry."

There was a mad dash to claim containers—apparently, the thought of crunching embryo heads with your booted feet was a tempting one.

Aidan and Rebah wound up paired at the last vat. "After you," he suggested after they'd taken off their shoes and socks and tugged on the white plastic coverings. Rebah, he noticed, had shiny purple toenails.

She ignored his outstretched hand and practically leapt into the vat on her own. "Ewwwww!" she squealed as her feet sank into the grapes, a shudder running through her body and out through her shoulders. "This is really horrible!"

Aidan followed her in and tried to hide the grimace that sprang to his cheeks as he, too, came into close contact with the grapes. "You remember that old show *I Love Lucy*? That episode where she's stomping grapes? I think she had a lot more fun than we're having. I suspect we've been sold a faulty excursion package."

"I mean, wine really is a special, wonderful drink, and perhaps this is simply the appropriate sacrifice grapes need to make to produce it for us. Only through pain comes beauty and all that, right?"

"I wonder if one can purchase cruelty-free wine that's been made with purely voluntary grapes?"

"Even if we could, I bet it wouldn't taste as good," Rebah pondered.

They stomped and slid their way from one side of the vat to the other, as all around them other Happy Valley guests whooped and exclaimed at the weird sensation under their soles. Once, Rebah slid in the grape mush and if Aidan hadn't reached out to put his hands on her waist, she would've gone over. "Um, thanks," she said with a blush.

"Just didn't want you to get juiced."

"Oh, I plan on it after this."

Michaels clapped his hands and called his troops out of their vats, suggesting they let their feet drip off a bit on black mats that were spread out for draining purposes. They could see golden-reddish juice running down the trough and through the tubes as it pooled in the collecting container. "You know, I'm not sure it's wise to see how the wine is made. It's a little too close to the sausage-making process," Michel mused in his deep voice. Aidan realized those were the first words he'd heard from the jazz man in a while.

"That was the most strenuous part of our journey," Michaels called. "Next stop is actually quite boring. The fermenting agents are added, but due to, ahem, regulations, we are only able to offer you the opportunity to press a button—it's all automatic. And then we do some bottling, and finally we end in the tasting room."

"Tasting room, excellent." Rebah brandished her wineglass that, unbelievably, she'd managed to carry with her this far.

"Anyone want a sip of wine juice?" asked Michaels. A few people clustered around the holding container as he operated a spigot and handed out tiny porcelain cups of the liquid from within.

Rebah sniffed, crinkled her nose, and tasted. "Erm," she judged.

This was a pretty consistent reaction.

"My feet still feel weird," said Jasper. "I can't get past the sensation that I've done something violent to those poor grapes."

The fermenting step was as boring as Michaels had promised, with everyone taking turns pushing a button and watching through a clear plexiglass wall as an assembly-line arm dumped a cache of chemicals into lined-up barrels. "I think we're ready to reunite with our original impressions of the drink of the gods," Rebah muttered.

"Understood." Michaels nodded, breathing an obvious sigh of relief, and led the group to a cozy room with one wall opened to the fresh spring air, the vineyards stretching off in the distance and blue skies promising a fair night. They settled around high-top tables and a waitress came by with a tray full of wine in gleaming glasses that the guests accepted with smiles. Aidan took a glass but simply set it in front of him on the tabletop. Rebah drank hers almost immediately and gestured to the waitress to keep her supplied. "This was lovely," she told Aidan.

"And illuminating," added Verity, who'd joined them at their table.

"And sobering," said Jameson, Verity's ever-present partner. "Darling, I feel as though we should establish a nonprofit solely for the purpose of rescuing vineyard grapes before they are pressed into a service they did not choose."

"That's a heartwarming idea, dear one, but it does seem to me that we cannot save everything that needs saving, and if we had to choose an organism to leave behind and continue to be of service, a grape might truly be the best bet."

"Huh. Have you always been this wise?" The two philanthropists gazed fondly at each other, and Rebah shifted in her seat. This was getting awkward.

"You know, I think I'm going to pick out a case or two for the B&B," said Aidan as he rose from his seat, leaving his full wineglass where it sat.

At the bar, he waited for the waitress to bring him the list of wines available for purchase. He glanced back at Rebah and discovered she'd drunk his wine. Now she was chatting animatedly with Verity and Jameson—perhaps trading notes on places they'd traveled, nonprofits they believed in, or the fate of jungle cats. Set against the glowing late afternoon vineyards, the scene before him was a reminder of what lovely things could come through if you worked hard enough.

It was also a reminder of what he might be losing.

Chapter 17

The weary winemakers trickled out of the van when they arrived back at the Happy Valley. Making wine was exhausting, especially when you felt compelled to taste so much of it after the final stage of bottling had been accomplished. Aidan watched with a half smile as his crowd of revelers made the trek up the front porch stairs and through the door. Funny how all of those people started out acting their parts, and now he was pretty sure they'd simply become whoever they'd pretended to be at the beginning.

He'd already announced that there was no sit-down dinner but that people were welcome to help themselves to the salad and appetizer bar he'd had Milly set up in the dining room and, sure enough, that's where most of the crowd headed. No one would ever guess that these apps had come out of the basement freezer where they'd been stored the past six months.

Milly had had a revelation a few hours ago and texted Aidan with the idea.

Mr. C! Dude! Your appetizer supply! In the freezer!

He'd immediately known what she meant and tapped back:

Brilliant!

There had been a moment about six months ago when Aidan had thought he'd had the energy to get back into cooking, and that moment had coincided with a neighbor calling up to see if he could help them out with a weekend barbecue by producing a load of appetizers for their guests; just an easy, friendly catering gig, nothing to be scared of. And Aidan had accepted the job, forced himself to enter the kitchen, and made a few hundred Beef Wellington bites, spicy vegetarian meatballs, Gruyère and hazelnut crackers covered in bacon jam, rosemary and garlic pinwheel cheeses, and Spanish ham croquettes, among other delectable bites. He'd been about to cart the entire shebang three houses over when the neighbor called and canceled due to a "marital disruption" that really should have been dispatched before they'd planned an intimate barbecue for two hundred. At least, that was according to the neighbor woman.

So, Aidan and Apple had eaten an excellent dinner of divine appetizers, given buckets away to Kye and Sharon and the kids, and frozen the rest.

Six months later, the appetizer bar was a hit at his faux grand celebration weekend.

Aidan hesitated on the front porch steps as he listened to the delighted exclamations coming from within. He remembered what it was like to cook for a crowd and have them enjoy it. So simple, this act of preparing food and feeding people. But Aidan knew of no greater joy, except maybe seeing his daughter happy. How could he have forgotten about this part of being a chef?

"People sound happy in there," Rebah said behind him. She, too, had lingered in the fading day. "You do a good job with this, you know. I know you think you were secondary to your wife's talents, but honestly? You're kind of the heart of this place."

"Yeah, but you weren't here when Jessica was running the show."

"True, but I heard about this place. People loved it. But look—people are loving it now. You're good at this. I've stayed at a lot of B&Bs and there's some quality that the best ones share. I don't even know what to call it, but it has nothing to do with the buildings or amenities and everything to do with the people." A burst of laughter floated from inside and swirled around them before releasing into the sunset sky. "These people love it here."

He wanted to explain that those people were hired, that their level of enjoyment had nothing to do with him and everything to do with the paycheck they'd each be receiving at the end of the weekend. But how could he? How could he reveal that the entire weekend was a lie?

"Hungry?" he asked instead.

"I could eat," she answered with a smile.

Inside, Rebah helped herself to some grappa-cured striped-bass mini pizzas and a glass of wine, then wandered out back where the band was setting up once again, tuning their instruments and nodding at each other when they hit the right note, murmuring amongst themselves about set lists and trying a new ballad. She found a spot on a bench where she marveled at how young they were, so confident and capable. So completely occupied within the sphere they belonged to. Boutique, too, who wandered through the guests with a platter on offer, chatting and laughing with people easily twice her age. When had Rebah lost that confidence? She couldn't remember the last time she'd felt like she knew what she was doing.

"Hey." Apple plopped next to her on the wooden bench, her own plate of appetizers balanced in her hands. "Everything good? How was the winery?"

"Oh, man, this is so good. Your dad is a genius with food, you know that, right?"

"Well, I know he has his days. And this day is one of them. Did you try the salmon pâté?"

"Actually, I'm planning to eat about a bucketful."

Apple popped a choice bite into her mouth and chewed thoughtfully while more people gathered around the yard. The band slipped into a drawling tune that was heavy on the bass, and Kai started his low, growling lyrics that, even if you couldn't understand the words themselves, seemed to convey a sense of righteous indignation and immense sadness.

"He's good," Rebah commented.

"Yup. That's my guy." Apple smiled. "I wish he had a little teensy bit more motivation. I mean, I know he's only nineteen, but music is a young industry. If he doesn't get his act together, he's going to miss his chance."

"Well, plenty of people make it big at a later age. Look at Sheryl Crow. She was thirty-two when she finally had a hit. And she was a woman. Your man? He's got time." Rebah considered for a moment. "But wait, I thought these guys were some kind of successful boy band from Europe."

Apple coughed around her mouthful of pâté. "Well. I mean. Who gets to define success, right? And, yeah, we're together, but it's usually a long-distance thing. Which is good since I'm going to be gone next year anyway." *Saved it*, she thought, kicking herself.

"Gone?"

"I'm going to Barnard." Apple couldn't help but beam when she said those words. She was finally getting used to the idea and could even picture herself packing up her things and boarding a plane, but it was still such a fresh concept—leaving. Her home, her boyfriend, her dad.

"Congratulations! That's fantastic. Man, what is your dad going to do without you?"

"He'll have plenty of help. Milly's terrific, and of course Kye and Sharon will never go anywhere, at least not until the kids are grown up."

"No, but I mean—you guys are buds. You're close. Don't get me wrong, it's not really the kid's role to worry about the parent, but I imagine he might go into a tailspin those first few months."

"Do you really think?" Apple's forehead creased in a wave of worry.

"Just something to keep in mind. Maybe call home once in a while, even after you find your crowd."

"It will be weird. I mean, since Mom died, he's never really had anyone else."

"No?" Rebah tried to sound nonchalant, but she was surprised to find she really was interested in who else had been in Aidan's life. She took a sip from her glass of wine.

"A couple of dates, I guess, all of which seemed to end badly. And there was one time a woman he'd known at cooking school started emailing and then she had a dozen summer squash delivered here and it was supposed to be a romantic gesture, but Dad had no idea what it meant. So, he made soup. But apparently that wasn't what was supposed to happen, and this chick got super offended. Over soup."

"Soup?"

"Soup. Sometimes my dad inspires women to fly their freak flag a little too high."

Rebah wondered what color her freak flag might be these days. And whether she could keep from flying it too high.

"But, yeah, we're close." Apple trailed off.

"And, hey, you've still got a few months before you leave, right?"

"More like one. There's a summer semester option that I'm going to take. It's basically field trips to Washington, D.C., Boston, Philadelphia—they want us to have a grounding in the history we're going to be studying."

"You're studying history?"

"Well, I'll be prelaw. Which means, yes, I'll be studying history. And English, and political science, and psychology, and . . ."

"Yeah, you'll be busy."

"Yeah, but I hope I'll still have time to practice piano. I'd love to get a gig playing in a nightclub or something. Can teenagers do that?"

"Well, I'm sure there are places that would let you play even though you're underage but, Apple? That's a lot on your plate."

"I can handle it."

"Of course you can, but do you want to wither away from stress at such a young age?"

"You're making fun of my name, aren't you?"

"What?! No! I'd never—" Then Rebah saw Apple's smirk and realized she was being teased.

They were cracking up as Aidan came over. "I get nervous when women are laughing near me," he said. "I always feel like maybe they're laughing *at* me."

"No worries, Dad. We're laughing at the ridiculous name you and Mom saddled me with. I'm going to go play a few songs with the band. And Kai looks like he could use some water. He gets parched up there."

Aidan took her place on the bench and Rebah noticed how her breathing changed. It was no longer easy and friendly as it had been when Apple occupied the spot next to her; her breath was carbonated now, and she could feel a crop of goose bumps rise along her skin.

"If you had to choose between twenty years alone on a deserted island or twenty years at a party with all of your best friends, which would you choose?" she asked, more in an effort to distract herself than anything else.

"That's an interesting question. Does anyone choose the deserted island?"

"Would you?"

"I might. I mean, I love my friends, but twenty years of a party? That sounds like a very specific hell." Aidan took a bite of the mint brownie ganache bar he'd brought with him. He held it up to her as an offering, and she hesitated only a fraction of a moment before delicately plucking a nibble of it from his fingers with her teeth. She grunted in appreciation at the bloom of taste on her tongue, and Aidan smiled at her. "Okay, yes. Deserted island. As long as it's equipped with a kitchen. And a stereo. You?"

Rebah considered. On the one hand, would it be a wise idea to choose her own solitary company for twenty years? On the other hand, with the names and numbers in her current contact list that she still thought of as actual friends—the party might not be any more populated than her island.

"How about we share an island? You can cook, and I can judge."

Aidan smiled. "Perfect."

They were peaceful together for a minute. Kai and the band had moved into a faster piece of music, and Jasper and Mackenzie were dancing, swirling together and pushing apart and reunifying all over again in a different shape, the two of them like magnets using their poles to great effect.

"I feel like I need to say something about the last time you were here," Aidan said.

"You mean the time you called me a drunk and embarrassed me in front of a roomful of people?"

"Yep, that's the one."

"Yeah."

"Yeah."

They were quiet again as they watched Apple take a seat at the electronic keyboards and warm up with a few scales. Kai eased his band into a ballad and Apple played along, adding a texture of sophisticated sweetness to their sound. Rebah glanced over at Aidan, who was looking at his daughter as though she were the most incredible thing he'd ever seen. She realized how deeply he cared—about his daughter, yes, but also about this place, these people who had gathered for however brief a moment. He simply cared.

"Look, Aidan, I don't want you thinking I'm a drunk. I don't even drink that much. I mean, yes, when in wine country I do drink wine, but I never even touch hard alcohol. Except maybe once in a great while, at a party or something. Or after a really rough day."

"Rebah, I didn't mean . . ."

"No, I need to make sure you understand. I'm not an alcoholic. I never drink and drive, I never drink more than I can handle, and I always drink responsibly. Wine is a delight, but it's not a tool."

"You know what? You're absolutely right. And I'm sorry for ever making you feel embarrassed. I really, truly don't want you to feel uncomfortable in my home."

Rebah looked carefully at Aidan's face. Did he mean that apology?

Was he truly trying to make amends? All she could spot in his expression was a sense of peace, concern, and, possibly, resignation. He was being authentic. But was it coming with a price tag?

She deliberately lightened the tone of the conversation. "The only discomfort I might ever feel in your home comes from eating too much. Oh, man, I can't even imagine another bite at the moment."

"Then how about a drink?" Aidan rose from the bench and performed a fancy twirl to the rhythm of the music before extending his hand to take her plate. She laughed and relinquished it. "Milady, can I interest you in a glass of wine?"

"I thought you'd never ask."

"Excellent. Back in a tick."

In the kitchen, after adding their plates to the growing pile in the sink, Aidan gazed at the collection of bottles in the wine rack Milly had stocked just the other day when they realized they'd be needing supplies for guests. Aidan had wondered how he'd feel about alcohol being so close, but it was interesting—he wasn't even tempted. There was zero desire on his part to have even a sip. He wasn't under the illusion that he was cured—he was no fool. Of course, if he started, he'd be hard-pressed to stop. But the fact that he didn't even want to start was heartening.

"Don't get cocky, weirdo," he whispered to himself. He chose a bottle of *Conn Creek 2007 Cabernet Sauvignon*, worked the corkscrew, and poured a generous glass for Rebah. Then he found a bottle of grape juice in the fridge and poured a healthy slug into another wineglass. He wasn't ready to reveal this part of himself to her yet. It was just . . . too much. He brought both glasses and the bottle back outside.

"Cheers," he said softly, presenting her with the wine. He set the rest of the bottle on the floor next to the bench. Across the yard, Kai and Apple were having a contest to see who could hit the highest note.

"Oh, thanks," she answered and took a plentiful sip. She sighed. "I needed that."

Aidan reflected on the several tastings she'd partaken of at the winery but didn't say a word. This wasn't his battle. He had no role to play in this particular arena.

"How did you and your wife ever find this gem?"

"Ah. That's a story."

"I'm waiting . . ."

"Right. Well, you know how some people grow up with really happy childhoods? A mom, a dad, a few elderly relatives, a slew of siblings, family dinners every night, and holidays that are so sweet they make your teeth hurt?"

"Hallmark childhoods!"

"Right. Oh, shit, did you have one of those?"

"Not exactly. I mean, my parents both worked a lot, but I spent a lot of time with my grandfather, and he was good to me. I wouldn't say that I've got smooth, dewy skin, unblemished by the horrors that can be family relations, but it's also nothing horrendous."

Aidan tried not to think about Rebah's dewy skin. "Great, me, too. Certainly not unblemished. My parents died in a car accident when I was very young, and my grandmother raised me. She's the one who first taught me how to cook. We'd work together in her tiny apartment kitchen—all these vegetables from the local market, spices ground by her friend the spice maverick who lived three doors down, goat freshly slaughtered a few streets over in someone's illegal backyard slaughterhouse. Great times."

"Illegal backyard slaughterhouse?"

"Yeah, it was amazing. Pretty sure they got shut down, though."

"Well, health hazards and all."

"But back then, it was all the rage."

"Um—in certain circles?"

"True dat."

"True dat?" Rebah barked out a laugh. "Oh, my God, are you a rapper?"

"Ha! Only in certain circles."

Rebah bent to fetch the bottle of wine and refresh her glass. She offered it to Aidan, but he lifted his own drink to show her how little he'd managed to ingest.

"So, there were always people at my grandmother's apartment, and we'd cook these enormous meals and someone always had a guitar and someone else could play the spoons, so it was like a constant party."

"Hey, like this place." Rebah gestured at the lawn, where guests were dancing, laughing, eating, drinking, and chatting. She was right.

But Aidan couldn't help but mark how much time had passed since the Happy Valley had actually felt happy like it did now. "I went away to school, but I'd always come home on break, and it stayed like that. People, so many people, all the time. And some of them I was closer to than others, but they were family, right, and you love your family."

Rebah nodded.

"And then my grandmother died. And I was just destroyed. She was old, she had heart trouble, and her death was the best death you could possibly imagine. She died in her sleep after a normal day. Just gone. And I was sad, but I was also really, really relieved that she didn't have to go through the shit that so many old people have to endure. She didn't have any long hospital stays or have to go to a nursing home. She was just Nana, and then she was gone, and it was peaceful." Aidan took a long sip of his juice. He'd almost forgotten it wasn't wine and was hugely relieved to find he'd already made the choice not to drink.

"With Nana gone, I didn't go back to the neighborhood very often. I went to Europe for a year, and then I traveled to wherever the work was. I focused on my craft. And when I did finally land in San Francisco for longer than a few days, I took a walk and paid my respects to the building where we'd lived. Where she took me in. And that's where I reconnected with Charlie."

"Charlie?"

"Charlie. Charlie was my grandmother's boyfriend, but I didn't know it when she was alive. I had no idea this grand romance was taking place under my nose. Stupid, right?"

"Well, maybe you were distracted by other things? Like being young. Young people, sometimes they don't see much beyond their own hands."

"Charlie was sitting on a folding canvas chair outside my old apartment building and he recognized me. And scared the hell out of me. He was about three hundred pounds and had about a head and a half on me and he rears up out of his chair and starts shouting at me, and I'm like, 'Whoa.' I'm so confused. But it's his voice that tweaks my brain—he's got this gravelly voice that sounds angry, but then it swoops up into this falsetto sound, and he starts hugging me and saying 'Where you been? Where you been?' and I recognize him. It's Charlie. He'd gained a little weight."

"But you still didn't know that he was your grandmother's boyfriend."

"Nope. Not until he takes me down the road to a bar and we start drinking beer and he tells me the story of his life, the story of my grandmother's life, basically the story of my life. He tells me Nana never wanted me knowing that the two of them were close. She want-ed to be sure that I never thought I was second to anything. That I'd never feel neglected. So they kept their relationship secret from me. It's kind of awful. The person I loved most in the world thought she was protecting me by denying herself the chance to live with the man she loved."

"Oh, God, that is sad. I'm so sorry, Aidan." Rebah put her hand on his arm. It was an automatic reflex, though she wasn't really prone to touching people she didn't know very well. And how many people did she really know all that well? But it felt natural to feel his skin under her fingers as he spoke.

"Yeah. It was kind of a brutal afternoon. But Charlie and I—we grew really close after that. I visited him a lot and we'd eat dinner or just drink at that same bar. He told me so much about my grandmother that I never knew. Then, he died, right before Jessica and I got married. Actually, I was going to bring her to introduce them. We were supposed to have dinner. He was invited to the wedding. But then I got a call from one of his kids—he had, like, dozens—that he'd died. And he died exactly the same as Nana. Went to sleep and never woke up."

Rebah squeezed his arm again and then used both hands to steady her glass to her lips.

"And you're sitting there thinking, *This is a really great story, Aidan, but what the hell does it have to do with how we came to the Happy Valley?*"

"Well, I wasn't going to be rude. And it's a wonderful story, even if it is sad."

"So Charlie turned out to be a fairly wealthy person, even though you'd never know it from the way he dressed, the places he liked to go eat, his general habits. Apparently, he was one of those people who never spent a penny and read personal finance magazines on the sly and so he knew how to invest. And when he died, he left me a chunk of money. Even with all of those kids and grandkids, he wanted me to have a little something of my own. He left money and instructions to keep cooking and buy property. So, when Jessica and I decided we were ready to make the leap into home ownership, and she was pushing hard for a place we could run a bed-and-breakfast out of, we had at least some of the cash to get started."

"It's such a fairy tale."

"And there's one final paragraph. This particular place was on the market for about a decade, mainly because a woman died here. But it turns out that woman was Charlie's Great-Aunt Mavis, who moved here in the forties with her rich husband who was eventually gunned down by the mob. Great-Aunt Mavis lived out her days in the house and died of old age—as a matter of fact, she passed in the same room you're staying in right now."

Aidan sipped his juice and looked sideways at Rebah, who appeared puzzled, then awkward, then horrified, then questioning, and finally suspicious. "Aidan Cisneros, are you making up stories to scare me? Because you should know, I've battled plenty of ghosts on my travels and haven't been bested by even one."

Aidan laughed long and loud, and across the yard, Apple looked over. He seemed so happy. More than happy, he seemed . . . free.

Chapter 18

Rebah and Aidan tiptoed down the front porch steps. Rebah giggled and held her finger to her lips. "Shhhhhh . . ." she tried to say, but it came out in a splutter of uncoordinated air and spit, and she and Aidan just laughed harder.

They'd decided to take a stroll. Or, rather, Rebah had decided it was time for a stroll and Aidan hadn't really wanted her wandering around by herself after finishing off the bottle of wine. Besides, he was enjoying himself. He enjoyed being with her. It was easy, even with the layer of complication.

Rebah grabbed a second bottle from the rack in the kitchen and they scooted out the front door, down the steps, along the driveway, and across the road until they came to a spot where a break in the hedge allowed entry to a neighboring vineyard. "I hope Jake isn't out checking his grapes this time of night," Aidan said, slightly worried they'd be caught by his neighbor. Not that they were doing anything really wrong, it was just that he'd never snuck into a vineyard at night with a beautiful woman and he felt very much out of his depth.

"I'm sure it's fine," Rebah whispered.

As they crept along the dusty track between the vines, Rebah tripped but quickly caught herself, and Aidan steadied her with his arm. She kept her hand in his even after her feet were behaving again. "Look," she said, pointing up.

The word "stars" wasn't really adequate for what they were seeing above them: a thick layer of creamy light, textured and deepened by the blackish-blue depths of the sky, no moon, just an endless sea of cosmic dust. "You know, as many times as I've seen it, this view always makes me grateful to be alive," said Aidan.

"Yeah." Rebah squeezed his hand. She swirled her thumb against the outside edge of his finger, up and down, up and down, in a gentle stroke.

Aidan bit his lip, trying not to shiver, but he failed. The sensation crested from his hand, up his wrist, along his arm, into his chest, and out with a gentle murmur of his shoulders.

Rebah squeezed his hand harder.

They stood a moment more and then started walking again, picking their way in silence until they got to the far end of the vineyard where Aidan found a grassy patch to sit on.

"I didn't mean for this to happen," he said quietly.

"Oh! I mean—is this okay? We can go back if you want?"

"No, I mean—okay, this is all so confusing."

"Listen. To the night sounds."

Aidan listened. He could hear breezes gently rustling the scrubby bushes that grew along the edge of the vineyard, the light rushing sound of cars in the distance, faint music coming from his house, a clicking noise that he imagined was produced by an insect, and the thrumming of a heart. His heart.

"Rebah, I have really loved having you here this weekend," he started.

"And against all expectations, I have really loved being here. This has been fun. Not just fun. It's . . . I've really liked . . . I know this sounds funny, but . . ." Rebah suddenly leaned over and planted her lips on Aidan's. She was clumsy with wine, but Aidan didn't care. He only felt the bloom of warmth in his chest. Her lips were a hot point of contact and the rest of him floated free, untethered from the anxieties of the world.

"Oh, I didn't mean—" Rebah pulled away.

"Sorry. Was I?" Aidan tried to see her face in the dark.

"Does it ever feel like we don't finish half our sentences to each other?" She giggled. "Is there something wrong with us?"

"I'm pretty sure there's absolutely nothing wrong with us." He leaned in and resumed the kiss, deeper this time, and his hands moved of their own volition to her jawline where they lightly framed her face.

"Oh," Rebah whispered around his mouth.

Then he pulled away. He felt like he was getting sucked into a whirlpool of emotion, one he might not be able to find his way out of.

Rebah blanched. "I'm so sorry. I don't know what I was thinking. I always do stupid stuff like this. I act without thinking it through and then I make a fool out of myself and now you're mad and you're going to hate me. I can't stand that I do this, and I can't stand that I did this to you. I'm so sorry, Aidan, I'm so sorry."

"Oh, Rebah, sweetheart, you have nothing to apologize for."

"But I have a really strong feeling I'm screwing everything up."

"Why just you? You do know I kissed you, too."

"But I started it."

"Here, I'll start it this time."

And again, their lips met, this time with a different kind of newness, one that was questioning, answering, wondering, greeting, and reassuring. Deeper, deeper, and then Aidan took a gusty breath through his nose and broke away. "Rebah, I'm sorry."

"Oh!"

She gasped so hard that Aidan turned to her, worried she'd put her hand on a piece of glass or something. But he could see, via moonlight, that the pain in her face had nothing to do with punctured flesh.

"I told you. I mess things up."

"It's not that. It's just that I haven't done this, felt like this, for a long time. Years. Since my wife."

"Oh, Aidan."

"So when I say it's not you, it's me, I really do mean it. You have absolutely nothing to be sorry for."

They were quiet for a moment, looking up at the stars, listening to the night noises, and specifically not turning to each other in the dark. Rebah took several swallows of wine and then swayed slightly.

"You're smart, Aidan. Smart to stop. I really am terrible at relationships and your first one should be with someone who knows what she's doing."

"Do you really think anyone knows what they're doing?" He laughed softly.

"I think I'm the only person I know who doesn't have a handle on things. Next year I'll be thirty and I have a job I used to love, but lately, I'm not sure I still believe that. And all of my friends have moved into these lives with other people, different people I don't even know, and they have partners and babies and they have jobs they really love and there's this way they look at me, like they know what could help me but they can't tell me because I haven't gotten over the wall yet. I haven't leveled up."

"I know, you've talked a little about this before, but is it really how you feel? Your blog—it always looks like you're having an amazing time. I mean, you've got a new guy gazing at you adoringly in every post." Aidan hesitated a moment, not sure he wanted her to know just how much time he'd spent poring over photos of her on the Internet. That afternoon, he'd gotten curious about her life. The weekend had been a shock—he couldn't quite believe how much he wanted to spend time with her, and only her. His goal of getting a good review and selling his place had paled in contrast to Rebah's light. And he was in the lucky position of falling for a woman who had a well-documented public persona, so he'd dug into it, just him and his laptop and a tall glass of cranberry seltzer. "You have this smile like you are just loving the hell out of whatever you're doing, wherever you're doing it, whether you're riding an elephant on the grassy plains of Kenya or snowshoeing into a crevasse in Denmark. You carry more sheer joy than anyone I know."

Rebah turned to him with eyes wide and clear and softly wailed, "But none of it's real! Those men are hired! They do it because they get paid, or they do it because their business is going to get a mention in my blog! Don't you understand? My whole life is a lie!" She let her head fall on Aidan's shoulder and he tightened his arm around her.

He'd never thought for a moment that the joy he'd seen splashed across her website was anything but authentic. But he realized, as he took in the coconut scent of her hair, that her traveling life might be every bit as fake as this entire weekend he'd invented to impress her. "So why do you do it?" he asked when her breathing had evened a little bit.

"That's what I've been asking myself for a while," Rebah sighed.

They sat in the dark a while longer, neither wanting to break the spell of near peace that had fallen like a weighted blanket. The day had been long. The place they were at was far different from where they'd started early that morning. And they didn't know where they were headed.

Aidan and Rebah finally made their way back to the house and found that the rest of the party had died down, only a couple of souls still remaining in the backyard, strumming guitars and singing deep-throated ballads about incomprehensible characters and their nefarious deeds. Aidan only hoped his neighbors within earshot would be forgiving. It was past midnight, long after the time for quiet. He looked out the window at the remaining partiers and wondered if he should shut them down, but he didn't want to leave Rebah's side, even for a few moments.

Rebah seemed to shake off all remnants of moroseness and suggested they open another bottle. Aidan obliged, again filling his own glass with juice.

Rebah was too enthralled by a framed photo on the wall next to the front door to notice Aidan's glass held something other than wine. "Who was the photography buff?" she asked, expecting it was another wonderful aspect of Jessica that would make Aidan's face turn soft and wistful.

"My grandmother," he answered. "She loved two things. Well, three, including me. Okay, four, including Charlie. She loved cooking, and she loved photography. Everything in the house is her work."

"Even the photo of the woman in the downstairs bathroom? Of the crying woman?"

Aidan looked at her in surprise. "Yes, that's hers. What did you think of that one?"

"It was compelling but uncomfortable. I felt like I was intruding." Rebah took a deep swallow of the wine, followed by a deep breath. "A lot of portraits make me feel that way, like why do I have the right to look so closely at someone?"

"Well, but that's the magic of art, right? It lets us settle our gaze in a way that isn't socially acceptable in real life."

"But why is it acceptable when the person is a two-dimensional image on a wall?"

"Because the person doesn't know?"

"But how is that different from spying on someone through a window? Something, I admit, I love to do. But again—it makes me feel awful! Like I'm doing something horribly wrong!" She grimaced.

"But if they never know, if they never find out about it, where's the harm done? And besides, isn't that what you do with writing?"

"Wait, what? What do you even mean?"

"Well, you watch, you describe, you decide what to include and what to leave out. And then you put it up for the world to see, to judge." Aidan reached out and brushed a loose strand of hair from her forehead. Without any forethought, he simply swept it away, as though it was the most natural thing in the world. *Huh*, he thought. *What exactly am I doing?*

Rebah didn't seem to notice. "Yeah, but the people I write about, they know I'm writing about them."

"But they don't have the choice to not be written about, right?"

"Well . . ."

"They just have to hope you approve."

"This is about that review, isn't it?"

Aidan looked at the photograph Rebah had been admiring. It was a snap of an old man walking his black poodle alongside a river. At least, the old man was centered in the image as though Nana had meant to capture that figure at that moment. And she had, but the more interesting figure was off to the right and behind the man.

A small boy was being attacked by a swan. His face was a blur, but his posture was all agony and panic, and the swan had an outline of vicious intent. You knew, anyone looking at the photo knew, that the swan was quite capable of doing damage to the child.

"Why didn't she drop the camera and stop the swan?" Rebah asked.

"My grandmother—I told you about her. She loved everyone, cooked for everyone, but she also had a side to her no one was allowed access to. And that's the side that took this picture." Standing there with Rebah lightly brushing his side, he could almost smell his grandmother's preferred scent—Farouche by Nina Ricci. As a boy, he'd been able to smell it even before she entered the room.

"Do you have that side?" Rebah asked, looking sidelong at him.

"Oh, God, no. I'm not a photographer."

"That's not what I meant."

"Yeah, I think I know what you meant."

"Do you think I have that side?"

"The cold, calculating side?" Aidan immediately regretted his words when her eyes flattened and narrowed. "No, absolutely not."

She turned away from him in search of the wine bottle and poured another glass while he tried to calculate how much she'd had by now. Nearly two bottles, plus all of the tastings she'd downed at the stomp-your-own-grapes vineyard. Jeez. When should he start to worry?

"I do, actually," she retorted. "I have a very uncaring side. In fact, all my sides are uncaring."

"I can't imagine that's true. And maybe we can talk about your caring side tomorrow morning, but it's late. I wonder if it's about time for bed. Not together, I mean. Sleeping in bed. In separate beds."

Rebah snorted slightly. "You think I'm too drunk to know what's going on here, but you, you are the one with no idea."

"I completely admit I have no idea what's going on most of the time." He bowed out to the kitchen for a minute for a bottle of ice-cold water and came back to slip her now-empty wineglass from between her fingers and replace it with the bottle. She immediately took a long, deep sip like she'd been parched for years. Then she sighed and smiled up at him. She turned and started up the stairs, then paused to look back to see if he was following.

Aidan looked at her for a long minute. Just looked.

Rebah shivered under his gaze.

Aidan stepped up to join her on the stairs and took her hand. They climbed together to the second floor.

He used his set of master keys on Rebah's door while she stood behind him and breathed lightly, looking up at the corner of the hallway that had been hastily re-papered only two days before. Aidan, after he'd opened the door, followed her gaze and discovered that the new paper was peeling away from the wall and hanging as though in defeat.

"Huh," she said.

Please let her be too drunk to notice a bad wallpaper job, he thought.

"Okay, in we go," he said aloud as he guided her through the doorway. She stumbled slightly on the threshold so he steadied her, taking the bottle of water back. She righted herself and threw her arms out as though to embrace the room.

"I really love my room," she said. "I love how it kind of wraps its arms around me whenever I come in. I love how it smells fresh and just slightly of pine-scented bleach. I love that it's here in your house." She landed her bottom on the bed and faced him, her arms still out.

Aidan understood: This was an invitation. The second one issued that night. And he was so very, very tempted to accept it, to bend toward her and lean her back onto the white coverlet, run his fingers through her long, coppery hair, and breathe as deeply as he possibly could into her neck.

He wanted, was desperate to test his teeth on her earlobe, her shoulder point, the swell of flesh just above the neckline of her blouse. He wanted to travel under her blouse and discover the smell of the secret space between her breasts. He wanted, he wanted, he wanted.

"Water?" he asked instead.

"Water," she answered.

He handed her the bottle. And she drank, deeply, then handed it back to him.

He could see that her tightly held control was seeping from her muscles. Her face was growing gentler and more malleable, affected by the moods that crossed underneath her skin. Her eyes closed, longer than a blink, but opened again to shoot him a knowing gaze. Even drunk, this was the smartest woman he'd ever met.

"Thank you for hanging out tonight," she said. "I do really like you." And with that, she scooted up toward the pillows and tightened herself into a snug ball of body, gone from the world.

Aidan slid off her shoes, tucked the quilt up around her shoulders, and turned off the bedside lamp. The quilt—it was the same one that she'd spilled wine on that terrible weekend. Now, Aidan searched his gut for any residual anger but felt only a surge of protectiveness toward Rebah. He knew his next move should be to go downstairs and lock up the house, herd any stragglers back to their rooms, check on Apple, and make a plan for morning. He knew he should at least make his way to his own room. But he was stalled, there, standing over this beautiful woman.

This wasn't supposed to have happened.

He hadn't felt a surge of feeling like this in a very long time. Honestly, he hadn't felt much of anything toward anyone since Jessica died, except for his daughter. And that feeling? Vastly different from this feeling.

Tenderness welled in his throat as he gazed at Rebah's sleeping face. He didn't want to leave her side.

So he took the pillow from the side of the bed opposite her still form and settled into the wingback chair by the window, a woolen afghan around his shoulders. His last thought before he plunged into a much-deserved sleep was to wonder if anyone had put the leftover appetizers in the fridge.

Chapter 19

As someone who spent as many nights in foreign beds as she did in her own, waking to wonder where she was never felt unusual to Rebah. But Sunday morning found her wondering something else: *Where is he?*

Even before opening her eyes, she knew she was alone in her bed. She assumed he'd gone back to his own room after she'd fallen asleep. It was silly to think anything else. Why would he stay when she hadn't even been conscious? She shivered and tucked her feet up closer, discovering that someone had taken off her shoes the night before. Aidan. She smiled to herself.

Still cold, she sat up to fetch another blanket from the bottom of the bed, and that's when she saw him: Aidan, stretched on the chair with one arm flung over the side, as though he'd been reaching for her in the night. His other arm was shaped delicately over his face.

Rebah watched his chest rise and fall for several rounds, admiring the taut spread of his T-shirt and the cresting muscles in his forearm, the way his chest sloped toward his belly, his angles poking out from under the skimpy blanket. She turned her attention to his face and drew her eyes along the defined edge of his cheekbone, the gentle shadows of his closed eyes, the scoop of hair that languished on his forehead.

She'd known he was cute, but she'd never realized he was gorgeous.

Aidan snored lightly in his sleep and his muscles came to life in a stretch. Rebah quickly lay her head back down and closed her eyes, trying to appear as though she were still in deep sleep. But she listened: a sigh, a scuffle of feet, a turn in the blanket. And then only his steady breaths. Still asleep.

She crept out of bed and brushed her teeth in her bathroom, checking her face for any obvious signs of puffiness or leftover exhaustion. She splashed some water in her eyes to chase away the lingering effects of the wine she'd drunk the night before and then found a hoodie to wrap around herself as she sat back down on the bed, unsure what to do. This was not a feeling she was familiar with. She looked back at Aidan's sleeping form and discovered—he wasn't sleeping.

"Hey!" she yelped, surprised.

Aidan sat up, worried. "I didn't mean to scare you."

"Oh, God, no, I just thought you were asleep. I don't usually scare that easily. Not a yelper."

They both fell quiet, all the sweet drama of the night before turning into an awkward sludge between them. Rebah remembered mortifying flashes of kissing him, inserting herself into his arms, forcing him to touch her, kissing him even after he told her no . . . A bile-ish taste rose in her mouth, and she had to look away from his eyes.

"You okay?" he said, rising from the chair to sit next to her.

"Aidan, I'm really sorry about last night."

"What do you mean?"

"I shouldn't have kissed you. I knew you weren't ready, but I was selfish. I wanted you. And I didn't listen when you told me no."

"Rebah, honey, that's not quite what happened."

"I remember—I wasn't drunk. I kissed you, you said no, I kissed you some more. I feel awful about it, and I hope we can go back to being friends. I just want to forget last night ever even happened."

She pushed her hair away from her face and tried to calm the stormy breath threatening to erupt from her chest. She wasn't usually like this! She was not a person who lost control. Even at her harshest, when she was gouging new eye sockets in the face of some lost taxi driver or an incompetent host, she was fully in tune with her actions, with her body, with her mind. Even drunk. But this—what she was feeling, what she was wanting—was enormous.

She forced herself to look Aidan in the face and was surprised by the sheer wash of tenderness coming from his eyes. "Rebah, I like you. I want you. I want to kiss you. I said stop last night because, yes, I had to get past thinking about Jessica, but also, I wanted to be sure you really wanted me."

This time? The kiss lasted.

And lasted.

And lasted.

The kiss turned into touching, which turned into Rebah slipping the hoodie off, and then her T-shirt, and Aidan sliding his shirt over his head, and both of them tackling the issue of pants, and then they were together in the bed, one body breathing a long sigh of relief and satisfaction.

Aidan jaunted down the stairs feeling quite excellent. Better than he'd felt in half a decade. Nothing quite touched his current mood. Unless it was Apple getting into college. And even that . . . nope. This was better.

His good mood lasted until he got to the kitchen door and heard arguing behind it. He paused, recognizing the voices of two of Mariah's actor friends—the philanthropists, maybe?

"Darling, truly, I think you are mis-seeing the entirety of the opportunity here," Jameson was saying.

Verity sighed deeply and belligerently.

"No, really, listen to my words. Your aunt, she's left you one hundred thousand dollars to do whatever you want, correct? I'm simply pointing out that we could split that money, give half of it to any charity of your choosing—your choosing, dear, not even my choosing—and with the other half we could buy that splendid couch we spotted at von Hermert's. That's all I'm saying!" Jameson's voice took on an up-squeak quality at the end of his sentence.

"Well, darling, while I see how the purchase of a luxurious item might move us some measure of distance toward a more comfortable living room, I must insist. We are nothing if not philanthropists, correct? How to come to terms with ourselves if we drop that amount of money on something that has no use beyond our walls?"

Aidan rolled his eyes and then pushed into the kitchen. It was a disaster. Bowls, glasses, pots, plates, syrup smeared on the countertop, an unknown substance dripping from counter to floor, the scent of burnt toast.

"No, it's fine, really. I'll just maneuver myself around you so you can keep arguing in my kitchen, no problem," he shot out as he squeezed behind Jameson, who was tucking into a stack of frozen waffles while Verity used her fingers to eat cornflakes from a bowl. His sarcasm was ignored by the couple, so he chose to express his dismay by running the water at an aggressive rate and scraping food debris into the compost bucket with exaggerated noise. He was ready to have his home back to normal. *Well, a different kind of normal,* he thought, remembering Rebah.

He'd finally cleared a space and begun to work on some breakfast for himself and Rebah when Kyle came bursting through the swinging door.

"Aidan, there you are," he said. "Yeah, I was hoping we could have, you know, a word?"

"Little busy here trying to make French toast with human obstacles," Aidan grunted. He flopped a piece of batter-soaked bread into a buttery pan and the crispy smell of heaven entered the equation, causing everyone in the kitchen to take a breath before remembering their grievances. "Can it wait?"

"Yeah, that's a no. We really need to chat. Like, now."

Aidan looked at his friend and recognized that particular slant of eyebrow that meant something serious had caused a seismic shift in

Kye's world and he'd do well to move this up in priority. He turned off the burner for the French toast, bemoaning the fact that the interruption in heat would likely add a layer of sogginess he was desperate to avoid.

"Okay, Kye, what's going on?" he asked as he followed him into the living room, then just about choked on his words as he came face-to-face with none other than Jax Pitts. "What the hell are you doing here?"

"That's not really the reaction you want to show the genius who's found a buyer for your business," Pitts sneered.

"A buyer?"

"Well. Potentially. Is that French toast I smell?"

"Yeah, I'm making French toast, but wait . . . how could you have found a buyer already?" Aidan was distracted by thoughts of the delicious morning he'd shared with Rebah, the smooth scent of her skin, the delicate flicker of her eyes as he'd slid over her.

Then Jax Pitts's sneer shook him out of his stupor of remembrance. "I have my sources. Now, I just wanted to check one thing. Full basement, right?"

"Well, yeah, that's where we keep the laundry, but, wait—I'm still not sure why . . ."

"Right, point me to the door and I'll descend."

"I'm sorry, but no. I'm making breakfast. We have guests. We are still an operating business."

"You don't seem to understand. You might actually have a buyer. Isn't that what you wanted?"

"Shhhhhh . . ." Aidan cut him off and gestured toward the front porch. He managed to usher him out the door, communicating via eyebrow for Kye to keep his eye out for Apple. Or, really, anyone. Kye's eyebrow answered back, but then he wandered into the kitchen and Aidan had no idea if he'd understood any of their silent conversation. Sometimes, Kye missed stuff.

"Look, Mr. Pitts, I appreciate you trying to make this sale, but now isn't a good time. No one knows I'm selling, and if they find out before

I'm ready to tell them, it could mean a lot of hurt feelings. You got me?" Aidan wasn't sure why he thought appealing to Pitts's emotions would work on any level.

"Ahhh . . . and by no one, you mean that lovely daughter of yours?"

Aidan sighed. "Exactly. And she's here, somewhere, likely to come around any corner and wonder who you are and why you're here. So maybe we can continue this conversation another day?"

"Say no more, Mr. Cisneros, say no more. I'll be as discreet as an early fog. As quiet as a fat hedgehog. As invisible as a—"

"Yes, I get it, it's fine. Just take off, please. Give me a call and we'll set up a time to really talk things through." Beyond worrying about Apple discovering the real plot behind the weekend, Aidan was having serious worries around the idea of selling. It was what he'd wanted— how else would he pay for Apple's tuition?—but the weekend had been thoroughly enjoyable. He'd learned how much he loved having people gather around him, cooking for others, having conversations beyond "How was your day?" It was ridiculous to even consider, but he couldn't help the thought from wiggling into his mind: Could he pull off keeping the place and running it as a B&B once again? Without Jessica?

That didn't quite catch before something else slid under the door of his brain: Would Rebah be a part of that new, shiny future?

"I'll just take a measurement, maybe two, and snap a couple of photos and be gone like a grasshopper in October."

Aidan sighed. There was no getting rid of the man. "Fine, just please be unobtrusive."

Pitts made puppy eyes as though unobtrusiveness was his middle name and whipped out his phone to take the pictures. Aidan gritted his teeth as he went back inside and tried to revive his French toast, which lay miserably in its pan. The morning wasn't going how he'd hoped it would. At least the arguing couple had disappeared.

"Aidan?" Rebah asked from the doorway.

"Hey!" He twirled around and couldn't help but scoop her into a hug that he felt from his crown to the soles of his feet. God, it felt so good to press a woman's body against his own. And not just any woman—this one.

"I'm really happy to see you," she mumbled against his shoulder.

Aidan held her apart from him and looked at her freshly show-ered face and form, at the delight that beamed out of her eyes at him, only him.

"Let me feed you," he said. "I've got batter mixed up for French toast and it'll take just a minute to cook a few pieces on the skillet." He turned back to the food and clicked the burner control to level four.

"Oh, wow. I guess I'd better up my exercise regimen so I don't gain too much weight while dating a chef."

Aidan whirled around to face her. "Dating?"

"Oh. Right. We haven't really had that discussion. I'm sorry, it just slipped out. I'm really not a needy person."

"No, I love it. Dating. I haven't dated anyone in so long—I might be really bad at it."

She dipped her chin and threw him some side-eye. "Yeah, I don't think you need to worry."

He smiled and leaned in for a kiss. For a moment, they were the only two people in the world.

"Oh! But what I really wanted to tell you was that I've decided to give the Happy Valley a stunning review on *Rambling with Rebah*! How's this for a headline: 'Champion Chef Offers Charm, Cheese, and Even the Chance to Fall in Love.' Or 'Wine and Dine but Get in Line at the Happiest B&B You'll Find.' Or how about 'I Ate My Words— And They Tasted Amazing.' I mean, the possibilities are endless."

"Oh, honey, but how does that work now that we're, you know . . .'"

"Dating?"

"Yeah. Isn't it a conflict of interest? Won't your readers think you're just writing good stuff because you want to get in my pants?" Aidan laughed at himself, but underneath his teasing he was being perfect-ly serious.

"You know what? My readers are going to love the fact that Rebah Reynolds found love in a place she never expected."

"Love."

"Oh."

"Yeah."

They stood together quietly until the butter in the skillet started to smoke and Aidan had to put the pan in the sink and flush it with water to keep it from becoming a fire hazard. Once the emergency had been diverted, he turned back.

"Love?"

"I know, I know. This isn't the way these conversations are supposed to go, and you don't have to say anything, not a damn thing. I'm going to go back to my room, write the review, pretend I didn't just mortify myself for the eightieth time this weekend, and then we can talk, okay?" She blew him a kiss as she went back through the swinging kitchen door.

Aidan didn't have time to ponder what that conversation had meant, exactly, before he heard a crash in the living room and dashed out to find a crumpled body at the foot of the stairs, Kye and Rebah standing over it, her face aghast. "I was just about to head up and he fell down!"

Jasper lay with his upper half on the floor and his bottom half on the last step, his purple velvet dressing gown flipped up to show off his hot chili-pepper silk boxers and his skinny white legs that ended in puppy dog slippers. "Jasper?" Aidan gasped. "What happened?"

Jasper couldn't stop giggling long enough to reassure his audience that he was okay but laughing required breathing, so they assumed he was fine.

"Jeez, Jasper, this isn't the way to ensure a long and upright life." Aidan tried to pull the man to his feet, but he was having none of it. Instead, he pulled down and Aidan nearly toppled on top of him.

"My darling!" cried Mackenzie from the top of the stairs. He flew down in his matching purple velvet bathrobe and landed in a protective stance over his boyfriend's body. "Nothing to see here, folks," he said, glaring. Jasper seemed to have fallen asleep.

"Whoa, Mack, he's fine," Kye assured him. "He was just talking and laughing. I think he needs to sleep it off and maybe wake up to a few aspirins, but other than that, no harm done."

"Except to his goddamn dignity." Mackenzie began maneuvering Jasper into a tight kind of extended football hold under his armpits so he could drag the sleeping creature up the stairs. "Do yourself a favor, my friend," he grunted at Aidan. "Never fall in love with someone who loves to drink. No matter how darling they are when sober."

"Hey, you want some help?" Kye asked before Aidan had time to respond to advice that could not have been better timed.

"Certainly, thanks."

The three men lumbered up the stairs, and Aidan gazed after them with a quizzical expression on his face.

"Well, that was bizarre," Rebah said as she scooted past him to make her own way up. "Drunk people, there's no telling what they'll do. Am I right?" She blew him another kiss and scampered upstairs.

With Rebah safely secured in her room and Jasper and Mackenzie upstairs, Aidan finally thought he could afford a minute or two of thinking of nothing. He went back into the kitchen and found it empty of occupants, which was good news since he didn't think he had the patience to have any more conversations before finding some food. The French toast was never going to materialize—he knew better than to try a third time—so he simply scooped some guacamole out of a tub in the fridge and spread it on a soft tortilla with some salsa, rolled it up, and called it breakfast.

He took it out on the front porch, where he'd hoped he'd be alone. No such luck.

"Why are you still here?" Aidan practically shouted.

Pitts didn't look the least abashed. "I told you earlier: Pictures. Descriptions. Sales. Sales, my friend, sales."

"And I told you, I want you gone. This isn't the time."

"Well, you might change your mind once you hear what I have to say. The buyer—he's very, very interested. Hungry for the place. Very motivated. And compliant in all areas but one."

"Which is . . ."

"Money."

"Oh, well, of course."

"My buyer is really interested in spending a tad less than what we were hoping."

"Well, then, no deal."

"I do think you should consider his offer, though. I mean, one good weekend does not a revival make, am I right? There's still a steep slope ahead of whoever invests in the property."

As much as Aidan hated to admit it, Pitts was right. He'd had one good weekend, and that was with forking out buckets full of money and hiring people to have a good time. The sinking feeling in his gut told him that his dream of running a successful business again might be premature.

"It's still a good purchase," he pointed out, weakly.

"Sure, sure, you and I know that, but my buyer, he's careful. He's a cautious man. Longtime business dealer. So he knows—he's seen how fortunes can dip."

Aidan clenched his fists and realized, too late, that he was still holding his breakfast wrap. Guacamole and salsa squished out and landed on Jax Pitts's shoe.

"Er . . . your food," said Pitts, holding his leathered heel away from his body as if to avoid contaminating all other parts.

"Huh." Aidan made no move to remove said food. Instead, he took a bite of his gutless wrap and spoke around the tortilla. "You can tell your buyer, pay the full price or no deal. There are plenty of other people who will be interested in my place. I'm not going a penny below what I need to sell this place for, what this place is worth. Have a great day!" This last line he said with an exaggerated smile, still chewing. He turned and went back into the house, unwilling to share air space with the man any longer.

Pitts watched Aidan's retreating back, shaking his head with barely concealed contempt. He fished a white handkerchief out of his jacket pocket and wiped the offending food off his shoe, dropping the soiled cloth into the bushes alongside the porch steps. Then he took out his phone and punched in a number. "Yeah, he's not taking the bait," he said, looking up at the house. "We're going to need to turn some screws."

Chapter 20

Rebah closed the door to her room and fell face-first onto her bed in a position of extreme mortification. *Why did you use that word?* she moaned to herself. *Why did you tell him you loved him? How could you possibly have gotten so caught up that you let* that word *slip out?*

Even as she admonished herself with all the negative energy she could muster in her current state of bliss, she knew: There was no way she could have hidden that particular feeling from that particular man.

She sat up and reached for her phone. She was overwhelmed with the desire to tell someone—other than Aidan—what was going on. How she felt. Why she had an intense desire to look at apartment listings in this neighborhood. And, if she was being honest with herself, she needed someone to talk her out of her headlong rush toward everything that came next, because she'd read enough books and seen enough movies and witnessed enough drama to know that this feeling was not where the story ended. This feeling was the start of the story and the rest of the narrative had to be approached with something akin to caution. Right?

Her thumb hesitated over her messaging app. She scrolled through her contacts and then scrolled some more. She switched apps and took a look at her social feeds. She checked her email. She checked the weather. She went back to Messenger and started tapping out a text to Jocelyn.

YOU WILL NOT EVEN BELIEVE!!! she wrote but then erased her words. She tossed her phone beside her on the bed, slipped her yellow legal pad out of her satchel, and turned to a fresh page. "When you land at the Happy Valley Bed & Breakfast," she wrote, "you'll discover a world you forgot could exist, a world that blends fun with fascination, comfort with adventure, and laughter with love. At least, that's what I found." She broke off and shook out her hand. It wasn't quite right. But it was a start.

And it was better than trying to find someone in her phone to share her feelings with. Maybe she would have better luck talking with some of the characters there at the Happy Valley? She wouldn't talk to Apple, of course—not about her dad! What about Sharon? Sharon was that special mix of fresh and funny and wise. Would it be totally weird to rely on her new boyfriend's best friend's wife for advice and some grounding conversation about what came after? Rebah hadn't even talked much to Sharon, but maybe Sharon was one of those women who listened to anybody. Rebah headed down to the backyard in search of a human sounding board.

The backyard was quieter than it had been all weekend. No music circled among the trees or down the garden rows. You could hear birdcalls from deeper in the woods and the faint, lonesome sound of traffic from the general direction of the highway. In a corner of the porch, Michel and Buttercup were sipping cups of coffee and trying to keep the pages of a newspaper from being snatched away by the slight breeze that played with the lavender fronds and teased Rebah's hair.

Rebah felt a letdown as she realized the party was over. She felt like a skydiver who'd suddenly reached the ground only having just opened her eyes. Could it have been only two days since she had first walked this ground and encountered Aidan, not even suspecting how large his presence would loom in her mind a mere thirty-six hours later?

She turned and took in the house, the porch, the patio with fairy lights strung along the columns, the wildly beautiful and beautifully wild garden where vegetables and herbs made their own choices. She could just catch a glimpse into an upstairs window and spotted a flash of pink and wondered if Apple was watching her. Not that Apple often wore pink. But she was someone who watched. And Rebah understood that—she was someone who watched, too. She had created an entire career out of watching.

She sank onto the wooden bench and sighed, trying to imagine herself as someone who stayed in one place for longer than three weeks at a time. She took a deep breath. What would that look like? What would she be like? Who would she turn into?

She closed her eyes and let her mind drift without direction while she simply observed her thoughts, the reactions in her gut, whether or not goose bumps arose on her skin. She pictured herself there, at the Happy Valley, waking in the morning and setting the breakfast table, greeting strangers-turned-friends as they wandered into the dining room for coffee, chatting with people about the day before, the day ahead. And Aidan, she saw Aidan carrying platters of steaming pancakes, French toasts frosted with powdered sugar, buttery eggs, and triangles of toast with side crocks of homemade jam. She saw him looking up, spotting her, smiling at her. That smile—that was where she wanted to live for the rest of her life. That was the face she wanted to see in every room she occupied until the end of her days. That man.

Rebah opened her eyes and looked around with new perspective. She knew what this place had once been, and she understood what it was now. But also? She'd peeked into the future.

She rose from the bench and hustled back across the porch, not even noticing that the two people in the corner had fallen asleep over their newspaper.

"Aidan?" she called into the house. "Aidan?"

"Rebah!" he called back. He was just coming in from the front porch and his eyes, when he found hers, were alight with a certain kind of recognition. "Hey, you."

"Hey."

They both paused and looked at each other.

Then another man came through the door behind him, closing it with a sharp bang.

"Hello," said Rebah, puzzled at this stranger who hadn't been a part of the weekend party. "Can we help you?" she asked. She noticed, even as she kept her face smooth of emotion, the "we" she'd uttered so naturally.

"Well, I hope so. Maybe you can help me convince this man to take the offer on the table. After all, you're Rebah Reynolds, of course. You know about value."

"Excuse me?" Rebah saw Aidan's face grow wan, but she was still so caught up in tendrils of happiness she couldn't see the crumbling that had begun on the upper edges of the picture she'd been painting in her mind.

"We've got an offer. A fair offer, reflective of what this place is worth," said Jax. "One weekend does not a thriving business make, Aidan!"

"An offer—for the house?" she asked.

"Well, yes, and the business," Pitts remarked. "That's what this weekend has been all about, honey. Aidan here needed to make some kind of grand, last-stand gesture to make this place worth enough to sell. He's got tuition to pay for, you know. And no one wants to buy a failing B&B. I've got to say, this place saw more action this weekend than it has all year."

Aidan's face was getting whiter and whiter. "Rebah," he choked, turning away from Pitts to face her.

But there was no joy to be found in her posture, her expression, or her eyes. "Wait. You said your business was doing really well," she accused Aidan.

"I know I did. And, yeah, that was a lie." He swallowed hard. Rebah wasn't sure she wanted to hear whatever came next. "Since your review a year ago, we've tanked. It's been bad. And when I ran into you in the city, I couldn't stand to admit that you had single-handedly brought my business down."

"But then where did all of these people come from?" Rebah put her hand up to her mouth. "Oh, my God. Did you hire them? Are they actors? Was this whole weekend a trick?"

Pitts looked blissfully amused, his head swiveling from Aidan to Rebah and back.

"What? No!" Aidan automatically defended himself. "I mean. Well, yeah, all those people were actors. No, not all of them, some of them were Apple's friends. But I didn't mean to trick you. I just thought if you would come and see how well the place was doing, you might . . . " He trailed off.

Rebah looked sick. "This whole weekend was a lie to get me to write a good review so you could sell the Happy Valley for more money?"

Aidan's whole body slumped. "It started out like that, but right now, that's the furthest thing from my mind. This weekend has been life-changing for me."

"Right, because with a stellar review you can sell the place for more than it's actually worth and get on with your pathetic life." Rebah felt that familiar stirring in her chest, that white-hot anger that had always been useful in certain circumstances, like a starving cheetah she could keep in her back pocket and take out when she needed to replace tough emotions with sheer fury. But what tough emotions could she possibly be avoiding right there, right then? She had been lied to, betrayed. My God, she'd nearly decided to alter her entire life around this conniving coward standing in front of her. Well, she was done. "You . . . you are a grade-A asshole. I can't believe I fell for the shit you were dishing out this weekend. And you know what? Anything decent I said about this place? It was said in a moment of blindness. I'm going to write a review that will ruin you for good."

"What is going on?" cried Apple. She teetered on the last step, having come downstairs with her phone held aloft, tears streaking her broken face. "How the hell did this get out there? What did you do?"

This last accusation was thrown at Rebah, whose anger paled in the face of the girl's obvious distress. Rebah never meant for Apple to overhear anything. She had no idea how much the teenager knew about her father's ploy, but her bitter vitriol didn't extend to the young friend she'd made over the weekend. No one was that good an actress at age seventeen.

"This is all over Instagram! All of my friends are tagging me in it! This is disgusting, and I can't believe you'd do this to me!" Apple shoved her phone toward Rebah, who took in a doctored photo of Apple and Kai standing slightly apart in the backyard, framed by twinkly lights, sharing an obvious moment of love and trust in a gorgeous setting. It would've been lovely but for the obvious string of spit that connected their mouths and the doodled words above their heads: "Lady and the Tramp." Whoever had done this had decided that Apple was the tramp.

"Oh, my God, honey, I have no idea how this happened. I would never do this!" Rebah cried.

"But it's your photo! You showed it to me when you took it! And then you added gross spit to it!"

"I didn't change a thing to it. I sent a lot of pics to my boss for the blog. Maybe someone at the office got ahold of it and thought it would be . . . funny?" Rebah felt sick that this could've happened.

"There's a link, you know." Apple's eyes lost their wounded patina and turned opaque with her own brand of fury. "A link to a review of the Happy Valley. And I'll give you one guess what kind of review it is."

"But I haven't submitted a review! I haven't even finished writing it! I barely started it!"

"It's a total bomb. You killed us, Rebah. You murdered us."

"Hold on, Apple," Aidan interrupted. "Rebah says she didn't write a review and I believe her, and besides, she said she was going to write a glowing one. It's been a good weekend."

Rebah snorted. "Yeah, a great weekend perfectly manufactured to impress."

"Let me see your phone." Aidan took Apple's device, scrolled up, found the link, clicked, and skimmed the headline and author. "Do you know a Stewart Starr?"

"*What?*" Rebah exploded.

"Oh, shit," Aidan muttered as he read more. "This is . . . I can't believe . . . Who the hell is this guy, and how did he get this stuff? He's got pictures of the whole weekend. The parties. The balloon ride. The winemaking. Even—" He broke off from the car accident of a review and looked Rebah in the eye. "Even shots from the walk we took in the vineyard last night."

Pitts pulled out a dining room chair and settled in to watch the drama unfold. He was enjoying this.

"Let me see." Rebah pulled out her own phone and began scrolling. This was all a ridiculous mistake. She pulled up Stewart Starr's home page and found the offending review. *Over It! Your Guide to Has-Beens, No-Longer Hots, and Other Spots to Avoid!* And the number one bed-and-breakfast to avoid?

The Happy Valley.

It was awful. Horrible. Every scrap of information she'd sent back to the office had been manipulated and distorted, twisted and bent so that what readers saw was a wildly obnoxious series of lies, all backed by altered photo "evidence." Where had they even gotten an image of a baby pouring baba ghanoush over its head to photoshop into the scene of that first dinner with the carnival food? And what were these videos of humping dogs interspersed throughout the review? Rebah tasted a disgusting metallic flavor in her mouth that had nothing to do with how much wine she'd drunk the night before.

"Aidan, I—"

But Aidan's look of fury stopped her. He'd been reading, too, on Apple's phone. "How could you?"

"No, I—"

"'A place where dreams go to die, like the rats that lay rotting in the basement.' Really? You had such an amazing time this weekend that you thought to celebrate like this?"

"But you—"

"'If you're looking for a cross between hell and torture, look no further than the Happy Valley, where the "happy" is nowhere to be found but the "valley" is deeper than it is wide.' Rebah, this is obnoxious."

"I didn't write it!"

"It came from your office. It used your photos."

Rebah took a deep breath. Something deep inside her, a hard finger of broiling desperation, rose up and took control. She was done. Everything was over. Time to burn the place down. "Look, you have absolutely nothing to be complaining about. I wish I had written that review. You lied to me every moment of this weekend, you led me on, you made me believe things I have never allowed myself to believe, and it was all a scam to sell the place."

Beside her, Apple reared back and shot a look at her father.

"Rebah, you are a drunk, a coward, a liar, and a thief," Aidan started, "because you very nearly stole something I shouldn't have ever let you near—my true opinion of you. You talk about this weekend being the result of my lies, but what about you? You've been lying for years! You lied in the first review you ever wrote for this place! Remember? I bet you don't, actually. I bet you can't remember a thing about your first visit here because you were either drunk or hungover the whole time. You're a goddamn alcoholic and I never should have agreed to let you come here again."

"Agreed to let me come? You were the one who begged me!"

"Ha! You wish. Nope, I was tricked into it just as much as you were by Kye."

"You don't even have control over your own so-called friends! You are so pathetic that their idea of helping you is to bring back the person who single-handedly ruined your business in the first place!"

"You are such a narcissist you wouldn't even know what a friend was if it bought you a drink! Oh, wait, you'd stick around for that, wouldn't you? Because you're a drunk."

"Who the hell are you calling a drunk? I see the way you cling to that token in your pocket. I saw the look on your face yesterday at the winery. I know you, Aidan Cisneros."

"You don't know shit about me."

"Oh, you don't think so? I know you're a dad just this side of dead-beat whose own daughter does more to keep this place running than you ever bothered with. I know you are pining—pining!—for the life you used to have and that's kept you from even trying to figure out the life you have now. I know that you claim to want to move on and find love and be a good dad, but the truth is, you're failing and you've been failing since the day your wife died and you're never going to not fail because you don't have the goddamn courage to look an inch past your own nose." Rebah took a deep breath and steadied herself, prepared to unleash a second wave into Aidan's roiling face.

Pitts spoke before she could continue. "Listen, gang, before we set up the wrestling ring for the next round, how about I help clear a few things up? Not for your sakes, but simply because the time has come for you, Aidan, to accept the realistic offer on the table so I can collect my commission." He rose from his chair and dusted off his hands as though he'd been in contact with something ill-advised. "No, Rebah Reynolds did not write that smashing review, but her company did use her material to come up with it. Why? Because my buyer is only willing to write a check to cover the real worth of this place, not the value that would be assigned to it by a stellar review from none other than our Rebah."

"I'm not *your* Rebah!" she snapped.

"How would the buyer be able to guess that Rebah's company was going to post a bad review?" demanded Aidan.

"Ah. Well. The company and the buyer are basically one and the same."

You could hear the early-spring bluebottle flies buzzing against the windowpanes in the living room after Pitts made his announcement.

"It's just business. Buy low, then make the place popular again with a series of comeback stories. Travel journalism and the B&B business—a match made in money heaven. And Stewart Starr was really quite happy to help out when you seemed to falter, Ms. Reynolds."

Aidan turned with a concentration of cold fury. "Out."

Pitts clapped his hands as though taking his departure was all his idea and turned elegantly for the front door. "I'll be in touch for signatures," he sang, and Aidan responded with an elevated pitch of his previous direction.

"*Out!*"

Then, he turned to the two women standing in front of him. Apple was looking at him with wet, hurt eyes that registered confirmation that what she'd suspected of the adult world—that it was a cold, dreary place devoid of love and kindness, where people's actions were dictated by money and power—was utterly and terrifyingly true. "Apple," he began, but she whirled around and stormed up the stairs.

"Don't you think you've done enough damage for the day?" Rebah said icily.

"Why are you still here?"

"Why are *you* still here?"

The two lost souls looked at each other for a minute more, anger, sadness, disappointment, and sheer exhaustion fighting for hierarchy in their features. What had they just lost? What were they about to lose? Both suspected they wouldn't know the true cost of the weekend for a long, long time.

"I'm going," Rebah said hoarsely and she turned away and headed up the stairs.

"Rebah!" Aidan couldn't help calling after her. She stopped but didn't turn around to face him. "I'm angry and hurt, but I want you to know I wasn't lying about everything this weekend."

Somehow, his words made her hurt worse. She ordered her feet to carry her up the rest of the stairs to her room so that she could pack. Ten minutes. A weekend she thought had changed her life, her very soul, and she knew it would only take ten minutes to wipe all traces of herself from her room, all traces of the room from herself. *Well, you know how practiced you are at this,* she reminded herself as she threw a bra in her bag, followed by her jeans and hiking sneakers. But where this skill usually inspired pride, right then she just wanted to lay back down on the bed and cry.

Instead, she grabbed her bags and made her way out the door, down the stairs, and back out to the driveway where her rental car waited as though the weekend had never happened. And she never heard Apple's choked whisper, "But, wait," from behind the glass of her upstairs bedroom window. Crying, she eased the car onto the road and sped away.

Chapter 21

Aidan's dark mood matched the storm clouds he encountered when he strode out of his home and down the front steps, got into his Jeep, and headed down the road. He had one goal: to drink. A lot.

It had been five years since he'd crossed the threshold of a bar, but as soon as he dragged himself into Nate's Eats, he knew it was the perfect place to piss away five years' worth of sobriety. The back corner of the place played host to a middle-aged woman scribbling in a notebook and sipping a glass of red wine. Two college students sat with their heads close together over a phone, hitting each other on the arm every so often in a display of power Aidan didn't understand. But he didn't care about understanding. What he needed was at the bar.

"Whiskey, two shots, and a Corona," he told the barkeep, an older man with a crossword puzzle spread out in front of him, the paper anchored by a sweating glass of clear seltzer water. "As soon as humanly possible."

"Rough day?" the barkeep asked as he lined up two shot glasses on the bar. A few dips of a bottle and a flick of an opener and Aidan was supplied with exactly what he'd asked for.

"Rough is an understatement. Disastrous doesn't even come close. The worst day. The absolute worst day. And I'm a man with a dead wife." Aidan downed the first shot, the second shot, and chased them with a sip of beer.

"Sorry to hear that," said the man. "I'm Jack. You need more to blot out your day, you let me know."

"Thanks, Jack. I just can't believe how stupid I was to let her back."

"Your wife?"

"What? No. No, not my wife—the writer. This writer that I knew was bad news. I knew she'd screw me over, but I let her come anyway. Hell, I bent over backward to impress her. Oh, God. I even . . . I mean. It's not something I'm used to doing. Or telling people about—"

"Slept with her?"

"Yeah."

"Damn." Jack poured another two fingers of whiskey without being asked.

"Damn," muttered Aidan. "You'd think in your forties you'd know better, right?"

"Hell, I'm in my sixties and I still make mistakes."

"What I'm really mad about is how screwed we are. Me and my daughter. This whole thing, the whole weekend, the whole setup, it was all for her, it was all so we could sell the place for a good price and my little girl could go to the college of her dreams. That's all I wanted."

"And what were you going to do? After selling your place and sending your daughter to college?"

"Well, the world was my damn oyster, right?" Aidan finished his beer and waved the bottle at Jack. "I was thinking I'd move east and get an apartment near her college. So she'd have a place to stay if she needed to, you know, get away for a while."

"And you think a college freshman is going to want her dad within shouting distance of her dorm room?" Jack chuckled, setting another bottle of beer in front of his customer, and Aidan joined him.

"It's been a long time since she needed me, but the habit's hard to quit. You got kids?" Without realizing it, Aidan managed to throw back another shot and settle into his second beer.

"Huh, six of them."

"Six kids!"

"Yeah, they just kept coming. Only one of them is related by blood. The others, well, my wife and I both have trouble saying no to kids. Or to anybody, I guess." Jack chuckled again.

"So, can I ask—if you don't mind my asking—I'd just, I'm dying to know. How did you pay for everyone? Never mind college, even just, you know, food?"

"Yeah, I don't make a whole lot now doing this, but this is really a retirement role for me. I used to own two bars downtown, The Jenny and The Kate. You ever been? We closed up maybe seven years ago."

Actually, Aidan did have a distinct warm reaction when Jack mentioned The Kate. He was sure he'd been there before, back when drinking was something to be pursued and accomplished. Could be that in another lifetime, he and Jack had already crossed paths.

"So I did that when the kids were growing up and it was tough. Never enough time on either end of the day, and certainly never any time for me. But we made it work. Becky, that's my wife, she did most of the heavy lifting when it came to the kids, and I was always grateful for that. I got great kids."

Aidan felt a sweeping sensation when he thought of Jack's wife. He imagined someone with long blond hair and smoky eyes and smile wrinkles, dressed in corduroys and a sweater, someone who laughed as easily as Jack and baked really amazing pies. Maybe she was also a social activist, writing up leaflets and making phone calls after the kids had gone to bed, keeping her hands in important work even while she made sure all six children ate enough vegetables and read for at least half an hour every night.

Jessica hadn't been anything like that. She was far more polished, moved with easier elegance than the wife he'd invented for Jack, but she had that same kind of capability. He missed her so much.

"Jack, I need another shot," he said, only slurring a little.

"What's your name, son?"

"My name's Aidan."

"Listen, you sure you want another shot?"

"Just one more. Promise."

"Okay, Aidan. One more shot and then we're going to sit and talk some more and I'll brew some coffee."

"Jack, I think you are the only decent person in the world. You and Mrs. Jack. The only decent persons."

Jack chuckled again as he poured one last shot.

Chapter 22

*A*pple watched out her bedroom window as Rebah slammed out of the house and roared down the road. She clutched her old pink blanket in her hands, the weave tightening around her fists as she clenched them harder.

She watched Mariah lead the weekend revelers out to the front yard and hug each and every one before they, too, disappeared into cars and left. Mariah took off on her electric bike. Everyone was leaving. The weekend was over. And it had been terrible, ruinous. Nobody was even saying goodbye to her. Of course, that could be because she was hiding in her room, but still. No one, she would bet, had even thought to wonder where she was.

She was still standing at her window holding her blanket when Milly and Sharon and Kye met briefly in the driveway and had a conversation that involved a lot of shrugging shoulders and animated hand gestures.

And then Boutique came out the front of the house and looked up toward Apple's window and shaped her fingers into a heart over her chest and made the universal sign for "I'll call you later." Then she climbed into a decaying Nissan truck.

She still couldn't believe the whole thing had been such a lie.

What had Dad been thinking? How could he have thought of selling

this place? It was ridiculous. Where would he go? He belongs here at the
Happy Valley.

She sent a quick text to Kai to let him know she was going to spend the day at home and, no, he didn't have to come over. She didn't know if he'd seen the meme yet. He wasn't on social a lot and it was absolutely possible that he hadn't discovered it and Apple was totally going to take advantage of his ignorance to figure some things out before they had to have a conversation about it.

God damn Rebah.

Even a long, hot, soapy shower, with several pauses in scrubbing to allow for tears to fall, didn't wash off the feeling of betrayal. Apple stood in the spray and tried to find a new way of looking at the whole stupid situation.

Maybe Dad was having some kind of midlife crisis.

Maybe grief over her mom's death had finally caught up to him and this was his way of working through it.

Maybe Rebah had made him so crazy, had ensnared him in some kind of weird sexual attraction trap, that he'd gone off his rocker and the crazy was starting to show.

Maybe Kye and Milly put him up to this.

No. Impossible. They would never do that.

What reasons would her dad ever have to sell the Happy Valley?

Apple finally got out of the shower, dried off, and put on some bright green flannel pants and an old T-shirt of her dad's. She checked her phone—no texts. From Dad, from Kai, from Rebah.

Why would she even want a text from Rebah?

Despite the mortifying events of the last few hours, Apple heard her stomach complain and realized she was starving. No action had sounded from downstairs in a while—she had a feeling everyone had fled the scene of the crime and she was alone in the house. Which suited her just fine.

A few minutes later, her top half was deep in the fridge, sniffing out leftovers that would not only ease her hunger but also taste amazing, a way of making up for the shitty day. Mini beef tourtierès. Honey-mint lamb skewers. Crab salad tapas. Milly had defrosted everything, it seemed, but none of it called out to be eaten. Apple wanted nothing her father had cooked.

She pulled out a jar of peanut butter and one of jelly and got the loaf of store-bought bread from the top shelf of the pantry. She smeared so much jelly on one slice of the bread that it oozed out the sides when she slapped the more thinly applied peanut butter slice on top. Perfect. A glass of milk and she was ready to eat.

Instead of going back up to her room, which had started to feel too much like a cage, she slid her plate and glass on the wooden kitchen table and sat, feeling very adult all of a sudden. So what if her dad had lied to her, betrayed her, gone back on his unspoken promise to forever protect this special place from outside forces so it would always be here when she needed to come home? So what if the person she thought was a new friend turned out to be truly evil? So what? Her whole world was changing anyway, with college coming and her life finally starting. Who the hell cared anymore?

As she chewed, she gazed across the table at two photos on the wall, one color and one black-and-white. The color one she knew was of her mom. And, technically, Apple, too, since Jessica had been pregnant at the time of the shot. She was leaning against a fence and the Golden Gate Bridge stretched behind her. It was certainly not the best picture of it ever taken, but you really couldn't take a bad photo of such an iconic symbol. "Sure, a symbol of capitalism and unfair labor practic-es," Apple muttered under her breath, even though there was no one around to share her ever-seething outrage over inequality.

She had never felt comfortable looking at this picture that was both of her and not of her. She remembered a lot about her mom. The way she started so many conversations with "Did you know" and then went on to explain something that, yes, everyone already knew. Like the fact that the bananas you bought from the grocery store were all clones of each other. The way she would say, for example, "Apple, I think you need a room makeover," and then three days later, Apple's bedroom would be shiny and new and exactly reflective of her personality that year. Horses at seven, Paris at nine, feminism at twelve.

Yes, Apple remembered a ton, but seeing a picture of her mother before she was a mom, before Apple was able to form memories, was disconcerting.

The black-and-white photo, though—Apple had different feelings about that one.

She knew her dad's parents had been killed in a car crash, and she knew he'd been raised by his grandmother, but she died, too, before Apple got to meet her. She knew her great-grandmother only through the photos that hung on the walls of the B&B. The images let her see through her great-grandmother's eyes: the desperate woman in the downstairs guest bathroom, the small boy being attacked by a swan, and this one, her favorite. Great-Grandmother had shot straight on from across a busy street and captured the open windows of an apartment building, each with a figure boxed into its own space as though frames had been applied to the residents of the building. A grizzly, unsmiling man in a white tank, his once-strong arms sagging against the sill as they propped up their seemingly mean owner. A young woman in a silky soft dress with a scar running down the side of her face, her eyes turned to the sky as though unable to bear the sight of ground-level living. An older woman looking straight at the camera, eyes shining and mouth sloped in a delighted chuckle, offering what looked like an orange to whoever looked at the scene. A boy, a very little kid, trying to climb onto his sill while a young dad scrambled to pull him away from the edge, the boy laughing and laughing and laughing, the dad not laughing.

Apple had always thought the smiling old woman in the photo was her great-grandmother, that somehow she'd set up a timer or magically managed to be in two places at once to include herself in the photo. But Dad had told her that, no, the older woman was her great-grandmother's neighbor, who excelled at baking raisin bread and reading the tarot. But that was her great-grandmother's living room window. And by extension, his boyhood living room window. That had always given Apple such a strange feeling, to know her dad had likely rested his own forearms on that windowsill and leaned out to look the world over.

Apple picked up her phone and sent the link for Rebah's horrible review to Kai. Might as well get this over with. His first response was:

Dude.

I know, right? Sucks.

You ok?

Apple thought for a moment. Was she okay? She was mad, sure. But strangely, she was kind of okay. The review was a disaster, her dad was a disaster, but she didn't have to accept this whole situation as her disaster. She texted back a rolled-eyes emoji, knowing Kai would understand that she was just over the whole thing.

For a second, swallowing the last of her milk and brushing crumbs from the table in front of her, she felt a flash of claustrophobia. Suddenly, her legs wanted to move faster than humanly possible, just shoot out across the kitchen, into the yard, down the drive, and away, all the way across the country to Barnard. She was so ready to leave this damn place.

She cleaned up her dishes and was heading back upstairs to her room when she stopped with one foot on the bottom step. Barnard.

Barnard was expensive.

Tuition was insane. Room and board even more so. Books, fees, expenses.

That's why he wanted to sell the Happy Valley.

Apple thumped her bottom down hard on the step, reeling with the sudden realization that her dad's lies and betrayal were actually all in service to . . . her. And her education.

How could she have been so stupid? So blind? How could she have suspected him of all the awful things she'd suspected him of?

She groaned and dropped her face into her hands. This was all her fault.

A commotion outside distracted her from her misery. She looked up just in time to see her dad stumble through the front door. Behind him, Kye kept his arms out just in case Aidan took a sudden swerve toward a hard surface.

Dad is drunk. Dad is drunk. Dad is drunk. Apple's eyes widened and a choked sob escaped her lips, a sob that stretched across the room to yank Aidan's chin from his chest so he was forced to stare into his daughter's eyes. *Dad is drunk.*

Apple shook her head slowly and the look on her face was one of profound sadness, deep pity, and not a little regret.

She slowly turned and crept up the stairs, as though the less pressure she applied to her steps, the less damage might exist in the room that was already brimming with it.

Aidan planted his feet on the wide wooden boards of the living room floor and tried to keep from swaying. When the low sound of thunder rumbled outside, he thought he was imagining it.

"Shit," Aidan mumbled.

"Yeah. Shit," Kye agreed.

"I have screwed up so, so much."

"Yep."

"I mean, I have really screwed the pooch."

"Oh, yeah."

"Totally ripped off the curtains."

"Demolished."

"Drove the car into the lake."

"Drowned."

"Kye? I don't know what to do."

Kye sighed and rested his hand on his back. Aidan felt the warmth of his friend's palm even through his shirt and it just broke him. He leaned forward and let the tears come, a generous rush of saltwater that bathed his face and neck in a wash of release. The torrent only lasted a few moments, but as it petered out and Aidan could stand up straight again, he realized that had been exactly what his body and mind—and heart—had needed.

"I have to fix this," he said calmly, making a move to follow his daughter.

"You're absolutely right, but I just want to check: You sure you can handle those stairs?"

"Kye, you're my best friend. You're my brother. I got those stairs."

Kye let him go, watching as he stumbled only a little on the first step before drawing tall and tackling the rest of them as though his life depended on it.

Chapter 23

Apple's room still boasted the décor that had been decided on and accomplished by her mother six years ago. They hadn't gotten around to changing it before Jessica died, so vintage posters of Women's Equality Day in 1970 and framed photo reproductions of Susan B. Anthony, Alice Stone Blackwell, Elizabeth Cady Stanton, Emmeline Pankhurst, Sojourner Truth, Harriet Tubman, and Gloria Steinem lined the pale-yellow walls. Along the ceiling line Jessica had handwritten in elegant script quotes from Ruth Bader Ginsburg, bell hooks, and Malala Yousafzai.

In the face of all that feminist power, Aidan wanted to feel supported and confident, but to be honest, Apple's room had always reminded him a little too sharply of his dead wife, and—it was hard to admit—he'd taken to simply avoiding the room. There was so much of Jessica in there, still, despite the addition of posters of starlings in flight and pages of printed-out samples of Clara Schumann's handwritten scores that Apple had taped to the walls. And he knew that if Jessica were alive today, she'd be crushed to see him that way.

But she wasn't there. Jessica was dead. And Aidan had to fix this.

"Hey," he said softly as he knocked on the open door. "Can we talk?"

"You know, Dad, I get that things are hard and you have this disease. You're an alcoholic and that means this is the way you react to hard things, but it just sucks, okay? It really sucks that you went out and got drunk today!" Apple shouted this last line. She was sitting on her bed, clutching her old pink blanket to her stomach.

God, she reminded him so much of her mother like that. The same reproach in her eyes. But in Apple there was an anger, a hard anger that Jessica had never shown him, despite all the reasons he'd given her.

"Apple, I am really, really sorry. So, so sorry. I messed up." Aidan paused, drew himself up straighter, and tried to clear his head. "I'm sorry about drinking, yes, but also about this whole weekend. It was incredibly stupid of me. I never meant to do anything to hurt you. You've got to understand that I'd never hurt you if I could possibly help it."

"You say shit like that but that doesn't erase the fact that you. Are. Drunk."

"You're right, it doesn't. I messed up. Badly."

"And I am so sick of your apologies! Endless apologies, for not taking care of guests, for not cooking breakfast on time even though it's *in our name*! Bed and *breakfast*!"

"Oh, man."

"You are always sorry for something, but guess what would be so much more useful? Way more useful than apologies. If you changed your goddamn behavior."

Aidan felt a flood of shame—he was drowning in it.

"Because we can't have a relationship built on apologies. No one can."

"You are so, so right."

"It's just—it's time for you to knock it off. I'm all out of forgiveness."

For a moment the room was thickly silent as Apple's anger and resentment swirled around them, enveloping everything in a film of black-barbed feelings.

"Can I just say," Aidan pleaded, "that I know it looks like this weekend was all for my sake, but that isn't true. Everything I did, all the stupid shit, I did it because I wanted to make things better for you." He paused. "Except for getting drunk. That was just me making a really, really shitty decision."

"Um, really shitty."

"I can't believe I just tossed five years down the bottle."

"Oh, Dad."

"But that's on me. That's nothing to do with you."

"I know."

"I'm not going to apologize again, but I do want you to know that I didn't go get hammered because of anything between you and me. It was Rebah. I was miserable that I treated her that way. And this place—I'm miserable that I can't be what your mom wanted me to be. I just want you to know that."

"I do. Actually, I really do. I'm not even that angry about this weekend. I get it."

"Wait—you do?"

"I figured it out, Dad. Admittedly it took longer than I would have liked but, yeah. You want to sell the Happy Valley to pay for my college."

Aidan sat beside his daughter on her bed and they shared a quiet moment. Then he spoke again. "Since your mom died, all I've wanted was to make it work for you."

"Yeah, but, Dad, in the process you've completely neglected yourself. I mean, I get that staying sober is a lot of work, and being a dad is a lot of work, and this place is a lot of work—even with you being a half-assed owner—but you've still managed to let yourself just . . . go."

"Wait, what?"

Apple sighed gustily and held her pink blanket up to his face. "It's like my pink blanket. My pink blanket has worked so hard at staying pink it forgot to stay clean."

"I'm like your pink blanket?"

"It's a freaking metaphor."

"Right! Okay, I'm pink, I'm a blanket, and I have to work hard to stay pink, and so I . . . get dusty?"

"And you lose a corner," Apple said, showing him a frayed edge.

"I think I can fix that for you."

"Wait, Dad, that's the point. Here you are, again, fixing something that's right in front of you. Pink Blanket's corner. Your drinking. Instead of fixing things that are deeper down. Like your relationship with the entire world. Your relationship with me."

"Oh, honey. Shit. I just . . . everything was so much easier when your mom was alive."

Apple nodded and a tiny smile tempted the corners of her mouth. "Oh, I know."

"Everything. Not just running this place, which was like your mom's superpower, but being with other people. Being with you. Not that you're hard to be with—"

"Dad, it's okay, I get it. You don't have to apologize for expressing your feelings."

"Yeah, I know. But with Jessica here I felt like I was always myself. I wasn't just this guy who'd lost his parents and was raised by a grandmother and wanted to know how to cook. I was Jessica's husband, co-owner of the Happy Valley. I was me."

"Except . . . you were also drunk a lot."

"Except I was also drunk a lot."

"And when you're drunk a lot, that's kind of a sign that you're not really happy with who you are."

"Well, it's a little more complicated than that."

"But not a whole lot more."

"I really was happy with your mother." Another roll of thunder erupted outside, and rain began to hit at the window.

"But maybe you weren't happy with other parts of your life. You can love someone and not love what they love. Mom was pretty anal about this place—it had to be a certain way, her way."

"But she was amazing at keeping this place up to standards."

"Her standards, sure, which were incredibly exacting. You know what was fun about this weekend? You know why everyone had such a good time? Because it was so relaxed. People danced and laughed and a couple glasses got broken and people got drunk and it was great! Until it wasn't."

"Huh."

"Mom's idea of fun was a lot different. It was a lot more tightly wound." Apple held her pink blanket up to her face and rubbed her cheek on the softness.

"But there's a lot I should've done differently. This weekend and for the past five years. Ten years. Twenty. Listen, one thing I know is that part of getting sober is understanding that drinking is a way of hiding. And staying sober is a long process of not hiding. Of revealing." Aidan took a shaky breath and wished he had a glass of water. Maybe some crackers.

"Okay, and what have you revealed?"

He stood to pace the room. The conversation was taking its toll on him. He'd give anything to be in a meeting right now. Meetings were a safe place to speak, but speaking here, in front of his daughter, the person he cared for most in the world, didn't feel safe—it felt dangerous.

"I think I'm a person who means well but never really gets it right," he finally said.

"And?"

"I think I'm a person who doesn't tell people enough that I care about them."

"Or?"

"Or show them. Apple, I really, really love you. That's what this whole weekend was about." He let himself simply look at his daughter's face, not with shame or anger or even sorrow. Simply with presence and humility. And honesty.

"I know, I really do know, and I really do love you, too."

Aidan stretched his arms open and Apple stood to meet them. He breathed in her teenager self, the shampoo and a hint of the backyard and something inexplicably Apple.

"But look." She pulled away. "I know that Barnard is up in the air because of money and everything and that who knows what will happen to this place, but understand this, Dad: I'm not going to stay here forever. I'm ready to leave. I *need* to leave. I need to figure out who I am, just like you need to figure out who you are, and I can't help you anymore. You want to keep going with this place, great. You want to sell, great. It's your choice. But I don't really feel like wasting any more time helping you carry something you just need to put down."

Jesus, when did this girl get so wise? But Aidan knew—she'd been like this since birth. In fact, the first time he'd met her, he'd gazed down at that scrunchy face wrapped in a hospital blanket and searched her half-open eyes, which widened into knowing as soon as he found them. Since then—that's when he knew his daughter held knowledge he couldn't even begin to imagine.

He looked at her and said, "I get it. I totally get it. And, Apple, I can't even tell you how much I appreciate you for everything you've done and everything you've been. And I can't wait to see what you do next, whether it's college or the open road or going straight to the White House to fix the country."

Apple grinned. "There's an idea."

"If anyone can do it, you can."

"One more thing, Dad?"

"Anything, Apple, pretty much literally."

"You need to take a shower and eat some pickles or something. You smell like booze."

"Huh. Pickles. You are pretty smart."

"And I need to text Kai and let him know I'm okay."

"Did he see the picture?"

"Yeah, we texted about it earlier. He doesn't care about it. He cares that I care, but otherwise, if it isn't music or skateboarding or vaping, he's not affected."

"Oh, jeez, do you and I have to have the vape talk? Because I'm exhausted."

"You've met me, right? Would I risk any precious brain cells on chemical alterations?"

"How'd you get so smart?"

"Must've come from Mom."

"You've got that right. Love you, sweetie."

"Love you, Dad."

While Apple and Aidan were having their heart-to-heart, Milly was down in the living room, packing. A large cardboard box sat with its flaps open on the floor in front of the cabinet while she chose a wooden troll, wrapped it in three times more newspaper than it really needed for a buffer against the world, and tucked it into the box. She'd been at the job for an hour and there were still dozens of the things in the cabinet. She hated using that much newspaper, but Jessica had loved those ugly trolls and so she would protect them.

"Whoa, Milly," Kye chirped as he came in from the kitchen. "That's a job and a half."

"Yeah, well, I figured I didn't want these getting forgotten until the last minute and then someone rushing to do the job and Jessica's trolls getting smashed up." Milly sniffed. "And anyway, these things collect dust and it's a real pain to dust them."

Kye didn't point out that it looked like no one had dusted them in some months, years even. He did ask, "You do know Aidan hasn't sold the house yet, right? Or did something happen while I was home with the twins?"

"No, no new news, but you know it's going to happen. I want to make it as easy as possible for Mr. C. And for Apple. I just feel so sorry for these kids, you know?" Milly said in a sad voice.

"Apple and Kai?"

"No, Apple and Aidan. I mean, after all this time, leaving like this. Like this place was nothing special. This place is the most special place ever, and no buyer is ever going to see that and pay what it's worth."

"Yeah, the market isn't exactly happy to award sentimentality," Kye said, scratching the back of his head.

"And, jeez, poor Apple. I mean, to be all 'I'm going to the school of my dreams!' and then to be like, 'Whoa, no school for you!' I mean, I know I'm never going to college and, honestly, that's fine, I have zero interest in sitting in a classroom or reading books I don't want to read or listening to people I don't want to listen to—but Apple? That girl is freaking smart. And the world needs her brain!"

"Yep. We do have problems that need solving. I was reading the other day that we're looking at wildfire seasons that are going to be exponentially worse than anything we've seen before because, you know, drought. And the climate crisis."

"Right? She's the kind of person who could be like, 'Here's what you all need to do to curb climate change and here's how to get the money for it,' and, boom. Problem solved." Milly reached into the cabinet and claimed another troll, this one carved to wear a tuxedo, its hideously grinning face clashing with its debonair, but still stumpy, body. "I never really got why Jessica liked these things so much."

"That was Jessica. She could see the beauty in a rotten squash."

"Right?!"

They were quiet as Kye plucked a girly troll from the cabinet and blew the top layer of dust away.

"Hey, remember when Jessica got the idea to start doing wine tastings here as part of some kind of romantic getaway package?" Milly asked.

"And Aidan got so drunk during the tasting he was supposed to be hosting that he ended up telling some really tall lady that she made a better coat rack than sex symbol?"

"And Jessica got so mad at him she made him sleep over at your place? She would've made him sleep on the porch, but she didn't want guests to trip over him in the morning."

Kye choked up with laughter. "It's funny, but also kind of sad. Aidan's drinking got in the way of a lot. I always wondered—what might Jessica have accomplished if she hadn't been married to Aidan?"

"What? What kind of wondering is that?" Milly shook her head at the ridiculousness of Kye's wondering.

"No, I know, God knows I love them both, but there was an element of fantasy to their marriage. You've got to admit it. She loved him, and he loved her, but he held her back. He holds himself back, and before he quit drinking he was an even bigger set of brakes, and she felt that."

"I get they didn't have the perfect marriage. I mean, who does? I don't think I'll ever trust marriage. Too much work for not enough return. But they were good together, weren't they?"

Kye still held on to his troll. He gently stroked the top of its head while looking toward the ceiling. "Mostly? But when one person in the marriage is more of a burden than the other, they can love each other all they want and there's still a downward drag. Think of what Jessica might have done if she'd married a guy who was sober more often than not, who was ambitious enough to make a simple concept like adding a wine-tasting component to a B&B work. Think what she could have done."

"Kye, you're a nut. Mr. C is your best friend." They went back to boxing up Jessica's collection of trolls. "Is he even keeping these?" she asked.

Kye hiccupped. "I can't really see Aidan putting these on display in a new apartment."

"Oh, sure, he'll put them beside the Depression-era butter dish and the flapper dress from the twenties."

"Do you think Apple will want them?" Kye pondered.

"Oh. Let's not even burden that girl with the thought of taking them."

"Yeah, if anyone needs to get free of her childhood . . ."

"Listen, I was thinking about something," Milly said, shyly. And shyly wasn't Milly's style. "Do you think he'd accept if I offered to help?"

"What do you mean? You're working every day. And I know you're working more hours than you're getting paid for. You're already helping."

"No, I mean helping financially. Like, a donation. No, I mean a loan. I've got, like, a lot of money."

"Really?"

"Well, sure. I mean, my apartment's cheap and I eat all my meals here and the only money I spend is on my lizards. When you don't have a lot of expenses, it can add up."

"And you're thinking of giving it to Aidan?"

"For Apple. For school."

"Huh." They worked together silently for a while longer. It was a revelation to Kye that Milly had money. He'd always thought of her as struggling, but in a fun, carefree way. He wondered how much she had. Then he wondered how much he had. Huh.

He pulled out his phone and shot off a text to Sharon. The answering ding came quickly. He sent another text. The ding came even faster this time. Milly looked over. "Who the heck are you having such a fast conversation with, Kye? That's pretty different from your usual pace." It was true. Text Kye and you might get a response in a day or two.

He tucked his phone back into his pocket. "I was just texting Sharon to ask how much money we have."

"You don't keep track of how much money you have?"

"Nah, that's all Sharon. But listen. I know I've got my own kids to think of, but they're still years away from college, and you know? If the situations were reversed? I've no doubt Aidan would sell a kidney to get money for one of them."

"He does love them." Milly put an extra layer of newspaper around one particularly delicate troll.

"How about we join forces?"

"You want to help, too?"

"I've got about twenty thousand sitting in a savings account."

"I already figured out I can spare thirty-five thousand."

"Damn, girl."

"Independent woman with low expenses, remember?"

"So we're doing this?"

"We are so doing this."

Kye and Milly shook hands as though they were strangers who needed to seal the deal with skin, when in reality they'd had each other's trust for nearly a decade and this was simply another link in their chain of family.

Chapter 24

"Mr. C!" The next evening, Milly dashed across the driveway toward the house from her junker car, her neon-yellow hair flying behind her in two ponytails. "Hold up, Mr. C. Damn, you move pretty spry for an old guy."

Aidan stood framed in the front door, his hands full of dead marigold heads he'd been plucking. He grinned at her as she paused at the bottom of the porch steps to catch her breath. "I happen to know there's an éclair left over from this afternoon's baking marathon if you need some incentive to make it up the rest of the way."

"Oh, man, éclairs. Who thought up éclairs? Who decided, let's mush some cream into the pastry stuff and coat the whole thing in chocolate and then just release them on the unsuspecting citizens of the world like they're not ticking time bombs waiting to go off in our arteries? Sure, I'll take half. Give the other half to Kye. He's behind me somewhere."

"What have you two been up to?" Aidan asked.

"Scheming!" called Kye from the door of his pickup truck. He ambled out and up the drive, pausing to take in the sky, the house, the ground, and finally made it to the porch where Aidan and Milly were watching him just a tad impatient. Without further ado, he handed Aidan a white envelope.

"What's this? Oh, God, you two aren't quitting, are you? Is this your notice?" Aidan ripped open the envelope but only grew more confused. "I don't get it." In his hands was a check for fifty-five thousand dollars.

"We know it won't cover the whole four years, but it'll get her through a semester at least, right?" Milly's face was as eager as a puppy's.

"You're giving me money?" Aidan asked, still not getting the gesture.

"We're loaning Apple the money. For school," Kye explained.

Aidan's face melted into a mess of gratitude. His friends didn't have much time to appreciate his emotion before he pulled the two of them into a fierce hug that was tight enough Milly gave out a little yelp.

He didn't have the breath to express how grateful he was, not just because of the check—which he couldn't accept—but because of how they'd been his foundation ever since Jessica died. Without them, he knew his life would've been much harder, much more harrowing. He breathed in the chemical smell of Milly's ever-changing hair and the woodsy smell of Kye's dungarees and wished there was some way he could let them know how much they meant to him.

Kye broke free to clap him on the back. "Aids, you know we love you and that girl of yours and we would do anything in our power to help. Sharon's part of this, too. And besides, it's just money. All's it does is sit in a bank. Where's the fun in that? Let's put the cash to work buying an education for Apple!"

"You guys are amazing." Aidan took a deep, shuddering breath and stepped back. "I love you both so much. You'll never even know how much. But I have to say no."

"What?!" Milly gasped in dismay. "That's not how this conversation is supposed to go!"

"I can't take your life savings."

"You're not taking it, we're loaning it to you!"

"Seriously, Aids, we've already thought it out and talked it through. The money is Apple's."

"Come with me." Milly grabbed one hand of each man and led them, through the front door, up the stairs, and down the hall to Apple's room. "This is what's at stake, Mr. C. This isn't the time for stupid pride." She knocked gently at the door, and when there wasn't an answer, she eased it open.

Apple was sleeping soundly—she'd been going to bed early these days. Her shades were pulled, but a night-light left over from the year after her mother died still glowed from the far wall. Aidan remembered the nightmares that afflicted his girl every time she slept that year, the wails that inevitably rose from her exhausted soul only moments after she finally succumbed to dreams. The nightmares had subsided, just like the school therapist had said they would, but the night-light stayed, burning into the dark long after its bulb should have naturally run its course. Now, in its bluish sphere of illumination, Aidan could see the rise and fall of the old pink blanket over Apple's form as her tiny soft breath filled the room.

"That's what's at stake," Aidan agreed, whispering. Apple deserved this. "Okay, you guys. I accept your incredibly generous offer. But please know I will pay you back every cent."

"Dude, no doubt," said Kye.

Early the next morning, Aidan just couldn't wait for Apple to wake up. So he started packing. He knew it was weird. But sometimes dads were weird.

He found Jessica's old hiking backpack on the top shelf of his bedroom closet and beat the dust out of it to make sure it wouldn't make Apple sneeze. No one ever guessed this about his wife, but for all her impeccable taste in décor and her gift for entertaining, she'd loved the great outdoors and had spent many hours hiking, camping, canoeing, and even hunting. Her dark green backpack, with a bright orange–flowered piece of canvas patching up one side, had seen a lot of action back in the day.

As he took it into Apple's room, he laughed to himself, remembering the first time he'd been treated to the sight of Jessica weighed down by it, it being almost half her size. He loved the idea that now it was Apple's turn to use it, to take it wherever she might wander.

"Dad?" Apple's voice, slightly incredulous but still sleepy, alerted him that he'd woken her up by accident.

"Hey, hon, sorry, it's just me. We're um . . . packing."

"Packing? It's, like, barely morning."

"Yeah, that's right. I know, so weird, right? I mean, how do I know what you'd bring to college? But I wanted to at least give you your mom's old backpack."

"You know college doesn't actually start for another month, right? And besides. I know we can't afford it. There's just no way." She sat up and stretched, her black Eminem concert T-shirt as rumpled as her loose hair. She gave him a look as though suspecting him of finally diving off the deep end.

"Nope. You're going. It's decided."

Apple sighed as though she couldn't believe he was still that delusional. "Dad, let's drop it, okay? I really don't want to revisit all the reasons this isn't going to work."

Aidan sat at the end of her bed as she went to her dresser and started winding her hair into a messy bun, checking her work in the mirror. "Actually, it is working," he said to her reflected image. "The gears of change are already turning."

She whipped around to face him. "Don't do this, Dad!"

"I'm serious, Apple. Kye and Milly loaned us some money. I already paid the deposit on my credit card. I'm selling the Happy Valley, and I know it will bring enough to get you on your way. There are other, more trustworthy realtors to talk to. And I'm going to get a job. You, Apple, my daughter, your mother's pride, are going to college. Because you've worked hard and deserve it."

For a moment, Aidan watched five years' worth of emotion run rampant on her face, all kinds of conflicts and protests and—hope. Hope that this was true, that what was happening was a good thing, that Aidan was finally stepping up and being the kind of father she needed.

"Are you sure?" she croaked but didn't get any further because she choked up on tears.

"Yes, sweetie. I've never been more sure of anything in my life. Let's get you to college."

Apple flew into his arms and hugged him with all the power she contained in her seventeen-year-old soul, which was really quite considerable, and Aidan knew he'd keep that moment with him the rest of his lifetime.

Chapter 25

Rebah had been back in her house for a month but it still felt as though she were visiting. How could that be?

She used to love her house. A large ranch with a two-car garage on a cul-de-sac in New Jersey, a giant kitchen she never used, a master suite with a hot tub that she used a lot, a pool, a yard that always looked decent, if not inspired, thanks to the crew she hired to cut and tend it. But after coming back from California, she couldn't get comfortable there.

She'd thrown herself into trying to make the place feel more like home. Including throwing a dinner party, which turned out to be a painful exercise in saying goodbye to some former friends. She'd invited people she used to know—Jocelyn and Mark, Tammi and Craig, Kristin and Jeremy. All people she shared memories with: dancing beachside on a spontaneous trip to Jamaica, doing shots at an airport bar during a layover in Chicago, laughing until the early hours on lawn chairs by the pool at their rented villa in Tuscany. People she had loved as best as she knew how. But when they'd gathered at her house a week ago, there'd been an invisible wall between her and the rest of them that she hadn't been able to scale, no matter how she'd stretched and reached. She'd even had the damn thing catered from the Mexican restaurant down the street that everyone had raved about, but even that, apparently, had been a misstep. "You hired out for the food?" Kristin had asked with barely concealed scorn. "That's so . . . single of you."

"I didn't really have time to cook today," Rebah had defended herself, taking an extra-large gulp from her wineglass.

"Well, you could have always made this potluck. We'd have brought stuff. You know, you don't need to impress us."

"Oh," Rebah had answered simply. Truth was, she *had* been trying to impress them. It felt like she was always trying to impress somebody.

The evening didn't get better and had ended early with her friends making excuses that involved dog walking and babysitters.

Rebah had also tried repainting her downstairs bathroom in an effort to quell the nagging feeling that something wasn't right. But the burnt orange she chose to cover the delicate lavender ended up feeling garish and wrong.

A deep cleaning—she decided that's what her house really needed—a big spring cleaning blowout. But she couldn't stand the thought of doing it herself, so she called in some help, ignoring the niggling sensation that this was similar to hiring a restaurant to cook the food she served at her dinner party.

And now, a team was scheduled to descend on her place tomorrow morning, so it was time to do some initial pickup. Nothing big, just clearing the way for the professionals. Trash bag in hand, she cleaned the dining room table of old mail, takeout containers, and menus, plus several empty bottles. In the living room, she swiped the coffee table of paper plates, plastic cups, and several more empty bottles.

The bag was already full—and heavy with glass.

Next, the bedroom. Armed with a fresh bag, she picked through the bottles on her dresser, bedside table, and under the bed. Even the bathroom needed a sweep—four empty wine bottles balanced on the edge of the tub.

That had to be it.

No! The sunroom off the side porch. Rebah liked sitting out there, sipping a glass of wine or sometimes something stronger, watching the sun set over her neighborhood and the streetlights come on, one by one. Out by her favorite lounger, she collected seven or eight empties and a dozen or so lipstick-stained glasses.

Four bulging trash bags later, she felt as though she'd climbed a mountain and found the view from the top horrifying. Who was drinking all of this alcohol? It couldn't be just her. She wasn't an alcoholic. But where did all these empty bottles come from? For a moment, she entertained thoughts of people breaking into her house while she was traveling and having riotous parties, but she dismissed the scenario as improbable as soon as she let it in.

I'm doing that thing, she realized. *That thing where people find really ridiculous excuses for something they know deep down is their own fault.*

Oh, God. She didn't want to do this.

She bolted into her bedroom and ransacked it, looking for her running clothes. Tossing bras and T-shirts and shorts over her shoulder, she finally came across what she needed—and nestled against her favorite running skirt was another bottle of wine. This one still had a couple of glasses in it, but for the life of her, she could not figure out how a half-full bottle might have gotten into her dresser drawer.

Running clothes abandoned, she took the wine to the living room and sat on the couch, holding it up to the light coming through the windows, letting the liquid slosh back and forth, back and forth, a wave of relief just inches from her mouth. A powerful yearning nearly folded her in half so she gently set the wine on the coffee table, only recently cleared of its own collection of bottles, and pushed her palms against her eyes. This couldn't be who she was. What she was.

Rebah looked around her beautiful home, the vaulted ceilings and creamy trim and crystalline windows. Her gorgeous home that she spent so little time in. And the realization that she was lonely—heartbreakingly, achingly lonely—flooded her entire body and soul, and she started to cry.

* * *

"There," Kye said, giving a post one last smack with a rubber mallet.

"Thanks for doing this," said Aidan.

"I still can't wrap my head around it."

"I know, man. Me either."

The white For Sale sign with green lettering felt awkward and out of place on the lawn of the Happy Valley. When Aidan turned to head back inside, the house seemed disappointed, as though he'd failed it. It's just a house, he reminded himself, and shot a look of apology at the place, just in case there was some kind of soul under the clapboard siding and rusty-pink trim. But it had to be done.

The house was no stranger to goodbyes this month. It had watched as Apple dragged her suitcase and her mother's hiking backpack—stuffed full of her entire life—to her dad's Jeep, where Aidan had waited to drive her to the airport. She had looked back one last time as they pulled out of the driveway.

"It's funny," she said. "For so long I have been so anxious to leave and start my real life. And don't get me wrong, I'm all Barnard-or-bust over here. But I know I'm going to miss this place."

"And, man, this place is going to miss you," Aidan answered. He'd done a pretty good job of holding it together the last few days as he helped her decide what to bring, what to throw away, and what to leave for him to pack up and move into storage. "Definitely a lot of endings coming through right now."

"And beginnings," Apple reminded him. "How about for this ride we think about the beginnings?" She dug around in the back seat and came up with a bag of dill pickle potato chips. "A new road snack in honor of new beginnings."

Aidan smiled at his favorite person in the world. "Deal. Beginnings!"

And then they'd blared Mozart, Simon & Garfunkel, Billy Joel, and Prince all the way to the airport. At the security gate, they'd shared a long hug, and in that hug they both did a lot of forgiving and a lot of releasing. Then Apple had resettled her bag, said, "See you," and walked away.

It was that easy and that hard to say goodbye.

Aidan had decided to sell the place, for real this time, to take the first offer that came along. It was the only way forward that he could see. He also needed to find steady work so he could keep paying for higher education. And getting rid of the Happy Valley was the first step.

Well, one of the first steps. There seemed to be a lot of them. He'd been applying to restaurants and hotels in the area and looking for a new apartment at the same time. Kye and Sharon had said he could stay with them until he found a place, assuming the Happy Valley sold quickly (a presumptuous presumption), but Aidan knew their space was already tight with four people. And to be honest? He needed a space that was his own. A place he could cry if he needed to, swear in anger when necessary, and mourn everything he felt like he was losing.

He'd been blue since that weekend. The infamous weekend of music, dancing, hot-air balloons, horseback riding, winemaking, and Rebah. And not just because Apple had moved away. In his rawest moments, he could admit to himself that he missed Rebah.

That weekend together had been the most fun, the most meaningful time he'd had since Jessica died, and he couldn't stop replaying certain moments over in his head: watching Rebah on the other side of the sky during the hot-air balloon ride, offering her some of the first food he'd managed to cook all year, seeing her amazed face when she took a bite, walking in the neighboring vineyard in the dark with only moonlight as a guide, holding her hand for the first time.

And, of course, making love the next morning.

Before it all went to hell.

But! New beginnings! Aidan shook off his lingering doubts yet again and clapped his friend on the back as they walked up the drive. A crash sounded from inside the open door and the two broke into a run, arriving just in time to see Milly disentangle herself from a large pile of pots, pans, spatulas, and other cooking paraphernalia.

"Milly! What are you doing?!" Aidan cried.

"Packing!" Milly cried back, raising her hands in frustration. "But I made the box too heavy."

No damage done. Except for a broken ladle handle and a saucepan that was now slightly oval instead of round. *Meh*, Aidan thought. He had a hard time getting annoyed at either of these two people who'd saved his daughter's academic career. And, on a deeper level, his life. Not just this month. The last five years.

Pleasant Dale Park was exactly as pleasing as it sounded, which was why Rebah went there to try and remember how to breathe when everything got to be too much. She sat on a certain bench overlooking a man-made pond and forced herself to quit looking inward and gaze at the flocks of starlings that crowded the maple trees along the edge of the water. The mom pushing a carriage while trying to wrangle a determined toddler away from the pool's edge with bribes of cookies. The teenage boy jogging in pink shorts and lavender tank top. The feeling of stone-cold granite under her jeans. The kiss of sun on her face. The gentle wisp of breeze on her neck. These were the things she needed to notice in order to stay grounded.

Sometimes, it even worked.

But not so much this morning. She hadn't slept well last night. She'd been getting increasingly irritated emails from her boss, well, bosses, and she'd managed to dodge his, well, their, frequent phone calls, but yesterday, distracted, she'd accidentally answered on the first ring and was confronted by the depth of her dilemma.

"Ah, Rebah. My favorite ghost."

"Oh, hey, Frank. Yeah, sorry about not getting back to you. I've just been super busy working on my house and doing some real hard-core self-care. I know I owe you some emails and—"

"Oh, it's not just emails that you owe me. Rebah, dear, I'm not sure you fully understand the extent of my disappointment."

"Oh?" Rebah swallowed. She hated this. She hated anyone express-ing disapproval of her actions. But this was one of the things she'd been working on, right? She tried to look at the phone call as an opportuni-ty to exercise her new mental muscles. "We need to talk, Frank."

"Oh, you need to do more than talk, sweetheart. You need to write. You owe us work. We haven't heard a word from you in a month. Nothing after that shit show in Napa Valley that Stew had to clean up, and now you think you need to talk? What you need, Rebah, is to get back to work."

She took a deep breath and steadied herself with one hand on the wall. Rooted—she tried to feel rooted, to the carpet beneath her bare feet and the painted plaster under her hand. She could do this. "Frank, I quit. I'm done."

Silence on the other end of the phone.

"I have decided that this lifestyle just isn't healthy for me right now."

"Healthy?! You want to talk about healthy?! How about the health of your bank account?"

"I'd appreciate you not threatening me with financial matters you know nothing about."

"Oh, I know how much we pay you and I know how much you like to spend on your extravagant lifestyle."

"I think you mean you're aware of how much I earn, but make no mistake—you aren't privy to my financial health and well-being." She took another deep, cleansing breath. "I'm done with you and the blog. I quit."

"But—you're Rebah! What becomes of *Rambling with Rebah* with-out Rebah?"

"Not my problem. I don't ramble anymore. Goodbye, Frank."

She'd been so proud of that phone call. Her fingers had hovered over several contact names, all people she might have once called to celebrate her successful disentanglement from a job that didn't make her happy anymore. But she didn't tap on any of them.

Instead, she'd done her best to make pad thai from scratch and watched *When Harry Met Sally . . .* for what might have been the five hundredth time in her life. Not a bad evening.

But the doubt had done its work in the early hours of the next day, waking her at the ungodly hour of three a.m. and not allowing her to slip back into any sort of numbing sleep.

So there she sat. On the bench in a beautiful park. Watching the world go by. Feeling untethered and not a little panicky. What was she going to do?

Well, first, she was going to distract herself. She pulled her phone out of her pocket and scrolled through social media. People with dogs, cats with dogs, interesting trees, flowers displayed on a clean wooden table, pithy quotes meant to inspire (they didn't), children, more children, and even more children. People living full, happy lives. Rebah didn't know how they did it.

She came across Apple's feed and, with major trepidation, clicked back in time to that weekend. That weekend. Rebah couldn't think about it without a whole flood of emotions and memories. And while she was working hard to feel her feelings as they came and to quit throwing up walls to block anything that might hurt on any level, her hands shook slightly as she found the photos Apple had posted of that time.

Rebah looked up and across the pond. She smiled as the toddler finally made it to the edge of the water and splashed right in, his mother yelling behind him. And he didn't stop with wet feet. He plopped down on his bottom and began to roll and laugh in the chilly late-summer water.

Right. Be brave, she told herself. *Just plop down and roll around.*

So she scrolled through Apple's photos. The band playing in the backyard. Dinner that first night—all that fried food! What had Aidan been thinking? Shots of Kai making goofy faces. Shots of Kye making goofy faces. There was Milly with that crazy blue hair. Oh, the hot-air balloons! Apple had posted a video of their takeoff and Rebah could hear herself laughing hysterically as she and Apple clung to each other—not that it had been a bumpy trip, but just the thought of leaving Earth had sparked a hilarity in the two of them. She'd been such a good kid, Apple. And there was Aidan, smiling at his daughter while she filmed him getting out of his own balloon. He was so handsome.

Rebah caught herself. The whole weekend had been a lie. He had lied to her. A lot. That was unforgivable.

Another video. This one from the horse barn. Aidan and Rebah were talking, the two of them leading their horses away from the camera. In the video, Aidan leaned closer and said something to her, but she wasn't listening or looking at him. She was watching something outside the camera frame. And Aidan was watching her. On the bench, Rebah watched him watch her and the look on his face was . . . adoring. Aidan was looking at her with real love. That wasn't a lie. There's no way he would have been acting at that moment—he'd had no idea they were being filmed.

Rebah scrolled through the rest of the photos and found more evidence that something deeper had been going on, something deeper than the story she had told herself about those three days. A shot of Aidan with his hand outstretched toward her. An angle that showed a half smile he'd let sneak onto his face while he watched her taste his amazing frittata. And another video where Apple had captured the two of them slipping away for a moonlit walk when they'd thought no one was looking.

While she was scrolling, a notification popped up that Apple had posted another video, and without really thinking about what she was doing, Rebah clicked to view. Apple! Rebah was truly thrilled to see her. And she looked so good! She was sitting at a piano in what looked like a practice room, playing a few bars before talking at the camera.

"Just wanted to tell everyone out there the story of how I got to college. See, I have a pretty great dad. A somewhat misguided dad, sure, but he's got a really excellent heart. My mom died almost six years ago and ever since, he's been juggling taking care of me and taking care of our bed-and-breakfast, and it was really, really hard. On both of us, but especially him. I mean, yeah, I'm a handful, but you should try satisfying every wish and whim of paying guests 24-7. And with my mom gone, he didn't even really like it anymore. And then, when we found out I got into Barnard, he decided to sell the place so he could pay for my tuition."

Rebah's eyes crinkled as she began to realize what that weekend had been—a last-ditch effort to sell the Happy Valley for enough money to send his daughter to college.

"So he got this freaky scheme to throw a really fabulous party over a whole weekend and invite a famous travel blogger to come so she'd see how amazing the Happy Valley was and someone would want to buy it and then we'd have enough money for school."

Apple's face got a little sad at that point. Rebah could tell it was hard for her to say.

"But it didn't really work out. I mean, he did everything he possibly could, but, well, some emotions got in the way and the weekend ended on a pretty sour note. Things were said."

Rebah felt a stab of guilt, remembering some of the things that had come out of her mouth.

"But my dad isn't one to quit, or to let pride get in the way. He kept fighting, and we have some really great friends who helped with that fight, and look—I'm here! I'm at the college I've wanted to go to since I was a kid. Barnard. Next stop? Who knows? But I do know that whatever I decide and wherever I go, my dad is going to be right there with me, supporting me any way he can. It's just who he is."

The video ended.

Oh, shit. That's why Aidan had been trying to sell. That's why he'd developed such an elaborate ruse to fool her into writing a good review. But she'd ruined it by assuming he was all about hurting her. She had been so self-centered—she'd never even thought about what else was going on in his life.

Rebah clicked over to her photos and scrolled through all the shots of amazing locales around the world. Then she scrolled back to the photo of Aidan and her, strolling in a Napa Valley neighborhood, al-most holding hands as they headed out into the dusky unknown.

Huh.

Aidan looked around the living room of the Happy Valley. The place hadn't looked that good since Jessica had lived there. Freshly cut flow-ers stood in elegant arrangements around the room, a professional coat of paint had done wonders, and a new arrangement of furniture had really opened up the whole downstairs. Jessica's ugly wooden trolls were now housed on an elegant Shaker shelf that almost made the little guys seem cute. He brushed some pollen from the shiny surface of the table and then brushed it off his hands into the air.

Pitts knocked on the front door as he opened it. "Okay, are we ready?" he asked.

"Sure, just let yourself in," Aidan answered.

"I have this theory. Once you're a motivated seller, the place is no longer yours. It belongs to the person who can make a sale happen. And that's me." Pitts scanned the downstairs with a practiced eye.

Aidan could feel that practiced gaze take in his self, too. Did he measure up? *It doesn't matter,* he reminded himself. *You're done. You're out of here. New life.*

"Okay, looking good," Pitts said.

What was going on with Pitts? This wasn't his usual egotistical self. Aidan figured that because he was willing to accept any offer, even a low one, he'd slipped on Pitts's list of priorities, and that was why the agent was acting so strangely. But Pitts knew the deal. The only inter-est had been from people unwilling to pay even close to half what the place was worth. Business had tanked, the Happy Valley was now just a shell. And Aidan wanted out.

"So when is this buyer coming?" he asked.

Pitts looked at his watch. "Any minute."

A car pulled up outside and Aidan expected Pitts to jump to greet the prospective buyer on their way up the front steps, but he stayed where he was, nervously twitching his shirtsleeves down and checking his watch.

Footsteps on the porch.

"Hello?" a voice called out. A woman's voice. But a familiar woman's voice.

Then the door opened—Rebah!

"Wait, what?" Aidan gasped.

Rebah drew herself up to her full height and took a deep breath. "I'm your buyer," she said. And her voice wavered only the slightest bit.

"You're the buyer." Aidan couldn't believe it. He glanced around widely, convinced there were cameras trained on him, that an audience was watching this whole thing unfold while eating popcorn and laughing hysterically. "You're the one paying half what this place is worth."

"Actually, I'm the one buying half the place for exactly what it's worth."

"What the hell are you talking about?" Even as he felt a surge of anger mix with his confusion, he couldn't help but notice how gorgeous Rebah looked, her skin glowing, her rust-colored hair caught in a shiny braid, her eyes bright with what looked like joy. What was going on? And why did he want so badly to hug her? They were enemies, weren't they?

"I know—this is a pretty gigantic gesture. But, Aidan, I need to tell you something. I never felt the way I felt that weekend I stayed here. And I tried to convince myself that you had lied to me for your own selfish reasons and that you wanted to hurt me, but I know—you were just being the best dad you could be. And I fell in love that weekend. I fell in love with you. And I fell in love with the Happy Valley. This place is incredibly special, and not just because your wife worked so hard to make it that way, but because of you. I want to be a part of that. I could never take her place, but I do feel like there's room for me here. With you." She took a deep, shuddering breath, and Aidan saw just how much this speech was taking out of her.

She reached into her front pocket and dug out something small and round and held it up in the palm of her hand. "Ten days."

"You're sober?"

"Yep."

"Rebah, I never meant to hurt you," Aidan began, but she held up her hand.

"Actually, you don't even need to say any of it. You have a very articulate daughter who has done a fantastic job explaining exactly what I got wrong about that weekend. What we both got wrong."

Aidan let out a breath he hadn't known he was holding. "Oh, sweetheart," he said, and opened his arms. Rebah stepped forward into his chest, his heart, his life. She was finally home.

Epilogue

"**I** don't think you understand what an amazing opportunity this is," Pitts barked at them as he strode up the front porch stairs. "Really, you can't even begin to think about passing this one up."

Rebah, standing at the top of the steps, glanced back at Aidan, who leaned against the open front door's frame. She smiled at him, and in that smile, he recognized the glint of icy humor that was always within her reach.

"No, really, Pitts, tell us more," she drawled. Next to her, a golden retriever puppy thumped his tale at his mistress's voice. Baggins was a new addition to their small family, but already neither Aidan nor Rebah could imagine life without him.

The house around them was vastly different from the home it had been a year ago when Aidan and Rebah's new chapter had begun. New siding, new shutters, the addition of a side veranda, and native plantings all scheduled to bloom on a domino schedule. From the front porch, Pitts couldn't see the scene, but extending out from the backyard was a grassy field and a new barn, where two pinto ponies were happily grazing. Rebah was teaching Aidan how to ride in their spare time. It turned out Rebah had a talent for creating a sense of place that people wanted to be a part of. All those years of traveling to premier destinations had formed in her an instinct for beauty and functionality that she applied with precision to the Happy Valley, a home she was proud and grateful to call her own.

As for Aidan, the past year had seen him rip out of the cocoon of his own making. *What had I been waiting for?* he often wondered to himself. The easy answer was Rebah, but he suspected the sharp interest he'd felt for food, community, and life itself for going on thirteen months now was a more complex result of hiding for almost five years. He'd been the walking dead, performing the motions, keeping the world at bay—even his daughter—until a crack appeared in the exterior that one weekend. And since then he'd watched as the crack spread and, eventually, his entire glass dome had shattered, exposing him to the cuts and kisses of the world at large. He'd braced himself as best he could, but it turned out that feeling everything was preferable to feeling nothing.

"A million five," Pitts wheezed. The past year had seen his girth grow, though perhaps not his net worth. The Jaguar in the driveway was last year's model.

"Huh," Aidan mused. "That's it?"

"That's it?" Pitts repeated. "That's it? That's all you have to say? With that kind of money, you can send your kid to school and still afford to retire in Italy. Or Nova Scotia. Wherever it is you people want to go."

"Thing is, Pitts, we're happy here." Rebah smiled at Aidan, who felt that familiar flood of sheer joy her smile always sparked in him. "There's no place we'd rather be."

Pitts's shoulders sank in a sign of deflation. "You sure you won't consider? It's a really good—"

"Opportunity." Aidan stepped onto the porch and put his arm around Rebah's waist. "We know. But if you'll excuse us, we have an event to get ready for."

"Oh? Another weekend party? What's the occasion? Trying to impress an influencer?" Pitts couldn't quite hide his bitterness. You could practically see his desperation for a hefty commission oozing out of his worn suit.

"Something like that." Aidan looked at Rebah. "Actually, we're getting married tomorrow."

"Would you like to come?" Rebah asked Pitts. Aidan lifted his eyebrows at her in surprise, and she answered with a softening of her eyes. "It's a pretty small event. Mostly just family and close friends, but if you'd like to drop by . . ."

Pitts sighed. He knew what his answer was supposed to be. "No, thank you. Working weekend for this guy. You know, got to push the paper, hustle the houses." He let his gaze roam up and around the property. It really was a beautiful spot. "So, I guess I'll be going. Let me know if you change your minds . . ." He gave up and turned his back on the Happy Valley, trudging back down the front steps and across the smooth new gravel to his dusty, once-loved sports car. It took a couple of tries to get it started before he could drive away.

"What do you think, soon-to-be Mrs. Cisneros?"

"About what, Mr. Cisneros?"

"You sure you don't want to sell the place and retire to Italy? Or Nova Scotia?"

Rebah smirked at the man she'd grown to love more than she'd ever loved anyone. "You know I'd follow you to the ends of the earth, but really? I'm not sure we'd find any happier place than here. Besides, we've got a busy day ahead of us. You heading out to pick up Apple soon?"

"First thing on the list: pick up Apple from the airport."

"Actually, that's the second thing."

"Did you want me to make breakfast first?"

"Nope. First thing on your list is to kiss your bride."

Rebah caught Aidan's face in her hands, and as their lips met, a dozen crows burst from the black walnut tree at the far end of the driveway and swooped into the blue sky, calling out in voices that could, if one were happy with the state of the world, sound like joy.

Addison J. Chapple Collection

(Comedies and Romantic Comedies)

ISBN: 978-1-933769-74-5

Two friends travel to Somalia, impersonate Navy SEALs, take over a village, and steal treasure from pirates. Easy! Until it all unravels.

ISBN: 978-1-933769-76-9

Determined to outdo their rich friends, a couple plans the "wedding of the century" in the tiny island nation of Milagros. But when civil war breaks out, the true meaning of love and friendship will be tested as the bride, groom, and all of their guests are sent running for their lives.

ISBN: 978-1-933769-72-1

Inspired by a hilarious true story. When a brilliant but bankrupt conman chooses an aging aristocratic French family as his next mark, he must convince them to engage in an all-out battle with an enemy that doesn't actually exist in order to swindle them out of their entire fortune.

ISBN: 978-1-933769-78-3

In this irreverent action-comedy about stereotypes, two female FBI officers must pretend to be a gay couple in order to infiltrate 'Dykes with Bikes' after the NSA uncovers a terrorist plot involving the motorcycle gang.

ISBN: 978-1-933769-80-6

A wild and off-beat comedy for those entrenched in the wonders of quantum physics or the migratory habits of UFOs. When a science professor learns her father willed all his money to a wacky New Age cult, she must prove the organization is fraudulent and discredit the cult's charismatic and ever-so-sexy guru in order to gain her inheritance.

ISBN: 978-1-646300-78-5

When a neurotic statistics geek gets invited to his 25-year high school reunion, he spends his life savings remaking his identity to wow his old classmates. Only one tiny problem: his new persona gets him mistaken for a drug kingpin and forces him to go on the run with the very people who used to make his life miserable.

Santa Ana is an absurdly hilarious and magical tale about the masks we wear . . . and those strange California winds that blow them all asunder.

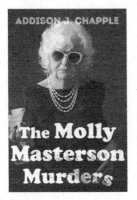

ISBN: 978-1-646300-80-8

When a disgruntled son hires an incompetent hitman to kill his mother, the wrong Molly Masterson keeps getting murdered. Inspired by true events.

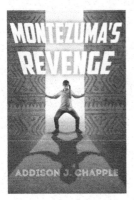

ISBN: 978-1-646300-79-2

When four middle-aged men answer an ad to search for Aztec treasure, they are drawn into a cartel plot to smuggle artifacts out of Mexico.